"*Phenomenal Girl 5* kept me up late turning pages. Kudos to debut author A. J. Menden for creating a fully realized superhero world with a well-rounded cast of characters complimented by a sharp-witted narrator that you can't help but want to spend time with."

—Julie Kenner,
Bestselling Author of *Deja Demon*

SUPER LOUSY TIMING

In all those years of living, Robert had definitely mastered the kiss. His was slow and soft, but with enough passion behind it to make me light-headed. I found myself drifting backward to rest against the closed door for support, pulling him along with me, kissing him back. Our tongues danced together, and he tasted faintly of coffee and brandy.

"We should not be doing this," he said against my mouth between kisses.

"And yet we're not stopping."

He reclaimed my mouth, and I felt a little sigh of pleasure escape. I had been crazy about him for weeks, never dreaming he was into me. Not really. But he thought I was sexy? I wasn't going to analyze how it happened; I was just going to enjoy it.

Of course, that's when alarms started going off. All the villains in Megolopolis were teaming up.

FOUNTAINDALE PUBLIC LIBRARY DISTRICT
300 West Briarcliff Road
Bolingbrook, IL 60440-2894
(630) 759-2102

A. J. MENDEN

PHENOMENAL GIRL ⑤

LOVE SPELL   NEW YORK CITY

To Mara and Cordelia, who are already "super" girls.

LOVE SPELL®

November 2008

Published by

Dorchester Publishing Co., Inc.
200 Madison Avenue
New York, NY 10016

If you purchased this book without a cover you should be aware that this book is stolen property. It was reported as "unsold and destroyed" to the publisher and neither the author nor the publisher has received any payment for this "stripped book."

Copyright © 2008 by Amy Mendenhall

All rights reserved. No part of this book may be reproduced or transmitted in any form or by any electronic or mechanical means, including photocopying, recording or by any information storage and retrieval system, without the written permission of the publisher, except where permitted by law.

ISBN 10: 0-505-52786-3
ISBN 13: 978-0-505-52786-8

The name "Love Spell" and its logo are trademarks of Dorchester Publishing Co., Inc.

Printed in the United States of America.

10 9 8 7 6 5 4 3 2 1

Visit us on the web at www.dorchesterpub.com.

Acknowledgments

So many people to thank for putting up with me! First off, thanks to my super agent Michelle Wolfson and my amazing editor Chris Keeslar and assistant editor Alissa Davis for pulling me out of the "slush" to take a chance on me and the book. And a big thanks to all of the good people at Dorchester for all of their hard work.

A big "wow" to artist Judy York for her, forgive me, *phenomenal* cover art.

I've got to give it up to my extraordinary team of betas: Laura Tennant, Andrea Greynolds, Jolene Craig, and Rachel Lane because without their encouragement, nothing would get written.

A huge amount of thanks goes out to Kelley Armstrong for creating the Online Writers Group on her website and introducing me to a community of talented people who have been such a source of help and support over the years. To all past and current members of the OWG, big hugs around. You guys rock!

Extra love goes to Susan Charman for going above and beyond the call of duty as crit partner and being an endless supply of encouragement.

And saving the best for last, thanks to my family for always encouraging me on my road here. Especially my husband, Jeremy, who reads everything I put in front of him and always has an opinion on what I should do next, and Mara and Cordelia, for being so understanding about Mommy's need for writing time.

PHENOMENAL GIRL 5

CHAPTER ONE

"Phenomenal Girl Five? Doctor Rath will see you now."

I glanced up at the trim, petite secretary complete with stereotypical bun and nerdy glasses. I studied her for a moment, trying to figure out who she really was, before her tapping foot and impatient look prompted me into action. I quickly put down the magazine I was pretending to read and stood, smoothing out my white linen skirt, checking to be sure my suit jacket hadn't slipped and wasn't showing any unnecessary cleavage. Doctor Rath was supposedly old-school when it came to heroines: a little T&A went a long way, but too much and you were considered a woman of loose morals, and heroines had to have impeccable morals. At least, they did if they wanted to join the Elite Hands of Justice.

Anyone who was anyone was a member of the Elite Hands of Justice. Based in Megolopolis, the EHJ were *the* superhero team of the country, maybe even the world. They were the team to which everyone turned when aliens threatened invasion, villains tried their world-domination schemes, and apocalypse was nigh. Other teams might deal with garden-variety villains and stop a terrorist or two, but it was the EHJ whose pictures were in every newspaper and tabloid. Heroes worked their tails off to even be considered for an interview whenever a position came up. I had applied at every chance, endured several pre-interviews, and received numerous "We'll keep you in mind in the future" letters to finally make it this far: an interview with the big man himself. Rath had been the driving force behind the EHJ for twenty years. Possessing super-intelligence, he was the perfect man to plan strategies to keep one step ahead of whatever villain wanted to blow up or rule the world that day.

The secretary led me into a large, lush office decorated in the finest style, antiques amidst computers, holo-screens, and other gray bits of hardware I couldn't identify offhand but that I was pretty sure were so high-tech not even the military had access to the designs.

Doctor Rath sat behind an indecently large desk. At sixty-five, he had matured into a distinguished gentleman. He was six feet tall with wide shoulders and a muscular, trim frame evident through the fine charcoal gray Armani suit he wore. His dark gray hair was pulled back in a slick pony-tail, and his eyes were the same dark color.

He consulted the folder in front of him. "Phenomenal Girl Five, correct?"

"Yes, sir."

He motioned to the chair opposite the huge desk. "Please sit."

I did, making sure to sit up straight and ladylike, legs crossed demurely at the ankles instead of half underneath me, like I did at home.

"As you know, the Elite Hands of Justice are looking to expand the team," Rath said, shuffling through papers on his desk and coming up with a file folder. "There has been a shift in the last couple of years, and more and more young teens are showing up with powers. Where it used to be one in every hundred thousand people had powers, it has accelerated to one in every ten thousand. That may not sound like a lot, but when you factor in that there are more than three hundred million people in this country alone . . ." He trailed off. "We have a lot of policing to do. Not that every one of them is going to turn to a life of crime—or a life of heroics, for that matter—but we need to keep an eye out."

He flipped open the folder and studied my PR photo. "This is your costume?" He stabbed a finger down on it, resting on my bustline. I stared, unsure if he was doing it on purpose or if his finger had just happened to land on the amplest part of my body.

He kept staring at me and I remembered I was supposed to speak. "Yes, sir."

"A little different than the previous Phenomenal Girls."

"I am my own person, sir. And the previous costume was a bit impractical."

"How so?"

"A miniskirt, halter top, and go-go boots aren't exactly good for flying, sir." You couldn't concentrate on fighting crime when you were constantly worried your breasts were going to pop out of your impractical top, or that someone was looking up your skirt as you flew by.

He gave a slight nod and gestured back down at my photo. "And this black leather getup is?"

"Well, it's slightly more aerodynamic."

"It doesn't look much like a costume."

I stifled an eye roll. Of course he would say that. My male teammates had almost said the same thing. S&M vibe aside, the body-hugging black leather pants and vest covered more skin than all the costumes of the rest of my female teammates combined, and that wasn't even counting the matching fingerless gloves that stretched up to my biceps. The women of our set tended to strut around in outfits that either looked like lingerie or something rejected by a cage dancer. The male contingent liked their women looking like eye candy. Personally, I never bought into the strategy of surprising criminals by distracting them with cleavage. I wished my costume could be less tight. While still in perfect shape, I had the kind of body that had a little extra padding and without careful monitoring could easily go to fat.

"Well, the black sets off your blonde hair nicely, and gives you a certain look. We want someone memorable to the public." He eyed the photo and then gave me the same critical stare. "You always wear that much makeup?"

I sighed. Yes, I knew my chosen field was a man's world, but give me a break. "With all due respect, sir, I don't see how my love of dark eye makeup and red lipstick has any bearing on whether or not I'd be a good addition to the team."

Rath seemed a bit taken aback. He stared, mouth hanging open for a moment, then snapped his teeth together with a click and cleared his throat. "Well, er . . ." He shuffled some papers in the folder and pulled one out. "Your work with the Red Knights and the Power Squad is impressive. Your apprehension stats are beyond average and your power levels are above a seven, which is excellent. Strength and flight, correct?"

"Yes, sir."

He nodded, more to himself than me. "Yes, excellent." He took out a blue piece of paper and read it, then spoke in a brisk tone. "Based on your pre-interviews, the Magnificent, White Heat, and Aphrodite have already given their approval for your membership, which only leaves my decision." He leaned back in his chair and eyed me critically.

I should have kept my big mouth shut about the makeup. Contradicting the boss was not the way to win a job. My heart was pounding so fast I swore he could hear it. Still, the EHJ's three major players had given their approval, and that had to count for something. I sat up straighter in the chair, hands folded neatly in my lap, and tried to look interested but not overeager.

When I didn't wilt under his gaze, he gave me a slight smile. "I think I can okay you for preliminary membership."

"Thank you, sir!" The words burst out excitedly as I forgot about maintaining my calm, cool expression. "You'll be pleased with your decision, I guarantee it."

"Don't thank me just yet." He chuckled. "You did read in the standard contract we sent over that you must perform two years of training before you are considered a full member of our roster, correct?"

Okay, so I hadn't read the contract that thoroughly. My usually pinpoint-accurate lawyer mind had instantly started gibbering with excitement and I had barely given it more than a once-over.

"I think I remember something like that in between the liability clause and the alias patent agreement," I said, hoping I sounded confident.

Rath nodded absently, as if the details were no matter, and continued with his orientation speech. "It's a standard clause, as two years seems to be what works best, but we do promote early on a case-by-case basis. We require all new members to work with the Reincarnist. 'Tour of duty,' they like to call it, but we've all done it. I suppose you've heard the rumors about him?"

Who hadn't? "The papers say he's quite eccentric."

"You're being kind. 'Mad' is what the papers say, and there are those both on and off our team who would agree. But he's the smartest man on Earth and no wonder, possessing the intelligence of the ages. Unfortunately, the business of being reborn does have its drawbacks, as he forgets a bit with each new life. However, you're getting him at a good time. He's been Robert Elliot for twenty years now, so you won't have to face working with him at the start of a new life. It's always hard on those that get him at that age."

"I thought he was reborn as a young man of twenty, sir, not a baby," I said, confused.

"Oh, he is, but he's usually a little confused at first, and forgets how the magic works." He waved a hand dismissively. "Ah, but you won't have to worry about that. He's forty, in the best shape of his life, and smart as a whip. I am confident you'll get along just fine. Getting training from the Reincarnist really hones your detective skills—always helpful to a hero—as well as your powers. He's officially on the inactive list, but he does special assignments for the team as well as some patrolling of his own sector. You'll live with him in his house in Covo City—not a hardship, let me tell you. The man is always a billionaire playboy, no matter what life he's in. And this way you can work with him on his assignments."

I nodded, a growing worry forming in the pit of my stomach as I recalled all of the newspaper articles I had read about the Reincarnist. Pushstar had washed out of the program because of him, and this after years of working with Fantasmo, who was about as nuts as they came.

I reminded myself how long and hard I had been working for this opportunity. Forcing away my doubts, I stretched my lips into a smile that I hoped didn't look as sick as it felt. "Sounds great, sir."

"I'll have Gladys work up your papers and clearance level. Have you notified the Power Squad yet?"

I blushed, thinking about how fun that conversation would be. "I didn't want to count my chickens before they were hatched, sir." Forget about the fact that I had been hired and the team now needed a replacement; Turbyne, our leader, was going to be super pissed I had even gotten a callback when his multiple applications to the EHJ hadn't even garnered so much as a preliminary interview.

Rath seemed to understand. It probably wasn't the first time a new hire's old team had sore feelings over their promotion. "I'll have Aphrodite notify them that you are working with us from now on. Your address is correct on your application form?"

"Yes, sir."

"Good. I'll send someone over to your apartment to pick up your things. We can make arrangements to sublet if necessary."

"Sir?"

"Your training starts today." He stood. "We're off to the Reincarnist's."

CHAPTER TWO

The Reincarnist's mansion was the perfect hero/billionaire playboy bachelor pad. The elaborate home was on the edge of Covo City, surrounded by a private forest and placed, fortresslike, at the top of a hill. After going through a series of security systems that would put the government's to shame, our car made its way through the expansive grounds to come to a stop in what looked like a parking lot for the rich and famous. Hundreds of thousands of dollars in cars lined the driveway in front of the house. A servant was detailing a black Escalade.

Rath and I got out, pausing to admire the vehicles. "Are there people visiting?" I asked.

"No, he just likes cars," Rath said. "This is just part of his collection. Today must be wash day."

We climbed the staircase leading up to the front door. A butler in black tie answered the door before we reached it.

"Good day, Doctor Rath. Phenomenal Girl Five." He gave us a slight nod of greeting. "I was told to expect you."

"Good morning," Rath said, stepping past the butler into the entranceway. "Miss Livingston, this is Mayhew, the Reincarnist's butler and personal assistant. Should you need anything, he can take care of it. He's been in the business of helping oversee our preliminary members since he was your age."

"Welcome, Miss Livingston," Mayhew said solemnly.

"Your things arrived moments ago, and we are preparing your room."

"Thank you."

"He downstairs?" Rath asked Mayhew, and at the butler's nod motioned for me to follow him. "Let's introduce you to the man himself."

I followed Rath down the hallway and into the library. My heart hammered in my chest. I was finally going to meet the legendary Reincarnist.

Rath walked over to the large bookcase lining one wall. Hundreds of leather-bound books filled the shelves. Moving along the wall, he pulled out volumes seemingly at random.

"He'll teach you the code," Rath said as he pulled the last one, and a hidden panel next to the shelves slid open, revealing a gel pad. Rath placed his palm on the scanner and the screen lit up, confirming his identity in blocky type: RATH, DOCTOR BENJAMIN. A loud click sounded, and he moved to guide me away just as the bookshelf slid open. Beyond it, a wide staircase sloped down into blackness.

"This way," he said, starting down the steps without hesitation.

I followed, eyes trying to adjust to the surrounding inky darkness. The stairs flattened out into a long hallway lit by small lights in the ceiling. At the end of the hall, I came to a stop, and my jaw dropped.

I had expected some sort of creepy cave, not the opulent room that met me. The walls were calm beige, with intriguing and priceless paintings lining them. Antiques and ultramod furniture were spaced throughout. Muted classical music played out of invisible speakers. More bookshelves lined the walls, but the tomes filling them were worn with age and use. Some were spread out on a nearby table, splayed open as if the reader had just stepped away. Unlike those in the library above, these books were not for show.

At the other end of the room, technology ruled. Off to one side was a fully equipped lab. A large flat-panel monitor flanked by smaller models covered one wall. And sitting in front of the monitors was a man. He glanced up at one of the smaller monitors, looked down and scribbled something in a notebook lying on the table in front of him, and then turned his attention back to the monitor. He was mumbling to himself.

"Robert," Rath called.

The man continued mumbling, checking the monitor again. "Coffee in the earth," he said distinctly, then jotted something in his notebook.

I took a step back. Maybe the rumors of the Reincarnist's madness were true.

"Robert!" Rath said, sharper this time.

That seemed to catch his attention. He turned, still looking not all there. Recognition crossed his face and he lost his distracted air. "Ben, old friend!" He got up and came over to embrace Rath in a friendly bear hug. "It is good to see you."

Nervously I watched the man that was to be my mentor. I had seen pictures of him in newspapers, but he was so different in person. At least a foot taller than my 5'5", he was powerfully built, with wide shoulders on a solid frame that was barely contained by the dark, expensive suit he wore. His black hair was laced with gray. He had a very commanding presence, as if you could sense his true age.

He turned his attention on me, and a warm quiver shot to the pit of my stomach. He wasn't pretty-boy handsome, but there was something about him that caught my feminine attention. He had the softest, kindest brown eyes I had ever seen. He gave me a slight smile, very boyish, causing that tingle to intensify.

"And who is this?" His voice was deep and warm, the kind of voice you could imagine whispering sexy things to you in the dark.

God, I was done for.

"Robert, this is your new partner, Phenomenal Girl Five," Rath said, since I was too busy staring to speak.

I got a hold of myself, offered a hand, willing it not to tremble. "It's an honor to meet you, Reincarnist."

His large hand swallowed mine up in a warm handshake that was all man, but not so much so that he was crushing my fingers. "Why is your alias Phenomenal Girl Five?"

His directness flustered me. Well, he flustered me altogether. "Th-there were four Phenomenal Girls before me. They've all either been killed or retired, and I had powers similar to theirs, so . . ."

He nodded, looking distracted again. "I do not use an alias. You may call me by my last name, Elliot, unless I say otherwise. Do you understand?"

Taken aback by the apparent cooling of his welcome, I stuttered, "S-sure."

"Excellent. And what is your real name?"

"Lainey."

"Lainey what?" He sounded as if he were losing patience with me already.

"Lainey Livingston."

"Well, Miss Livingston, we shall get to work straightaway. Ben, I have a break in the Donner kidnapping." He motioned for Rath to follow him to the monitors. I stood there, uncertain whether I was supposed to go with them or stay put. I felt very awkward.

"I analyzed the dirt scraped from the child's shoe," the Reincarnist was saying. "There is coffee present." He leaned over the computer keyboard and typed a few things. A chemical equation appeared on one of the small screens, and a large map of the city on the large screen. "There used to be a coffee factory at this location." A red dot appeared on the map. "The authorities will need to sweep that area."

Rath nodded. "I'll let them know, but you may be needed as well."

The Reincarnist shrugged and went back to studying the monitor.

Rath turned his attention on me. "Well, I'll leave you two

to it. Good luck, Miss Livingston. Robert will be informing me of your progress. I'll be in touch. Robert, the Hands miss you at meetings."

"They will continue to do so," the Reincarnist replied absently, tapping at the keyboard and mumbling to himself. "No fingerprints shown, but a detection spell . . ."

Rath shook his head. "See if you can get him to emerge from his cave occasionally, Miss Livingston. Other than to patrol or walk crime scenes, I mean." He clapped Elliot on the back, forcing his attention away from his computer. "How you keep up the playboy persona is a mystery to me."

"I throw lavish parties, I say hello, and I leave. Mayhew or my current partner takes care of the guests." He glanced over, his gaze as effective as any stasis beam as it ran up and down every inch of my body, appraising me. My throat went dry as other parts of me did the opposite. "She will do in that respect."

"Keep me on the guest list."

"Of course. It was good seeing you, Ben."

"You too, Robert." Rath nodded to me. "Let me know if you don't receive all of your things." And with that, he disappeared down the hall toward the stairs we'd come down not so long ago.

Leaving me alone with the Reincarnist, whom I was supposed to call Elliot. I was having lustful thoughts about someone I wasn't even allowed to call by his first name.

The only sounds were the classical music, the clack of the keyboard, and the scribble of pen on paper. Feeling awkward, I looked around, wondering what I was supposed to be doing. I don't think mentally drooling over my new boss was part of the job description.

He finally glanced up at me, startled, as if he had forgotten I was there. "Miss . . . Livingston. What exactly is it you do again?"

"E-excuse me?" Was he angry I was just standing there? I had no idea what my job as his partner would entail. At least his noticeable irritation with me was cooling off my crush.

"Your talents. Your powers." There was that annoyed look again.

"Oh!" My face flushed with embarrassment. "Flight. Super-strength."

He frowned. "We will have to make do."

"What's wrong with my powers?" I blurted, my own annoyance coming out.

He stared at me, as if amazed that I didn't know. He held my gaze long enough to make me uncomfortable, then cleared his throat and said, "Well, nothing is wrong with them per se, but they are powers based on brawn, not brains. Training with me will be good for you. I will teach you to use your intellect, but I am afraid you will not be much help to me."

Now it was my turn to stare at him. "Did you just call me stupid?" That pretty much doused the last of any lustful feelings I'd been having. Why did I have to go and be partnered up with a sexist pig?

"I do not mean to offend, Miss Livingston . . ."

"Because I graduated at the top of my class from the best law school in the country," I interrupted, steamed. Here it was again, the same prejudice I got from every man I met. "Don't let the blonde hair and the big boobs fool you. There is a brain in my head, one that I use on a regular basis, and not for figuring out what lingerie makes for the best costume."

Now he was staring at me as if I was crazy. The crazy man doubted *my* sanity. Wonderful.

"I know about your academic accolades, Miss Livingston. I checked your background before you came here. I only meant that mental powers, such as telepathy, for example, might be better suited for a partner of mine. I did not mean to imply that you were stupid."

"Oh." Maybe he hadn't, and I had just jumped to that conclusion. "Well, the next time you fight Jihad, maybe you'll think differently when I lay him out flat with one punch."

A slight smile crossed his face at the mental image of a punched-out archnemesis. "Yes, well, the trick is to find him first. Which is what we will attempt to do, when we are not patrolling or doing investigative work for the Elite Hands of Justice and the police. Now, I have more work to accomplish, so I will have Mayhew show you to your room. Take some time to settle in, and I will see you at dinner. We dress for dinner at this house. I assume you have the proper attire?" He pressed a button on his desk.

My business suit was out of the question. "Well, I . . ."

"If not, tell Mayhew, and he will order something appropriate. We will be doing some entertaining from time to time." He frowned. "It is a necessity, I am afraid, for a man of my stature. Dinner is seven o'clock sharp, in the dining room. Afterward, we will go on patrol."

I nodded. "Alright. Seven it is. It's a date."

He looked alarmed, and then cleared his throat. "You may go."

Gee, may I? "Um, good luck on the coffee grounds and all that."

Paging through his notes, he nodded, but it was obvious that he had forgotten about me already.

I turned to leave and almost bumped into the butler. Freaky. Where had he come from?

Unmoved by my surprise, Mayhew gestured toward the passage leading to the stairs. "This way, Miss."

We passed through the hallway, and this time went up a large staircase. The upstairs of the mansion was just as ornate as the downstairs, and had many rooms. The butler stopped in front of a set of double doors. "The master's suite," he said, opening one so I could see in. The room was enormous, done in sumptuous reds and golds.

"Your room will be across the hall," he added, closing the

door to Elliot's suite. He moved across the corridor to the facing double doors and swung them wide. "It's better for you to be close by, in case the two of you are called out in the middle of the night."

I nodded as I stepped inside, my breath taken away. The room was the size of my entire apartment. A large buttery leather couch bisected the room and faced a large flat-panel television mounted over the fireplace. Bookshelves on either side were filled with CDs, DVDs, and books. A closer inspection proved that it was my own personal collection. Apparently, the supermovers had arrived before I did. The other side of the room was taken up by a king-sized bed covered with a spread done in deep greens and yellows, like the rest of the room. An enormous walk-in closet already housed all my clothes. Directly across from the closet was a large bathroom, complete with a Jacuzzi tub.

I had died and gone to heaven.

"I trust everything is to your liking, Miss Livingston?"

A bit embarrassed to see Mayhew still standing in the doorway to witness my gawking, I waved aside formality. "Lainey, please. Miss Livingston sounds like an old maid living with her hundred cats. And everything is fabulous, but you know that. Your decorator has a good eye."

The butler smiled. "Mister Elliot does what he can."

I stared. "The Reincarnist—I mean Elliot—did all of this?"

The butler nodded. "Yes, Miss Lainey."

I looked around again, weighing my surroundings against the man I barely knew. "Interesting." Was there anything the man couldn't do? Well, except hold a conversation without sounding arrogant.

"Do you have a dress for dinner, Miss Lainey?"

Some of my newfound glow started to slip away. "Yes, I have a dress. I met the President in it, so I think it will do for dinner." Maybe my nerves were making me extra irritable, but neither of them had to act like I didn't know how to dress or handle myself in the company of the elite.

"Should you require anything at all, do not hesitate to ring," Mayhew said, unperturbed. "If you need help dressing, I can send up one of the maids. Also, the workout facilities and the pool are at your disposal in the downstairs left wing."

"Thank you."

"I shall leave you to get acclimated." He left with a slight nod, shutting the doors behind him.

The doors had barely closed before I launched myself onto the large bed. Working with the Reincarnist might not be a picnic, but the amenities were definitely making up for it.

It wasn't like it was going to be such a hardship working with him, either. Regardless of the vibe he gave off, it was an honor to work with the smartest man alive, and hey, he'd earned the right to his arrogance.

There was also the little flutter he gave me in the pit of the stomach.

Oh no, I ordered myself. *Don't go there. Crushes on the boss do not work out. Ask anyone.*

Still, I couldn't wait to wow him at dinner tonight.

Or at least show him I wasn't a poorly dressed dolt.

CHAPTER THREE

I descended the wide staircase, keeping a steady hand on the banister. It didn't help; my four-inch heels still caught on something invisible to the human eye, and I almost fell down the stairs. Klutziness, thy name is Lainey. Swearing under my breath, I tightened my grip on the banister and continued gingerly down, probably looking like a kid wobbling in her mother's shoes. I had never mastered the sashaying walk most women seemed to be born with. Maybe it was because I had never had a mother to guide me to womanhood, but there was something boyish about my manner, despite being amply blessed in the bosom area. I was meant to kick butt, not be eye candy.

I made it to the hall without falling and stood outside for a moment, checking to make sure every inch of the black designer dress was in its place. Satisfied, I took a deep breath, opened the door to the dining room, and walked in. A large table took up most of the space. At one end sat the Reincarnist, reading a newspaper. He glanced up and folded the newspaper, setting it next to his plate.

"Good, you are on time." He rose and walked over to me. I felt his eyes travel my body, assessing me as he approached.

See, I'm not a slob, I thought. Aloud, I said, "Where is everybody?"

"Pardon me?"

I gestured to the room. "We're in this huge room, all dressed up. I thought you were having company."

"Not tonight, no."

"So why are we dressed up?"

He looked at me as if I were beyond understanding. "I told you, we dress for dinner in this house. Long ago, people used to dress up for dinner and not lounge about in jeans and T-shirts." He pulled out a chair at the other end of the table from his place and stood waiting for me to take it. I looked blankly at him. Why would he seat me so far away?

"Sit down." He motioned to the chair.

"Seriously?"

He frowned. "What do you mean?"

"It's just the two of us. You're all the way down at the other end of the room!"

"The acoustics are very good in here. One can carry on a conversation quite well, though I am afraid I have gotten used to dining alone as of late."

I gave up and sat down. So my life for the foreseeable future was going to be spent dressed up for meals in an enormous hall with a companion who didn't like to talk. Not that I would have been able to hear him, anyway.

"Maybe I should bring a book or something," I said, more to myself than him, as he retook his seat at the other end of the monstrous table.

"Pardon?"

"Exactly."

He rang a bell and Mayhew appeared from the door behind him. "We are ready."

"Of course, sir." He disappeared again.

I examined the array of utensils in front of me. Good thing I had practice eating at fancy political dinners, otherwise I'd be feeling overwhelmed by the sheer number of forks.

"Do you always wear black?" Elliot asked, his voice echoing

off the walls. Okay, so maybe the acoustics *were* good in this room.

"Huh?"

He motioned to my dress. "I have seen photographs of your costume. And your dress. Do you always look as if you are in mourning?"

I glared at him in outrage. He made me get all dressed up and then he was going to complain about what I was wearing? "I went to meet the President in this dress, and he didn't seem to think I looked like I was going to a funeral."

"The President was probably admiring the assets the dress shows off."

That was it. The gloves were off. No way was I going to sit there and be insulted and somewhat sexually harassed.

"You know, for the smartest man alive, you certainly are an idiot when it comes to women," I said, my voice calm.

Mayhew, who had walked in at just that moment, was standing stock-still, shooting quick glances at his employer. I calmly stared at Elliot, waiting for his response.

His lips twitched suspiciously. He found my outburst amusing? "I do apologize, Miss Livingston, I meant no offense. You are correct. I am not an expert in women's fashion. I only meant that you might want to try wearing a bit of color once in a while. I am sorry to have upset you."

The danger past, Mayhew set the first course down in front of me, winking. *He knows his employer's crazy,* I thought. *Maybe at least I have an ally in him.*

"Apology accepted," I said. "I'm sorry I said you were ignorant."

This time a smile did break out. "Actually you are correct, Miss Livingston. I may have lived forever, but I still do not have the best social skills. A side effect, I am afraid, of spending too much time in the lab and with books."

"Maybe you should get out more. When you're not tracking down villains, I mean."

"Maybe I shall. Do try the wine, it is an excellent vintage."

I sipped it. It was good; not too heavy. "So, speaking of the lab, how did it go with the coffee grounds?"

"We shall see tonight. The police have searched the surrounding area where the child was last seen, as well as the one I pointed out today, and found nothing. Tonight I want to try a detection spell on-site, and see what I can find. I may need you to fly around and check the buildings."

I speared a piece of lettuce. "So I *can* be useful to you?" I said, a slight hint of humor creeping in my voice.

"That remains to be seen. I want to determine how strong your investigative skills are. But first, let us enjoy our meal. No more business discussion at the dinner table."

"Is that what heroics are to you—business, not pleasure?"

"Fighting crime is our job, much the same as it is for a police officer or a judge. And having studied extensively in criminal psychology and forensics, not to mention my magical advantages, I get many requests for help from the police, and that is also my job."

"I thought you were old money," I said, and then bit my lip. He probably didn't like the billionaire playboy stereotype being shoved in his face.

He laughed. "My dear girl, Robert Elliot might be called 'old money' by society, but who do you think earned and invested it for all of these years? I have worked very hard for all of this."

Well, now I felt stupid. "Of course you did. It's just a hard concept to wrap your mind around, someone living multiple lives and retaining the knowledge from each."

"I do not remember everything," he said with a distracted air. "Many of the details are fuzzy. For instance, I can tell you I fought in every major war in the United States, but not who my commanding officers were."

I shivered. "Sounds a bit spooky to me."

"Why? You do not recall every bit of your life in perfect detail. Could you tell me what happened to you on this date fifteen years ago?"

"No, not exactly." I would have been eleven, so I could hazard a guess that my classmates at the School were probably torturing me, but I got his point. "So I guess death doesn't really scare you, huh?"

"Why would that be?"

I toyed with my napkin. "You know you'll come right back, right?"

"Not exactly." He frowned. "There is never a guarantee the life I am living will not be my last one. Or that if I do come back, that I will retain any memories at all or just become a blank slate."

I shivered. *Yikes.*

"We could talk about my long life for years, but I would rather hear something about you," he said. He obviously wanted to change the subject.

I let the approaching main course of beef Wellington distract me. "There's probably not much to say that you don't already know."

"Pretend I know nothing about you."

I took a bite of the delicious beef, determined not to let my past ruin my appetite . The sting had gone out of my history awhile ago, but I still hated talking about it. I settled on giving the edited version. "My powers are the result of a power plant accident that killed my dad. My mom survived long enough for me to be born."

"I am very sorry."

I picked at my food. "I never knew them. I don't know if that makes it better or worse. But I like to think that they would be proud of the work I do."

"I am sure they would be."

Pushing aside the melancholy that always cropped up when I talked about my parents, I continued. "My powers manifested at eleven, and I was sent to live at the School." I eyed him. "Which you founded."

He nodded. "A couple of lifetimes ago, yes."

"I've worked with both the Red Knights and the Power

Squad, and now I'm working with you." I held up my hands. "That's me. Not as exciting as fighting in World War II or learning the black arts."

He winced. "Do not use that term, if you please. That is for unenlightened people, of which you are not one, who think magic is the direct route to damnation."

"So I'm enlightened now, am I?"

"Anyone who graduated from law school at the tender age of twenty-four is enlightened." At my shocked look, he added, "I said I researched your career. I told Ben to accept you the first time your application went through, but he thought Pushstar was a better choice. We both know how wrong he was."

"Pushstar's washout was legendary," I said, stunned by the revelation that *he'd* wanted me to make it into the EHJ. The Reincarnist had told Doctor Rath to accept me? Why? And then why had he been so derisive about my powers? And asked me my name? He had to believe I was intelligent and capable if he had recommended me in the first place. "So you *do* know everything there is to know about me."

"Not everything." He put his folded napkin down next to his plate and pushed back his chair. "We should get ready to patrol. You can assist me in setting up the detection spell."

I retrieved my own napkin from my lap and stood up. "Sounds great. I've never actually seen anyone use magic before." I followed him out of the cavernous dining room into the hall and up the stairs toward our suites.

"Yes, they do tend to segregate the magic students at the School, do they not?" He moved at a brisk pace. "Just do what I ask, and you shall be fine. I will wait for you to change."

Leaving him in the hallway, I went into my suite and dressed in a hurry. My black leather costume and thick-soled boots were with the rest of my clothes. Pulling them on, I slicked my hair back into a tight ponytail and bounded back down the stairs to the foyer.

"Okay, I'm ready. Let's patrol," I said when I found him downstairs. Damn, and I'd dressed fast too.

Elliot slid a vial into his jacket pocket. "Excellent. We can . . ." He trailed off, seeing me. "Why are you wearing that?"

God, did he think he was a fashion critic? "I thought we were going patrolling. It's my costume."

He shook his head. "Just as I do not use aliases, I do not use costumes. Neither will you in my company." He motioned to his outfit: a simple dark suit, long trench coat, and a fedora. "We try to blend in with the crowd as much as we can. All the better to sneak up on a villain."

"How do you keep villains from finding out who you are? No wonder this place is so heavily guarded!"

"Confusion spells. This hat." He smiled. Was he teasing me? "And how exactly does tight, black, leather clothing and no mask protect your secret identity?"

Okay, so he had a point. "I have no one to protect. They find out my secret identity, the only person they're going to hurt is me. But I'm not as high-profile as you. I don't have any archnemeses."

He sighed and rolled his eyes. "The language we speak is so over-the-top, do you not think? Archnemeses, secret identities, villains, super-aliases . . ."

I shrugged. "Our lives are over-the-top. We're heroes. It's what we do. I can bench-press an elephant and you live forever and cast spells. That's over-the-top."

"Do you at least have a jacket to wear over that?"

"Got just the thing. Won't be but a minute." I turned and flew back up the stairs, literally, to return only moments later in a lightweight black coat that was fitted to my waist and then flared out.

"Oh, that is *so* much better. That certainly blends in."

"Sarcasm is no one's friend," I retorted. "I'll wear civvie clothes next time. Let's go."

CHAPTER FOUR

We walked outside into the chill night air.

"Which one of your cool cars are we taking?" I surveyed the line of vehicles.

My comment got a genuine smile out of him. "You think my cars are cool?"

"What are you, modest? You know they're cool. You've got a 1957 Corvette Roadster, for God's sake."

I could tell that I was winning him over. "A woman that knows her cars. I am impressed. Most women would call it 'that cute little red car.'"

"Please, give me some credit. Besides, I'm a sucker for anything retro."

He gave me a quick look. "Really? Anything?"

Surely he didn't mean that the way I thought he did. In either case, I pretended I didn't have a clue to any hidden meanings. "Clothes, music, cars—I like anything vintage. Of course, you probably bought this when it was brand new."

"No, not that one. I bought it a few years ago from a collector. The 1952 Hudson I bought new."

"You have a Hudson? Where?" I looked around.

"It is in the garage. I will take you to see it when we get back. But first, we have work to do."

"So, which car are we taking?"

"I do not like to drive any of my cars down to where we are going. I would worry about it being boosted."

Somehow, the word *boosted* mixed in amongst his proper speech threw me. "So, what, you have a junker you drive to patrol?"

"Not exactly." He reached out and took hold of my arm. He pulled a vial from his coat pocket, poured out a handful, and threw the contents into the air. "*Apra il portal.*"

"Italian?" was all I was able to get out before a thunderclap filled my ears and I was hit with the sensation of being turned inside out while hanging upside down. If not for Elliot holding on to me, I would have fallen. As it was, I steadied myself on his arm, bent over in severe pain and nausea, and tried not to throw up.

"Wh-what was that?" I managed.

"Teleportation spell. I should have warned you it was going to be unpleasant," he said as I breathed in and out slowly, the rancid air not helping matters.

"The dentist is unpleasant. This is worse. Doesn't it bother you?"

"The dentist?"

I shot him an annoyed look and tried to straighten slowly. My head swam again, and this time I did fall to my knees, feeling my stomach revolt. *I will not throw up*, I told myself.

"I am accustomed to inter-dimensional travel," he said. "You will become so as well. The first couple of times are always the worst. Do you want me to perform a healing spell?"

"No more spells," I gasped. "I'll be alright. Just give me a few minutes." I looked around from my position on all fours on the concrete. "Where are we?"

"In the old industrial district. The dirt scraped from the missing child's shoe was matched to here. There used to be a coffee plant over there." He pointed to somewhere I couldn't see. "The members of the Elite Hands of Justice are all occupied at the moment, and this is in my jurisdiction, so I told Ben we would do a quick search for the child."

"How long has the kid been missing?" I found that I was now able to sit up. Progress!

"Two days. The police have not been able to turn up anything yet. She was abducted during the day, in front of a lot of witnesses, at the park on Seventh. Her mother was watching her, but she had a baby with her as well. The baby cried, the mother went to pick it up, she looked around, and her six-year-old was gone. Witnesses said they saw a strange man looking at the girl minutes before she disappeared. One of the shoes she was wearing at the park turned up on the front step of her house that evening, as if from nowhere. No fingerprints were on the shoe."

I got to my feet, watching as he pulled another vial out of his coat pocket and began to shake what looked like salt around him in a circle. "How do they know the kidnapper took her here?"

"Why else would she be here? Her mother lives on the other side of town. No reason for a child to be down here." He took out another vial. "Can you stand back, please?"

I did so. "But why would the kidnapper send her shoe back?"

"To taunt the police." He took a deep breath, closed his eyes, and spread his arms out wide. "I am going to cast a detection spell to see if I can find the girl."

"What do you want me to do?"

He opened his eyes. "Stand there and be quiet. If the spell pinpoints one particular building, I will have you do a flyby, then we will go inside. If the spell centers around several buildings, we will have a large area to search." Closing his eyes again, he spoke. "*Trovi il innocent.*" He poured the contents of a vial on the ground in another circle around him, then made one large puddle in the center that he then stood on.

"Is that blood?" I squeaked.

He ignored me and continued. "*Lustro di innocence.*"

I jumped as my skin suddenly felt warm, like the sun was shining on me even though it was night. I looked down at my arm and realized I was glowing. "What is going on?"

He glanced over and his eyes widened. "At least I know now you are not corrupt."

"Excuse me?"

"My spell casts light on those in the area that are an innocent."

"But I'm not a . . . I mean, I've . . ."

He rolled his eyes. "The spell speaks of your *soul*, not your virginity or lack thereof."

I blushed furiously at his matter-of-fact tone. Good to know my heart was pure, but did I have to go and blab that my body wasn't?

"Now, go fly around the buildings and see if you can see any light."

"But what if she's not by a window?"

"I will keep working the spell. As long as I am in the circle, it will continue to get brighter. If she is in a building, it should give the building a slight glow. Circle around a couple of times and then come back and tell me if you saw anything. It takes a lot of energy to run this spell."

"What about me?"

"What about you?"

"I'll be a big bright glowing thing in the sky. Won't that kind of warn the bad guy that we're coming?"

He smiled. "Good thinking, Miss Livingston. I will have to filter you out of the spell." He reached forward, plucked a hair from my head, and dropped it in the center of the puddle. He reached back into his coat, pulled out another vial full of powder, and with a few soft words in Italian, I felt the warmth fade from me.

"There we are. Remember, circle a few times, and if you do not see any glow, come back here."

"Got it." I took off into the air.

After circling a few times, my eye caught on one of the buildings. There was something faint, almost like steam, rising up from it. I landed easily on the roof. It wasn't steam, it was light; the same that had radiated off of me.

A thought dawned on me as I stood there. The Reincarnist had said the spell worked on those whose souls were innocent.

He hadn't been glowing.

I didn't have time to mull that over, because the light below me went out. I looked back in the direction from which I had come. Had Elliot quit the spell?

Oh, God. What if the girl had just died? Or had she somehow been corrupted? I hurried to the door on the roof, broke the lock, and headed inside. Something had gone wrong.

The building was dilapidated. It looked like junkies and squatters had taken up residence at one point—dirty needles and stained mattresses lined the floors. But there was no sign of anyone, innocent little girl or no.

I deliberately hovered over the floor, so my footsteps would not sound my presence. Most of the doors had been ripped off, which saved me from having to open one blindly. But at the end of the hall was a closed door, and a dying glow was coming from it.

I hurried forward, sailing past the other doorways, ignoring them for the one obvious one.

"What's your hurry, do-gooder?" a voice growled from behind me, and I was yanked backward by an unseen force.

I was slammed through the wall, plaster and wood breaking around me. A man stood in the hallway, staring into the room through the hole my body had made. A red ball of energy crackled in his hand.

"That sweet little thing sure did taste good," he said, the light from the ball giving his features a red glow as he stepped into the room with me.

I jumped up and he made a motion with his hand, stopping me in my tracks, hovering in the air. I tried to move but couldn't. It was as if my muscles had forgotten how to work.

"Stay still," he said. As he neared, I could see black tattoos covering his pasty white skin, all some sort of arcane symbols the Reincarnist would probably recognize. His lank black hair fell into eyes that were also black—and not just his pupils; the corneas were black as well. I shivered in revulsion.

He studied me like a kid ready to pull the wings off an insect. "You're not the magic-user." He made a motion and my body went flying to him, stopping only inches away. Up close, he smelled of decay and sulfur. He sniffed me, and I almost threw up. He smiled at my revulsion and ran a finger across my cheek, trailing down my arm to my breast.

"You smell sweet, too," he said, sharp teeth like knives showing in a hateful smile. "You wouldn't believe how many do-gooders actually have no good inside them." He gave my breast a hard squeeze, and then slid his hand so that his palm was right over my heart. "That little thing was just a snack." His hand glowed red again. "You will be the main course."

A searing pain worse than anything I had ever experienced tore through my chest and in deeper. I heard someone screaming, a gut-wrenching sound that seemed to go on forever. My mind could barely comprehend that it was me.

Then what looked like a glowing white thunderbolt blasted the villain in the throat. He gasped airlessly, head snapping forward, and he lost his hold on me. I collapsed bonelessly to the floor, my whole body tingling as if I had been electrocuted. Clutching at his throat, my assailant glared hatefully at the man in the doorway behind him.

The Reincarnist.

As I tried to drag my injured self out of the way, I heard Elliot's commanding voice. "Syn, you have stolen from your last soul. Come without a fight, and I will not ruin you."

Syn still couldn't speak, but his bottomless black eyes conveyed his intentions even as he made a quick but intricate gesture and a black splatter of light shot from his outstretched fingers and into Elliot. I had a feeling it was not only an attack, but something obscene—like the magical equivalent of giving someone the finger.

Elliot grunted as the sizzling blast hit him straight in the chest, but he didn't take a step back, nor did he betray any of the pain I could tell he was feeling from his slightly widened eyes. But then his dark eyes darkened further, with an odd magical glow that elicited a whimper out of me as I scurried to get out of the way. There was something dark and scary lurking under my partner's calm demeanor that I had a feeling, if ever released, would be ten times scarier than the villain in front of me.

His tone of voice only furthered that conviction. "Fine," he said. He stretched out a hand in Syn's direction and growled two words, "*Legatura magica.*"

The instant the words left his mouth, Syn collapsed onto the floor next to me, convulsing. Elliot himself slunk back to lean against the wall, breathing heavily and looking pale beneath his 1920s detective hat.

I staggered to my feet and over to him. "Wh-what did you do to him?"

"I bound his magic according to our old laws. He will not be able to access his abilities anymore."

"You can do that?" I was impressed. It had seemed so easy!

He nodded. "I am one of the few who can. It takes a lot of will to do such a spell, especially after the power drain he hit me with."

Oh. So maybe it hadn't been that easy. Now I was concerned for him. "Are you going to be okay?" I asked.

He gave me a reassuring smile that didn't reach his eyes. "I will just need to rest for a few days." All I had to do was look at his pale face and the pain he was masking, and knew he was lying. But I knew how much male heroes wanted to look invincible, even when they weren't, so I said nothing.

He straightened and ran both hands down either side of my body, but not touching me, almost like he was feeling up my aura. A warm quiver of desire shot straight through me. "He did not get much."

"Much of what?" I half-whispered.

"Your soul."

That shot me back to reality. "What?"

"He uses magic to steal your essence and feast on it. It gives him power. He escaped to the Higher Planes once before, but not this time." He took a deep, steadying breath. "He may be powerful, but he is still only a child. I have been doing magic since before this country was founded."

"We need to try to find the girl. There was a light at the end of the hallway, but it was very faint." I started toward the hall.

"Do not bother," he said. I turned back, and saw the dark look flitting in his eyes. "You do not want to see what is in that room."

I froze. "Oh, God. Why not?"

"She is dead. I saw you land on the roof and followed you here when you did not return. I thought you could handle him long enough that I could get her out, so I went in." He cleared his throat. "I found her body."

My stomach rolled, but I tried to stay professional. "I've seen dead bodies before." A sad but true fact in this business.

"A child?"

Well . . . I shook my head no, trying to keep from crying.

"Then trust me, you would rather not see it. It is always worse to see a child."

We hadn't been able to save a six-year-old kid. It wasn't fair! I felt tears run down my cheek and angrily swiped them away. "I'm sorry. It's not professional to go to pieces like this."

"Do not apologize. I rather appreciate that it affects you still. It means you are not so jaded that you are incapable of empathy for those we are trying to save."

"It's just that not being able to save an adult is sad, but not being able to save a child is devastating. At least to me."

"I would agree," he said.

"We need to call the EHJ." I swiped the remainder of tears away and took a calming breath.

"They are all on a mission to outer space." He handed me a handkerchief with monogrammed initials on it. Who still carried handkerchiefs?

"Seriously?" I wiped my eyes, twisting the handkerchief in my hands. "God, why don't they do some actual work in this country or on this planet for a change?"

He smiled. "That is what we are here for."

"What are we going to do with him, then?" I pointed to Syn without looking. *I know what I'd like to do with him, lousy child-murderer.*

"See you in hell, bitch!"

What?! We both whirled in time to see Syn, who had gone from passed out on the floor to alert and mobile in the space of a second. I had a fraction of a second to react as he came at me with a wicked-looking blade.

"*Arresto!*" Elliot ordered, and the madman froze on the spot. "I cannot keep doing this all night. The magic is taxing me to my limits. He should not have been able to recover that fast."

"Tell *him* that," I growled. "So, what are we going to do?" I took a deep breath, trying to pretend I wasn't shaking.

"Give him to the authorities, I suppose. I will call a man I know on the police department. Someone needs to collect the . . ." He cleared his throat. "The body."

Our eyes met and I saw my pain echoed in his. So the child's death really was affecting him. I wasn't sure if this surprised me.

"We have to hold him until the police arrive?"

He nodded.

"Alright." I walked over to where Syn still stood frozen, and punched him. He hit the wall hard and went down, unconscious.

Elliot nodded. "Good thinking."

I kicked the knife away, out of Syn's grasp, but didn't touch it. Elliot dialed a number on a cell phone and spoke with someone. He sounded angry as he hung up.

"Pendergast is not working tonight, so they are sending Deburt."

"Deburt on the take or something?" I half laughed.

"No, he has issues with our kind and does not like me personally. He will make this more difficult than it needs to be. I am sorry your first night on the job has turned out to be so rough."

I shrugged. "I'm used to it. Nothing ever goes smoothly for me. I would be more worried if everything went according to plan."

"Still, we came expecting a missing persons case and you ended up getting a chunk taken out of your soul."

"I'll live." Then, alarmed, I asked, "Won't I?"

"He took just a bit, like a fingernail."

"So it's survivable."

"Lots of things are survivable."

I didn't like the tone of that. "Is there any way to fix it? I feel a little weird, walking around with a fingernail-sized hole in my soul."

He looked me over for a long moment. I felt like his gaze was shooting through to my essence and inspecting that missing piece. He nodded, as if I had passed some unspoken test, and said, "I can heal you."

He laid his palm over my heart, much like Syn had done. I hoped he wouldn't feel it speed up at his touch. He closed his eyes and breathed deep. I could feel the heat from his hand all the way through the black leather I wore, causing my breathing to quicken.

"Should you be doing this?" I stuttered. "You said yourself, the spell you just cast took a lot out of you."

"This will be the last magic I do for the night, then," he said. "*Guar l'anima.*"

Something warm spread through my being for a moment, a good feeling, like standing in front of a fireplace on a cold day, and then it was gone. I felt cold and involuntarily arched toward him to try to recapture the warmth. He gave me a slight smile and lightly clapped me on the shoulder. "You should be alright now." He leaned back against the wall and closed his eyes.

"Thanks." I felt very strange after the spell. I had an almost overwhelming need to reach out and touch him, to retain that momentary closeness. I wrapped my arms around myself instead and shivered.

"You are welcome." He kept his eyes closed.

"Why are your spells in Italian?" I asked, trying to fill the void in conversation.

"It is the language in which I learned them." He didn't open his eyes, but his mouth quirked in a slight, teasing smile.

I returned the expression, even though he couldn't see me. "Obviously. So . . . every magic-user learns spells in different languages?"

"You learn the spells in whatever language your teacher uses. Mine happened to be Italian, but this was centuries ago."

"So, can anyone learn the spells?"

"Only those born with the gift can access magic."

"So, is the Reincarnist thing a part of you, or is it magic you've done?"

His eyes snapped open. "You think I would do this to myself on purpose?" His voice held a darkness that was surprising.

I masked my discomposure by shrugging. "Everyone wants to live forever."

"Only those that do not know what it truly means to do so."

I was taken aback for a moment, and then I blurted, "Why didn't you glow? When you did your spell, you said it showed innocence of the soul. It worked on me. Why didn't it work on you?"

His smile was sad, but he did not fail to answer. "When you have lived as long as I have, you do not escape without a little tarnish on your soul. If you want the truth, usually only children will shine. It is very rare to see it in an adult; we all lose our innocence bit by bit."

"But I'm nothing special," I protested. "Trust me, I'm not."

"Someone thinks otherwise, Miss Livingston."

"Lainey," I said. "I think after everything we've been through tonight, you can call me Lainey."

He nodded. "Alright, Lainey. When we are alone together, you can call me Robert. Elliot when we are out like this."

Hey, it was a start.

The sound of sirens could be heard pulling up outside the building.

"Prepare yourself," Robert said. "Here comes Deburt."

Deburt had an obvious chip on his shoulder. The policeman glared at me as if I had committed the felony, not been one of the victims. "Of course *you* would be here, Elliot, but who the hell is she?" he growled, killing the myth of the jolly fat man. Well over three hundred pounds, Deburt was about 5'7" in stocking feet, just a little taller than me, so I had the height advantage with my high-heeled boots. His black hair was slicked back in fifties greaser-style and he had a thin mustache. His dark eyes barely skimmed my face and instead fell to rest on my breasts. Oh, great. It was going to be one of those conversations.

"This is my new partner," Robert said, sounding like a tired parent who senses his toddler is about to throw a fit. "She will be joining me on my investigations."

"I'm sure she will." Deburt leered at me.

Robert gave him a dark look. "It is too bad Pendergast is not working tonight."

"He's off. Sorry I'm not willing to kowtow to your vast experience," Deburt said sarcastically to my breasts. "You capes are an arrogant bunch, believing we should be grateful any time you collect one of the numerous nutcases you create."

"First of all, my eyes are up here," I said, pointing to my face. The other investigators snickered and he shot them a nasty look. "Second, is either one of us wearing a cape? I don't think so. And third, we didn't create the psycho nutjob that butchered that little girl and almost did the same to me. We were just trying to help find her, and I would think you'd be happy for any help you can get." After having a piece of my soul ripped out, I had no patience left to deal with getting ogled by a skeevy guy who probably had to pay to see a naked woman. "Besides, you wouldn't have wanted to try to take this guy down by yourselves. I'm super-strong and got my ass handed to me."

"You look fine to me," Deburt said, giving extra emphasis to the word *fine*.

"Well, that's because he used magic."

"Uh-huh. Magic." He acted as if I had told him Santa Claus was real.

"Yes, magic. And then Elliot saved me."

Deburt looked at my boss. It was a welcome relief to my breasts. "With magic, I suppose?"

Robert gave a slight nod. "I can go over the crime scene with you, if you wish."

"That'd be nice." Deburt's tone said otherwise. "Let's go." He pointed to the detectives with him. "You three take her statement. Make sure she doesn't go anywhere. They're still suspects until we get this matter settled."

Like they could stop me, I thought.

Robert must have sensed my mood, because he stepped over to me, laying a gentle hand on my arm. Though my coat and gloves covered my skin, a warm thrill of delight still ran through me.

"Cooperate with them," he said in a low voice. "But if they get too accusatory, request your attorney be present."

"I don't have one," I whispered.

"The Elite Hands of Justice do. And you are a part of them now."

I nodded, and faced the three remaining cops with a dark stare. Living in foster homes and with hero teams all of my life, I had learned that if you came on strong with a take-charge attitude, you wouldn't be walked on.

The two older cops, one with graying hair and the other who bore an eerie resemblance to the rapper Qpid, had obviously dealt with the super set before, judging by the way they went about the business of securing the crime scene. They ignored my presence, leaving me to the young cop who was staring wide-eyed at me.

The newbie seemed to remember he was supposed to be taking a statement and not gawking, and cleared his throat. "Alright ma'am, what's your name?"

"Phenomenal Girl Five."

The gray-haired cop nudged Officer Qpid. "I told you that was her."

"N-no, your real name." Newbie was clearly rattled.

"You don't need to know that information."

"Yes, we do."

"Kid, have you ever heard of secret identities? It's not much of a secret if everyone knows."

The other two cops snickered at this, enjoying the hassle I was giving their coworker.

He pressed on. "Can you give us a statement as to what happened here?"

I ran over the whole story with him as Qpid bent over Syn.

"And you engaged in combat with the assailant?"

"Yep."

"And he attacked you with a knife and with magic?"

"Yes. He ripped out a chunk of my soul."

"Of your soul?"

"After confessing to assaulting the girl, yes."

"And you knocked him out?"

"After Elliot healed me."

"With magic?"

"You say that like you don't believe it," I said. "Trust me, Junior, magic is very real."

The younger officer glanced back at his partners, who were helping a handcuffed Syn to his feet. Suddenly, with an insane howl, the villain lurched out of their grasp and launched himself, teeth bared, at the younger police officer.

I shoved Junior aside and punched Syn in the face again. He went down screaming, his nose shattered. I grabbed him from behind, picking him up by the collar of his shirt and his cuffed hands, and held him in the air as he bucked and screamed. "Want me to take him down to the police car?" I asked the three astonished cops.

Robert was outside by the police cruiser with Deburt, and he didn't even look surprised as I walked out holding the crazed villain in front of me like a bag of garbage, the three cops following in my wake. Deburt, who was clearly having a nasty conversation with whomever was on the other end on his cell phone, shot me a glare as I passed. From what I could infer, he was being told to leave us alone.

"Is everything under control?" Robert asked as Officer Qpid opened the door to his car and I tossed Syn in the backseat.

I nodded. "Of course." The two older police officers waved their thanks and got in, dragging Junior along with them.

"Good. If the police have matters in hand, we have other business to attend to. Let us know if we can be of further use to you," he said to Deburt. "Good night." He strode away.

"See ya," I called back to Deburt, and followed my partner.

"Robert," I said as we cleared the warehouse. "What else do we have to do tonight?"

"Go home and get a good rest," he said with a boyish smile.

I couldn't help but grin back.

"Who was that waste of a badge Deburt talking to on the phone?"

"The police commissioner. He is an old friend. I think the gist of the conversation was that we caught a dangerous criminal and Deburt should be grateful for the help." He held out a hand. "Shall we?"

I took it with caution, remembering the teleport here. "I'm not going to get sick again, am I?"

"No, because we are taking a cab home." He pulled a cell phone out of his jacket pocket and dialed a number. "I need to rest before I do more magic."

I was bone-tired and more than a little bit freaked out. Good to know I wasn't the only one who had been tested to the end of their limits in the space of one night.

CHAPTER FIVE

The next morning I woke up in that dazed way you do when you've forgotten where you went to bed. Sun was peeking through the thick draperies, and with a yawn I got up and plodded over to throw them open. Bright light greeted me and I yawned again, holding a hand up against the blinding sun. What time was it? I hadn't been able to sleep well, with thoughts of that poor little girl and her family running through my head.

A knock sounded on my door a split second before Robert came barging in. I jumped, startled.

His glance flicked over me in an instant, and he frowned. "Do you sleep until ten every day?"

"Only on mornings when parts of my eternal essence were sucked out the night before," I retorted, crossing my arms over my chest, keenly aware I was only in my silk cami and boxers—and that they were a bit on the see-through side in the right lighting.

He didn't appear bothered by my near-nakedness. "Well, get dressed and hurry along. Mayhew has a late breakfast waiting for you in the nook and Detective Pendergast is stopping by to speak to us at eleven."

"About the murder?"

"Yes. He has a few questions about the statement you gave. I thought I told you to cooperate."

"I did!"

"Not giving your name is not cooperating."

"It's called a secret identity! *Secret!*"

He fixed me with a dark look. "If you are going to be my partner, then you must learn to be up front with the police. These moronic super-aliases are more trouble than they are worth. They cast an air of suspicion on you that you do not want. We work with the police, not against them. Besides, was it not you who told me you did not wear a mask because you had no one to protect?"

"I wasn't . . . I'm not . . ." I gave up.

He pulled a notebook out of his jacket pocket and flipped it open. "I also told you last night to circle a few times and come back to report what you saw. Instead, you went inside and engaged Syn."

"Yeah, but . . ." I trailed off. He was right. That wasn't a good move on my first day. "Wait, are you critiquing me on my performance last night?"

"I am supposed to be training you."

"I know, but . . ."

"Yes?"

"Can I at least get dressed first?"

He looked me over again and flipped his notebook shut. "We will discuss this more later. For now, get dressed, eat, and meet me in the library at eleven sharp." He turned on his heel and left.

Fuming, I whirled around to my closet, got dressed quickly, and ran a brush through my tangled hair. On my way out, I nabbed a book off the shelf, clutching the slim volume to my side as I went down the stairs.

Just where in hell was the nook?

"Miss Lainey?"

I turned to find Mayhew walking up to me. Thank God.

"I'm lost," I said by way of apology. "I'm sorry I missed breakfast. Robert said you had something waiting for me in the nook?"

He raised an eyebrow at my use of his boss's given name.

"Yes, right this way, Miss." He turned and led me down the hall, through a set of double doors, through the kitchen, and into a small eating area overlooking a garden.

A feast of gourmet coffee, croissants, fruit, an omelet, and crisp bacon awaited me. I hadn't been hungry, but seeing all that food made my mouth water. I sat down and dug in.

"If there is something you would rather have for breakfast in the future, please let me know," Mayhew said. "I just made what Mister Elliot likes."

"This is fine. And I'm sorry I wasn't up earlier. What time do you usually serve breakfast?"

"Mister Elliot likes to eat at seven, followed by his daily workout routine."

"Seven? Seriously?" I blurted. I took a sip of coffee to cover my blunder. "I mean, I'm not usually up that early, we keep such late hours."

"He doesn't require much sleep," Mayhew said. "But I believe his former associates have usually had breakfast between the hours of eight and nine."

That was better, at least. "I'll be up at eight, then."

"Very good, Miss," he said, whisking my plate away.

I sat and sipped my coffee, grateful for a moment alone to collect my thoughts. Remembering the book, I flipped through it until I found the page I wanted. I had read it so many times, the book could turn there on its own.

Lost in thought, I didn't hear anyone walk into the room.

"You are reading?" Robert asked, surprise in his tone.

Irritated, I gritted my teeth. "Yes, I read. Don't let the shock of my being literate kill you."

"You should not take every comment I make as a personal insult directed at you." He grunted as he sat down across from me and poured himself a cup of coffee. I remembered last night had taken its toll on him as well, and my anger cooled.

"I thought I was the only one who brought a book to meals." He gave me that slight boyish smile.

"Oh." I was embarrassed. He was right, I needed to relax or the only kind of impression I'd be making was that of the crazy variety. "I was kinda antisocial in my childhood and teenage years. Books were my friends."

He nodded in understanding. "So . . . you would not be offended if *I* brought reading material to dinner?"

"Only if you promise to lighten up on the dress code. And do you have any other room in the house to eat in that isn't an entire hall?"

He smiled. "A more casual atmosphere can be arranged."

"Great." I toasted him with my coffee mug and went back to reading.

"So, what is it that so engrosses you?" he asked, looking over at the slim hardback.

"Oh, it's poetry." I shrugged it off. "From the Romantic era."

"Who is the poet?"

"William Graves."

A look of complete surprise crossed his features. "Really? Why him?"

"He's my favorite. At school we had to do reports on these assigned poets, and he's the one I got. Something about his work really spoke to me. It all has this innate sense of loneliness that I connected with. After all, what teenager doesn't feel alone in their problems—especially one with superpowers who lost her parents? Anyway, I just completely dug his work, and we had to read a poem to the class and explain what it meant. So I read this one." I pointed to the page to which the book was open.

He slid the tome around to read the title. "'Theft of a Moment.'"

"I told everyone it was about this man's desire to take a chance, failing to do so, and how he hoped the next time he'd be able to act but was afraid he would let it pass again. My teacher said no, that's not what the poem's about; it's about the failure to overthrow the corruption of the politicians and the Industrial Age's birth. We got in this huge fight because I wouldn't back down, and I got an F."

"I cannot imagine you not backing down," he said with mild sarcasm.

"Known me one day and already you know me too well."

He paused a moment. "Well, if it helps to hear, you were right and your teacher was wrong. I happen to be sure of it." He got up from the table. "We must go. Pendergast will be waiting."

Surely he wasn't suggesting what I thought. I scrambled after him.

"Did you study Graves?" I asked, keeping in step with him.

"After a fashion, yes."

"Did you know him or something?"

"Or something."

I stopped. "*Were* you him?"

He turned back to look at me. "Lainey, there are a lot of lives I have lived whose memories are but a dim spark, almost like a half-forgotten story or a dream I once had. That is not a truly *shared* life."

Okay, if that didn't sound like the meanderings of a poet, I didn't know what did. "So you were him."

He paused at the door to the library. "Let us save ourselves a lot of trouble, shall we? From time to time, I might mention something historical, of the past. Let us assume I know what I am talking about. Whether or not I was that person or had that experience, or just read about it in a book, is irrelevant. So, when I say that you understood your poem and your teacher did not, it is true, and how I came about the information is not important. Alright?"

I nodded, feeling even more confused. "Okay."

"If it helps, think of my former lives as relatives. After all, they all had different names and faces—and as I say, not all the same memories. Now, back to the matter at hand." He opened the door and walked in.

I followed after him. No wonder everyone said he was crazy. I'd be crazy too if I were him.

Detective Pendergast was in his fifties, slightly overweight, with gray hair that almost looked silver. He was flipping through a notebook when we walked in.

"Good morning, Detective Pendergast," Robert said, giving his hand an enthusiastic shake.

Pendergast responded in kind. "Good to see you again, Mister Elliot."

"Can I get you anything? Coffee, tea, something to eat perhaps?"

"Coffee would be great, thanks."

"I will ring Mayhew." Robert busied himself at the desk.

I walked up to Pendergast. "Hi. Lainey Livingston."

He took my hand in his firm grip. "Nice to meet you. I take it you are his new partner?"

"I just started yesterday."

"Pretty eventful first day."

"You have no idea."

"Then you are Phenomenal Girl Five?"

"Yes, sir."

He flipped through the notebook again. "Why didn't you tell the detective on the scene your real name?"

"He asked for that information in front of someone who had attacked me."

"Duly noted, Miss Livingston." He scratched something down in the notebook.

"Is there anything I or my partner can do to help out your case, Pendergast?" Robert asked, coming to stand very close behind me. I twitched at the proximity.

"Syn was more than happy to brag about what he did to the girl, and to your partner for that matter. The D.A. won't have any problems prosecuting this case." Pendergast accepted the coffee cup Mayhew brought him. "Thank you.

Everyone knows Deburt has a grudge against capes." He winced, as if remembering to whom he was speaking. "Sorry, those of the powered persuasion."

"He has had problems working with me since the Grivinci case," Robert said.

"We do appreciate all the help you have given us, make no mistake about that," Pendergast said. "Your expertise has been invaluable, and we don't want one bad apple like Deburt to ruin our relationship."

"It will not, but I appreciate you saying so."

"Syn said something else during his confession that I thought you needed to be aware of." Pendergast cleared his throat and glanced down at the notebook. "He said the EHJ needed to be more concerned about what went on in their own backyards than in space." He flipped the notebook shut. "Are the charter members of the Elite Hands of Justice off-planet?"

My blood ran cold. "How would he know that? That's not the type of thing released to the public."

"Someone must have told him they were away." Robert tapped a finger on his lips in thought.

"I think this Syn was egged on by someone else," Pendergast said. "Someone who was aware of the EHJ's activities."

"But who would know that information?" I asked.

"Other than their legions of publicists?" Robert said darkly. "That is the trouble of keeping too public of a profile; almost everyone knows where you are at all times. I am surprised villains have not taken advantage before this. Although we did not know they were going off-planet until yesterday . . ." He trailed off, lost in thought, oblivious to Pendergast's and my presence. "It is a matter that needs to be addressed."

"Well, you may be receiving a summons to court," Pendergast remarked.

"Of course. Whatever you need, do let us know," Robert said. "We will be keeping an eye on things on our side."

"Like I said, we appreciate everything you do. I'll see myself out. Thank you for the coffee. A pleasure to meet you, Miss Livingston." He nodded to me and left the room.

I turned to Robert. "There's no way a villain knew the EHJ went off-planet just by reading the newspaper."

"Syn could have used surveillance. Though, with the wards and Mindy's many inventions, any bugs should have been picked up. There is one possibility . . ."

"What?"

"Someone close tipped Syn off."

I stared at him. "You think someone in the EHJ switched sides?"

"I did not say that. It does not have to be one of the members. It could have been a member of the housekeeping staff, or one of the public relations assistants, even the barista in the building's coffee shop. But we cannot eliminate any possibilities yet." He moved past me to the bookcase. "I shall see if I can get in touch with Ben, and apprise him of the situation."

"Anything I can do to help?"

"Yes. A woman from the Poverty Society will be coming at one to discuss plans for the charity ball I give every year. I do not have time to deal with her, so can you take care of it?"

"The *whole* ball?"

"Yes. I generally like to have my partners take care of social events for me."

"How sexist of you."

"My partners have sometimes been men."

I smiled at that. "Alright. Help some chick throw some party. It'll be easy."

He laughed. "See me after she leaves. I may have an easier time of it than you will." He pulled the proper books and the door swung open. "I will be downstairs." He disappeared into his lair, leaving me to wonder just what I had in store.

CHAPTER SIX

Exactly at noon, a black-haired tornado burst into the library. Startled, I looked up from the psychological profiling book I was leafing through.

"Robert, darling, I was just . . ." She trailed off. "And just who are *you?*" She gave me a look as if I was something she had scraped off the bottom of her designer shoes.

She was pretty in a spoiled-rich-girl way. Model skinny, with perfect skin and glossy black hair. What I hated most were her eyes. I've always thought it wasn't fair I was born with blonde hair but not blue eyes. Hers were the bluest I'd ever seen.

Remembering I shouldn't be rude to a guest of Robert's, especially one who called him "darling," I squared my shoulders and took a step forward.

"Lainey," I said, reaching out to shake her hand. She recoiled as if I had licked it first. Feeling awkward, I lowered it. "I'm his new . . . assistant." It's not as if I could say *crime-fighting partner*, now could I? Who knew how much she was aware of?

"Oh." She looked relieved that her precious Robert wasn't lowering his standards to socialize with me. "Then be a dear, take my coat and bring me a cappuccino. I swear, that butler of his is worthless." She threw her coat at me, revealing a skin-tight black dress with a scoop neck so low that, coupled with the push-up bra, it was amazing the objects on display didn't reveal that last critical inch. She took a compact out of her tiny little designer bag and checked her reflection. Yes, she was still hot. Nothing had changed since she walked in. "Do tell Robert that Victoria Dupree is waiting for him."

"Robert was . . . called away on other business," I said. "He sent me instead."

She paused, a tube of lipstick just inches away from her mouth. "You're not serious?"

I shrugged. "I'm afraid so."

"But we're supposed to be planning the benefit together!" Victoria glowered at me. Did she think I was hiding him somewhere, so he wouldn't get to see her spectacular cleavage, which she'd probably spent all day glittering and pushing up just right? She might be a sublimely gorgeous stick figure, but at least I had her beat in the chest area.

"He said I was to take over for him. He's too busy with his work."

"But I have an appointment. And I'm an old friend of his. He can make a little time to see me. All I really need to do is ask him one teeny question about the party and the rest I can handle. Now, go tell him I just need to borrow one minute of his time and then I'll get out of his hair. I know how time-consuming his work can be."

"What does he do?" The words slipped out of my mouth before I could stop them.

She blinked in surprise. "What?"

"Robert. What exactly does he do for a living? Since you're an old friend and all."

Her eyes flashed blue fire. "We don't discuss business. And I don't think it's appropriate for his assistant to be using his first name in such an intimate fashion. His last assistant always called him Mister Elliot."

I shrugged. "What can I say? He likes me better." Or he had until I went and insulted his girlfriend. But if she were his girlfriend, he wouldn't have foisted her off on me. "Now, if there is any message you would like to leave for Robert,

I'd be happy to take it. And I'd be glad to help with your benefit."

"Just tell him I will be calling him later. I'll arrange for a private dinner to discuss matters further. Away from this house." She snatched her coat from my grasp and clicked off, stilettos echoing out into the hallway. "He needs to put the help in their place!" she shot at Mayhew, who was holding the door open for her.

I'd rather fight your garden-variety villain than a psycho society woman any day.

Seeing the butler still standing there, I flashed him an apologetic look. "I'm the help that needs to be put in their place, not you, Mayhew."

"Don't worry about me, Miss Lainey. Miss Dupree has been after Mister Elliot to fire me for over a year now."

"He's not going to be mad I antagonized her?"

Mayhew chuckled. "I doubt that. He tries to antagonize her every chance he gets, just to shake her off. She's been vying for the title of Mrs. Elliot since they met."

I'm sure she has been. "And he doesn't want that?"

"The master doesn't have time for romantic attachments, and they would be . . . complicated."

"The hero thing. I hear ya." It was one of the reasons I had focused on my career and let the romance factor slide. Not that I never dated, but heroes as a general rule tended to date inside the family, so to speak. No one understands why you have to cancel dinner to fight some loony in pajamas more than another hero. They might even join you. "So, where is Robert anyway?"

"Out in the garden, doing some exercises."

"Did he get through to the EHJ?"

"I believe so, Miss Lainey, but you will have to ask him."

"Thanks, Mayhew. I go . . . this way?"

"Through the kitchen is the best." He gave me a wink.

"Thanks." I'd get the layout of this mansion someday. Out in the garden, Robert was doing something that looked like Tai Chi, eyes closed in meditation. He was whispering something I couldn't quite catch as I walked up. I didn't want to interrupt, but he had said to meet him.

Finally I cleared my throat. "So, did you get in contact with Rath?"

He opened his eyes and focused on me. "Yes, I did. He is going to keep an eye on the members, make sure nothing is out of the ordinary. And they are going to instate new security measures with all of the staff in the building immediately. Has Miss Dupree left already?"

"Yeah. I kinda pissed her off."

"Really? What did you say to her?" The corner of his mouth twitched.

Even though Mayhew was sure he wouldn't be angry, I wasn't. I took a deep breath. "Well, she was really upset I wouldn't let her see you, and then I questioned your close friendship." I meet his gaze. "I probably shouldn't have, and I'm sorry I upset your friend."

"You probably should not have?" He laughed. "That is an interesting apology, Lainey. And you are correct in assuming she is but an acquaintance of mine and not a close personal friend." He went back to exercising.

I watched him go through the motions. "Is that Tai Chi?"

"Something like it. It helps to focus and balance the magic energies. After last night's activities, it was sorely needed." He finished the movement and eyed me. "You should try it."

"Maybe if I had magic."

"Perhaps you do and do not realize it. Some live their whole lives and never know of their capabilities. No matter how many tests the Elite Hands of Justice persuades the populace to run to check for 'powers,' there will always be those who slip through their fingers." He sounded somewhere between annoyed and amused by this.

"I was tested when I was a kid."

"Humor me," he said, hands clasped behind his back.

I shrugged. What harm could it do? I'd always wanted to take up Tai Chi anyway. "What do I do?"

He came to stand behind me. "You start off in a stance like this." He put his hands on my waist, bringing my hips to a centered position. He moved his hands up to my shoulders, squaring them, then left one lightly on the small of my back.

"Now, shift your weight onto your left foot and pivot to the side, and move down while extending your right arm . . ." He led me through the exercise, a series of slow movements, all the while staying right beside me, every so often correcting a move with a small touch. I felt my body growing warm, and not from the exertion.

". . . And center position, hands together in front of you." He followed the movement along with me, hands slightly on my hips again. The urge to lean back against him was almost too overwhelming to control.

His hands left my hips, and traced a line up my body without touching it, much like he had done the night before. "It is faint, but it is there."

My breathing went shallow. "What is?" I turned to face him, daring to look into his eyes.

"Magic. I doubt you could ever cast a spell, but it is there."

"But they tested me at school."

"Maybe it did not show up until you matured." He again traced the outline around me, somehow setting my skin on fire without even making contact. The magic scans at school never did *that*.

I leaned forward. I couldn't help it; it was like an involuntary reaction. For a moment, it seemed as if he was going to lean in to kiss me. And God, did I want him to. But then he moved away, arms behind his back again.

"Thank you for taking care of Miss Dupree for me."

"Well, I don't think I scared her off for good," I said, not liking the mention of the society chick in our fading moment. "She said she was going to arrange a private dinner for you to discuss things away from your uppity servants. Or something to that effect."

"I will just be too busy for her calls. Mayhew will have to take a message."

"That's cold."

"To Miss Dupree?"

"To Mayhew."

He laughed. "I need something to keep me busy so I do not have to speak with her. Would you like to go into town with me?"

"We don't have to teleport, do we?" I asked, cautious.

"No, I still need to let my powers rest after last night."

I frowned. "Are you sure you're alright?"

"Fine, fine." He waved away my concern. "You will be glad to know that since you do have a spark of magic, your body should adjust to teleportation travel quicker."

"I'll wait to test that theory. Can we take one of your cars?"

"How about the Roadster?"

I did a little bounce. "You don't have to ask me twice. Let's go!"

"I will tell Mayhew we will eat dinner in town."

"Great!" I said. That sounded a bit like a date. Okay, it was probably more like two coworkers grabbing a bite at some local diner, but still . . . he was turning down an invitation with the skinny rich girl to have dinner with me. It wasn't like that happened all the time.

CHAPTER SEVEN

"This car is awesome," I said, running a hand along the dashboard.

"Thank you," he said, flashing me a quick grin. "It is one of my favorites."

"So, let me ask you something," I said, eying him. "You've lived for hundreds of years, and you retain the knowledge of the ages . . ."

"Knowledge of the ages, eh?" he repeated with a soft chuckle. "Is that what the public relations representatives for the Elite Hands of Justice say?"

"It's what the textbooks say, my friend," I replied, reaching back to pull the ponytail holder out of my hair, letting it fly loose in the wind. (Yes, it tangles, but it is an exhilarating sensation.) I turned to catch him staring at me as if transfixed.

He snapped his eyes back to the road. "So, is there a question in there?"

I turned my head, feeling a self-satisfied smirk cross my face at catching him watching me. "I just want to know if the 'I have no social skills or tact' line is an act, or have you really learned nothing about people in all those years?"

"Well, what do you think?" he asked, turning on to the town's main drag.

"I think it's more of a test. I think you like to see how people react."

"You think I am manipulative?"

I laughed. "I've known you for about a day now, and I *know* you're manipulative!"

"Let us just say, I have had years experience of suffering fools, and I do not do so lightly anymore. If that is lack of tact . . . I would suggest that people who act a certain way deserve to be called on it."

"Interesting. So you were feeling me out?"

"Pardon?"

"Yesterday. Were you just making all those snarky comments to get a rise out of me?"

"Snarky?"

I rolled my eyes. "Never mind. It's like pulling teeth!"

He laughed, and I smiled in spite of myself. We already had an easy, comfortable way of being together, and after everything we had been through, it seemed like we had known each other for weeks instead of a measly twenty-four hours.

"Thanks for taking me into town," I said. "It's nice to be able to go somewhere without having to fly in. Or teleport, for that matter."

"Well, you can borrow one of my cars whenever you want. My former partners liked to use the '67 Mustang."

"Really?" I tried to keep my car giddiness internal, yet couldn't help but grin. "I'll hold you to that promise."

"I am sure you will."

"So, where are we going?"

"My favorite restaurant. Tuscani's."

Okay, so this wasn't a quick bite at a diner with a coworker. I was glad his quirk of always dressing up had compelled me to do the same before we left the mansion. "I've heard about it but never been."

"I am surprised you have not."

"It's a little out of my price range."

"Then are you not glad you have a wealthy partner footing the bill?"

"You're a generous date," I joked. Then I realized what I'd

said and tried to backtrack. "Not that this is a date. I just meant that you're not cheap like the guys I've actually dated." I snapped my mouth shut before more damage could be done.

Either he didn't notice my embarrassment or he chose not to acknowledge it.

"So if you do not go to good restaurants, where does your usual date take you?"

"Out for pizza, I guess," I said. "It's been so long since I've dated, I don't remember. My focus has been on the work lately." Okay, so my focus had *always* been on work, but he didn't need to know that.

"A focus on work is not a bad thing. Look where it has gotten you."

"True. My friend Selena always said I have tunnel vision. I set my sights on a goal and ignore everything else to achieve it, and I've wanted to be in the EHJ since I discovered I had powers."

"Determination and drive can both be good qualities," he observed.

"I just don't want them to overtake me completely. I want to meet someone eventually. I don't want to become one of those reclusive heroes who only live for the job and barely come out of their secret hideout."

He gave me a pointed look as he pulled up in front of the restaurant. "Ouch."

I knew I could babble on and get myself in deeper, or I could be brutally honest. He was one who liked to dish it out, so I hoped he could take it.

"I don't mean to be insulting, but no, I don't want to end up like you. My father died before I was born and my mother shortly after, so I've never had a family. I'd like to have one someday. Not now," I quickly amended. "I want my career first, of course. But I know I need to set my tunnel vision sights on that at some point, or I'm going to spend my whole life alone."

"I have had a family many times over," he said. "And I am still alone."

He opened the door and got out, but not before I caught a glimpse of the sadness and pain in his eyes. I felt a wave of sympathy for him. It must be hard to lose everyone you care about and still continue on.

A valet opened the car door for me, and I got out and followed Robert. The doorman held the restaurant door open for us to pass through, and then we were inside the dark mahogany of Tuscani's. People came for the cozy atmosphere of this current "it" restaurant—which was heightened by the fires burning in hearths in every corner—and of course to be seen.

"Mister Elliot, so good to see you." The maître d' glided up to us. "Right this way to your table."

"After you," Robert said, putting a light hand on the small of my back. Was he finding excuses to touch me, or was it innocent? I couldn't tell. I wished this were one of those moments when he was brutally honest.

We were escorted to a cozy little table in the back, near one of the fireplaces, but not near enough that we would roast. The waiter came to take our drink orders. I deferred to the voice of experience, and Robert ordered us a bottle of wine I assume was a vastly good year, considering the way the waiter's eyes lit up.

He returned with the bottle and glasses. They went through the whole rigmarole with the cork, tasting the wine, all while I studied the menu and tried to figure out what to order. No prices were listed; I guess if you needed to know, you couldn't afford to eat there, so it was impossible to tell what the most expensive item on the menu was and avoid it. There's an assumption about the woman who orders the lobster on the first date—Oh, but this wasn't a date. The romantic atmosphere was making me forget.

The wine was pronounced drinkable, and I sipped it while

Robert ordered his food in Italian. He could cast spells in the language and order dinner; he was handy to have around.

The waiter turned his attention to me. I looked at Robert. "You've been here before, order me something good."

He nodded, spouted off something in rapid-fire Italian, and the waiter disappeared, menus in hand.

"You will take a chance on my tastes?" he asked.

"I trust anyone with such fantastic taste in cars."

He smiled. "So, tell me something about one of your teams. The adventures you have had so far."

"Only if you'll tell me about working with the EHJ."

"Alright. You go first."

I was hesitant at first, but as he nodded and laughed at appropriate times, seeming genuinely interested, I got more into the storytelling. I never thought my life was all that exciting, especially to someone like him, but somehow I managed to blab straight through the several courses.

". . . And then, Ignition and Titantrix start throwing cars at each other. Cars! We're all trying to calm them down before more collateral damage is done, and then they pick up the team leader Ripshot's car," I said as the waiter removed our plates and gave us salads. *Salad after appetizers and two main courses? Fancy restaurants confuse me.*

"So, then what happened?"

"Well, of course he's mad, but there's not much he can do about it because his power is more battle strategy–based than strength. So he tells me to go get it. I didn't want to get in the middle of a lovers spat, but what could I do?"

"What did you do?"

"Well, I grabbed the car away from them and they both turn on me—How dare I get involved in their business?—and then the police show up, guns out, and that's when everyone else takes advantage of the distraction to tackle Ignition and Titantrix to the ground. The police are all just staring, like, 'What the hell is this?' We're heroes, we're not supposed to be acting like children! Although the median age of the Red Knights was about seventeen, so we weren't that far out of kid-range, though we were all super-geniuses or had been sidekicks for years. Anyway, Ignition and Titantrix are hauled off to jail, and the whole time I've been holding the car up. I finally get to set it down, and as soon as I do, Ripshot's all over it, checking to see if his baby's been injured. And he turns to me and says, 'You scratched the hood, Phenomenal Girl Five.'"

"I can imagine how that was concluded."

"So, yeah. I punched him." I took a nibble of salad, wanting to save room for dessert. "And so now everyone's mad at me, big surprise, and we spent the ride back home in the Knight Jet in utter silence."

"Why was it not a surprise they were all mad at you?"

I shrugged. "I was always the odd man out. My teammates all wanted to save the world, of course, but they also wanted to gossip about who was dating whom and go to the clubs in their off-time. I was Brainy Lainey with her nose stuck in a book who wanted to be in the EHJ when she grew up. I didn't fit in with the regular kids at my public school because I lived in a foster home; then it was because I had powers, and once I got to the School, it was because I was younger than most of them, a bit on the chunky side, and a big nerd." I sighed. "You ever feel like you don't fit in anywhere?"

He stared at me. "What do you think?"

I gave a soft, humorless laugh. "Oh, yeah. Forgot who I was talking to, the king of loners."

He took a drink of wine. "Sometimes it is better to be apart."

"That doesn't make it any less lonely."

"No, it does not," he agreed.

I eyed him over the rim of my wine glass. "Okay, let's not ruin this good food with brooding. Now it's your turn. Tell me about working with the EHJ."

"What do you want to know?"

"Well, for starters, why'd you quit?"

"I did not quit, obviously, since you are here."

"Why were you taken off the active members list, then?" I rolled my eyes. "Mister Literal."

"That is not necessarily a less brooding topic of conversation. And I do not know if I should explain it to you."

"Why not?"

"It might discourage you from joining."

"Are you kidding? I'm already in, Robert. I've been working toward this my whole life."

"That is exactly why I do not want to ruin it for you."

"It's not going to ruin it for me, I promise."

He sighed and took another sip of wine. "Well then, to tell you the truth, the fun went out of it."

"That's it?" I leaned back in my chair. "I was expecting a big revelation and you just tell me that you were bored?"

"That is all, but that is enough. The Elite Hands of Justice became very political. It became more about helping the right kind of people, making the right impression, hiring the right hero who would get noticed and bring some connection to the team, than about helping people. And when there were not enough high-profile cases in America to suit them, they started doing work overseas. When they got bad press about interfering and trying to take over the world or some sort of rubbish, they decided to opt for space travel."

"Aliens aren't going to say 'Those weird Earthlings are interfering'?"

"I am sure they do, but their press releases and opinion polls do not reach us."

I laughed. "And I can tell you aren't into politics."

"You live long enough, you find out that politics are a meaningless waste of time and energy. Karl Marx once said that religion is the opiate of the masses. Now he would say our publicized political system is the opiate of the masses: people parroting the rhetoric of their designated side, never bothering to check the facts for themselves or allowing anyone to disagree with them, because their side is always right."

"Oh, did I set off a rant?"

He laughed. "Sorry."

"It's okay. I'm very anti-partisan too. I think both sides are equally ridiculous."

"I have fought in one too many wars over the years— some that were actually trying to stop evil, and some that were not. And some worthy causes and soldiers were spit upon because of politics. I thought the Elite Hands of Justice were the last bastion of good faith—of people trying to right wrongs, regardless of what others thought, just to make the world a better and safer place. And the people respected them for it."

"But not anymore."

"I am not saying they are not still seeking to make the world a better place, just that they care now about what others think. And now no one respects them for it."

"Well, you're not discouraging me," I said, taking a forkful of the delicious cheesecake that had appeared at some point during his tirade.

"Well, I am glad, then. I think someone of your determination and idealism would be good for the team."

"Thanks." My cheeks warmed at the compliment and the way he looked at me when he said it. "And you know something else? I think you should go back, too."

"Whatever for?"

"To change it. You've had a hand in picking and training these new recruits; you probably know them better than their teammates. You know who's decent and who's not. Get rid of the waste and turn the team back to what it stood for."

He laughed. "You make a convincing argument."

"But you should finish training me first. Then you should come with me."

"You want me to come with you?"

"Well! This is the last place I expected to find you!"

We both jumped as a huffy tornado stood by our table, fuming. It was Victoria Dupree.

"Good evening, Miss Dupree, and how are you?" Robert said. His tone was pleasant and yet still conveyed that he couldn't possibly care.

"I thought you were unavailable for dinner." Victoria's tone was shrill. "And then I find you out with some little tramp young enough to be your daughter!"

I stared at her in shock. Wow, talk about overreacting.

"My assistant and I had matters to go over in town and we decided to stop to eat before returning home."

She gaped at me. "You're that rude girl? Never mind, I don't care. Robert, I need to speak to you."

"Well, I am busy, but if you would like to call the house tomorrow, I am sure Lainey can set up an appointment for you."

"And you'll show up this time?"

"If it is about that trifling party, then no. Lainey is taking care of that."

"*I'll* take care of all of that," she hissed. "I need to speak to you about private matters."

I was uncomfortable watching this exchange. She was just a little too wound up to only be bent on snagging him. That was more the tone of an ex.

"Fine, then. Call the house tomorrow. Lainey will check my schedule and pick a convenient time."

I nodded. "First thing on the agenda tomorrow. *Robert.*"

She shot me a nasty look at the use of his name. I maintained a bored expression that only seemed to irritate her more.

"Fine. I will," she snapped, stomping away.

Robert and I looked at each other. And then burst out laughing.

"That was dinner and a show," I said, trying to stifle my giggles before I started snorting.

"Get her an appointment for fifteen minutes, no more. That is about all I can stomach."

"She'll love the 'rude girl' even more."

"She needs to give up the idea of ever landing my money."

"Well, I hate to tell her this, but coming over and throwing high drama all over the place is not a way to win friends and influence people," I said with another laugh, tossing my hair back. "Wow, I've never been 'some little tramp' before. It's kind of exciting."

He leaned forward to speak in my ear. "Do you think you could have this much fun with the Elite Hands of Justice?"

I smiled. "Nah. Only with a man old enough to be my father. I think her math skills leave something to be desired, unless you've been fathering kids at the tender age of fourteen."

"Unlikely, since I have not been fourteen since my first time around. And every woman on this planet is young enough to be my daughter. Including the woman right over there."

I turned to look where he was pointing, at a grand woman dressed to the nines who had to be pushing ninety.

We both started laughing again.

"We'd better get out of here before the second act begins," I said.

CHAPTER EIGHT

When I descended to Robert's lair the next morning, after a quick gulp of breakfast, he was already surrounded by mountains of files. Did the man ever sleep?

"Good morning," I said, taking the chair across the table from him. "Anything I can do to help?"

He gave me the barest acknowledgment. "No, it is my usual busywork from the Elite Hands of Justice. Time to run the magic-level estimates again."

"Pardon me?"

"Every year, the Elite Hands of Justice takes all the intelligence they have on every magic-user in the country, from students to villains, and has me work up a profile on each to estimate how powerful their magic ability is or will be, and then enter it into our shared database." He gestured to the large computer screen behind him.

"That sounds a bit intrusive and paranoid."

He gave a slight shrug. "Magic-users are the most dangerous of all powers. Our abilities are only limited by our knowledge and strength of will. There is more potential to become drunk on power and take advantage."

"So they depend on your expertise to single out who's the most likely to become a threat?"

"Something like that, yes." He tossed me a newspaper. "Take a look."

I caught it. "Is this a broadening-my-horizons thing or something important?"

"There is something inside you should take a look at."

"Uh-oh." I spread the newspaper out on the nearest table not covered in books.

"Page Twelve," he suggested, riffling through the contents of another file and scribbling down a note.

I flipped through the pages, expecting to see a celebrity or a member of the EHJ in the famous gossip column. Instead there was a photo of Robert leaning in to whisper something into a glamorous blonde woman's perfect shell of an ear. She was laughing, and they looked like they were sharing an intimate moment. The caption under the photo read: "The infamous Robert Elliot was seen out canoodling with a hot blonde at the über-hot Tuscani's."

"Holy hell!" I shrieked. "That's me! I'm the hot blonde!"

He grinned, glancing up at me from the files. "I thought you would get a kick out of that."

I read the rest of the caption out loud. "Sources close to Elliot say the blonde is a colleague, but they're looking a little too cozy at the intimate nightspot to be only friends."

What would he say to the obvious chemistry the photo captured?

He shrugged. "You will get that on occasion. The paparazzi like to take a photo out of context."

So much for chemistry.

"Everyone on the Power Squad is going to freak out, even though I'm unidentified," I said.

"You will not be unidentified for long. The paparazzi have caught wind of you; now it is only a matter of time before they identify you. Might as well get used to it."

I folded the paper, tucking it under my arm, intending to clip the photo later. "So I'm a star now, huh?"

"To those that read Page Twelve, yes, you are."

"*Sir, you're wanted on the phone,*" Mayhew's disembodied voice interrupted from an unseen speaker.

Robert dug a cordless phone out from under a stack of files. "Robert Elliot. Good morning, Detective Pendergast." He paused, listening, and then looked troubled. My heart sped up. Something was going on. "Yes, I understand. We will be there shortly." He hung up and looked at me. "Syn is gone."

A spike of fear shot through me, echoing phantom pains of Syn tearing at my soul. "What do you mean, 'gone'?"

"As in no longer in his cell. He just disappeared. Pendergast wants us downtown to investigate." He was already heading toward the door.

"I thought you said you wiped out his magic," I said, rising to follow him.

"I did."

"So how did he get away?" I struggled to keep up with Robert's long, purposeful strides down the hallway and up the stairs to the main floor.

"I do not know. That is the purpose of our investigation, is it not?" He stopped walking and looked at me. "Can you work this case, Lainey, or is it too personal?"

"What do you mean?"

"I mean, after what happened with Syn, will you be able to investigate this case with a clear head? Not allow emotions to cloud your thinking?"

I frowned. "I'm a professional, Robert. I can do this."

He gave me a nod and a slight smile. "Let us go, then."

"Should I change into my costume?"

"To see the police? I think not. They already have differing opinions of our work, and we do not want to stand out further. In the future, I think you should save the costume-wearing for patrol situations."

I shrugged. "Leather chafes after awhile anyway."

Robert glanced at me. "Indeed."

We stepped outside and I watched as he prepared the teleportation spell.

"Are you okay now to do this?" I asked.

"I am fine, Lainey," he said, in a tone indicating that I wasn't to question his health, magic-wise, again.

"Do you always do this outside?"

"Yes. It would damage the carpets otherwise."

I smiled. "Can't argue with that logic."

"And I thought you could argue with anything."

Before I could retort, the spell took effect and we were transported into the police station.

The room spun, and I grabbed hold of a nearby desk, breathing deep and closing my eyes in an attempt to ward off the nausea. At least I wasn't throwing up. I was making progress.

When I opened my eyes, I noticed the entire squad staring at us, open-mouthed.

Robert looked bored by the attention. "Can you direct me to Detective Pendergast, please?" he said to the nearest officer, a woman with cropped red hair and freckles.

"He's back by the holding cells," she said, pointing in the appropriate direction.

"Thank you very much." He headed off without hesitation, causing me to scramble along between desks and the officers who were now over the shock of our arrival. I heard one of them mumble, "Capes," as we passed.

"You take the lead on this," Robert said as we walked down an industrial gray hallway that led to the cells.

"Me? Why?"

"You are supposed to be training with me, are you not? I need to see how you handle this type of thing."

"Alright." I tried to not look nervous as we entered the room and Pendergast noticed us.

"That was fast," he said, moving to shake hands.

"We teleported down," Robert explained. "I assumed time was of the essence."

"Correct. We dusted for prints already, but considering the cell was still locked, I don't think you'll find anything. It's as if he just disappeared into thin air."

I peered inside the cell. It was standard, nothing out of the ordinary. Except for the fact that it was missing its inmate.

I checked the lock to see if there were any physical signs it had been tampered with. There were none. I glanced up at Robert.

"Is there any way you can do a spell to see if the lock was magically altered?"

He nodded. "Good thinking. Keep going."

I looked around in the cell for a clue, anything to explain how Syn just vanished. As I turned to look back at Robert, who was running a hand over the lock and whispering some words in Italian, I noticed a security camera.

I pointed to it. "Was the camera on?"

Pendergast nodded. "We already checked. One minute he's there, the next he's gone."

"Could someone have tampered with the tape?"

"We don't use tapes anymore; the footage is downloaded onto a hard drive."

"The lock was not altered," Robert said to me.

I frowned, biting my lip. There had to be something to lead us to him.

"Can we see the footage?" I asked.

Pendergast nodded. "Follow me."

Moments later, seated around a computer monitor, we watched as the prerecorded Syn stalked around his cell like a caged animal, soundlessly ranting to himself. I shivered, remembering the searing pain he had inflicted. Unconsciously, my hand moved to rest over my heart, where he had taken an eternal piece of me.

On camera, Syn raised his head to look up, as if hearing someone approach. Then, in an eye-blink, he was gone.

"Can you slow it down?" I asked the detective who was manning the computer.

"Sure thing." He typed something and the footage started over again, running a bit slower this time.

"Can you do frame by frame?"

This time, as Syn looked up, a blur appeared in front of him. Then he was gone.

"Freeze it!" I pointed to the blur. "There, what's that?"

"Someone teleported him out of the cell," Robert said from behind me. He leaned over and tapped the screen. "That is a teleportation signature."

"He couldn't have done it himself?"

Robert shook his head. "I took away his magic ability."

"So it was someone working for him."

"Or someone he was working for." Robert gave me a faint smile. "Excellent work, Lainey."

I grinned at his praise. "I don't suppose you can trace where the signature came from? Or who it belongs to?"

"Not entirely. I do not recognize the genetic signature, so it is someone new. Teleportation spells leave a residue, at both the entrance and the exit. I can do a spell to search for residue within a certain radius from this building. It fades the further from the two points you travel."

"So let's try it."

As we walked back to the cell, I couldn't help but be proud of how I was handling myself, showing Robert I was more than just blonde hair and a physical powerhouse. I had a sharp mind, too.

Maybe he'd want to keep me around . . .

I shook those thoughts from my head as I watched him enter the cell and hold out some sort of amulet, dangling it from a chain. He spun it in a slow circle, and as its arc widened, I began to see a glow form in its wake. A faint ball of light appeared along the outer edge of the path.

"It is there, but barely," Robert said. "Outskirts of the city, probably near the dump."

"Tell Bob to send a squad out to the dump," Pendergast said to the detective next to him. "Move."

As the police force snapped into action, I whispered to Robert, "If they find him, will they be able to handle him?"

"He is powerless, but that does not make him less dangerous."

"Maybe we should tag along?"

"You do not want to let go of this case, do you?"

I shook my head. "I want to see it through to the end."

He studied me and then gave a slight nod. "Then we shall."

We appeared just a short distance away from the dump. The police still hadn't arrived on the scene, but then again, they didn't have teleportation access.

Of course, they didn't have to suffer the aftereffects either. I swore and fell to my knees, stomach roiling and head pounding.

"Your body will get used to teleportation travel soon," Robert promised.

"Good to know." I got to my feet and nearly fell over again. He reached out to steady me. I held on to his arm and breathed deep, realized that was a bad idea outside of a dump, and shuddered.

"Do not worry, soon this will be second nature to you," he said, tone light. "You will be wondering how you ever got around before."

I smiled at his attempt to make me feel better. "Do we wait for the cops?"

"This is your show, Lainey. Tell me how you want to run it."

"What we're dealing with is magic, and that's a bit out of the police's league, so I say we go in."

"Then we go."

The stench from the dump was overwhelming. I tried holding my breath for as long as I could, and finally gave up. There was nothing to do but try to find some way to bear it.

"Here," Robert said, passing me a small jar. "Dab it under your nose. The police use a similar trick, except this is magic and neutralizes the smell instead of covering it up."

I did as I was told and found that it worked. "Thanks. So can you pinpoint where the teleportation spell came out?"

He nodded. "This way." With a few mumbled breaths, he rose up to float in the air, above the garbage. I followed, glad I didn't have to step in God knows what.

I glanced at our surroundings. "Whoever teleported him isn't still hanging around?"

"Could be, but they would have likely attacked by now. Still, it is a good idea to keep your guard up. It should be right over . . ." He trailed off. "There." He pointed to the flagpole next to the fence. Instead of a flag flying in the breeze on top, there was an impaled body.

I knew my mouth was hanging open, but couldn't stop myself. "He didn't do that to himself by messing up the teleportation spell, right?"

"The spells will not let you teleport into a solid object, no. Someone did that to him." Robert floated up higher. "Let us take a closer look, shall we?"

I couldn't help but feel a tiny bit vindicated that Syn had met an untimely and painful end. But whoever or whatever had done this to him was probably much worse.

Robert studied the body with a professional, detached gaze. "No sign of a struggle. Someone took him by surprise."

"But why go through the trouble of getting him out of police custody only to kill him? Seems like a lot of unnecessary work to me."

"So he would not reveal information to the police."

I studied the body. "Any idea who did this?"

"You tell me. You are the one in training."

I bit my lip and tried to focus on the details. "Well, I would think you'd have to be pretty powerful to do a teleportation spell from a remote distance."

He nodded. "A level seven magic-user at least." Seeing my confusion, he continued, "This is where my leveling work from this morning comes into play. One is low, ten is apocalyptic."

"Okay." I'm sure it was a helpful system, but it sounded really silly aloud, like a video game or something. "Well, there's not that many magic-using villains."

"Not many that are so powerful," Robert agreed. "Or running loose."

I had to laugh at that. "Brag much?" The Reincarnist had an arrest ratio that was almost unheard of.

"I do my job the correct way. Once they go down, they stay down."

I heard sirens. "Police are here."

"We will probably have to help them get the body down once they have finished taking note of the crime scene," Robert said. "Once we get home, I will help you run the statistics into the database to search for villains that fit the profile. Assuming whoever did this is not a first-timer."

"Villains do tend to be like a hydra," I said. "Take one down and two more spring up in his place." Something on the body caught my eye. "Wait, what's that?"

I floated up to inspect Syn's wrist. I started to reach out and heard Robert's curt "Gloves!"

I moved my hand back quickly. "I didn't touch anything."

"You need to start carrying a pair of exam gloves." He floated up to meet me, extending a pair of latex gloves that he had taken out of his trench coat pocket.

"How much stuff do you have stashed away in there?" I slipped the gloves on and reached out for Syn's wrist. Just touching him made me shiver. He was long gone, but I half expected him to come to life and start draining me, like this had all been some elaborate trap.

I turned his wrist over to see a strange burn mark, and the angry red skin made a pattern. It made a dragon.

"Robert, take a look at this," I said.

He floated up behind me. "Now *that* bears more investigation."

CHAPTER NINE

"Any luck?"

I tore my eyes away from the computer monitors I had been staring at for hours to glance at Robert. "I got some hits, but I haven't been able to narrow them down much."

"So what are their profiles?" He sat down in the chair next to me.

I worked the mouse and a series of mug shots popped up. "All of these magic users are level seven and above." I clicked to scroll through the pictures. "Some are heroes, some are criminals."

"Start narrowing down the suspects."

"These are the ones who are in jail or have had their magic neutralized."

He nodded. "Go on."

"None of them have been known to brand anyone or leave dragon symbols at crime scenes. They haven't gone by the alias 'Dragon' or any variations thereof. They haven't been known to work with Syn. You magic-users tend to stick to yourselves." I'd noticed that as I read through several files.

"You need to lump yourself into that category as well, now."

"Oh yeah." I had forgotten about that spark of power in me. I wondered if it meant there would be a file on me soon. "There are a few, however, who have worked in close proximity to Syn, and I've marked them for possible investigation. What about your old archnemesis, Jihad?"

"He is always a possibility, but he disappeared after our last battle five years ago."

He looked at the screens. "Do you want to eliminate the heroes?"

I shook my head. "Not yet. We've had too many of our own play turncoat, and it was a villain who was killed, so his murder could be seen as justice by the suspect."

"Good. Excellent. You are already better at deductive reasoning than most of the others I have trained. I practically had to hold their hands through the process; you take the initiative."

"Thank you."

"I am glad to see there is more to you than just a pretty face and muscles."

Did he just say I was pretty? I played it cool. "And there seems to be more to you than just super-intelligence coupled with a lack of tact."

A boyish grin broke out. "Well, of course there is."

"I'm sure."

"You left out good looks, for one," he added, either fishing for a compliment or teasing me. Or both.

I rose to the challenge. "And modesty."

"And athleticism."

"And obsessiveness."

"And charm."

"And bossiness."

"Well I am, technically, your boss."

"Oh, yeah." And I had a crush on my boss. Was there ever a relationship more doomed to failure? "Well, I guess we can't be friends then."

"And why not?"

"No one's ever really friends with their boss. Eventually the boss has to do something authoritative, and it upsets the subordinate."

"Well, I think the subordinate should be more understanding."

"And bosses don't like being challenged by subordinates."

"We know that is not true in this case."

"What do you mean?"

"You are mouthy."

"So are you!"

"And it does not bother me that you are. I rather like it, actually," he said, rocking on his heels, hands behind his back. "You are not mouthy in a disrespectful sense, like some of my previous partners were, nor are you a submissive mouse like many others. You are one of the most interesting people I have had the pleasure to meet in a long time."

I blushed. "Thanks. So I guess we can be friends."

"I think so, too."

I turned back to my work. "So what do we do now?"

He looked at the list and sighed, reaching over to take the mouse and coming tantalizingly close to me to do so. "Start checking into the suspects' last known whereabouts. The police are already investigating the two crime scenes to see if anyone saw anything suspicious, and Pendergast promised to let me know if they find anything. The next step will be asking around in the magic community. And I still patrol nightly, so we must continue with that. Maybe we can kill two birds with one stone."

"How's that?"

He clicked on the picture of the Virus. "Get into costume. We are going patrolling in Sector G. The Virus has been known to frequent a bar down there and has made it known how much he hates Syn. Maybe we can eliminate him from our suspect list."

"Shaking down a villain sure beats sitting in front of the computer," I agreed.

The area by the train depot was heavy in crime. Robberies, drug use, and rapes happened with regular frequency. You'd think with all the heroes in the world that places like this wouldn't exist, but reality was sadly uncooperative.

I hovered above a building, barely noting the prostitutes hawking their wares to passersby below.

"Are you not going to do anything?" Robert asked as I landed on the roof next to him.

"About what?"

"Them." He nodded to the prostitutes.

"Why? Is one of them a magic-user? A villain?"

He studied them, whispering a few Italian words under his breath. "No. Just civilians."

"Then what am I supposed to do with them? The police come by and arrest them, and when they get out, they get right back here to turn more tricks."

He frowned. "This is a good lesson for you, Lainey. Would you stop a robber?"

"Yes."

"Would you stop a rapist?"

"Yes."

"Would you stop a pedophile?"

"Yes."

"Would you stop a drug dealer?"

"I guess. I mean, if he was selling to kids."

"Why are you qualifying it? A drug dealer is still a criminal."

"There are so many drug dealers in the world, for one thing. If I made it my mission to search out every one, I'd be in it for the long haul and still never get them all. You could never get rid of all the drug dealers in the city, Robert, just like you'd never be able to get rid of all crime."

"But if you saw a drug deal going down, would you try to stop it?"

"In that case, yes."

"What about a purse snatcher? A mugger? They are all still criminals, victimizing the weak. The minute you begin qualifying which crimes you will stop and which you will not is the minute you start to not care about the people you are supposed to be protecting. You take a step closer to becoming more like *them*."

"Them who?"

"Heroes who have lost their way, like the members of the Elite Hands of Justice."

"You know, you *are* training me to become a part of that team, Robert."

"I do not want you to become like them, Lainey. I want you to be something better. I want you to be part of what brings them back to what they once were—a group of people who would do anything, even give up their own lives, to save the world and its people from themselves. That is why I personally chose you. I saw your potential."

Before I could think of how to respond, I heard the screeching of tires in the distance, and gunshots. They were coming closer.

I glanced over at Robert. "I'm on it."

Flying up into the air, I moved over the next building, dipped down toward the street, and sped down an alleyway. Two cars zoomed by me. One was trying to outrun the other, and both had guns blazing. Probably gang violence, and they were going to end up bringing innocent people into their fight by hitting someone with a stray bullet.

I followed after them, dodging the bullets as I went. I landed on the roof of the second car, and in an instant, gunfire flew up at me. I managed to avoid the spray, and punched my fist through the roof right above the driver as if it were tinfoil, then peeled it back. I snatched the gun out of the passenger's hand, wadded it up in a big metal ball, and tossed it aside. The passenger reached to take another gun from the guy in the backseat, and as he did so, I pulled back and hit him hard enough to knock him out. I tore the roof off, dived down, and punched the guy in the backseat—who was still staring in disbelief—before he could level his gun at me. It dropped to the floor as its owner slumped down, unconscious.

I turned my attention to the driver, whose eyes were darting to the rearview mirror to stare at me. His hands were in a death grip on the steering wheel.

I gave him a nasty smile. "Stop the car. *Now.*"

He did, so fast I was almost tossed out of the now-roofless vehicle.

Police sirens could be heard in the distance. The driver whimpered.

"Stay there," I said. "Don't move."

"I'm not going back to prison."

"And I'm not getting out of the car. I'm the one with the gun back here, so stay put!" I ordered.

The police pulled up behind us. The officers got out, guns at ready.

I held my hands up. "I stopped them for you!" The driver started to get out of the car and I reached out, grabbed his shirt, and pulled him back.

"What is this, cape night?" one of the officers said, coming over to take the criminal from me. He looked to be about my age and not yet worn down by the job. "We just got a call that the Reincarnist was turning over a car full of hoods."

"We're working together. I'm Phenomenal Girl Five. And since you're taking them into custody, I've gotta go."

"Typical big-time celebrity crime fighters," said another cop, this one older and balding, with a sour expression. "Leave us with the clean-up while you swan off to save the day somewhere else."

"Leave her alone. They're just trying to help."

"They get paid a helluva lot more money than we do to help. All because they won the genetic lottery," Bald Meanie said.

"Where was the Reincarnist?" I asked the nice one.

"About three blocks over."

"Thanks. I'll see you around."

"I'll keep an eye on the sky," he said with a flirtatious smile.

I flew off to find Robert, the two cops still loading up the hoods and arguing about capes as I went.

"Take care of everything on your end?" Robert greeted me as I landed on the sidewalk next to him. He was handing out cards for an outreach program to the prostitutes we had noticed earlier.

"Of course. Are we still on a magic hunt?"

"Hopefully not much of a hunt," he said. He nodded to a prostitute wearing a white vinyl skirt and bra and matching thigh-high boots, which, I was sad to notice, looked like something a former teammate of mine had worn. "Vivian here has seen our friend the Virus at a bar down on Randall Street."

"You gonna arrest him?" Vivian asked.

"We might take him into custody for the police," Robert said.

"You gonna beat him up?" She looked hopeful.

"It's not out of the realm of possibility." I cracked my knuckles for effect. Robert gave me a stern look.

"He deserves it. Beat up my man Alvin once."

"See?" I said to Robert. "He deserves it."

He shook his head. "We should go. Good evening, ladies." With a nod to them, he started to prepare the teleportation spell.

"He's hot," Vivian said to me, nodding to my boss. "And a gentleman. You're a lucky girl."

I started to correct her, then figured, why bother? "Thanks. Be careful out here."

Robert held out a hand to me as I approached. "Ready?"

"As I'll ever be."

CHAPTER TEN

We popped into existence outside of a seedy-looking bar. Not a surprise, considering where we were.

"Is this guy going to attack us the minute we step inside?" I asked as soon as I convinced myself I didn't need to throw up.

"I doubt it. He is supposed to have gone legit," Robert said, holding the door open for me.

Even in the dim bar light, I recognized the Virus. He was a bald barrel of a man whose arms were covered in tattoos of binary code. He slumped over a pool table, using a finger instead of a cue stick to point and shoot at the balls. His opponent just stared, unwilling to call him on the obvious cheating.

"Cyrus!" Robert boomed in an enthusiastic voice. "How have you been?"

The Virus's head snapped to attention. He gave a slight smile. "It's the Reincarnist!" he said, his voice pitched just a little too loud.

The room went silent in reaction, and I saw a few people throw money on the bar and leave.

"What can I do for ya?" the Virus said.

"You heard about Syn?" Robert asked, looking down at the pool table. He bent to eye the billiard balls.

"Yeah, someone took him out. You don't think I had anything to do with that?"

Robert's eyes flicked up to him. "Did you?"

"No, man, come on. You know I went legit."

"Maybe you had a relapse."

"Look, it's no secret I wish very painful things on Syn, and I can't say I don't want to shake the person's hand that offed him, but I haven't seen him since I quit. And as much as I hated him, I wasn't going to waste my time and energy tracking him down and taking him out. I have better things to do with my life."

"A level seven offed him," I put in, wanting to be a part of the conversation.

The Virus turned his attention on me. "So?"

"You're a seven, so that makes you a suspect."

He kept his eyes on me but addressed Robert. "Who's your little blonde friend, man?"

"My new partner."

The Virus walked over, looking me up and down like I was on display at a bakery. Suddenly he was no longer the lesser power he showed Robert; he was a dangerous villain who could easily take me out with magic before I could lift a finger.

He got close, almost touching me, but I knew I couldn't so much as flinch or he would take it as a sign of weakness. I stared him down and maintained a bored expression, even though my palms were sweating.

"She's something, isn't she?" he said, face only inches away from mine. He inhaled, sniffing me. "Got a spark of the gift. Isn't that interesting?" He looked back at Robert with a grin. "I'd love to see what she can do . . . Powers-wise, of course."

"Cyrus, do not make me hurt you in front of all of these people," Robert said, his voice a steel edge.

"Take it easy, Old One, I'm not going to hurt your pet." The Virus turned his attention back to me. "I heard old Syn took a chunk out of you before he went down for good. I'll bet that hurt."

"What, like this?" I head-butted him in the nose, and blood went everywhere. He howled and stumbled backward.

"You're gonna pay for that, bi—"

"ENOUGH." Robert held up both hands, and glowing, swirling blue fire sparked between them. All of the balls on the pool table shot into the pockets. The glasses and bottles at the bar clanked together, and a few shattered. A hard wind whipped through the room. My skin crawled and tingled like ants were crawling on it. The Virus took a step back.

"Who killed Syn, Cyrus?"

"I don't know, man!"

"*Sapete e mi direte!*" Robert's eyes were now glowing blue with magic.

"I don't know, Old One, I swear!" Cyrus was holding his head in pain. "Stop! I don't know! It was someone new, that's all I know!"

The wind died down and I felt a bit of the intensity in the room fade.

"Who knows more?" Robert asked in a calm voice, as if we had all been sitting around discussing the weather.

"I don't know! Ask Alessandro, ask Fantazia, they're the nosy ones. All I heard was a new player took out Syn. I'm out of the game, man, I'm out of the loop!"

"Was Syn working for this new player?"

"That's the rumor, but like I said, I don't know! Please!"

Robert took a deep breath, and all the power went out in the room. Literally. First the presence of his magic left, then the lights, the jukebox, the television—everything went out.

"Thank you, Cyrus. You have been most helpful," Robert said.

"Excuse me, but could one of you two fix the lights?" I heard a voice ask, possibly the bartender.

"*Luci sopra.*"

The lights snapped on and we all blinked.

"Thanks, Reincarnist," the bartender said.

Robert nodded to him, flicking a few hundreds on the bar

as he passed by. "For the damages." He glanced at me. "Come along."

He didn't say a word as he prepared the teleportation spell, but I knew he was angry by the set of his jaw and the fact that he kept avoiding my eyes.

"Do not ever do that again," he said the moment we appeared in front of the mansion.

"What?" Lucky for me the adrenaline was chasing away the usual aftereffects. "What did I do?"

"I had the situation under control with Cyrus, and you took that away with your grandstanding," he said, his voice rising with every word.

"He was up in my face trying to intimidate me, so I showed him I wasn't intimidated."

"And then I had to intimidate him to stop him from hurting you. You picked a fight with someone bigger, meaner, and more powerful than you, and that would have gotten you killed had I not been there. You should not rely on your teammates to protect you."

That stung. "I don't rely on anyone but myself, Robert. I've been fighting guys bigger and meaner than me for years now and I've survived for this long. I can take care of myself; God knows no one else is going to." I whirled around to walk up the driveway.

"You should have stayed out of it," his calm voice called after me.

I stopped, turning to look back at him. "I thought you were training me, wanted me involved in all of these cases."

"And I am training you to think in these kinds of situations, not to act rashly." He brushed past me on the way to the door.

"You got the information you wanted!" I snapped. "I don't know why you're so upset!"

He turned back. "I expected more from you." He slammed the door behind him.

CHAPTER ELEVEN

"Shut the hell up!" I screamed, raising my fist to punch the villain I had pinned down.

"Is the swearing and hitting necessary?" Robert asked.

"Yes, as a matter of fact, it is! You don't know the restraint I'm using right now to keep from dropping the f-bomb."

"Swearing shows one's limited vocabulary."

"No, swearing means you've run out of patience and are about to run your fist through someone's skull," I growled through clenched teeth. I addressed the villain: "If I were you, I'd start talking before you really piss me off." My whole life I'd had to remember to pull my punches so I wouldn't accidentally kill someone, especially in the heat of battle. But some days it was more difficult to control myself.

This was one of those days.

Okay, it had been one of those weeks.

Things between Robert and me had been a little forced since our blowup over the Virus incident. We had continued patrolling and following any leads we could dredge up about Syn's murderer. We weren't making a lot of progress, and the tension between us was almost to the breaking point.

The man I had pinned to the roof of an office building stared at me as if I had lost my mind. "Lady, you've got the wrong guy, I swear."

"Oh, really?" I lifted him off his feet and held him aloft.

"Then what the hell's this for?" I jerked a finger to the device that Robert held in his hand.

"It's just a garage door opener."

I gave him a shake. "So you just *happened* to be wearing military fatigues and carrying a garage door opener while hanging out on the roof of a building? And it's another massive coincidence that some lunatic named Death Dealer just called city hall and told them he would blow up the elementary school if they didn't wire one hundred million dollars to a Cayman Islands account? Oh, and oddly enough, your name is Bill Wyte, which is one of Death Dealer's aliases. Yeah, those are just random quirks of fate. Do I look stupid to you?"

"Well, you *are* blonde," he muttered.

"Funny man, you just said the wrong damn thing." I gripped him harder and flew straight up into the sky. It's a bit of a pull when you're carrying someone else, but that's where superstrength comes in handy.

"What are you doing?" Robert asked, floating in the air next to me using some sort of spell.

"Mr. Wyte here thinks threatening to blow up innocent children is a joking matter, so he's going to see what I like to do for fun," I growled.

"I do not think you are in your right frame of mind."

"Oh, I'm not, that's obvious." I climbed the sky harder.

"If you are going to work with the Elite Hands of Justice, you cannot fly off the handle like this. Someone is always planning to blow up the world or kill innocent people, and you have to learn not to let it get to you and do your job."

"I'm doing my job, alright."

Death Dealer, who had been silent, spoke up. "I don't know what you're planning, do-gooder bitch, but I don't scare. And that actually is my garage door opener. The bomb detonator is right here." He twisted the stone on his ring. "Say good-bye to the kiddies."

I dropped him. He let out a girlish scream as he fell.

"Tempo del freeze." Robert glared at me as everything around us stopped. There were no sounds of traffic and people below. There wasn't even the sound of the Death Dealer crying like a baby. I looked down at the villain, who was frozen in mid-fall. Robert had performed some sort of pause-time spell.

"You disappoint me, Lainey."

"He was going to blow up kids, Robert!"

"And I neutralized the bombs already."

"He doesn't know that."

"But we do. You cannot go around losing your temper and killing villains. We serve justice, we do not mete out punishments."

I knew he was right but wasn't ready to back down. "The justice system sucks. Why else are all of these criminals back out on the streets?"

He studied me. "Your pure soul is probably turning black as we speak."

"That's probably from having it snacked on." My anger was starting to fade, leaving me feeling embarrassed for losing my temper in the first place.

"I wonder. Maybe . . ."

"What?"

"Nothing. Are you going to do the right thing and go catch him? Let him serve his trial?"

I sighed. "Fine. The justice system better not screw this one up, because I won't be this nice to him the second time around."

"Letting him plummet to his death while you argue with me is nice?"

"He's not plummeting. You did some sort of pause-button spell to stop his fall; I could tell right away. My skin tingled."

Robert cocked his head, interested. "You can sense the magic?"

"That, and you speaking random Italian. Oh, and the no sound thing is another dead giveaway."

He ignored my sarcasm. "I froze time around us, but cannot do it for very long. Go catch him before I have to drop the spell."

I flew down to where the evil Bill Wyte hovered in the air, still frozen. He wasn't that far away from me; I could have caught up without the time displacement.

I grabbed him by the shirt just as I felt a cool tingle wash over my skin, and then he was shrieking again. The game was back on.

"Oh, stop it, you big wuss," I said, flying past one of the large office buildings downtown and heading toward the police station.

"You crazy bitch!" he screamed. "You dropped me!"

"And I caught you only at my partner's insistence. I would have let you become a little splatter on the concrete if I had my way. People who try to hurt little kids just for something as meaningless as money . . ."

"It was one hundred million dollars!"

"You'd better pray we get to the police station pretty damn fast."

Robert must have somehow contacted Pendergast, because he was waiting on the roof of the police station when I arrived carrying the sullen villain.

"Good afternoon, Phenomenal Girl Five," the detective greeted me.

"Hi, Pendergast." I landed, setting Billy-boy down a little harder than necessary. "Got your handcuffs ready?"

He handed me the apparatus and I snapped them on Death Dealer, who was whining about wanting his lawyer.

Robert floated down next to me. "Do you want a statement, Pendergast?"

"Just a short one. If Phenomenal Girl Five would help me take the prisoner into custody, I'd appreciate it."

"Not a problem." I jerked the villain to his feet. "Let's go introduce you to your buff and dangerous cellmate."

* * *

"How about a trip to The Grind?" Robert asked as we left the police station.

"Why?" Aside from our one dinner, nightly patrol, and crime scenes, I hadn't seen him go out anywhere. In the two short weeks I'd been working with him, I had made multiple trips to the coffeehouse for my caffeine fix.

"I think you could use it. And I want to talk to you about what happened." His voice was hard with barely concealed anger.

"Yell at me is more like it."

"Then you should be happy we will be in a public forum so I will not yell."

I was so getting fired.

The popular non-chain coffeehouse was situated in the town's shopping district. I kept silent as Robert teleported us to a small alleyway across the street from it.

The warm and comforting smell of brewing coffee greeted me as soon as I pushed open the door. Unlike some coffeehouses that had a dark and depressed atmosphere, The Grind was bright and welcoming. It inspired you to pull up a chair, read a book, and relax, not to check to make sure the goth students around you weren't real vampires.

The clerk behind the counter smiled in greeting. "Hello, Lainey." Taking in my appearance, he whistled. "Damn, you coming home really late after a night of clubbing or something?"

I pulled my jacket closer, realizing my costume looked out of place surrounded by businessmen and women who didn't like the corporateness of the big coffee chains. And that it was very pathetic that the clerk and I were on a first-name basis already. "Oh, just laundry day, George. You know how it is."

He nodded. "I've worn some crazy things because I was too lazy to hit the Laundromat. You want the usual?"

"Yes, please."

"And for you, sir?"

I jumped, realizing Robert had sneaked up close behind me in that quiet way he had.

"None of those elaborate and overly sweet drinks. Just an espresso, please."

I watched as George prepared my non-fat, sugar-free caramel latte, no foam, and Robert's espresso. When he set the cups in front of us, I looked over at Robert.

"I have no money."

He didn't even seem surprised. "Really?"

"Do you see room for cash in these pants?"

George burst out laughing.

Robert handed him some money. "Convenient excuse."

"You can search me if you don't believe me." I picked up my cup and headed to the back corner of the room, so that my firing wouldn't be witnessed by the half a dozen patrons clustered around the small tables at the front of the store, pretending to read the newspapers or tapping away on laptops and sneaking glances at us.

Robert sat. "Lainey, I am concerned about your behavior since the Syn incident. I am beginning to wonder if the Elite Hands of Justice and you are a proper fit."

My stomach plummeted. I'd known it was coming, and the thought of losing everything I'd worked so hard for hurt. But it was his disapproval that hit the hardest. "I'm having a bad day, okay?"

"You cannot attempt to kill people on a bad day. That is not professional. That is not how we do things."

"I know. I'm sorry. It just really got to me, this case. I can't stand anyone trying to hurt children, especially after what happened with Syn . . ."

He sighed. "You cannot save everyone. You cannot be everywhere at once. Even if you live forever, there will be lives that slip through your fingers. The question is, can you move on and try to help the next person, or will you let it haunt you for the rest of your life? Do you have any idea how insane I would be by now if I dwelled on everyone that

I failed to save over the years? The ones I remember, anyway?"

"I can't shut myself down, either," I said, my voice barely audible even to myself. "I can't become emotionless like you." The instant the words were out of my mouth, I regretted them.

"I am emotionless?" he said, his tone frosty.

Well, my big mouth had gotten me this far. I took a deep breath and plowed ahead. "You live in that mansion all alone except for your butler and whatever person you train for two years and then move along to the next one. You very rarely go out, and when you do, it is related to work in some way. You don't speak to anyone in the EHJ unless it's on business, and the only person who ever makes personal calls to you is a demented ex-girlfriend." At his raised eyebrow, I nodded. "You don't have to be the world's smartest person to know there used to be something between you and Victoria. No one throws a hissy fit like she did unless they're an ex or in major need of therapy."

"I would not discount that last option," he said, a hint of sarcasm in his voice.

"The point is, it's only business with you."

"And that is how it has to be, Lainey," he said, setting his lips in a firm line. "That is the only way I can live my life. Like I said before, sometimes it is better to be alone."

It occurred to me I had no idea if we were talking about the distance he kept between himself and the rest of the world, or the strange budding chemistry between us that existed even when we were angry at each other. Or both. Judging from the way he sipped his espresso and avoided my eyes, he didn't know either.

"You can't tell me White Heat or Aphrodite don't get too involved in their cases and don't want to ice a villain once in a while," I said, getting back to the subject at hand.

"Ice?" A hint of a smile came out at my particular slang.

"You know what I mean."

"I never said they do not have those feelings. But they do not act on them."

"Neither did I!"

"Because I stopped time."

"I would have caught him before he hit the ground."

"So you say."

"I know I would have."

"We cannot have a vigilante on the team, Lainey. If we wanted one, we would have hired Markus Vale instead of you."

"You did *not* just compare me to him." At his silent, condemning look, I exploded. "Markus Vale is a psychopath! Are you saying I'm becoming a psychopath?" I wasn't just being dramatic. Markus Vale was legendary among heroes— a former soldier who had decided to punish the "terrorists" in our country. Yeah, he took out criminals, but he also took out jaywalkers. Anyone who broke a law, no matter how small, was a criminal in his mind and deserved a death sentence.

He cleared his throat. "Idealism is a slippery slope. Once you begin to descend . . ."

"I don't need this." I stood up. "Don't worry about firing me, I quit!"

I downed my coffee in one gulp—no sense in letting it go to waste—and walked out, leaving Robert sitting alone at the table.

I made it a few blocks before I felt the tears begin to burn in my eyes. Swiping them away in anger, I walked faster. My emotions were in turmoil. I couldn't believe I had acted the way I had, losing my temper both with the Virus and Death Dealer, fighting with Robert, and quitting the job I had worked for my whole life. I did know better than to lose control with a villain; it was one of the first lessons I had learned in school. They killed and ruined lives. Real heroes were better than that. And I especially knew better than to lose my temper. Because of my powers, control had to be my top priority. I had even been told to watch myself in, um, *intimate* situations. Think watching the sexually transmitted diseases or the male/female development video in health class is an embarrassment? Try having your health teacher explain to you that you could snap your partner's back or worse in the heat of the moment. No wonder I didn't lose my virginity until I was in college; the guys that knew me were terrified.

And I never should have bashed Robert for being a loner. Who was I to judge? I was just as much of an outsider as he was. No matter how hard I pushed myself, no matter how much I focused on my career, deep inside me that lonely and awkward orphan still existed. And any comments about me becoming like Markus Vale came out of good intentions. He was worried about me, not trying to be cruel. Maybe I was just unused to having someone who cared enough to worry about me.

I ducked into an alley and then flew up to the rooftops. Finding a suitable one, I plunked down and had a good cry.

My skin tingled a split second before I heard Robert's voice. "It is okay, Lainey. It was bound to happen."

I quickly wiped my face, but knew it was useless; my red eyes and nose would show I had been crying. "My washing out?"

He shook his head and handed me a handkerchief from his pocket. "No, succumbing to stress. It happens to everyone. That is why you train for two years. After all, this is a very stressful job, even if you have been doing it for years prior."

"Everyone has a freak out?" I said, wiping my eyes.

He nodded. "You have done better than I expected after all that has happened with Syn."

"I wanted to be tough, to prove I could handle anything."

"Why?"

"To impress you."

"Why?"

"Because I wanted you to like me!" I blurted. "It's not like I have a lot of friends to back me up. And if we were friends, maybe you wouldn't tell the EHJ I couldn't hack it. But after what happened with the Virus and now today, I'll understand if you tell them to let me go."

He sat down next to me. "Lainey, I think you can more than just 'hack' it. There is potential for greatness in you. You could be one of the heads of the Elite Hands of Justice one day. That is part of the reason that I do expect more out of you than any of the other partners I have trained. Your idealism and determination can be one of our greatest assets. But idealism can also take a very dark turn."

He reached out and brushed a tear away from my cheek, an intimate gesture. "You are right, our justice system is not perfect, and criminals escape or get off through loopholes every day. It can make you think that all of our work is for nothing. That is why many heroes stop caring and focus on notoriety, like the EHJ, or burn out and walk away. Or worse, become like Markus Vale." He laced his fingers in front of him. "We fight the darkness of mankind every day, Lainey, and it is important to not become consumed by it."

I was aware of how close we were sitting. "You really think I could be great?"

"You are well on your way." He leaned in and my heart pounded an excited rhythm in my ears. Was he really going to kiss me?

He stopped short and brushed a kiss on my forehead. "Now, if you are not going to quit, I think we should be heading home. It has been a long day and it is not even noon yet."

"Okay." I dealt with the disappointment of another moment that we had both let pass by as I braced for the teleportation spell.

CHAPTER TWELVE

"We are going to do something new today," Robert said as I met him out in the garden a few days later for our daily centering kata.

"Why am I suddenly afraid?"

"You have no reason to be. We have been working the Syn case since it began, and are both succumbing to the stress. After your incident the other day with the Death Dealer, I thought we could use a slight change of pace."

I winced at the reminder. "So what are we doing?"

"Training exercises. Since your powers are primarily physical, I thought I would test your reactions, limits, and strengths and weaknesses in that area."

"Oh, God, we're not going to spar, are we? Because let me tell you, based on personal experience, the only thing that ever accomplishes is spinning off into real fist fights." I'd seen too many of my male teammates almost kill each other because they got tagged too hard during a sparring session and assumed it was done on purpose.

"Trust me."

He led the way through the grounds to a large building I'd assumed was a stable. Wrong. Inside was a state-of-the-art training facility that looked like something straight out of a comic book, with not only every workout machine known to man, but also a chamber with what looked like rotating hoops in the air and floor, and strange metal columns that popped up from the floor at odd intervals.

"You're not serious," I said. I also wondered what he kept this for.

"It is like an obstacle course. You have to fly through the hoops and dodge the columns to get to the other end of the room and push that button. It shuts down everything. Your objective is to do this without touching a hoop or column before time runs out." He pointed out video cameras. "We will record it so you can see what mistakes you make."

"I'm not going to make any mistakes. It's easy," I scoffed.

"Alright. Let me see you do it, then."

I positioned myself at the other end of the room. "I'm ready. Let's go!"

He pushed the button and everything started up. I watched for a moment, getting into the rhythm of the machinery, and then went for it.

I passed through the first hoop easy, curving my body to miss the column that shot up just as I flew overhead, and dove toward the ground to pass through the second hoop. I was right. It was easy. You just had to watch for the pattern.

I made my way through the grid, forcing myself to go a bit faster. Maybe if I went through his little system with a record-breaking time, he wouldn't make me do it again.

I cleared the last hoop and headed for the button. It was only a few feet away, and I stretched out my hand, ready to punch it—

—and hit what felt like an invisible brick wall.

I plummeted to the ground like a bird that had hit a window, and lay there in a daze. What had just happened?

Robert stood over me, holding one glowing hand up.

"What did you do?"

"Shield." He leaned over and punched the button. "Your time is up."

"That's not fair! You cheated."

He raised an eyebrow. "Are you going to complain to a

magic-user villain that he is cheating if a situation like this happens in the field?"

"No, I'm going to punch him in the face."

"Not if you cannot touch him. So what else could you do?"

"Distract him so he'll let his guard down. Throw a car or something big at him so he's occupied with that and then go hit the button, figuratively speaking."

"I myself would try something involving less property damage, but that might work. You did show good reflexes with the obstacles, and were making good time. But you forgot about one tool you have at your disposal."

"And that is?"

"Magic. Which is the next part of your training. If you would follow me, please?"

"Can I at least get a drink or a shower?"

He ignored me and we walked back to the house.

"You said I probably wouldn't be able to cast a spell."

"That is right; I said *probably*. I did not say definitely. So we shall try it and see what happens. And you should know your way around magic, since I am the highest-level magic-user today and you are my partner."

"You go around telling people that at parties? 'Hello, my name is Robert Elliot, and I'm the highest-level magic-user today.'"

"Of course not. I would say I *am* the highest-level magic-user today."

I smiled at the joke. "Of course, you're the one who ranks all of the magic-users, so it's a bit of a cheat, isn't it?"

He gave a soft laugh. "A perk of the job, but it does not make it any less accurate. I still rank a ten."

"Braggart." I returned his smile. Since my meltdown, things had still been somewhat tense. It felt good to be getting back on friendly ground.

"Well, even though it probably won't work, I'm game to try," I said as we descended into his lair.

"Good. First you are going to start learning Italian." He walked over to one of the tables and picked up some CDs. "Start listening to these during your free time."

"What free time?"

"Instead of watching television, you can do something productive."

I made a face at him. "Can't you just teach me the spells in English?"

"I could, but that is not how it is done. I was taught them in Italian, therefore I teach any pupils of mine in Italian. It is tradition."

"Alright. So I'm learning Italian." I watched as he went to a cupboard and took out a few vials and small bags. "What am I learning today?"

"I assume the School went over the basics of magic with you?"

"We had a class in rudimentary magic knowledge, yes." At his expectant look, I sighed. "Magical forces are all around us, but only a few people are born with the ability to tap into those forces and use them as their own. It's a power, like strength and flight are mine." He nodded and I continued, feeling like I was back in school again. "There are three effectors of magic: word, deed, and will. Word, hence your use of Italian. Deed can be a physical action, like a hand gesture, or a physical ingredient, like the powders you use in the teleportation spell. Will is taken from you."

"They can all combine, too. As a matter of fact, some of the highest-level spells will use all three. Will, however, is the key ingredient to any high-level spell. Understand that the spell powers itself from you on a physical and spiritual level. Many magic-users have died trying to perform high-level spells, like resurrection, for this very reason—it drains their bodies and their souls until there is nothing left. That is how I go about 'leveling' magic-users. The higher the level, the greater their capacity to do will spells and survive. Teleportation spells are mid-level magic, say a level five, and they only use word and deed. The mind spell I used on Cyrus is a high-level spell; no one below a level eight could work it, and it uses word and will. Word will work its way into most spells. That is why you need to learn Italian."

"So, what are we trying?"

"Something basic, since you are a level one." He motioned for me to sit in the chair in front of the desk and I did so. "Focus on the book sitting open on the table. Now you are going to raise it. Point to it, make a motion like you are picking it up, and say '*Libro di aumento*.'"

The book lifted off the table.

"Sorry about that. My magic made it do that just by saying it." He motioned for the book to settle back down and then nodded at me. "Try it now."

I took a deep breath, pointed, said, "*Libro di aumento*," and lifted my hand.

Nothing happened.

I swallowed hard. "*Libro di aumento!*"

Still nothing.

"I told you I couldn't do this."

"You have to believe you can. You are letting doubt cloud your power."

"You sound like a mentor in the movies."

"I do not watch television or movies. I find better ways of occupying my time."

"You've got all the time in the world. You're allowed to kick back, relax, and do something stupid, like wasting time watching television."

"I would rather waste time by going to a play or reading a book."

I shook my head. "Fine. Snub television. Be that way." I gave him what I knew was a flirtatious smile, and was delighted to see him return it. Yes, it was definitely better to be back on friendly terms.

"Try again. This time try to clear your mind. Think of nothing but the book, the words, and lifting it up."

I closed my eyes and took a few calming breaths. I opened my eyes slowly, focused on the book, pointed, and said with all the conviction I had, "*Libro di aumento.*"

The book lifted from the table, hovered there a moment, and then dropped back down again. My mouth hung open. Robert looked pleased.

"Very good. Better than I expected. Now remember, you do not use magic carelessly. As I said, you are using a bit of your will every time you work a spell. You do not want to drain yourself, or worse, become addicted to the power of spells. And I think it goes without saying that you should not use your magic to harm others." He held up a hand at my impending argument. "Yes, there will come a time in our business that you may have to use your magic to defend either yourself or someone else against someone who means harm magically. It is key for you to find a balance. Just as you cannot go around punching people who say the wrong thing, you also cannot go around silencing them magically. That kind of magic abuse is the way to downfall."

"Again, sounding like a movie mentor." At his frown, I held up a hand. "No using spells for frivolous reasons or to be a bully. I got it."

"It is not just yourself you could harm, but the environment as well. Too much inter-dimensional travel using teleportation can rip a hole between this dimension and the next."

"You mean we're going to another dimension when we teleport?"

"Briefly, yes. And that is why I only use teleportation spells for official business and do not use them to, say, zip around town."

"I doubt I'll be able to work a teleportation spell anytime soon."

"You keep practicing and learning Italian and I will have you up to a level four or five before your training is finished."

"Really?"

"Absolutely. In our spare time, I will have you work on both physical and magic training every day." He handed me a leather-bound book. "Here is a book of spells you can try on your own."

"Sure, what else have I got to do but read?" I joked. Between working on the Syn case, patrolling at night, and doing menial office tasks for him during the day, I was always busy.

"You knew how involved this job would be when you took it. The only place that villains are stopped without any hard work or effort is on Saturday morning cartoons."

"It really bothers you that there is no Reincarnist on the Elite Hands of Justice Morning Hour, doesn't it?"

He laughed. "Do I seem like I care?"

"They left you out for a wise-cracking teen sidekick that never existed. All I'm saying is that has to hurt. But you know what? I'm willing to put in the hard work and effort because I have a new power!" I did a little happy dance and noticed he was watching me in that way guys do when they are checking you out. I deliberately caught his gaze, just to see what he'd do.

He met my gaze and held it. The room temperature seemed to climb. I swallowed hard, my mouth going dry.

"Sir, Fantazia is on the line, returning your call," Mayhew said, popping into the doorway. He must have sensed something going on between us, because he cleared his throat and said, "I'm sorry, am I interrupting?"

Robert turned to him, hands behind his back, and once again, the moment had passed. "Not at all, Mayhew. I will take it in the library."

"Very good, sir." Mayhew turned and exited.

"She is one of the heroes on our list," Robert said to me, as if I didn't know. "She may know something about Syn."

"What would you like me to do?" I asked.

He smiled. "Start studying the CDs, *cara*."

"*Cara*? What does that mean?"

"Study the CDs and you will find out."

CHAPTER THIRTEEN

I hurried around the room, putting the finishing touches on my look for the evening. As busy as we had been in the past few weeks, I'd barely had the time to eat, let alone to prep for the social event of the season. I could hear noise downstairs; the guests had begun to arrive, but Robert didn't seem to mind. Apparently even though he was hosting the big party, he didn't have to be there to greet the guests. According to Mayhew, my boss would show up at some point during the festivities, thank everyone for attending, and tell them to have a good night. Then he'd disappear back into his lair before being forced to be too social.

It was going to be my job to mingle, though I was supposed to be going with him as his "date." I tried to ignore the fluttery feelings I got from the wording, as he'd made it clear when he asked that I was simply saving him from having to put up with someone else's company.

I was wearing a dress created by a heroes-only designer that cost more than three months' rent at my former apartment, shoes that weren't much cheaper, and I'd had my hair and makeup done like I was going to the Oscars instead of a benefit party. I nearly had a heart attack from hearing how much this evening was costing me, but as Robert had said, what else was I spending my money on? He was footing the bills for my basic necessities, and the EHJ paid very well, so I could afford to splurge.

It was nice to be able to take a night off from the usual routine of patrolling, helping the police when needed, and all the while still searching for a still-nameless villain. Not to mention cramming in magic training, like making books float, while still maintaining my daily workout of obstacle course running and swimming laps in the pool. Maybe seeing me looking the hottest I ever had would finally inspire Robert romantically. Doubtful, but hey, I could dream. I enjoyed just being around him. I had learned a lot in the month that we had worked together, and we were now good friends. Granted, I wished for more, but I was used to loving guys from afar.

Still, for the amount of money this evening was adding up to, I'd better get at least a dance with a hot guy instead of being ditched twenty minutes into it. No, for that amount, I should get a hot and heavy kiss in the coat-check room, and possibly felt up—but the likelihood of that happening was slim to none, so I'd settle for a dance.

I was checking my hair one last time and wondering how movie stars did this on a daily basis when I heard a knock on the door.

"Yeah, come in," I said, reaching for a blue velvet box sitting on my dresser. Inside was the most gorgeous piece of jewelry I had ever seen: a sapphire necklace surrounded by diamonds. Robert had a deal worked out with a jeweler to rent pieces for just such an occasion. I just had to return it in the morning.

I took out the necklace and started to fasten it around my neck when Robert appeared in the mirror behind me.

"Do you need some assistance?"

I jumped. "Yes, please. Make some noise when you walk, man! You scared me."

"It is the carpeting." He took the necklace from me and fastened it around my neck. "You look lovely, *cara*."

"Th-thank you." I was thrown by both the compliment and the Italian endearment. Thanks to my studies, I had learned that *cara* meant "beloved" in Italian. I tried not to read too much into that; I had once worked with a hero who called all the women "darlin'," and it definitely didn't mean anything other than he couldn't be bothered to learn our names. But the times I found Robert looking at me with a warm gaze he didn't even bother to conceal anymore gave me hope for some meaning behind the word.

"See how well color suits you?" he teased. "Get you out of costume and you are really quite stunning."

I couldn't resist. "So you're saying you want to get me out of my clothes?"

Heat flickered in his eyes. "Lainey Livingston, that would be a very inappropriate thing for me to say, being your boss." His wry grin said he knew I was teasing. But I noticed he didn't deny it, either. Interesting.

"You clean up very well in non-work-related clothing, too," I said, returning the compliment. Armani made a nice tuxedo, and Robert filled it out even better.

"Let us go and get this over with," he said, holding out an arm.

"Robert, we haven't even got there yet and you've already used up your social skills for the day?"

I took his arm and we left my room and walked down the hallway. Mmm, he smelled good up close like this. *Don't go there, Lainey.* "You remind me of those grumpy old men who are impatient at restaurants and complain loudly about how long it's taking."

"My dear, I *am* a grumpy old man."

"You're forty, that's not old, so you can't use age as an excuse."

"Compared to you, I am old."

"That's only fourteen years difference. And in a weird way that makes my head hurt, since you start over at twenty every incarnation, and you've lived as Robert Elliot for only twenty years . . . that makes you six years younger than me. So there."

"'So there'?" His grin sent a shiver of desire down my spine. "That sounds like the height of maturity."

"Hey, just because you can't use your advanced age as an excuse for your antisocial behavior doesn't mean you get to pick on my vernacular. I don't mention your never using 'don't' instead of 'do not.'"

"A long time ago, that was how one spoke. Everyone did not dumb down their speech with slang."

"I've heard you use slang!"

"Maybe I just talk that way to put people off."

"It works."

He stopped outside of the hall door. Inside, I could hear the party going full swing.

"Your lack of reverence is refreshing," he said, and dropped a quick kiss on my forehead. "*Se soltanto fossi libero amarli.*" He opened the door and led me inside.

"Wait, I didn't understand all of that." I was still dazed from the forehead kiss. Why did he keep doing that? Did he think I was three or something? My skin wasn't tingling, so it wasn't a spell he was working. "Did you say something was free?"

He ignored my difficulty with the Italian language and pulled me along to a group of society members. "Good evening Mayor Thompson, Police Commissioner Dunn. May I introduce my assistant, Miss Lainey Livingston?"

The mayor of Covo City shook my hand like most men do, as if it would break if he gripped it too tight, not realizing it was quite the opposite. "Nice to meet you, Miss Livingston."

"Nice to meet you too, Mayor Thompson."

"Please, call me Doug," he said in a booming voice. "How have you been enjoying working with our Mister Elliot?"

"Just fine, sir," I said, mind still on the Italian thing. What was that about? I really needed to study the CDs more. "It has been a learning experience."

"Nasty business with that Syn character," the commissioner said. "I heard you were injured during the capture."

"I'm fine now."

"Well, we must mingle," Robert interjected, antsy already. "Do enjoy the evening." He dragged me off to the next bunch of people.

In the same whirlwind blur, I was introduced to almost every muckety-muck in town in the space of twenty minutes. Grabbing a glass of champagne off the tray of a passing waiter, I tried to figure out a way to get Robert to slow down or otherwise stay with me at the party instead of going to his underground lair or room to hide. Hearing the orchestra start up a dance number, I had an idea.

"What lovely music," I said to Robert, who was trying to get away from talking to an extra-chatty society matron.

"Mmm . . . yes," he said distractedly.

"And oh, look, people are starting to dance."

"They generally do at these benefits," he said, as the society matron waddled off. "I thought she would never leave."

"You know, as the host, you should probably dance at least once," I said. "Before you go." *Come on, no one is this thick!*

"That is an excellent idea," a purring voice said, and Victoria strutted up to us. Well, she strutted up to Robert; she pretended I didn't exist, sandwiching herself between us and leaning up to give him air kisses and rub her amped-up cleavage on his arm in the process. Her black dress was skintight, leaving hardly anything to the imagination, but still appropriate in the way only designer dresses can be. "Well, darling, how do you like the little party I threw together for you?"

"For the charity, you mean," he said. "You know these kind of events are not my cup of tea, Victoria."

Victoria? What happened to Miss Dupree?

"That's why you need someone like me around, darling. I live for these things," she said.

"See, Robert, Miss Dupree wore black," I said, my irritation not well concealed. "I know you prefer color, but designers do make black dresses as well."

That caught her attention. She half-turned to acknowledge my presence. "Some women just don't have the coloring for black, dear," she said in a sugar-sweet tone. "On blondes it makes you look like death. It's too bad no one told you that before. But blue doesn't make you look quite as sallow. And your dress is very . . . quaint." She went back to ignoring me. "Well, Robert, I think your assistant is right, you do need to dance." She took his arm. "Let's go."

He didn't even protest, and she ushered him off, looking back to give me a catty little smirk.

"Who's the skank?" a voice asked behind me.

I whirled in shock. "Oh my God, I don't believe it! Selena!"

"In the flesh, girl! You look freaking amazing!" My old friend hugged me, and for a moment I was a teenager again. Selena had been my only friend at the School, and we had even joined the Red Knights together. We had tried to stay in contact over the years, but as we both moved up the hero ladder, it had become more difficult.

"Thanks! You look fabulous as usual." Selena had never gone through the awkward stage, even as a teenager. She was always a tall, regal-looking woman with a perfect figure and curves to kill for. Acne never touched her light chocolate skin. Why the prettiest and one of the most popular girls in School had chosen to ally herself with me, I'd never know; I just knew I was grateful. "So, what are you doing here?"

"The Fives are affiliated with the EHJ. We've all been asked to be preliminary members at one point or another but decided we liked freelancing instead of the corporate world. But I heard you've been named a preliminary member. Congratulations! I know it's what you've been working toward since we were kids."

"Yeah." I glanced back to Robert, who was dancing with Victoria. I frowned. "It's fabulous."

"I can tell." She followed my line of sight. "I've only seen pictures of the Reincarnist, but I must say, they don't do him justice. There's just something so *grrr* about him, you know?"

I turned away. "I hadn't noticed."

She laughed. "Is that why you look like you want to rip that skinny chick apart with your bare hands?"

I shrugged. "Okay, so maybe I have noticed. A lot."

She shook her head. "Same old Lainey, always rocking the crush on the hot, intellectual older guy."

"I don't know what you're talking about."

"Please! Once you started noticing boys, you always had a crush on a student teacher or some guy on one of the teams. I've never known you to date guys our age."

"You've never known me to date, period. I was in college before I actually had a boyfriend. *He* was my own age. Although all he did was cheat on me, proving why I never liked my contemporaries."

"And why was that?"

"They were immature. They never noticed Brainy Lainey. They went for the hot-but-no-personality girls. And the guys that think they're God's gift to women are cruel—like Brian Edwards, who locked me in the supply closet the day the EHJ came to visit the School."

"Yeah, but Brian Edwards is nothing, Lainey. He never got recruited to any of the teams and is probably managing a car dealership right now, while you are a member of the most powerful team in the country."

"Good to know all those dateless nights and Christmases spent at the School when the rest of you went home to your families were good for something."

Selena frowned as she watched Robert out on the dance floor. "Wasn't it that supply closet incident where you met the team talent scout who helped you out and got you all excited about becoming a hero? The *much older* talent scout?"

"I don't know if he was there scouting for people to join teams; he could have also been a substitute teacher or something. I never got his name; I was too busy getting out of that locked supply closet. But he was nice, and he said I could still be a hero, while those bullies could never be."

"Whatever, he was cute, he was older, and he came to your rescue. All I'm saying is, I'm not surprised you've got a thing for your cute-but-older partner—who, from what I've heard through the grapevine, came to your rescue during the Syn incident."

I stared at the floor. "It's not like it's reciprocated."

"I don't know about that," she said, nodding in his direction.

I gave a casual glance over my shoulder to see him looking at me while dancing with Victoria. I turned my attention back to Selena. "You see? He has the super-skinny debutante. I'm just a friend."

"No, I'm not buying it," she replied, still watching. "The chemistry between you two is a little too thick to be only friendly."

"He's with her, isn't he?"

"I was watching. He didn't exactly want to go with her. And trust me, babe, you don't give your friends the 'I want to throw you down on the table and screw your brains out' look. He's giving you that look right now."

My head snapped to look, but he looked away as soon as he saw me noticing.

"It was probably aimed at you, Selena. And is that the way they teach you to talk at the Five?"

She rolled her eyes. "I work with four other women on a daily basis. The lack of men is making me super horny, and I don't switch sides. But he was looking at you, no question."

"Well, he won't be sticking around much longer," I said, taking a bit of satisfaction out of that. "He wants me to circulate for him so he can go hide in the Reincarnist Cave, so she won't have her nasty little hooks into him for long."

Three dances and one trip to the bar with her later, he didn't seem to be in any hurry to leave. And it was official: I had been ditched. No hot make-out sessions in the coat-check room. I hadn't even gotten a dance. I had blown a couple of grand for nothing.

"This sucks," I said.

"Lainey, just go over and tell him you need to borrow him for a second, then go into an empty room and jump him."

"And in what reality did I turn into you?" I wished I could be bold and go after what I wanted. Instead, I was always watching as the rest of the world made their moves. I was more like the man from William Graves's poem, always hoping I'd take the next moment, but knowing deep down that I'd let it pass by like always.

Selena checked her watch. "I've gotta split, hon. I've got a trip to the Dominican Republic in my future. Michelle knows a guy who's in business down there and is worried there's going to be a government coup. He somehow convinced her we could keep an eye on his business interests, protect the people, and work on our tans at the same time. I'm more interested in trying to help the poor people trying to live their lives. I'll call when I get back."

"Be careful, okay?"

"Don't worry about me. I'm nigh indestructible, remember?" She winked at me. "Good luck with the Reincarnist." She glided off, lovely as ever, leaving me on my own.

While my date enjoyed the evening with another woman.

I was just getting angry enough to leave when I heard a male voice say, "Who is he?"

"Excuse me?" I turned to see an attractive blond man in an all-black suit standing before me. Tall, with an athletic build, he stood with that casual yet suave awareness some men master. He had blue eyes and a slight dimple that would make a girl swoon.

Only, I wasn't swooning. My mind registered there was an attractive man before me, yet I didn't get any tingly feelings. Maybe it was because I got a sense he knew he was attractive and used it to his full advantage.

"Who's the idiot that left you unattended?" he said. "Because I have a feeling you didn't come here alone."

Or maybe I have bad-pickup-line awareness. "I came with *him*." I pointed to where Robert was standing talking to Victoria.

He followed my direction and did a double-take. "You're not serious."

I nodded. "Afraid so. He's my boss, though, so it's not like a real date or anything." I don't know why I felt the need to qualify it like that to a random stranger, like there was no way I'd be here on a date with Robert.

The blond guy laughed. "Good. I was going to question your taste if you were dating him. And I'd have to wonder what else was wrong with him that he ditched you for her."

Thank you, hot guy! Now why don't I find you as attractive as I should? "I'm Lainey Livingston." I held out my hand to shake.

He kissed it instead. Smooth. And yet it did nothing for me. "Simon Leasure." He leaned in closer, lowering his voice. "Inferno, from the Elite Hands of Justice. So you're Phenomenal Girl Five."

Now I recognized him, and I instantly went giddy from being in the presence of one of *them*. "Of course, I didn't recognize you without the costume . . . and I've only seen pictures of you." *God, Lainey, act like a professional!* "It's so great to meet you!"

"The pleasure is all mine. Your pictures don't do you justice." He stood close to me. "So you're the latest victim of the Reincarnist. We've all been there and made it through the experience relatively intact. I'm just glad you're not his girlfriend. I couldn't bear the thought of someone as lovely as you going to waste on him."

"No chance of that," I mumbled.

He laughed, mistaking my meaning. "He's a real piece of work, isn't he? If it helps, think of your time here like a fraternity initiation—survive two years of him without losing your mind and you're in."

"He hasn't been so bad," I said, my tone a bit defensive. "He's been nice to me."

"That'll change. But let's not waste our time talking about him." He turned his movie-star-caliber smile on me. "You know, when Rath and Kate made me come here, I thought I'd die of boredom, but now that we've met, things are looking up. Would you like to dance?"

A hot guy had just asked me to dance. The night had taken a decidedly better turn.

I smiled. "I'd love to."

As he led me onto the dance floor, I caught Robert's eyes. He was frowning.

What was his deal? He ditched me and then had the nerve to look upset that some hot guy my own age asked me to dance? Well, like Simon said, I wasn't going to waste my time thinking about Robert. I was going to enjoy myself.

After a couple of dances, Simon and I walked to the bar to get drinks. I felt very cool as I ordered my Cosmopolitan and sipped it in the company of a guy who looked like a movie star. Except, he didn't make my heart race like Robert did.

Forget about that, I ordered myself, *and enjoy the hot male attention. You've already had your dance; a hot kiss might be in your future if you play your cards right!*

"So I've been team leader on several missions," Simon was saying. "The way things are going, you could end up working for me someday."

"Really?"

"Paul's grooming me to be the next team leader. I'm trying to take the lead on some of the higher-profile cases. It's all about getting the right kind of exposure, Lainey, remember that."

"Uh-huh." So, he was attractive but full of himself. Typical.

A beeping sounded from his pocket, and he reached in, pulling out a communicator. "It's the EHJ."

"Oh, is it something serious?"

He looked at me as if I was slow. Duh. Of course if they were beeping it was serious. "It could be about the Kremordians. We've been off to space lately, trying to help a group of aliens with a peace treaty."

Because there's no countries on Earth that need of help in that department. "I've heard."

"I'm sure you have. The Reincarnist always has made a big deal about our space missions. Just because he doesn't want to expand his horizons . . ." He trailed off. "I'd better be getting back, they'll need me. But, assuming I don't have to go into space tomorrow, would you like to go to dinner?"

You know your life is strange when your would-be date's possible reason for canceling is space travel. I glanced in Robert's direction to see that he was again frowning at me.

I turned back to Simon with a big smile. "Sure. I'd love to."

CHAPTER FOURTEEN

I ate breakfast, worked out, and practiced magic by myself the next morning. Robert was nowhere in sight. That could be taken in any number of ways, but since the last time I'd seen him he was heading out to the garden with Victoria Dupree, I was expecting to see her do the walk of shame at any moment. Only, in her case, it wouldn't be the walk of shame. More like the strut of pride. When I still didn't see him at lunchtime, I didn't know whether to be disgusted or impressed.

In either case, I was in a dark mood as I sat in the library, answering Robert's correspondence. It was a job his assistants always did, but one I had let build up in favor of other more heroic pursuits. I took a moment to get the mental image of Simon Leasure acting as a secretary, and just couldn't conceive it.

Robert was well-known in different circles—for forensics and criminal profiling in the law enforcement arena, and for his spellcasting skills in the world of sorcery. As a result, he was always getting requests for this book or that lecture circuit. He usually turned them all down. I did my job and wrote the proper no-thanks replies, but in my mind it was a different story.

No, I cannot come to your party because I am too busy screwing a stick figure.

No, I cannot give a speech at your committee meeting because I am an antisocial jerk.

No, I cannot coauthor your book because I am too lazy to even reply to my own letters and I make my overly jealous colleague do that.

I have no right to be jealous, I reminded myself. *He can date whomever he wants, even stick figures with hideous personalities.*

That task finished, I started toward the door, only to be met by Robert.

We both froze. He took a step back and then seemed to relax. I, however, tensed more. All my pep talk about not feeling jealous went out the window.

"Good afternoon," he said.

"Hey. Correspondences done. I was downstairs earlier and the world hasn't exploded, so we're cool. I'll see you later." I started to bypass him and he moved to block me.

Annoyed, I glared up at him. "Is there something else you need?"

"I am sorry I was not around this morning to give you instructions."

"It's not so complicated a job that I can't do it on my own." I winced after I said it. That was more than bordering on rude.

"You do a good job, Lainey." He clapped me on the shoulder. *Great, I'm one of the guys now.* "I am sorry to have shirked my duties for most of the day, but I was meditating."

"Is that what you kids call it nowadays?" I moved to slip away.

"What?" He blocked me again. "What did you say?"

"Nothing. I'm just . . ." *jealous.* "Cranky."

"Did you think 'meditation' was an euphemism for sex?" He laughed.

God, Mister Blunt! Anyone else would have softened that statement somehow. "Well . . ." I tried to think of the least embarrassing way to say yes.

"Because unless I am having sex with myself, I was upstairs alone, transcending to the astral plane." He looked amused at my discomfort.

"It's not my business anyway," I muttered, desperately wanting out of the conversation.

"Who did you think I was with?" he continued, not letting me escape.

"I didn't . . . I don't . . ." *Oh, the hell with it.* I gave up. "Victoria Dupree."

"God, why?" The look of astonishment on his face seemed genuine.

"Well, you ditched me for her all night, for one thing!" I said, a trace of anger escaping.

"You were going to circulate for me, remember?"

"And I did, but a gentleman doesn't ditch his date to go off with another woman, even if his date is just a coworker."

"True," he conceded. "But I tried to get rid of her all night. She stuck to me like an annoying parasite."

"You didn't seem to mind." Why had I just said that? Why didn't I just scream 'I have a not-so-secret crush on you!' and get it over with?

He seemed to not know how to reply. Not that I blamed him.

"Forget it." I waved him away. "Like I said before, I'm cranky, so just ignore me. 'Meditate' with Victoria or don't, it doesn't matter to me."

"I can tell." His lips quirked in amusement. "And yet, I saw you were not unattended for long last night."

"Well, my old friend from the Red Knights showed up, but she's not exactly the same as having a date."

"That is not who I meant."

A knock on the door interrupted us, and Mayhew stepped inside. "Miss Lainey, there is a phone call for you."

I picked up the receiver, angling away from Robert so he couldn't eavesdrop. "Hello?"

"Hello, Lainey. This is Simon Leasure, we met last night."

"Oh, hi!" I said in an overly cheery voice, and then lowered my voice. "I was just thinking about you." Robert cleared his throat behind me. God, was super-hearing one of his powers?

"Good things, I hope."

"Of course." I let my voice sound a bit more flirty.

"Is the Reincarnist hovering right behind you?"

I started to half-turn and about ran into Robert. "Yes," I said, giving him a pointed look.

"Yeah, he seems to think he has to listen in on every conversation you have."

I covered the receiver. "Do you mind? A little privacy, please."

Robert moved backward slightly, hands behind his back. "Sorry."

I gave him one last glare and turned away from him again. "Sorry, go ahead, Simon." I ignored the annoyed cough behind me.

"Well, the good news is that we didn't have to go to space. It was something easily fixed without leaving planetside."

"That's great."

"So, since we're on the same planet, how about dinner tonight?"

"Sounds great." I'd take dinner with a hot guy over grousing about someone who liked stick figures.

"I'll come by around eight. Will he have a fit if you play hooky from patrol?"

I glanced back at Robert, who was now seated at one of the sofas, glowering at me.

"It shouldn't be a problem," I said. "I'll take care of it."

He laughed. "Wish I was there to see it. You'll have to tell me about it tonight."

"Alright. I'm looking forward to it."

"Me too."

We had barely disconnected when I heard, "Who was that?"

"God, he's right, you are nosey." I walked across the room, determined to make my escape this time.

"That had better not have been Simon Leasure." He sounded like a disrespected parent as he said it, and it made my blood boil.

"And what if it was?" I crossed my arms as I turned to face him, completely up to taking on the challenge he was dishing out.

"I saw him latch on to you last night the moment my back was turned." He was standing, arms behind his back and every muscle in his body tense, dark eyes flashing. He didn't even bother to conceal his anger.

"He was nice enough to hang out with me after you ditched me for Victoria," I retorted.

"Simon Leasure is an over-privileged brat with a chip on his shoulder for anyone in a position of authority over him. His senator father never made him take responsibility for any of his actions, and so he uses people to his advantage, especially women. This is just another way for him to try to get back at me—through you."

"Oh, so no man would ever want to go out to dinner with me just for my company?" I snapped. "Just because *you* don't find me attractive doesn't mean that my being asked out by someone who looks like a movie star is a vendetta against you. Some men *do* find me attractive, Robert, as hard as that may be for you to believe!"

He looked as if I'd hit him. "It is not like that at all. I just know Simon better than you. I am not trying to suggest . . ."

"Spare me the attempts to backtrack out of calling me repulsive," I interrupted. "Now, I have a date tonight, so . . ."

"You cannot go."

I gritted my teeth. "Excuse me?"

"You have to work tonight."

"I'm allowed some nights off, Robert! Last week you let me stay home from patrol to watch the season finale of a television show."

"Well, for this you cannot."

"You have no right to tell me what to do."

"Wrong. I am your superior until your two years of train-ing are completed, and then Rath becomes your boss. So technically, yes, I do have the right."

"A boss can't tell me who I can and cannot date."

"Romance is distracting, and you do not need any distrac-tions right now. Your training comes first, above all else."

"Work's always come first for me, and I'm tired of it." With that realization, a wave of calmness settled over me. I took a deep breath. "If you want, I'll do a quick patrol when I get back from my date, but I *am* going. I don't care if you two hate each other, you can't stop me. Fire me if you want, but be sure to tell Rath that it was over having a friendly dinner with a future teammate. In case you've forgotten, Robert, I'm not staying here to be your sidekick forever. I'll be joining the EHJ on a full-time basis soon." With that parting shot, I shoulder-checked him, knocking him out of my way, and headed upstairs to hide out in my room until it was time to get ready for my date.

"You seem tense," Simon said at dinner. "Have another glass of wine."

I looked at the half-full glass that I had barely touched. "I'm okay, really. I just had an argument with Robert."

He sighed. "We never saw eye-to-eye, either. He's too far behind the times. But Rath will never kick him out because of their history, and Toby's nostalgic for him because he helped found the team back in the forties. But the rest of us just put up with him and his old-fashioned ideals and wait for him to die. Again."

That was harsh. I shifted uncomfortably in my chair. "Did you have problems working for him?" I asked, deter-mined to know why they hated each other.

Simon drained his glass. "Did I ever. He wouldn't take the least little suggestion I made, had me working all the time, and then took all the credit for it, and expected me to act like an old man. I was young and wanted to have fun and he didn't see the need for it."

"He told me you were an arrogant little opportunist who uses women. And that is a direct quote."

"That sounds like something he'd say about me." Simon gave a mirthless laugh. "I just wanted to get ahead on the team and he didn't. I did what I needed to do for the actual team leaders to take notice. I took only the best cases, held elaborate press conferences, and got a publicist and an agent, all to get better exposure. And it worked. As soon as I graduated to a full member, I became one of the standbys of the team. I was going on all the missions, like the space thing I was telling you about, when normally they stick you with monitor duty and base camp work for the first year or so."

"And the using women part?"

He shrugged. "I'm not going to lie, Lainey, I date a lot. It's hard not to. We're like a movie star and a rock star rolled into one. I'm young, and the only commitment I've made is to the Elite Hands of Justice, so what's wrong with that?"

"Nothing," I said. But there was no way I was going to be another notch on a bedpost.

"The women throw themselves at me and, hey, I'm a hero, I will always catch a hot woman if she falls." He laughed at his own joke, and I shifted uncomfortably in my seat again and started looking around for the waiter to signal for the check.

He launched into a long tale about some mission to space, how he alone had saved the day and had hot alien women offering themselves up to him, but I tuned him out, instead thinking of Robert and the fight we'd had. Just because Simon was full of himself didn't mean Robert could tell me what to do, especially in the romance department. I was allowed to date whomever I wanted.

The waiter must have noticed my eyes screaming for help, because he brought the check. I pounced on it, calculating my personal total and giving the waiter a generous tip. Simon didn't even fight me on it, and I noticed when we left that he barely gave the waiter five percent of his share. So he was cheap, too.

Simon babbled in the car all the way home. He never asked me anything about myself, not that I cared. The women he had bragged about being with must have only been in it for one thing, and it wasn't his scintillating conversational skills. I didn't care how hot he was, I wasn't into casual sex with someone so self-centered.

We reached the mansion, and I knew the awkward moment of the date had arrived. Knowing the type of guy Simon was, he expected to kiss me. I didn't want him to, but I was going to have to work with him again, and couldn't be rude and run into the house without a word. I was going to have to find a tactful way to get out of it.

He pulled up to the line of cars and parked right in front of the mansion.

"He still loves to trot out those cars," he said. "Do you know how many times I had to wash those damn things like I was his servant? Makes me want to key them."

"Don't you dare," I snapped. Seeing his wide eyes, I tried to soften my tone. "Those are gorgeous cars. It would be sacrilege to hurt them because of him."

"Oh, you're a fan of cars?" At my nod, he smiled. "I'll have to take you for a spin in my new Ferrari. Custom made."

"Sounds nice," I said, but didn't mean it. I like old cars, not the modern designs.

"Does he make you drive that old junker car around town?"

"I haven't seen any junkers."

"He had some POS from the seventies he made me use when I had to run errands for him. The only time I was allowed to touch these cars was to detail them."

Thinking of Simon detailing the cars made me smile. "Well, I have the Mustang, so . . ."

"He lets you drive the Mustang?" Simon looked angry. "Just figures he'd let the hot chick drive one of those cars while I got stuck with a beater." Then he must have realized he had insulted me, and changed tones. "Not that you don't deserve to drive around in a Mustang . . ."

"It's okay, I get it." *You're an idiot.* "Well, thank you for taking me out tonight, Simon. I appreciated the change in scenery."

He smiled. "I'll bet. You just hang in there, Lainey, I'll see what I can do about getting you full-member status before two years." He leaned forward. "And I'm just a phone call away."

"Thanks. I appreciate it." I just wanted out of the car. "Well, goodnight . . ." I trailed off, seeing Robert open the door of the mansion.

Simon grabbed my face in his hands, turning it to face him, and kissed me. It wasn't gentle or even passionate: it was all tongue and saliva, lacking in technique and clearly for Robert's benefit. I pulled away, wiping my mouth off with my hand, and scrambled out of the car. "What the hell was that? A little finesse is appreciated, not drool." I think Robert's lack of tact was rubbing off on me.

He frowned. "No one's complained before."

"I think we're just better suited as friends, Simon."

He looked me over and turned on the one-hundred-watt smile. "We'll see, babe."

Robert stood at the front door, hands behind his back, giving Simon the evil eye as he peeled off, unnecessarily burning rubber on the pavement and honking as he left. I passed by, keeping my head held high, preparing for the inevitable *I told you so.*

"How was your date?"

"Fine." I managed, as if I hadn't been drooled on.

"Did he show his true colors, or can he behave on a first date?"

I wasn't going to give him the satisfaction. "You just don't like him and the feeling is mutual."

"Did he talk about me on your date?" Robert's eyes twinkled with amusement.

"He was trying to commiserate with me," I said, annoyed that he found this funny. I immediately went for the low blow. "Sounds like you have a problem with your wards having a social life while you have none."

"Lainey, I am sorry for trying to keep you from dating. You are right, it is none of my business."

"That's right, it's not." *What brought on the change of heart?*

"And I have already been out on patrol, so you do not have to worry about it. Go to bed and relax. I am sure it has been a long night."

"Um . . . thanks?" This was leading up to something.

"I got another call from Fantazia. We have an appointment to see her next week. She may have information about our mysterious friend."

"Great."

"And you can take patrol tomorrow while I am out."

Alarms went off in my head. "Out?"

"Yes, I am taking Victoria to a concert and dinner tomorrow night."

It was like someone set off a bomb in my head. I went from calm to mental in two seconds flat.

"Are you kidding me?"

His expression stayed bland. "Why would I be kidding you?"

"Oh, my God, you have to be the most immature man I have ever known, and you're older than time."

"I do not know what you are talking about."

"You're doing that on purpose! I went out with someone you hated and you're going out with someone I hate to get back at me. That's so immature, Robert. What are you, eternally thirteen?"

"It is none of my business who you date, and it is none of your business who I date."

"Oh, my God! You knew I didn't like her so you deliberately picked her. Why does it matter if I date someone you don't like?"

"Why does it matter if I date someone you do not like?" His dark eyes bored holes into mine. "Are you jealous?"

"Yes." And God help me, it felt good to finally get it out in the open, even if it was going to mean weeks of awkwardness later. "Are *you* jealous?"

"Terribly." He slid one arm around my waist, pulling me in tight, his warm lips descending to mine. His other hand brushed my cheek in a gentle caress.

In all those years of living, he had definitely mastered the kiss. It was slow and soft, but with enough passion behind it to make me lightheaded. I found myself drifting backward to rest against the closed door for support, pulling him along with me, kissing him back. Our tongues danced together, and he tasted faintly of coffee and brandy.

"We should not be doing this," he said against my mouth between kisses.

"And yet we're not stopping."

"You are just so sexy it drives me crazy to not be touching you, *cara*. I do not know how I managed this long." He reclaimed my mouth again and I felt a little sigh of pleasure escape. I had been crazy about him for weeks, never dreaming he was into me. Not really. But he thought I was sexy? I wasn't going to analyze how it happened; I was just going to enjoy it.

The escalating passion between us threatened to build into something more explosive and powerful. My skin was starting to tingle in a delicious way the promise of something other than a kiss hinted at. I know I craved it, and I could tell he did too.

And of course, that's when alarms started going off.

We froze, still up against the door.

"What the hell is that?" I asked, still in his arms.

"Damn it!" He broke away from me and started off down the hall.

"Whoa, you're swearing, so it must be serious," I said, following.

"The only way to set off the inter-house alarms is for there to be a code red threat." He went into the library and started pulling books to get to the lab.

"That isn't the usual villain threatening to blow up city hall, is it?"

"No, it is usually a villain threatening to blow up the world." He descended to the lab, me at his heels.

"Should we call in the EHJ?"

"They are probably already dispatched. A code red requires more than one person." He hurried down the hall to the monitors and clicked a few buttons. "Oh, hell."

"What is it?" I tried to peer over his shoulder.

"It is a team-up."

"Excuse me?"

"About six level-seven villains have hit the town. We have major trouble."

I sighed. "So I guess it's time to suit up."

"It is unfortunate timing, but yes." He gave me a rueful smile. "It is too bad. We will have to continue our . . . meditating later."

I grinned at him and raised an eyebrow.

"It is what the kids are calling it nowadays," he said with a smile. I swear, the temperature of the room went up about ten degrees.

"These mood-killers are going down," I said, cracking my knuckles. "I'm feeling the need to kick a little butt."

CHAPTER FIFTEEN

Chaos couldn't begin to describe what I was witnessing. Robert and I blinked into existence at the nearest coordinates the EHJ could give us, and we were dropped into an all-out war.

"Thank God you're here," Aphrodite, one of the EHJ members, said, coming up to us seconds before a car dropped in the exact spot she had just been standing. The nausea I used to feel after a teleportation spell had all but stopped, but with World War Three going on around us, I felt woozy. I stumbled, and Robert caught me around the waist.

"Who is doing this?" he yelled over the din, keeping a tight grip on me.

"You name it, that's who. It's like every single high-powered villain we've ever fought decided to have a convention!" She glanced at me. "You there, Phenomenal Girl, are you alright?"

"Sorry, it's the teleportation," I said, standing straighter and moving away from Robert. "I'm okay."

"Good. You're on crowd-control, then. Try to protect any civilians and catch some of the debris they're hurling at us."

"*Schermo*," Robert said, as what looked like a chunk of a building came flying at us. My nerves tingled as I felt his magic take effect and an invisible shield came up around us. "*Transmutazione ad acqua*." The building chunk became water as it hit the shield.

"Case in point," Aphrodite said. "Robert, we need you with us to try to stop the villains."

"Very well." He turned back to me as she bounded off. "Be careful, *cara.*"

"This isn't my first rodeo, cowboy. I'll be fine. I swear I won't overly antagonize any villains, drop them from the sky, or get my soul eaten."

"Thank you." He gave me a look that warmed my insides.

"You be careful, too," I said, watching as he flew off after Aphrodite.

An explosion went off behind me and I heard screaming. Whirling, I saw another large energy blast hit a building. Civilians ran past, and I saw a few get hit with debris. Flying over, I dodged the airborne pieces to help.

A piece of concrete had shattered a man's leg, and a woman was staggering around looking dazed, a huge gash on her head. I flipped the concrete off of the man, gathering him under one of my arms and flying off toward the woman. I grabbed her by the waist just as what appeared to be half of a bus came hurtling at us. I barely dodged it, ducking down an alleyway and shooting up and over a building and down three city blocks to where several police cars and ambulances were gathered.

I dropped down in front of a paramedic, who stared open-mouthed at me. I guess the shock of seeing someone fly never gets old to civilians.

"He's got a broken leg and I think she has a concussion," I said, setting them down on the ground as gently as I could. A loud explosion boomed behind us, and several people jumped and started crying. Overhead, I saw what looked like the Magnificent, another member of the EHJ, and a villain I couldn't identify go flying past, shooting and dodging energy bolts. I turned back to the paramedic. "I gotta go."

I zoomed back to the chaos. There didn't seem to be any reason behind it, just villains tearing apart buildings and throwing the pieces at us and the civilians. What the hell was going on?

I saw Inferno blasting at a villain on top of a building. The blast caught the villain in the chest and he went flying backward off the roof. I flew up to meet Inferno, who was peering over the edge.

"Is he dead?"

He turned to me. "God, I hope so. You got tapped for this insanity too, huh?"

"What's going on? Have the villains suddenly gone more crazy than usual? It seems so random."

"White Heat thinks it's a distraction, so he and some of the others are patrolling the major hot spots: the White House, the Pentagon, the Bermuda Triangle . . ."

"The Bermuda Triangle?"

"It's a gateway to Hell. Some psycho opens the gate and we might as well give up." Screams could be heard down the block, and he swore. "I'm on it. You stay on this end." He took off and I hovered in midair, unsure what to do.

I heard a cry for help and turned to see someone hanging off a fire escape that looked as if it were ready to fall off the building.

"Hang on!" I yelled. A passing villain noticed and blasted at me with some sort of energy emission. I dodged at the last minute and checked on my civilian. He looked alright for a few more moments, so I circled back to the villain. He kept shooting and I kept evading. Just as I neared the rooftop he was standing on, a blast caught me in the side. Grimacing as the pain burned through my body, I yanked off a piece of the ledge as I plummeted. The villain looked down as if to watch me go splat. With a good bit of my strength, I winged the piece of ledge at him. It cracked him in the head and he fell backward.

I twisted in the air and zoomed back to my civilian.

The fire escape was making creaky noises as I came up.

The civilian turned panicky eyes on me. "Thank God! Help me, please!"

"Hang on!" I started toward him and a sharp pain seared into my back. I went flying into the fire escape and wall behind it. Groaning in pain, I looked back from where I had been to see the villain that I had hit standing there. He had shot me in the back.

"Are you okay?" the civilian asked just as the villain shot the fire escape out from under us.

We dropped, but I managed to pull my aching body together to grab the man and fly back up to the roof. The fire escape fell on a car below, its alarm screaming to life.

Reaching the roof, I dropped the man and collapsed. I was in so much pain that my mind was blanking out.

"Are you alright, lady?" the man asked, staring down at me. He was tall and thin, with a pocked face and oily hair. He looked like he should be in his mother's basement playing role-playing games online instead of hanging from fire escapes.

"What were you doing out there?" I asked, forcing myself to sit up.

"I heard the commotion and stepped outside," he said, helping me to stand. "You're one of those capes, aren't you?"

I nodded. "Yeah. Phenomenal Girl Five."

His eyes lit up. "Really? I've heard about you."

"That's nice." My nerves tingled, and I looked around for Robert, but didn't see him. Yet I still felt the sensation of magic gearing up. "I need to get you to safety. It's chaos out here."

"Not yet it isn't," the man said, and the difference in his tone made me look back at him.

Then I felt a searing white pain in my chest—worse than my back, worse than anything I had ever experienced. My entire body spasmed and I gasped. I looked down at the twisted dagger plunged into my chest, oddly noticing that its handle was in the shape of a dragon.

The nerdy-looking man now held himself with confidence. "I am Jihad, the bringer of chaos. The heart's blood of the pure soul spilled in combat is the next ingredient he needs for the spell. The fact that you're the Reincarnist's little protégé is just a bonus." He twisted the blade, jamming it further into me, and the edges of my vision went dark. "It was nice of one of your little cape friends to arrange this distraction for my real work."

I fell to the ground, my body limp, air completely gone from my lungs as my mind tried to process his words.

"The Dragon sends his regards," Jihad said, standing over me with a wild grin on his face. I saw a mark on his wrist, like the one I had seen on Syn.

Just before the blackness came, I heard the echoing of Robert's voice, but I couldn't make out the words.

CHAPTER SIXTEEN

In the midst of all the darkness was light. I focused on it, and it filled me with warmth, peace, and love. A figure appeared at the center of the light. She had hair that looked like it was spun from pure gold and her skin glittered like diamonds. Her brown eyes were warm and full of love.

I knew who she was, even though I didn't remember seeing her face. But I had once, because she had held me as she died, her body succumbing to the radiation that would eventually give me my powers.

"Mother," I said, reaching out, tears running down my face at finally seeing her.

Even though the space between us was forever, she somehow brushed my hand with hers. "Lainey."

"I'm dead, aren't I?" I asked, although the answer was clear.

"I'm sorry, baby."

"Is this Heaven?"

"Where I'm standing is. You are at the crossroads, which is why I can't hug you like I want to. But He said I could talk to you while you're in between. You won't be for long."

"You mean I'm going to Hell?" I asked, panicked.

"No, baby. You're coming here, someday. Just not today."

"So I'm not going to die?"

"Oh, you've died. But you're still needed on Earth. Someone's bringing you back. Really He's sending you back, but using someone else to do so. He likes to work through people, you know?" She smiled. "You've turned out so well, Lainey. I'm so proud of you."

My heart leaped at hearing the words I'd so desperately needed as I had pushed myself over the years.

A cloud crossed her face. "It won't be easy for you, at least not for a while, but He says it builds character. And He would know. Remember, sweetheart, that nothing wonderful ever comes easy. You have to work for it. And everything happens for a reason." She looked behind her again. "He says it's time. I love you, Lainey, and so does your father. Keep on making us proud." Then she started to fade, and the blackness came up around me again, the light fading into the distance.

I wanted to cry, but couldn't. The love and the warmth were fading from me now, and I was falling down, somewhere where it was harsh and hard and there was no peace. And then I heard words being spoken, over and over again. The voice was familiar. I oriented myself on those words.

"*Portila di nuovo me. Portila di nuovo me.*" Over and over it was spoken, until it ran together in one pleading breath.

Bring her back to me.

With a jolt, I had the sensation of settling into something that was dark. I panicked. I tried to struggle, but couldn't feel my movement, which only increased my panic. A presence calmed me, something reminiscent of where I'd seen my mother. It made me realize where I was.

I was back in my own body.

It just wasn't working yet.

I listened to the voice speaking Italian, over and over again, and I remembered who it was.

Robert. It was Robert. But I had never heard him like this. He sounded ragged.

"You need to stop now. It isn't working." That was Mayhew.

"It will. It is!" Robert snapped. "It has to."

"It isn't." Mayhew sounded sad. "No one has ever been able to make a resurrection spell work. It's only killing you."

"So what if it does? What the hell does it matter? I will only be back in a few moments anyway, younger and a bit confused, but I will be back."

"There's no guarantee of that, Robert, not anymore! This spell uses so much will, and after everything that's happened, all bets are off."

"She does not even have that chance if I do not keep doing the spell. *Portila di nuovo me. Portila di nuovo me.*"

"Robert, let her go, don't desecrate her memory by bringing back an empty shell. She's gone!"

"No she is not! I can still feel her." Robert sounded like he was going to break.

Silence followed. "You only wish you could, sir. You're blinded by what you want. But it isn't true. She's gone."

"She cannot be." Robert's voice was choked with emotion. "I love her."

I couldn't believe what I was hearing. He loved me!

I felt awareness seeping back into my body. Tinglings ran through my arms and legs and torso. My chest hurt. It wasn't my heart; I was aware of it beating again. Oh! My lungs. I needed air.

I drew in a shallow breath. And then another. I concentrated on trying to open my eyelids, but they felt weighted down.

There was silence in the room. Then . . .

"My God." That was Mayhew.

There was a sharp intake of breath, and then something jostled me.

"Is she . . . ?" Mayhew sounded terrified and awed at the same time.

I felt warm breath on my face and sensed someone hovering just inches from me. My eyes opened, just barely. I peeked through my eyelashes.

"Lainey?" It was Robert. He sounded so hopeful.

I forced my eyes open. Robert and Mayhew were staring at me, faces white.

Feeling was back in my body. I struggled to sit up, needing to move again. Robert, who had been sitting on the bed next to me, moved to help.

I remembered how to use my voice. "Wh-what happened to Jihad?" It came out sounding raspy.

Robert frowned at the mention of the villain. "He is dead. I killed him."

"Y-you did?" My voice was gaining strength. "But we don't kill."

"I came up there to find you . . ." His voice broke and he looked away. "He was in the midst of working a spell that would have sent the whole world into chaos. I had to kill him." He looked down. "But it was not the world I was concerned about when I obliterated him."

I reached out to squeeze his hand. "I'm touched. Really."

Our eyes met and locked. Robert smiled and gently rubbed his thumb across the back of my hand.

Mayhew cleared his throat. "I'll leave you two alone." He patted my shoulder. "Welcome back, Miss Lainey."

"Thanks," I said as he walked out the door, closing it behind him. I realized that I was in Robert's bedroom, in his bed. "How did I get here?"

"I brought you straight back here." Robert closed his eyes for a moment as if he were concentrating on staying awake. "You were dead, Lainey."

"I know. I saw my mother."

His eyes flew open and I thought I saw tears form. "Christ."

"Didn't see Him, but He was definitely there. And I will smack the next person who tries to tell me God doesn't exist, because I know otherwise."

"Stop." His hands were shaking. "I do not want to think about you like that."

"Hey." I hugged him. His arms tightened around me, as if he was afraid I would disappear. "But you brought me back.

And it's like it didn't happen, because I feel perfectly fine. I was tired at first, but now I'm all good."

"I am glad. I was afraid there might be side effects. No one has ever been able to do a resurrection spell before."

"You're powerful." I pulled away to look at him.

"Not that powerful."

"I'm fine. I think that's pretty powerful. And you're fine . . ."

"No," he interrupted. "I am not."

A cold jolt ran through me. "Did you use up all of your magic?"

"No." He looked so sad. "I am dying, *cara*. Resurrection spells are the ultimate use of will. It took all of mine to bring you back."

What? I felt a stab to my heart again, and it was no less painful than the real thing. "No. You can't be. You don't die!" A tear slid down my cheek.

"I die every time I reincarnate, Lainey."

"But it'll be alright," I said, clinging desperately to that hope. "You'll be back . . . Just a little different, right?"

"Likely, but there are no guarantees, I told you that before. There is always the chance this is my last life. But even if it is, it is all right." He rubbed his thumb over the back of my hand again. "I would not change a thing. I saw an awkward young girl whose classmates trapped her in a closet become a real hero."

I thought my heart had stopped again. "Oh, my God." I looked into those familiar brown eyes that were even more familiar now. "That was you. Back in the School. The recruiter . . ."

"I kept an eye on your career after that day because I knew you would be good for the team. That you had the makings of a real hero. And I was right."

I shook my head. "So weird that was you. You were what inspired me to work hard to *become* a hero. Only, I forgot it was you. Or I didn't know."

He managed a rueful smile. "That is a nice change of pace—someone forgetting me instead of the other way around."

"What are you talking about?"

He sighed. "Even if I do come back, I will be someone else." His dark eyes bored into mine. "Someone who will likely not remember you."

My heart hurt again. "Well, try."

"I do not want to forget you," he said, tone adamant. "You have been a good friend and an exceptional partner. Had this not happened, I would like to think you would have been more. But I cannot help what I remember or forget in my next life. It is an involuntary reflex, what gets stored away and what gets deleted. And in all of these centuries, I have never woken from one life to the next with the knowledge of a girlfriend or wife or children. I have never remembered them, and it was too painful for them to know I forgot. Most probably left without me knowing it. The ones that stuck around suffered. I have a son who hated me for a long time because I replaced his father and did not know him. I do not want to see you suffer like that."

I swallowed hard. "How long do we have?"

He sighed, closing his eyes. "It is coming soon. Maybe an hour at most."

"It'll have to do." I leaned forward, wrapped my arms around his waist, and kissed him as if the world was going to end—because for us, it was.

The kiss deepened, our tongues coming together, and I felt my breath quicken. I slid my hand up to his barrel chest. I began to work the buttons of his shirt.

His hand came up to catch mine. "God, Lainey, as much as I want to, we should not do this." He trapped my hand against him and I could feel his heart beating so fast, the quickened rise and fall of his breathing. He might protest, but he wanted me as badly as I wanted him.

"No, this is what you meant in your poem. This is our last chance to seize the moment."

"It will make it worse for you after I am gone, *cara*."

I shook my head, tears burning in my eyes. "It would be worse to never be with you at all. This time, I'm not letting the moment pass by." I spoke softer. "I'm in love with you."

His brown eyes burned with heat. "Lainey . . ."

"And I heard you say you loved me when you thought I was dead."

He stared at me in shock, and then nodded. "Yes, I did."

"Will you say it again?"

A tender look settled on his face. "I love you, Lainey."

Our lips met passionately, and in that moment, I finally knew how it felt to be loved.

We lay facing each other, not needing to fill up the silence with words. He traced invisible patterns on my bare skin, moving from my arm to my back, eyes on mine. I smiled, reaching out to brush the line from his jaw to his lips with my fingertips. I tried to memorize every feature of his face: the way his mouth quirked at the corners when he smiled, his warm brown eyes that held such emotion. It was the face of the man I loved, who had shown me, with such sweet and tender passion, just how much he loved me. I leaned forward to give him the barest of kisses, a light brush on the lips. He wrapped his arms around me, returning my kiss. I inhaled his scent, trying to commit it to memory, and how it felt when he held me.

Because soon he would be gone.

I took the moment to cling to him, sadness creeping in. He had made me forget, if only for a short time, what was coming next. We had to have burned up an hour by now.

He must have sensed the mood shift, because he pulled back to catch my expression. "Do not look sad now," he said, brushing a strand of hair away from my face. "You will give me a complex." He smiled, falling back into the old pattern of teasing me, trying to lighten the bittersweet atmosphere that had descended.

"You won't remember getting one," I said, sorrow in my voice as cold reality sank in. "You won't remember any of this."

He looked pained. "It is not guaranteed I will forget. It is just . . ."

"Likely," I finished.

"Yes." He cupped my cheek, meeting my eyes. "I am afraid this was a selfish move on my part."

"Don't say that. No matter what happens, I wouldn't have traded this moment for anything."

"I just do not want to hurt you, *cara*."

"You won't," I said, only knowing that I did not want to ruin this last bit of time with him. "I'll remember for the both of us. So even if you do forget, I'll make you remember."

His smile was wan. "The only thing I want is to remember this. Lainey, try to recall, if things get bad, the man who loves you will still be inside that new person. I will still be there, somewhere. And if I do not come back . . ."

"You will."

"If I do not come back this time, if this was my last life, then I am happy to have spent what time I had with you."

My tears fell as he kissed me, long, lingering, and full of emotion. It expressed everything we couldn't in those last moments.

When he pulled away, I knew our time was up. "It's going to happen soon, isn't it?"

He nodded.

"Does it hurt?" My throat was clogging with emotion.

"If it does, I will be beyond pain by then. It is a strange process, *cara*. I transform into a new person from the cellular level up. Everything in my body resets itself to that of a twenty-year-old. I do not know why." He got up out of bed. "There are a few last things I need to attend to, before . . ."

I nodded, wiping away my tears, wanting to be strong for him.

He got dressed, with me silently watching. Turning, he walked over, picked me up off the bed, and kissed me hard. I poured every ounce of feeling I had into that last kiss, feeling tears dampen my cheeks again and not sure if they were mine or his.

"Pretend I am coming right back," he said, forehead against mine, holding me against him. "Make it easier on the both of us."

"I love you," I whispered, clinging tighter.

"I love you too, Lainey," he said, slowly releasing me. I could tell it was as difficult for him to let go as it was for me. "I will always love you. And that is a promise." Then he turned and walked out the door, closing it behind him.

I made sure I heard footsteps going downstairs before I gave in to my tears, feeling the loss of him with such brute force that it tore sobs from my throat. I curled up with his pillow, breathing in his scent, shaking with grief.

After a few moments, I took a deep breath and forced myself to calm down.

"He's coming back. He's coming back," I whispered, like a mantra. He had to: he was the Reincarnist. That's what he did, he always came back. Yes, Robert was gone in a very real sense. But he would be back, just a lot different. And I was going to have to figure out very quickly how to deal with that.

The worst-case scenario was that he wouldn't remember me. It would be painful, but that was a simple fix: Just remind him. *I'm Lainey. I'm your partner and your girlfriend.* Was I his girlfriend? Was that presumptuous, thinking we had a relationship now that he'd been reincarnated into a new person? Well, what else was I going to say? *I'm Lainey and I'm your lover?* God, that sounded trashy, like it hadn't meant anything. And making love to Robert *had* meant something. *Girlfriend* sounded much better.

As I thought harder about it, I realized that loss of memory wasn't the worst-case scenario. The worst-case scenario was that he wouldn't remember me and then the new him didn't like me! Who knew how much his personality would change? Or what if he remembered what had happened and didn't like me? That would be awkward.

On the other hand, what if he came back too different, and I just didn't feel the same way about *him*? As much as I couldn't fathom that happening, it was as conceivable as any of the other scenarios.

Or maybe he would come back, different but similar, would remember everything, and it would all be okay.

Please, God, let that be the case.

I knew I was driving myself crazy with the possibilities of what was going to happen. I was sure of one thing, though: I didn't want to face it naked.

My costume still had blood on it, so I did a very girlfriend-like thing—I took one of his button-up shirts to wear as a nightshirt. It still smelled like him, overwhelming me. Tears burned in my eyes again and I wiped them away. I didn't want to be caught crying by a strange man that used to be my boyfriend.

I was still shaking and my limbs felt like they might collapse, so I slid back under the covers and awaited fate.

Fate was faster than I would have liked. I heard footsteps coming my way and sat up, heart racing. Two people were coming toward the room, talking. It was Mayhew and an unfamiliar voice.

"I should explain . . ." Mayhew was saying, and then the door opened.

And I came face-to-face with the new Reincarnist.

CHAPTER SEVENTEEN

I am ashamed to admit that my first thought was, *Wow, he's hot!* Still in the same somewhat understated way, but this version of Robert would turn more than a few heads. He was about six feet tall, with a wiry build that was subtly muscular, and narrow shoulders. He had light brown hair and a sexy five o'clock shadow that turned a boyish face into something rugged and slightly dangerous.

But his most striking feature was his eyes. This time they were a dark blue. Yet they were still soft, and at the same time penetrating. They say eyes are the window to the soul, and I'd have to agree, because when I looked into this stranger's eyes I saw Robert. It gave me hope that everything would be okay.

We stared at each other in silence for a long moment, and then he spoke.

"Who are you and what are you doing in my bed?"

I hoped my face didn't betray the hurt I was feeling. It doesn't matter how much you know something painful is coming, it is still devastating when it happens.

He looked so lost and confused, expecting me to fill in the blanks. I found my voice.

"L-Lainey," I managed, clearing my throat. "I'm Lainey. You were training me to be in the EHJ—that's the Elite Hands of Justice. I'm . . . your partner."

Is that all I am? I chastised myself.

"Lainey. I'm supposed to remember you," he said, and I was thrown by the use of a contraction in his speech. "I don't . . ." He trailed off, noticing my borrowed clothing, and his face drained of color. "Oh, God, we're not lovers, are we?" His tone was pure panic.

I felt like I had been kicked in the stomach. Bad enough he didn't remember me, but to act disgusted at the very thought? That killed me.

I tried to gather up a bit of my pride and come up with a plausible lie. "I was injured—well, dead, actually—and you brought me back. That's how it is that . . . you're here. You brought me here, said I should get some rest."

A look of relief crossed his face. "Oh. Yes, of course."

Mayhew was giving me a pointed look. I ignored him, wondering how much he knew and how much he assumed.

"I'll just get out of your hair," I said, gathering up my ruined clothes. "My costume was wrecked, and I needed to borrow a shirt. Sorry."

He waved a hand. "No problem. I'll have to have them tailored; I don't think they'll fit anymore as is. But, if you were . . . dead, you can stay and I'll just go to a different room. God knows I have enough to get accustomed to without inconveniencing anyone. You don't need to be up and about just yet."

"Oh, I'm fine. And you've been dead, too." The pain that spiked through me at those words brought tears to my eyes. "I-I'm just across the hall, anyway." I hurried to the door and grasped the handle. "I'll see you later."

"Goodnight," he said, like an afterthought, looking around as if seeing his surroundings for the first time. Which, I guess, he technically was.

I went to my room and shut the door behind me, feeling like my lungs were seizing up. God, this was worse than I'd thought. The Robert who had loved me was gone, replaced by someone who was repulsed by me.

I grabbed my poetry book off the shelf, clasping it to my

chest, my last link to our own "theft of a moment." I could still smell Robert's scent on my skin and the shirt I wore.

I curled up in a ball in my bed, alone, and cried myself to sleep.

I awoke in the morning knowing something was wrong, but forgetting in that first moment what it was. Then the pain was fresh again. Puffy-eyed, I stumbled around the room, found clean clothes, and headed for my shower. Hesitating, I stripped off the shirt I had been wearing and tossed it in the back of my closet. He wouldn't miss it, and I wanted something that still belonged to Robert and not the stranger who had replaced him.

In the shower, I let my tears fall again, feeling the loss gnaw at my heart. It wasn't fair! Why wasn't I allowed to keep anyone who loved me? First my parents had been taken before I even got a chance to know them, leaving me to be someone who forever kept people at a distance, making few friends and never connecting with any of the foster families that took me in. I had kept up a wall around my heart just so I wouldn't be hurt when someone else left, and had buried myself in my career. But I had taken a chance and fallen in love with someone who loved me back. Now that person was gone. Thank God I had thought to take precautions last night. That would have been the cap on an already lousy situation, if I had ended up pregnant. Then I would have lost both my career and my love, and would have been stuck with a responsibility I wasn't sure I wanted, certainly not by myself.

I stopped those dark thoughts as I turned off the tap and stepped out of the shower. I dressed, catching a glance of my reflection in the mirror. I looked like death, pale and splotchy with puffy red eyes.

I put on light makeup just to compensate, so I didn't have to face the Reincarnist, version 2.0, asking me if I had been crying.

I took a deep breath and squared my shoulders. I had to do this for my career, which was all I had. I had to numb myself while being around this new guy. We had to work together, and it wouldn't do to be crying every time I saw him. After it had became apparent that he had absolutely no memory of me and didn't even want to entertain the thought that we had ever been together, I knew my hopes of picking up where we left off were over. I especially recalled what Robert had told me while I was training with him: to think of his reincarnations as descendants, not as the same person. The man I loved had died saving my life. His progeny was going to be working with me now. We might become friends, but everything Robert and I shared had died with that lifetime. I had to finish up working with this new Reincarnist so I could move on to become a full-time member of the EHJ.

When I walked into the breakfast nook to find the new Reincarnist there with a bagel, a cup of coffee, and a book—so typical of Robert—my heart hurt.

The new guy glanced up. "Good morning," he said.

"Morning." I took the seat across from him.

"Have you had any ill-effects since the resurrection spell? Numbness, loss of muscle control, memory loss?"

If only. "No. Same as usual."

He smiled. "That's amazing. I must say, in the entirety of written history, no one's been able to perform that spell correctly. The side effects are so dangerous; either the resurrected comes back as a zombie with no will or mind, or is trapped in his own body, unable to control it, or the spell just kills the caster . . . Well, I guess it did that."

That put a damper on my appetite. I pushed my bagel away.

"I wish I would've written down all the variables so I knew how it worked—not that I'd ever be able to perform it again, but for posterity, you know?" He'd been speaking to himself; now he seemed to notice me. "No, you wouldn't know. Sorry. I don't mean to make light of what happened to you. I'm sure it was very traumatic."

I tried not to hear the contractions. "You don't remember anything that happened yesterday?" At the moment, I wasn't sure if I wanted him to remember or not. This new guy was not Robert.

"Everything's still a bit of a blur. I know about the EHJ, I know in my former life I was respected for criminal profiling and crime-scene investigation, and I remember how to work all of the spells I've learned, except that last one. It's like there was a power surge to my brain and I'm trying to reset all systems. Everything else is coming to me in odd little flashes." He cocked his head to the side. "There. There's one. I was a pirate once. Did you know that?"

"No."

"Neither did I." He frowned in concentration. "In 1716. Had my own ship and everything." He shook his head. "There. It's gone again."

I shivered. This was more than a little spooky.

"At least it's better than coming back as a total void, no memories at all. That resurrection spell really could've done a number on me, you know?" He shook his head. "No, I barely understand it, I don't expect you would."

Did he just call me stupid?

"But I'm afraid any training we were working on is going to have to wait until I get myself settled . . ." He trailed off and stared helplessly at me.

I stared back until I realized he was looking at me to remind him of my name. Because he didn't remember it.

I gritted my teeth. "Lainey. Lainey Livingston. Phenomenal Girl Five."

He had the good sense to act sheepish. "Right. Lainey. Sorry. Um, I'm thinking of using Wesley."

I blinked at the topic change. "Who? And for what?"

"For my name."

"Wait, Robert isn't your real name?"

He laughed. "My real name would sound very old-fashioned by today's standards. I change names for every life. The last one was Robert Elliot. This one I think will be Wesley Charles."

"Sure, if you want to be the guy with two first names," I said.

"Elliot is a first name as well."

"It sounds more like a last name than Charles."

He frowned. "I like it."

"Well, it's *your* fake name," I muttered.

"Yes, it is." He closed the book he had been reading, drumming his fingers on the cover, closing his eyes. The awkwardness between us was almost tangible. We were off to a fabulous start.

The silence grew heavy and I sipped my coffee, trying to figure out just how long I had to sit there and be polite.

He opened his eyes again and shook his head. "By the way, the memorial service will be on Friday." I watched as he stirred some cream into his coffee. I'd never seen Robert take it any way other than black. I didn't understand how something as basic as how you take your coffee could change.

Wait, what was he talking about? I tore my eyes away from the cup. "What memorial?"

He narrowed his eyes, rubbing a hand across his forehead like he was getting a headache. It was obvious he thought I was dense, giving me a flashback to my early days here. "For Robert, of course."

My stomach twisted. "You're going to set up your own funeral?" My voice rose in disbelief. "You're going to host it?"

"We have to have it for the people who knew Robert Elliot as Robert Elliot and not the Reincarnist, although I'm sure the members of the Elite Hands of Justice will attend. It'd be strange for the civilians to have him just disappear and me take over his things without any explanation. And it's not really *my* funeral, it's Robert's."

"So, what, you're going to pass yourself off as his son?"

"No, just his legal heir." He cleared his throat. "It might help you to think of me as your friend's son, and not him. That way you won't expect me to remember everything or act a certain way."

My laugh sounded bitter to my own ears. "We've had this conversation before."

"Excuse me?"

"Back when Robert and I were discussing one of your former lives, he said almost the exact same thing." I set my cup down on the table and stood, unable to take the strain of being around him anymore. "I get it, Mr. Charles. You're not him. That's obvious."

"Look, I'm sorry I don't remember you," he said, reacting to my icy tone. "And you don't have to call me by my formal name; Wesley is fine. From what I've been told by Mayhew and from what I've read, we were friends."

"Hold on," I said. "From what you've *read?*"

He held up the book he carried. "Apparently it took a couple of lives to figure out the need to write things down. A large number of the books in my library are diaries of my former lives. Including one of Robert Elliot. Sometimes it helps to read about my last life while everything's reordering itself in my brain. Helps me bring details back to the surface and make sense of it all."

My heart dropped into my stomach. "What does it say in there about me?"

He didn't seem to notice my anxiety. "It's all been complimentary. He didn't seem to be the type to allow for close friendships, and yet it is obvious that you were. Close, I mean."

I knew that was my cue to tell him the truth. I had told Robert I would remember for the both of us. And yet, I couldn't bring myself to talk about it with this complete stranger before me. I didn't know if it was residual hurt feelings from Wesley's apparent disgust at the thought of us being together, or worse, that I was angry with Robert for forgetting.

"Did he mention what happened last night?" I asked, hoping I sounded nonchalant.

"About your death?" A look of sympathy crossed Wesley's features. "No, the last diary entry he made was a couple of days prior. Mayhew told me he wanted to write down last night's events, but he just didn't make it. Robert told him about killing Jihad because he had murdered you, and Mayhew was there for your resurrection, so he told me about that. I don't know much of the details about the Jihad incident, but that's just as well. From what I remember of the EHJ, they don't like anyone on the team killing anyone. At least not without forms signed in triplicate." He gave me a weak smile. "Sorry. I shouldn't joke about that. Jihad murdered many people in his time, and someone needed to put a stop to him. He kept escaping from prison or jumping to higher dimensions while he hatched his next plot."

Though a part of me agreed, this sounded nothing like the man who had read me the riot act and compared me to a psycho vigilante for almost letting Death Dealer plummet to his death. The one who had cautioned me about being consumed by the darkness and had kissed me on the forehead so gently after . . .

"The EHJ may still speak with you about the incident for their files, so be prepared. If you're having any problems dealing with what happened, they have counseling services, I'm sure, for that sort of thing."

"I'm fine," I said, trying to ignore how unconvincing that sounded. "I just want to get back to work as usual."

"Alright. Let's go into the library then." He stood and strode down the hall, me following with less enthusiasm.

"I've made a list. I think it's a quirk, actually, list-making." He walked over to Robert's desk—his desk now—and picked up a creamy sheet of paper, handing it to me. I took it and stared at the perfect handwriting, completely legible, unlike

Robert's messy scrawl, which usually needed deciphering. I wondered if he had problems reading Robert's diary entries, or if he could read the words because he had once written them.

"Was Robert a list-maker?"

"Um, not really. He was very organized, but he didn't write everything down."

He looked very disappointed. "Well, that's the agenda for today. I'd like to get as much of it done as possible."

I frowned. He'd said it in his stuffy tone, like he'd be doing the work, but of course I would be doing it unless his tolerance for secretarial duties had changed. I skimmed the notes.

Make appointment with tailor for fittings. Notify associates of Robert's passing and funeral arrangements. Oh, God. I didn't know if I could handle that, calling up people and telling them Robert was gone. I skipped ahead. *Business associates to be notified of Wesley inheriting companies.* The rest was mostly about planning aspects of the memorial service: caterers, music, that kind of thing.

I looked up at him. "I've never handled this type of situation before. I have no idea what kind of flowers to get or anything."

"Oh, don't worry about that. I'll have Mayhew take care of the most of the memorial arrangements; you just take care of the other items on the list."

Great. So it looked like the bulk of my day would be spent writing death letters and assisting Mayhew in preparing my late boyfriend's memorial service. Although, if I could take comfort in any of this, and there wasn't much to be taken, I *did* get to tell Victoria Dupree that she never needed to darken this door again.

"Can you add 'buy more casual clothes for me' to the list? I'll write down my approximate size for you." He leaned against the table and rubbed his head like he had a migraine. "I knew Shakespeare?"

"What?"

He waved me away. "Nothing. I still want to tailor some of the suits. It's not that I mind dressing up on occasion, but every single day?"

Although I never understood Robert's need for formality, it hurt that this new version was going to wipe away all traces of him. His manner of speech, his clothes, his feelings for me . . .

"Fine," I said. "But we're both young *professionals*, and I can't respect a boss who runs around in designer T-shirts with pseudo-witty sayings written on them."

He laughed. "Thanks, I needed a bit of humor."

Mayhew entered the room. "Excuse me, sir, but Detective Pendergast is on the phone. He wants to speak to Mîster Elliot about one of the detainees."

Wesley looked at me. "Lainey'll have to take care of it until I'm formally introduced. She's the one who actually remembers what happened last night."

In more ways than one. "It's fine, Mayhew, I'll take it in here."

"Right away, Miss," he said and disappeared. A few moments later, the phone on the desk rang.

I picked it up. "Detective Pendergast, this is Phenomenal Girl Five."

"Ah, good morning. I don't suppose I could convince you and your partner to come downtown? We interrogated a few of the villains rounded up last night, and something came out in one of the interviews I thought you should hear. The Feds picked up the criminals early this morning to take them to the Holding Tank"—this, I knew, was the prison for powered villains—"but I thought this was information of a sensitive nature that the Reincarnist should deal with himself."

"I-I'll come over right away," I said, and hung up before he could say anything else. I couldn't tell Pendergast of Robert's death with Wesley sitting right there and listening in.

"Is everything alright?" he asked, flipping through a book.

"I don't know. I'm going to check it out."

"If you need any help, don't hesitate to call. I'm a bit out of it, but still capable of lending a hand, even while not at my best."

"It's fine. I'll let you know what happens." I shut the door to the library behind me.

"Did you tell him?"

I shrieked. "Jesus, Mayhew! What are you doing lurking out here?" I cast a quick look back to make sure Wesley hadn't heard me scream like a little girl.

"Did you tell him?"

"About what?" I continued down the hall, trying to brush the butler off.

He frowned. "About you and Robert."

"I don't know what you're talking about."

Now he was glaring at me. "Don't do that."

"Do what?"

"Pretend you don't know what I'm talking about."

"I don't know what you're talking about!" I hoped I didn't blush when I said it. I've never been a good liar.

"You already lied once when he asked you point-blank if you were lovers. I assumed you were just thrown by him changing, but I thought for sure you'd tell him the truth by now."

I snatched up the keys to the Mustang. I was already exhausted by this ordeal, and the day had just begun. "You don't know what you're talking about."

"Please give me a little credit," he said dryly. "I know he loved you. I know you had deep feelings for him as well."

"I loved him."

Mayhew's eyes were kind. "It doesn't take a genius to figure out what happened next. Before he died, Robert wanted to write something in his diary. He didn't get a chance. He wanted me to make sure he remembered you in the next life. That was the first thing I was supposed to ask him, if he remembered Lainey."

"And he didn't."

"No, but he seemed to know where to go to find you."

I gritted my teeth at the reminder. "Wesley doesn't remember me and he doesn't even like me. You heard him last night! I probably would have said something had he not asked if we were lovers with such complete and utter disgust."

Mayhew's features slumped in defeat. "Miss Lainey."

"This new Reincarnist doesn't need to know about what happened, Mayhew. That died along with Robert. Now, if you'll excuse me, I've got to go see the police." I turned and walked out of the mansion before he could see me cry.

CHAPTER EIGHTEEN

The noise and insanity at the police station was almost comforting. It was normal, everyday behavior, at a time when my life was turned upside down.

I gave my name to the officer at the desk, who called back to Pendergast. The nearby television was turned to a news conference, where none other than Simon Leasure was holding court over a bevy of reporters, letting them know how great a job he'd done and how he, single-handedly, had saved the day. God, had our date only been last night? It felt like a lifetime ago.

"Miss Livingston?" Pendergast walked up, looking around. "Where's your partner?"

"Can we go somewhere private?"

He nodded. "This way."

Pendergast looked worried as we sat in one of the interview rooms. "Has something happened?"

I nodded, looking down at my hands. "Robert was killed last night."

His face turned white. "Oh, God. I'm so sorry, I hadn't heard."

I shook my head. "No one has. I don't even think the EHJ knows." I broke off, tears coming. "Damn, I'm sorry."

"Don't be." He handed me a tissue. "I know how hard it is, losing a partner. Mine was killed in the line of duty last year."

"I'm sorry."

"Me too. I'd heard the Reincarnist took down that Jihad character."

"Yeah. One of the last things he did."

"One of the guys we had stored here last night was pretty irate about it. He's the one I wanted to talk to you about."

"Alright."

Pendergast clicked on the computer and scrolled through some black and white images. "Here is the footage from him last night."

The footage started and I saw a burly man with a military buzz cut slumped in a chair.

"State your name, please." That was Pendergast.

"Talon."

"Your real name, not your alias."

"That is my real name. It was the name he gave me on the day I was reborn."

"He?"

"My master. I joined with him, and I was baptized in fire and blood." Talon's smile was sinister. "Have you ever smelled human flesh burning?" He moved his arm and I gasped.

Pendergast eyed me. "What?"

"Go back. Now pause it." He did, and I tapped the screen where Talon had flashed a glimpse of his wrist. "He has the same marking that Syn and Jihad had."

Pendergast looked. "I can't believe I missed that."

"You weren't looking for it." Things were beginning to connect. "Go on."

"You want to tell us what you all were doing tonight?" Pendergast was asking on the recording.

Talon smiled. "Creating chaos, obviously. It's not as easy as it looks. You need just the right amount. Go too far, and it spins out of your control."

"I thought chaos was all about no control."

"There are some who can harness it."

"What were you using it for?"

"Something that is beyond your fragile human mind."

"Try me."

"It was just a component of something bigger." He sat back, arms across his chest, looking satisfied. "The Master will be pleased with our work."

"So you were all working together?"

"Not all of us. We hired some of the villain persuasion to help distract the heroes so we could go about our business."

"Who's we? You and this Master?"

"The Master himself cannot get involved yet. He is not ready. He is not prepared. My brothers and I go ahead of him." He seemed to fix his gaze on Pendergast.

"Was Jihad one of your brothers? Because I'd say he failed miserably."

"No, he did his part. The Old One cannot stop our Master, no matter how many of his servants he kills. Where one falls, another will spring up."

"Who is the Old One?"

"You know him as the Reincarnist. One day, my Master will bathe in his blood."

"Like he did Jihad's?"

Talon's face fell into a scowl. "The Old One should stay out of our business. He has problems in his own backyard. After all"—he smiled again—"it was one of his little capes that helped kick off our night of chaos."

I drew in a harsh breath as I remembered Jihad's words right before I died. Pendergast shut off the footage.

"This is the second time one of them has mentioned a traitor in our midst," I admitted.

"I know nothing about the inner workings of the Elite Hands of Justice," Pendergast said. "You and your late partner are the only two members I have ever met, and I trust you. But you need to watch your back."

I nodded. "Thank you for this, Pendergast."

"No problem. Please let me know if I can do anything, Miss Livingston."

And with a new reminder that someone was selling us out, I went on my way.

"Did you get everything taken care of with the police?" Wesley greeted me as soon as I walked in the door. He had a tumbler of scotch in one hand.

"Yeah. It wasn't much that we didn't already know, but it tied some loose ends together."

"You can tell me about it later. Write it down if you need to so you won't forget the details." He looked as if his mind was already occupied.

"You want me to write you a report?"

"Yes. If you could, that'd be perfect." He took a drink from the glass.

I eyed the drink. "A little early to be hitting the hard stuff, isn't it?"

"You try having half-memories of an eternal life keep popping up at random times and see how you feel," he snapped.

I glared at him. "Is basic manners one of things you forgot? Don't worry about the police or our case. I'm taking care of it." I turned and stormed upstairs.

CHAPTER NINETEEN

The next few days passed in a haze. I tried to avoid Wesley as much as possible and still do my job. Mayhew's disapproving gaze followed me wherever I went, but he kept quiet. I practiced magic on my own, ate meals alone, and even patrolled on my own, leaving when I knew Wesley was eating so I could give him a report of the sectors I'd covered later. For some reason, the criminal element had been quiet. Maybe after watching the big-timers get thrown down, they'd gotten scared.

Or maybe my heart just wasn't in fighting the good fight anymore.

I wasn't eating or sleeping much. Within days I had lost weight and had huge dark circles under my eyes. I was depressed and it was showing.

The day of the memorial dawned with a cold, gray light that fit my mood. I knew I had to attend and act like I was mourning my dead boss and not my lover. I hoped to slip away quietly and not stay through the whole ordeal. Through some quirk of fate, I had become more like Robert than Wesley was: I was the one who wanted to hide from social events.

A knock sounded on my door.

"What?" I asked, not bothering to get out of bed.

Mayhew poked his head in. "Mister Charles wants to know if you're coming down to breakfast."

"No." I rolled onto my side to face the wall. "I'll be there for the memorial."

"He wants to speak to you about the memorial."

I sighed. "I have the day off, remember? I don't have to do what he says today."

"You are destroying yourself for no reason."

"No reason?" I sat up and narrowed my eyes into little slits. "I think I have a damn good reason, Mayhew, so butt out. Most people are allowed to grieve for their loss and aren't told to act as if nothing happened."

"You're right, something has happened. To someone other than you, if you would care to get out of that hole you're wallowing in and notice. Someone is now adrift, completely lost in his life and confused as hell. And the one person who should be helping him, both on a personal and professional level, is instead avoiding him like the plague when she doesn't snap at him like a moody teenager."

I winced at the accusation, but wasn't ready to back down. "Like Wesley cares. He doesn't even know me."

"Just keep in mind who you're hurting, Lainey. Remember exactly who it is that you are treating so coldly." With that parting shot, he shut the door.

I threw a pillow at the door, swearing, hurting at the truth of his comments. How could he understand what I was going through? He didn't know how painful this was, looking at the ghost of Robert every day.

A steel determination set in. I was going to make it through today. And then I was going to take it one day at a time after that. I owed it to myself; I had worked too hard on my career to throw it all away over a guy. I was going to set my tunnel-vision sights on becoming a full member of the Elite Hands of Justice and getting the hell away from Wesley. And I was never letting anyone back into my heart. Robert was right—romance was distracting, and now I knew it could destroy you, too.

I got up and slid on my dress for the memorial. I was sure

it was going to raise a few eyebrows, but I didn't care. I was dressing for Robert, the last person that I would ever love, and he would have liked the burgundy color. I could almost hear him joking about not wearing black.

Taking a deep breath, I went downstairs.

Wesley glanced up when I walked into the breakfast nook, and then he stared, fork frozen in front of him.

I gave him a cool look, took my seat, and reached for the coffeepot, which held my usual breakfast as of late. And lunch. And dinner.

Mayhew set a plate down. I shook my head. "Not hungry."

"Eat and be quiet."

Wesley stared at him in surprise and I shot Mayhew a nasty look. He still looked as impassive as ever.

I picked up a piece of toast and took a bite. "There. Happy?"

He looked satisfied and went away. I chewed on the toast and sipped my coffee, finding that I did have a bit of an appetite if I forced myself to eat.

Wesley cleared his throat. "You look very nice."

"Thank you."

"It's an interesting choice for a memorial service."

"Robert would have liked it."

"The color suits you. And I think it's nice you wore color. I understand funerals are the living's way to mourn the dead, but it should also be about celebrating the life that has passed. All that stiff black clothing is not a celebration. We're both defying convention."

My gaze shot to him at that comment, and I noticed he was wearing a gray suit with a dark blue pinstripe and matching shirt. He did look nice.

My eyes flicked up to meet his dark blue ones, and I knew he was noticing me noticing him. I looked away, severing the connection.

"Lainey, I wanted to apologize for my behavior earlier this

week," he said. "I was rude. The first few days I'm back after reincarnating, I'm rubbish to be around, I'm afraid. My mind's trying to sort things out and it's distracting and painful. Especially since it seems like I get to keep detailed memories of those things I'd rather forget, and I lose happier things. But I'm doing much better now, and though my memory of the case we've been working on is vague at best, the diary is helping, and I'm sure you can help me fill in other blanks. We can get back to work as soon as you feel comfortable doing so."

"Alright." *This is for your career* was back to being my mantra. "Mayhew said you wanted to talk to me about the memorial."

"Yes. I know we're supposed to circulate, but can you stay with me? I won't know anyone . . ."

That's for damn sure. "You want me to introduce you to people?"

"Exactly."

"I'll introduce you to the ones I know." *And I'm ditching you at the first available minute.*

"Thank you, Lainey."

"It's my job." I got up and left before he could say anything else.

The mourners were circulating in the garden, nibbling on finger foods and speaking in hushed tones. Wesley and I stood out as the only ones not in head-to-toe black. I might have felt awkward, but I was beyond caring what those people thought. Let them think I was some oblivious employee not showing my boss proper respect.

"Miss Livingston," Detective Pendergast greeted me.

I hugged him. "Thank you for coming."

"Of course. It's such a damn shame about what happened. He was a good man."

"Yes. He will be greatly missed." I could feel the tension radiating off of Wesley.

"By a lot of us down at the department as well." Pendergast looked at Wesley. "Is this your boyfriend?"

"No!" I winced at how shrill that came out. "This is my new partner. Wesley Charles, Detective Pendergast. Robert and I turned over many a criminal to his care."

Wesley shook his hand. "A pleasure to see you, sir. I'm sure once I get my bearings, we'll be out trying to make your job easier again."

"Good to meet you. I'm sure you'll do fine work. Do you have one of those fancy aliases you people go by?"

"He's the Reincarnist," I said before Wesley could.

Pendergast gave me a strange look. "They like to use the same names over again?"

Either Robert's habit of staying out of the limelight was causing the confusion, or his powers were not well understood by the public. Or Pendergast was behind on his celebrity hero gossip. Either way, I rolled with it. "Well, I am Phenomenal Girl *Five*." I caught Wesley giving me an outraged look out of the corner of my eye. I ignored it and smiled at Pendergast. "It makes you a little concerned about the turnover rate that they've recycled my name five times?"

"It's not exactly the same," Wesley began.

"Well, welcome to the city," Pendergast said to him. "I have to get back to work, Lainey, but I wanted to stop by."

"Thank you so much for coming, Detective," I said. "I'm sure it would have meant a lot to Robert."

"I *know* it would have," Wesley said, and then as soon as he left, turned to me. "Why did you say that?"

"What?"

"Let him think I'm just some guy that happens to have the same alias?"

"Do you want to explain it to a civilian? Because it makes my head hurt."

Wesley might have said something else, but we were blindsided by the arrival of Victoria Dupree.

She was draped in an elegant black dress, complete with

black hat and veil. A veil, for God's sake! As soon as she walked in, she began loudly sobbing, dabbing her eyes with a prim white handkerchief.

I gritted my teeth and clenched my hands into fists at my sides, trying to rein in the impulse to punch her.

"Who the hell is that?" Wesley asked as she threw herself into the arms of a prominent businessman, wailing about the tragic loss.

"Victoria Dupree," I bit off, trying to force myself to calm down.

"*That's* Victoria Dupree?" He looked her over as if she were a specimen.

"You remember *her*?" Now I wanted to punch *him*.

He shook his head. "I read about her."

"Oh." If he had remembered her and not me . . .

"My God, I had exceedingly bad taste," he said, eying her with some displeasure.

I flinched. Okay, so ha-ha to Victoria, but he had just insulted me in the process. Only, he didn't realize he had. "I knew it," I said, glaring at her antics as she wailed about how she and Robert were supposed to have been going to a concert. He had actually made that date!

"Knew what?" Wesley asked.

"I knew she and Robert had a thing once, but he would never admit to it."

"Well, it was some years ago."

"She wanted to rekindle it."

"Trust me when I say that's never going to happen."

I had to smile at that.

"There it is," he said, almost under his breath.

"What?"

"It's the first time I've seen you smile. I've been wondering if I'd ever get a glimpse of the person I've been reading about."

I didn't know what to say. I just held his steady blue gaze, conflicting emotions draining me.

And then the celebrities arrived.

People started murmuring and we turned to see Doctor Rath, the Magnificent, White Heat, Aphrodite, and another high-ranking member, Sensei, walk in, all in impeccable dark clothing. Tekgrrl, another young member, trailed along beside Sensei, her wild magenta-streaked hair looking out of place with her sedate black clothing. Inferno was absent.

Doctor Rath eyed me as he walked up. "Red?"

"It's burgundy."

"For a funeral?"

"It's fitting for Ro . . . M-mister Elliot," I stuttered. Wesley shot me a strange look at the use of the less-personal name.

Doctor Rath turned his attention to Wesley. "So you're the new one."

"Wesley Charles." He looked at me to supply the name.

"Doctor Rath," I obliged him.

"Oh. You're him." Wesley seemed to brighten and shook his hand. "Good to see you, Ben."

I eyed Wesley. He didn't remember him on sight, so must have read something about Doctor Rath. I knew they had been good friends.

"Are you acclimating well?" Doctor Rath's tone was a bit less formal.

"As well as can be expected. The gaps in my memory seem to be a little worse this time, probably because I used up a lot of magic."

"I died," I supplied. "Robert brought me back."

"I know." Doctor Rath studied me with interest. "I heard about what happened with Jihad. I am sorry for what happened to you, Miss Livingston. You will be compensated, of course."

"Thanks." *So if you die, you get a bonus?*

"We will have to discuss everything that happened. A necessary formality, you understand. After you both get back on your feet, of course."

"Whatever we can do to help," Wesley said. "But I'm afraid I don't remember much."

"That's fine." Doctor Rath clapped a hand on his shoulder. "We would like to welcome you back into the Elite Hands of Justice. Robert wasn't interested for many reasons, but enough time has passed and we thought you might feel otherwise."

"I'm not quite sure how I feel just yet. But I will keep the option in mind."

Rath introduced him to the others, giving me a momentary break. They were all friendly to Wesley, but reserved. And they all looked on me with interest.

"Hey, sweetie," I heard before turning to see Selena walk up. "How are you holding up?"

I hugged her tight. "I'm so glad you came. When did you get back?"

"Yesterday. Heard what happened and the other Fives wanted to make an appearance." She nodded to four equally gorgeous women of various ethnic backgrounds mingling with the other mourners. "And I figured you could use a friend."

"Thank you so much." I led her away from the crowd so we could speak in private.

"So, do you want to tell me what happened? I only heard he was killed in combat."

I filled Selena in on the battle details, including my death and resurrection.

"Wow, Lainey. He sacrificed himself for you. He really loved you."

"I know."

"And the tragedy is you never made a move."

I looked down at the ground. "Well . . ."

"Oh, my God, Lainey! I knew you had it in you!"

"Well, it doesn't matter now because not only does he not remember me, he doesn't even like me."

As if on cue, Wesley walked up and cleared his throat. "Excuse me, Lainey."

"What?" I snapped, already exhausted.

"We're going to be starting the service soon."

"Fine." I saw Selena staring at me out of the corner of my eye.

"Would you like to say anything during?"

"No, I can't." I could barely even look at him, let alone get up in front of a bunch of people and talk.

"I think I'll just stand in the back," he said. "It is a little strange to be there, but I feel like I should be. You're welcome to stand with me, if you like."

"Thanks," I said, not really wanting to, but not wanting to sit in the front with everyone else in the EHJ.

Selena cleared her throat and nudged me. I realized what she wanted.

"Oh, Selena, this is Wesley Charles. He's the Reincarnist. Wesley, this is my best friend Selena Curtis, also known as Granite. We went to the School together and were in the Red Knights."

Selena shook his hand. "Nice to finally meet you."

"Ah, someone I haven't met and forgotten. What a welcome relief." He gave her a smile and then looked at me. "Well, I'll just be in the back." He motioned to the ballroom that had been converted for the day.

Selena nodded. "We'll be there in a minute." She waited until he left and then spoke softly. "He's good-looking."

"Yeah, he is."

"A lot younger."

"Uh-huh."

"That why you don't like him?" As my head snapped up to meet her eyes, she continued. "He was nice. To you. He doesn't have a problem with you; you have a problem with him."

"You didn't hear him after he came back. He acted downright disgusted by me."

"And you were downright rude to him just now. You're never like that."

"This is really difficult for me, Selena."

"I know, but it can't be a cakewalk for him, either. He flinched just now when you snapped at him. What you two had might not be dead completely if you snap out of it." Leaving those thoughts for me to mull, she got to her feet and pulled me along. "Let's go, hon."

I only half-listened to the service. Aphrodite, the Magnificent, and Sensei all said some nice things, as well as the police commissioner and a few other town officials. But then Victoria got up and started wailing. I heard people murmuring in sympathy and it turned my stomach. She shouldn't be the one acting like the distraught girlfriend, it should have been me! Selena squeezed my hand, either for comfort or to warn me not to go up there and kick her ass.

I had reached my limit. I turned away and Wesley looked over.

"She is a bit much, isn't she?" he said.

Selena caught the look on my face. "Lainey?"

"I need some air," I whispered, feeling tears burn in my eyes.

"You alright?" Wesley asked.

"I just need a moment." I turned and fled.

I made it outside to the garden before I started sobbing. Wrapping my arms around myself, barely even noticing the cold, I staggered along the walkway by the house, heading toward the garden, wanting to put enough space between me and everyone else to be alone with my grief. I slumped down on one of the benches in the garden and cried until I felt sick, never having felt as alone as I did at that moment. I had never known my parents; they had been absent all my life and I had gotten used to it, so their loss hadn't affected me like Robert's. But I had known a moment of being loved, of belonging to someone, and it hurt twice as much now that it was gone. The pain reminded me why I had closed myself off from everyone for all of those years. And why I needed to do so again.

I heard footsteps behind me and glanced back. "What are you doing out here?"

"I just wanted to check on you," Wesley said, holding his hands up as if to ward off blows.

I glared at him and wiped my eyes. "Just leave me alone. Jesus Christ, you're the last person I want to see right now."

He reacted as if I'd hit him. "Why are you being so hostile?"

"Maybe it's because you replaced . . . my best friend," I finished, dropping my eyes down to my lap. *Best friend* was still accurate.

He sighed. "Lainey . . ."

"You took everything about him away. You said it yourself, you're just his replacement. But you'll never be him again."

"Look, I know I said that, but it's not the entire truth. I'm still as much him as I am anyone else. What is essentially me has stayed the same since the dawn of time. The characteristics that made me the poet William Graves and Robert Elliot are still in me. I am still lacking in tact, I still think political shenanigans are a waste of time, and though I will always support Ben, I still think the EHJ has become nothing but a group of celebrities. Some aspects of my life I remember, most I've read, and some I just *know*, in the fiber of my soul. Like I know it's hurtful when you either avoid or spew venom at me. You're sad you can't see your best friend anymore in me and I act a bit different. I understand that. But I also know this is not how it's supposed to be between us. You're not supposed to hate me."

The retort died on my lips as I looked up and noticed the way he was standing, with his hands behind his back, like I had seen Robert do countless times before, a gesture, I realized in hindsight, that had been his way of keeping himself from reaching out and touching me.

I stared at Wesley, realization hitting me like a slap in the face.

Just keep in mind who you're hurting, Lainey. Remember exactly who it is that you are treating so coldly.

I had given myself license to be nasty to Wesley, forcing a wedge between us because he took away Robert. I had wanted to hurt him the way his very presence hurt me.

Lainey, try to remember, if things get bad, that the man who loves you is still inside that new person. I will still be there, somewhere.

"Oh, my God," I whispered, my entire being cold with shock.

I was hurting Robert. I understood that now. I hadn't truly comprehended his power until I witnessed it. Yes, Wesley in so many ways was completely different, but there were still some things about him that were the same, if I took the time to notice. And though he didn't remember a thing about me, deep inside, the part of him that was still Robert cringed every time I acted out; only Wesley didn't understand why it hurt.

"I'm sorry," I said, barely able to look at him in my shame. "I'm *so* sorry." I said to both him and the man he used to be.

I stood up and wrapped my arms around him in a stiff hug. It was awkward between us, not like it once was when I would have melted into his arms. He felt physically different, a different height and body type, but at the same time familiar. Like coming home and finding the walls painted a different color and the furniture rearranged.

He released me with a light squeeze. "It's not the first time I've had a friend or loved one not be able to deal with the new me, and I'm sure it won't be the last. I know I was difficult to be around there for a bit, and again, I apologize. And I'm sorry I won't ever be exactly the same person again. But we'll always share a bond, and we'll just have to find a way to deal with it and move on."

"What are you talking about?"

"The piece of my soul you carry."

I stared at him in shock. "What?"

"You mean Robert never told you?" Now it was Wesley's turn to look shocked. "He even wrote that bit down; I don't know why he didn't tell you. When he did the spell to heal your soul after you were attacked, he gave you part of his. That's why you have a bit of magic now. Because I have magic."

I couldn't believe it. Why hadn't Robert told me? I rested a hand against my heart, trying to sense it there: that part of me that used to be part of him.

Wesley patted my arm. "Take comfort in that, Lainey. There's a part of Robert that will always belong to you."

"A part of you, you mean," I said.

He gave a brief nod.

"I know you don't remember a lot about your previous life."

"Bits of it."

"And I understand that you're not one hundred percent Robert. But do you think whenever you refer to something that happened, you could phrase it like you did it? You know, like saying, 'When I did the spell to heal your soul,' instead of 'When he did the spell.' It might help me to remember that a part of my friend still exists in you."

He nodded. "Sure."

"Maybe we can be friends again." I thought we could. I might not have the same feelings for Wesley that I did for Robert, but friendship wasn't out of the question.

"I think I'm a likable guy." He flashed me a bright smile.

I returned the gesture, if only slightly.

He looked encouraged. "And I'd really like to meet the woman I've read about. She seems like a really interesting person."

"Maybe I could introduce you tomorrow," I said. "Today's been kind of rough."

"This whole week's been a painful blur," he agreed. "Let's

just forget about it and start over tomorrow. Maybe we could test my magic. And yours."

"That sounds like a plan," I said. It wouldn't sound like a date. Not again.

CHAPTER TWENTY

Wesley was not at breakfast when I came down the next morning. Figured. When I decided to stop avoiding him, he disappeared.

"He is downstairs," Mayhew said, coming up behind me with a plate of waffles. "He wanted to get some work done. He said you should have breakfast and meet him after."

I eyed the waffles and decided I was hungry.

Mayhew looked me over as he poured the coffee. "You're looking more like yourself today, Miss Lainey."

The truth was, I *felt* more like myself. The haze of depression hadn't dissipated completely, but I had decided to fake it until I felt better. Robert would have said something sarcastic about my black mood matching my clothes, and Wesley had been put off by my angst, so I was going to try to force myself back into my usual spirits.

"Well, who else would I be besides myself? I'm the one constant." That last bit didn't come out as bitter as it once would have. I took a bite. "Excellent waffles."

"The secret is to put just a bit of vanilla in the batter."

"You'll have to teach me to cook sometime. I'm hopeless in the kitchen."

He smiled. "That can be arranged."

Well, it looked like I was mending my relationship with Mayhew as well. "How's Wesley today?"

He looked surprised at the question. "He is doing better.

Things are more familiar today. He is concentrating on your training now, but after that he may decide to work full-time for the Elite Hands of Justice, or perhaps he will pursue more education or work with some of his business ventures."

"So he's putting his life on hold for me?"

"Yes. So I would suggest being a bit nicer to him in the future."

I frowned. "We buried the hatchet, so to speak, yesterday. We're going to try to rebuild our friendship." I tried to stress the word *friendship* to Mayhew. "And by the way, did you know about the giving me a part of his soul thing?"

Mayhew nodded. "Of course, Miss Lainey. He told me."

"Why didn't he tell me?"

"He believed it might frighten you. You were pretty shaken up about the whole incident."

"True. But he said I would have been fine without that bit of soul. Was that a lie? Is that why the resurrection spell . . . did what it did to him?"

"Well, that spell would kill anyone, usually without bringing back the recipient of the magic. From what he told me, the hole in your soul would have weakened it. Made it more susceptible to darken, less pure. He wasn't worried about the toll it would take on him; he knew he could handle it. But you are such a rarity, he wanted to preserve you." The butler cleared his throat. "And he was quite taken with you already."

"He had known me—*truly* known me—for only a couple of hours! No matter if he knew me at school."

"Miss Lainey, you treated him differently than anyone else ever has. You didn't fawn all over him and you didn't disrespect him. You didn't sit there and take his barbs, and you didn't agree with everything he said."

"That's just me."

"He appreciated 'just you.'"

I gave a half-smile and pressed a hand to my chest, trying

to feel the part of me that used to be him. "It's nice that someone did."

"I think he might well again, if you give him the chance."

I sighed and got up. "Alright. I'm off to make friends with the new boss-man."

I headed downstairs with my coffee still in hand, ready to put my best face forward.

I was thrown by the music that could be heard in the hallway to the lair. Instead of the classical or jazz I was used to, it was rock music. What was next? Rap?

I entered the room and, at the other end, sitting in front of the monitors, was Wesley. I had a flashback to how I first met Robert and shivered.

"Damn it!" he growled. Clicking on the keyboard could be heard, then, "Damn it!"

I got closer and saw the password screen on the monitor. He typed some more keys and got the *Password invalid* message again. "Damn it!"

"Problems?" I asked, coming to stand behind him.

He glanced back at me. "Yes. Don't feel bad, my memory loss of you is in good company, along with the password to my entire network."

I couldn't help it. I burst out laughing.

"Yes, because mocking my misfortune is so helpful," he said, a slight smile on his face at my mirth.

"I'm sorry," I said. "But you've got to see the humor in the situation. Didn't you write it down in your diary?"

"Obviously not."

"Well, what have you tried?" I asked, taking a sip of coffee, trying to remember if I'd ever seen Robert type in the password. I had my own password, but it had limited access.

"Oh, the usual and the obvious. Reincarnist, Elite Hands of Justice, EHJ, address, pet's name, password, 1234, God . . ."

"God?" I raised an eyebrow.

"For some reason, God is a lot of people's passwords."

"Religious reasons or ego trip?"

He laughed. "What do you think?"

"I'm not saying." I took a sip of coffee to further illustrate that point.

He smiled. "By the way, since we're starting over . . . Hello. I don't think we've met. I'm Wesley Charles." He held out a hand.

I rolled my eyes. "Cute. Hi, Wesley, I'm Lainey Livingston." I shook his hand. "And I didn't know you liked rock music."

"Everyone likes rock music."

"I'm just amazed at the non-instrumental music choice. Songs with lyrics. How progressive of you."

"I am twenty, you know."

"So, what's next? Rap? Death metal? Emo?"

"What is emo?"

"Never mind. What else can we try to get your computer working again?" I set down my coffee cup and leaned forward, reaching across him to try typing in a couple of things I could think of. Nothing worked.

"Why do you have to make everything so difficult?" I groused. "I use the same computer password for everything." I glanced back at him, and realized how much of his space I had invaded—not something you usually do with someone you're not close to. My shirt had ridden up, showing a bit of midriff, and his gaze was fixed on that patch of bare skin.

My body warmed and I straightened, pulling my shirt back into place. *Guys will stare at any woman showing the least amount of skin*, I reminded myself. Wesley himself didn't act like anything was amiss.

"Some people use their kids' names, pets' names, or even an old nickname for their password," I said, trying to get back to work.

"Hmm . . ." He typed something into the computer and *Password accepted* came up on the screen.

"What was it?" I asked.

"Benji," he replied, typing more, pulling up files. Most were of at-large villains.

It sounded like a pet's name. I shrugged. "So, are we going to get back to work on the Syn case?"

"Of course. Mayhew reminded me that we have a meeting with Fantazia. It got bumped back on account of what happened. I already spoke with Ben about the Jihad incident, and he may do a phone interview with you. Speaking of, I'd like for you tell me everything that happened, in as much detail as you can."

"He posed as a civilian. I tried to rescue him, he put a dagger in my heart." Harsh but simple.

"Anything unusual about the dagger?"

"The handle was shaped like a dragon."

Wesley put a finger to his lips. "Like the dragon we saw on Syn?"

"Reminiscent of, I guess. But he had a marking too, just like Syn's. Oh, and the guy the police had, Talon, had the same marking. And he mentioned working with his 'brothers,' specifically Jihad."

Wesley nodded. "So it's a team-up situation. Or a cult."

"Considering the weird branding, I'm thinking cult."

"So am I. Good to know we're on the same page." He gave me a slight smile, an echo back to whenever Robert was pleased with my work, and my heart skipped a beat at the memory.

Back to business. "Jihad mentioned a dragon," I said. "He said the dragon sent his regards. So I'm guessing we can assume that's his name. And Talon kept referring to his 'master.'"

Wesley scribbled this down into a notebook. "We'll have to ask Fantazia if she knows of a Dragon, or cult of the dragon. Did either of them mention anything specific about spells?"

I frowned in concentration. "Jihad said the heart's blood

of a pure soul spilled in combat was what he needed for a spell."

"His spell or the Dragon's spell?"

"He didn't specify."

"What about Talon?"

"That whatever they were doing was part of something bigger."

Wesley frowned. "Bigger, eh?"

I shivered as we came to the final piece of the puzzle. "Jihad and Talon both referenced one of the capes helping to arrange the distraction. That ties back to what we suspected when Syn knew the EHJ were off-planet."

Wesley looked disturbed by that. "That's something I'll need to speak to Ben about. They ran background checks on all of the employees at the buildings, but . . ."

"Maybe it's not a building employee," I finished. "It still could be one of them."

"I don't want to think that, but I agree."

We were silent for a moment.

"Is there anything I can do right now?" I asked.

"I'm going to talk to Ben. He's the only one there I trust without a doubt. In the meantime, I want to look through these files, refresh my memory. I don't know if anything will come of it, but you might look through the Sngetra Codex, see if you can find anything about the Dragon. Otherwise, we're free until patrol tonight—which I thought we'd do *together* for a fun change." He gave me a sideways glance.

I ignored the jab. "Well, I think I'll do a quick centering, and then I'll hit the books. I don't know how much help I'll be, considering most of them are in some ancient language, but I'll do my best."

"Alright," he said. "Get me for lunch."

"Okay." I turned and went into the workout room, having decided to do some magic alignment, as Robert had taught me.

I kicked off my heels and closed my eyes, taking deep

breaths and then beginning to run through the motions. I had barely run through half of the kata when I heard, "A rejuvenation spell, eh?"

My eyes flew open. Wesley stood at the back of the room, watching.

"What is?"

"What you're doing. It's a rejuvenation spell."

I shrugged. "It's just what R . . . you taught me."

"Did you ever try to cast any spells?"

"A few. I've gotten really good at getting a book to hover in the air. I can make a candle flame grow bigger or snuff out. I've been practicing the teleportation spell a lot lately. I'm not that powerful, and just started learning."

"Go through the kata again. Pretend I'm not here."

Like that was so easy. I closed my eyes and started going through the motions again, trying to forget there was a handsome, familiar stranger watching me. I sensed his approach. I tensed, feeling his body heat against me. I opened my eyes and glanced over my shoulder.

"What are you doing?"

"I'm just trying to get a sense of your power. Keep doing what you're doing." I felt his hands skim my body without touching me, like Robert had done before, causing a phantom tingle. It bothered me that he was standing so close, invading my personal space. I took a deep breath and almost whimpered. His scent reminded me of Robert, but probably because he used the same soap.

"Can I try something?"

"What did you have in mind?" I turned to face him.

"A spell. It's a two-person one. It would be helpful in combat situations."

"I can only cast low-level spells."

"Well, there's no harm in trying."

"Okay." I took a deep breath. "What do you want me to do?"

"Hang on just a second," he said, then turned and left the

room. He was gone just a few minutes, and then came back holding a vial. He sat down on the floor, cross-legged. "Sit down across from me, like this."

I did so. "Now what?"

He held his hands out, palms up. "Join hands."

I hesitated. I didn't know if I wanted to touch him yet.

He stared at me. "Is there a problem?"

"No, it's just . . . not going to work," I finished lamely.

"Don't worry about whether or not it's going to work. Just try it."

I nodded and joined hands with him. It felt strange to touch him. His hands were smaller than before and, unwillingly, my mind flashed onto a different set of hands running all over my body.

"Are you alright?"

"I'm fine!" I yelped, feeling my face flame.

He gave me a funny look, then closed his eyes. "Repeat after me. *Mia mente ad il vostro.*"

"I'm not sure what you just said."

"It doesn't matter, just repeat it. We should really get you some Italian lessons."

"I've been working on it. Or you could start translating it into English for me."

He gave me an expectant look.

I sighed. "*Mia mente ad il vostro.*"

He let go of one of my hands, picking up the vial and letting a bit of its contents run onto his index finger, and then traced a circle on my forehead. "*Mia mente ad il vostro.* Do the same thing."

I took the vial from him and let its contents run onto my finger. It was very cool. "*Mia mente ad il vostro.*" I traced a small circle on his forehead.

Our eyes locked.

The heat of his gaze made me slightly dizzy. Or maybe it was the spell. I sat back, needing distance.

Can you hear me?

I blinked. He hadn't said anything, and yet I heard . . .

Lainey, can you hear me? If you can, think yes.

Are you in my mind?

Yes, that's what the spell does. And it worked! See? You can do more than just simple parlor tricks.

Get out of my mind, Wesley! "Get out!" I yelled, flying to my feet.

He got up. "Sorry, I didn't think you'd react like that. I just thought it'd be handy in combat situations."

My head pounded. "I don't want you rummaging around in my thoughts."

"I can't do that. It's only what you think to me. I can only know what you tell me, and vice versa."

"Oh." I pinched my forehead. "I've got a migraine now. Thanks a lot."

"It's because you broke contact like that. It caused a bit of a backlash to both of us."

"Oh. Sorry. But are all spells designed to make you feel miserable after?"

He laughed. "They do take their toll."

"I can see why you chose this lifestyle," I muttered, rubbing my head. "You're not still in there, are you?"

"You broke the spell when you ordered me out."

"And it only works when I tell you something?"

"That's right."

"I guess it would be handy," I admitted. "And I can start trying spells with a bit more difficulty?"

"Yes. I'm not saying you'll be able to do them all, but you can try."

"Great." I turned and started for the door. "We'd better get back to work."

"Lainey?"

"Yeah?" I glanced back.

"Was there something in particular you didn't want me to know?" His face was impassive, like he had no idea what it could be and was just curious; but given what I had been thinking about moments before the spell, I wondered if he remembered something. Or suspected.

"No. I just like my privacy."

He nodded. "You still have it. I'll see you at lunch."

"See ya." I left him, my thoughts in a jumble.

CHAPTER TWENTY-ONE

I was dressed in my costume and ready to patrol, and Wesley was nowhere to be seen.

I sighed and tapped my foot impatiently. He had spent all afternoon in his lair except for the hour I made him eat lunch upstairs. Even then he had been distracted, barely making conversation, until I finally gave up trying. It was typical Robert behavior, and just seeing that bit of similarity made me feel better, but I still didn't know this version of him.

I gave up on waiting and stalked downstairs, where I knew he would be hiding. Grunge rock was playing as I walked in. There were stacks of thin books piled up on one of the tables, thick, dusty, leather-bound books on another, and the computer seemed to be flipping through villains at random.

"Wesley?" I said, skirting another pile of books.

He was bent over reading a book, sitting at the computer console. "Hmm?" he said, distracted, not even looking up. He probably didn't even realize I was in the room.

"I thought we were going patrolling."

"I'm sorry, what?" He looked up and all his words ceased. His mouth hung open.

"What?" I asked, feeling self-conscious, but in a way I wasn't used to. He was looking at me like I was a particularly yummy dessert he couldn't wait to devour.

"What are you wearing?"

"M-my costume," I said. He wasn't the same man who was disgusted at the thought of being with me now. "I thought we were going patrolling, so I wore my costume. I know you once had this whole 'going incognito' thing, but there's no point in being incognito when you're flying. We've had this conversation before, trust me." I pulled my short jacket closer to my body.

"It's very . . ." He looked me up and down, the heat from his gaze penetrating. I had the disconcerting feeling that he was undressing me with his eyes.

"Black leather?" I supplied weakly.

"Tight," he finished. "How do you get into that?"

"You've got to buy me a drink first," I said automatically, and then realized how inappropriate that old joke was now. My face flamed.

"I think there's some brandy around here." He tossed me a wry grin.

"Stop picking on me about my stupid costume."

"You think I'm picking on you?"

We had to get back to professionalism quick. "If you're finished being a bookworm for the evening, let's go patrol so I can grab something to eat. I'm starving."

"You missed dinner?"

"And so did you, and the reason why I missed it was I waited for you."

"You shouldn't have done that," he said, closing one of the books and stacking the others into piles.

"Well, I did. And let me tell you, I won't make that mistake again." I watched as he pulled a black leather jacket that I had never seen over his ribbed black sweater and blue jeans. With the beard stubble, which didn't seem to be going anywhere, he was very good-looking. Wait, was I checking Wesley out? "You're, um, wearing that?"

"You're wearing sexy black leather; I thought I'd join the club," he said with a smile, loading vials into the jacket's inner pockets. "Let's go."

Sexy black leather? I followed after him.

When we got outside, he stopped in front of his cars. "Which one do we normally take?"

He had to be kidding. "We don't. You have a thing about not taking your precious babies anywhere that doesn't have valet. You do a teleportation spell for us to travel anywhere to patrol. And then we walk or fly. Walking is a key factor."

"A teleportation spell. Right." He rubbed his hands together. "How do I do that?"

I stared. I knew my mouth had to be hanging open. "You're not serious."

"You're right, I'm messing with you," he said, lips twitching.

I made a face at him. "You grow a sense of humor, and it happens to be a bad one. Figures."

His smile widened. "Now you're starting to break out of your shell. I may not be able to remember everything, but this feels familiar."

"You tormenting me and getting a sarcastic remark as your prize? Oh, yeah, this is a normal run-of-the-mill day for us," I said, trying hard to be all business, and not smile back. I barely contained it, but not enough that he didn't notice.

"Good. I like someone who will talk back to me and not be meek and mild."

"You'll like me, then."

"I do," he agreed, and something in his tone made me meet his gaze. I shivered, seeing a hint of Robert there in the blue depths.

"Thanks." I jammed my hands in my coat pockets. "Shall we?"

"By all means," he said, and stepped closer to me.

He recited the familiar words, created the circle, and I felt the spell take effect. One second we were in front of his house, the next we were in an alley in the middle of the city. The queasy feeling I used to get had disappeared, but Wesley doubled over, turned, and immediately threw up.

"What the hell?" I asked, turning away and fighting not to join him. Anyone yaks, I feel the urge, too.

"Sorry," he said, holding on to the wall of the building, still looking down. "This body isn't used to transport-travel yet. And my magic has been reduced since . . ." He broke off.

"Since you brought me back," I finished.

"I'm not blaming you, Lainey, just stating a fact. Now let's get out of here, this alley isn't helping my stomach any." He said something under his breath and rose up to fly above the buildings. I followed after.

We drifted down the road, landing on rooftops to rest. Wesley needed a lot of breaks.

"You should have just let me do this," I said after the tenth time we stopped, annoyance creeping in.

"No, I need to be able to do it," he snapped back, almost panting, sitting down on a ledge. He was pale and sweating.

I softened. "God, Wesley, you're forcing too much. Like you said, your magic's weaker now."

"I can't afford to be. Something's going on."

I looked around. "There's nothing going on. This town is dead tonight. Not so much as a mugging."

"Nothing has felt right since I came back," he said, putting his head in his hands.

"Tell me about it," I mumbled.

"What?" He looked up, ruffling his hair in a cute way.

Whoa, why am I noticing he's cute when a day ago I practically hated him? "It's just all a bit hard to deal with," I said, sitting down next to him. "Dying. Having a piece of your soul. Your acute memory loss of me."

"It hasn't been easy on you, either," he admitted. "Not what you pictured when you joined up, eh?"

"You have no idea."

"I've been thinking about what Jihad did to you all afternoon."

"That's not the least bit creepy." I shivered, even though it really wasn't that cold out.

"Did he say *your* blood specifically, or just the blood of an innocent? I read about you having an innocent soul."

"He said the blood of the innocent, not me in specific. Would it make a difference?"

"I don't know. Maybe." He was shaking his head and muttering to himself. "I've read it somewhere . . . chaos spell."

"Wait, what'd you say?"

"Hmm? Oh, just that the blood of an innocent is part of an old chaos spell." He gazed off into the city night.

"Talon mentioned chaos a lot in the interview with Pendergast. About it being difficult to work with."

"Damn!"

"What? What is it?" I had a feeling things had just gone from bad to worse.

"Chaos spells using the blood of the innocent, part of something bigger, that all adds up to one thing."

"What?"

His blue eyes darkened. "An apocalypse spell."

"There're spells that cause the end of the world?"

"Oh, yes. Very powerful and dangerous spells. We may have lucked out for now, though."

"How's that?"

"I think I may have gotten to Jihad before he could finish. But there's nothing to stop this Dragon from trying it again." Wesley frowned, lost in thought. "I wonder why he didn't do it himself."

"Maybe in case it backfired?"

"Could be." He seemed to come back to reality and noticed the fear on my face. "Cheer up, Lainey, we get to save the world again. Just another day in the life of a hero," he teased.

For some reason, his flippant remarks loosened the choke hold fear had on me. "Such pleasant things happen when I'm with you, Wes," I said. "Soul-eating, death, possible apocalyptic spells . . ."

"I like it that you called me Wes," he said.

His tone made me look over to see him watching me intently. He looked as if he wanted to kiss me. He leaned toward me, and I felt my body moving toward him.

Oh, my God, what was I doing?

"Well, we're friends," I stressed, sitting back again. It was true. I couldn't harbor resentment against him anymore. I liked him. But I had to remind myself it wasn't exactly Robert sitting next to me. Robert had been like me: reserved, and always keeping people at a distance. Wesley frankly scared me a bit. Maybe it was his youth, but I could already tell he was a bit more aggressive. He had hit the wall around my heart, and instead of walking away, it was quite likely he'd just start tearing it down.

He took my rebuff in stride. "Yes, we are. And since I made you miss dinner, how about we grab something to eat?"

"Is anything open this time of night?"

"There's always something open. If I wasn't so weak, I'd teleport us to Italy. We could get a good meal and you could get some practice speaking Italian."

"Does that really fall into the 'not using magic for frivolous reasons' category?"

I couldn't tell if he got the reference or not. "Not really an option anyway, since I think I've used up enough magic for the evening."

"Do you want me to carry you, old man?" I teased.

"Ha-ha. You need to start working the teleportations."

"How about we go to Pizza Pi on Market? It's a college joint, so it's got to be open. We can eat ourselves sick and you can teach me some more Italian."

"Sounds good." He handed me the vials needed for the spell. "Just teleport us down to ground level, and we'll take a taxi to the restaurant."

"You trust me not to kill us?" I asked as I tossed powder into the air.

"Of course." He reached out to take my hand as I spoke the now familiar Italian words.

When we popped into existence on the sidewalk in front of the building, he was still holding my hand. He looked down at it, smiled, and rubbed a thumb across the back like Robert used to. And he didn't let go. My heart fluttered.

Oh, my God. Surely I wasn't starting to fall for Wesley?

"Lainey! Lainey!" He burst into my room later that night, looking frazzled.

"What?" I sat up, in an instant awake and ready for action. "What is it? Was there an attack somewhere?"

"I remembered something!"

My adrenaline cooled off. "What?"

"I remembered something about you that I didn't read in the journals!" Wesley looked as excited as a lottery winner.

Now my adrenaline was back on again. "What do you remember?"

"You went out with a guy I hate from the EHJ—Simon."

And now it was cooling off again. "That's it? That's what you remember?"

He deflated. "Well, I know it's not anything exciting, but it's something I remembered."

He was right, it was something. I glanced over at the clock. "Wes, it's four in the morning! This news couldn't wait a couple of hours?"

Now he looked like I kicked his puppy. "I thought you'd be thrilled, since you were so devastated I forgot you."

"I'm glad you remembered, just shocked. I barely remember the date, and I was the one who went on it." But what happened after was burned into my memory forever. "It's hard for me to get too excited about it in the middle of the night."

Now he looked sheepish. "Sorry. Go back to sleep. I'll see you in the morning." He shut the door behind him.

I fluffed my pillow and tried to settle back down. Just as I started to drift off, a thought occurred to me. *If he remembers that, what else is he going to remember? And do I want him to remember what happened after that date?*

Those thoughts were enough to keep me awake for the rest of the night.

CHAPTER TWENTY-TWO

"Now, a few things about Fantazia," Wesley said a few days later, as we stood in an alleyway in one of the seedier parts of town. Music from the nearby bar could be heard, along with raucous laughter and the sound of glass breaking. Someone was having a good time. "She does not involve herself in our fights—she is a neutral party."

"So she's like Switzerland."

"If Switzerland were a double agent, yes. She cozies up to both sides and listens. She will give us information about the villains for a price, but she will also do the same for them. So it's important to be very cautious about what you say around her. And do not antagonize her; she is very powerful and old. And she has a legendary temper. She was close to being as powerful as me—well, me before the Jihad incident, so I guess she's the most powerful now." He seemed a little sad about that.

I patted his arm. "It's okay, Wes. You're still big and bad."

"Thanks for the vote of confidence."

"You're welcome." I don't know why it felt so easy to flirt with Wesley now; maybe because he did it so often with me that it became automatic, but it scared me.

"Now, it's likely we'll see some magic-user villains. We may well see some of our Dragon cult members, too."

"Doubtful, since so far the ones we've fought have ended up dead."

"True. But we may see more villains with the marking. We may be in the room with the Dragon himself. The point is, we can't make a move against them while we are at Fantazia's, but neither can they."

"Spell?"

"No, Fantazia will kill anyone who fights in her place. We were invited, so we're under her protection. That's how she works. But if you see anyone with a dragon marking, try to memorize their faces and names."

"Got it." I looked back toward the alley. "So we go inside?"

He looked at me as if I was crazy. "No, that's a biker bar. We're going to somewhere a bit off the beaten path—a pocket universe."

"Fantazia created her own universe?"

"No, but she was the first one to travel there, so she claimed it. She's such a spoiled brat; what she wants, she gets. She's lived there for centuries, and brought it closer to this world so other magic-users can access it—I think to have company, mostly." He moved to the end of the alley and I saw a door appear out of nowhere. It was almost transparent; through it I could see the graffiti on the brick wall behind. A faint glow surrounded it.

"Stay close to me," Wesley said, and stepped inside.

I don't know what I expected a pocket universe to look like, but the expensive cathouse décor that greeted me—BDSM leather in particular—wasn't it.

The walls and floors were layered with thick red velvet. The furniture was all black leather, uncomfortable artsy-looking pieces surrounding small tables. In the muted candlelight, the people sitting around were hard to identify, which was probably the point. Emaciated-looking wait-staff floated between the tables, bringing refreshments and what looked like spell ingredients.

The patrons all stopped talking and looked up when we walked in. I tried to adopt a cool look of indifference like Wesley had, and scanned the bar for any familiar faces.

There were none. One by one, they all went back to conversation, though I thought I heard "Reincarnist," here and there.

"What are we supposed to do?" I whispered to Wesley.

"Remain calm. Get a drink and sit down. She'll send for us when she's ready."

I perched in one of the sadistic chairs and tried to act natural. A man with pointed facial hair sat with a bored-looking woman at the next table over, transforming something into a frog, a book, a kitten, an ice cube, and a baby dragon all in the blink of an eye. At the opposite table, a rumpled-looking man in a trench coat smoked a cigarette and argued with something that looked like it had walked off a sea monster horror movie set.

Wesley reached across the table and squeezed my hand. "Try not to stare." And once again, he didn't let go.

The man in the trench coat looked over at me and winked. I turned my attention back to my own table, where one of the wraithlike waitresses was setting goblets of red wine in front of us.

"'Lo, Old One," my friend from the next table over said, giving Wesley a nod. "Almost didn't recognize you. Haven't seen you round here lately."

"I've been concerned with other matters."

My friend blew out smoke. "I heard. Figured you're here to pick the old lady's brain for info." He smiled at me. "This your bird?"

"She's new to the magic-side." Wesley sidestepped the question. "Thought I'd show her the scenery."

"It's definitely improved." He eyed me like a hungry man eyes a steak. "You get tired of him, you're welcome to be my guest anytime."

A woman with milky white, almost translucent, skin glided up to our table. "Fantazia will see you now."

Wesley nodded and stood. "We're off." He took my arm in his, almost in a possessive manner.

"Cheers, mate." The man in the trench coat took another drag of his cigarette and started arguing with the squid creature again.

"Who was that?" I asked as soon as we were out of range.

"I've absolutely no idea. Someone I knew once."

"Good guy or bad guy?"

"In-between, I think." Wesley paused and looked back. "I think I lost one of my cars to him!"

"But he's not who we're looking for?"

"I don't think he's the type to do an apocalypse spell. Trick people out of cars, yes. Destroy the world, no."

As we followed the woman toward the back of the room, passing all the tables, I got a tingly feeling, as if someone was watching me. I stopped and gave a quick glance over my shoulder, but no one was looking in my direction.

"Something wrong?" Wesley asked.

I shivered. "No. Just got a feeling, that's all. Like someone was watching me."

Wesley gave the room a quick critical glance. "It's probably just the costume. But keep on guard, just in case." The corners of his mouth quirked up in the barest of smiles.

"You know, you keep mentioning the outfit, but I'm still covered up more than most of our kind."

"It's still eye-catching."

"I'll take that as compliment."

"It was meant to be one."

I didn't have to come up with a reply as our guide threw back a heavy velvet curtain and we were ushered into a smaller VIP-type room, this time in opposite-colored decor—black velvet wall and floor coverings and two bright red leather couches. Instead of candles, a bright spotlight shone down, illuminating the area surrounding the seating and casting the rest of the room into darkness.

Fantazia might have been old, but she didn't look it. In fact, she seemed about my age, with the kind of body men fantasize about, shown off to its full advantage in a barely-there black dress. Adding to the sex-kitten look were long, wavy brown hair and dramatic red lips. Her bare arms were covered in henna tattoos that looked like an ancient language I had seen in some of Wesley's texts. She was draped across one of the couches, with two scary looking henchmen hovering just behind.

She smiled and held a hand out to Wesley. "Good evening, Old One." I noticed her nail polish was red, too. She took the color-coordinating thing seriously.

Wesley bent to kiss her hand. "Fantazia. You're looking as lovely as ever."

"You wouldn't know, considering your spotty memory, but I'll take any compliment I get." She motioned for us to sit down. "I'm sorry I didn't come to the memorial, but after a few centuries, they tend to lose their meaning. But I like the new look. Boyishly handsome suits you."

"Thank you."

"You get the good looks no matter which life you're in." She gave a soft laugh. "Got to love those genetics."

"We can keep complimenting each other, or we can get down to business," I said.

I felt Wesley's smirk but ignored it. Fantazia just seemed amused.

"Oh, this one's good. I like her. She's got spunk." Her eyes narrowed in critical concentration, and she turned her head as if hearing something I couldn't. "Wait. Is that . . . ?" She slid off the couch and hovered nearby, running her hands over me without touching, like he had done before. "Oh, my. What have you done?" She shook a finger at him and made a *tsk-tsk* noise. I'm sure the color drained from my face.

"This little girl has a part of your soul! I can't believe you did that. Oh, but she's special, isn't she?" She patted my head as if I were a child. "A rarity. A pure soul. Didn't want to chance it getting tainted by leaving the wound open?" She went over to her couch again. "Always sacrificing yourself for the greater good, never mind the consequences. Did you find the last remaining bit of pureness inside you to give to her?"

"Stop it, Fantazia!" Wesley snapped, on his feet. Her goons stood to attention.

She raised a hand to stop them. "Easy, boys. He's not going to hurt me. He won't lay a finger on me, will you . . . I'm sorry, what's your name now?"

"Wesley," he said through gritted teeth.

She waited, a sweet but fake smile on her face.

"Charles," he finished. "And if the fishing expedition is finished, let's get down to business. You've got information for us; now tell me what you know and quit wasting my time." The light above us flickered. He could still do the scary power-surge thing. Maybe he wasn't as depleted in the magic area as he thought.

She dismissed her goons with a wave of her hand. "After everything, you can't believe that I would play *you*, Old One."

"I believe you've become selfish over the years and would do anything to further your own interests."

"That wounds me." She put a hand to her chest in mock pain. "Alright. We'll talk business, then. I've heard you've been playing with the Cult of the Dragon."

Wesley steepled his fingers in front of him. "Go on. Who is the leader?"

"The Dragon, of course."

"And what do they want?"

"What the Dragon wants."

"And what does the Dragon want?" Wesley looked like he wanted to reach over and smack her.

"To bring about the prophecy of Likghardt."

I blinked. "What the heck is that?"

She gave me a condescending smile. "He'll figure it out."

"What are the ingredients to the prophecy?" Wesley was leaned forward in his seat.

"Interesting choice of words. All are parts to the big puzzle. Each part must be assembled at the right moment. It builds, can't you feel it?" She held her arms out and smiled. "The magic is growing. Chaos and blood and death and rebirth, all joined together to bring out something wonderful. Or terrible. Depends on how you look at it." She smiled and got to her feet. "I have another appointment, so you will have to excuse me, Old One."

Wesley stood. "And what will I owe you?"

"If I can't do a favor for you, who can I do one for? And if the prophecy comes to pass, you'll have a whole new set of problems to worry about." She leaned forward and kissed him on the cheek. "Take care, *il mio creatore*." Her goons appeared and ushered us out.

"What was that all about?" I asked.

"Nothing." Wesley took my arm again and led me past the room full of guests and back to the real world. "I'd forgotten how infuriating she can be. She can't just come out with it; no, she has to be vague on purpose."

I sensed there was something going on other than just annoyance with her riddles, but I didn't want to bring up the obvious fact they had a past. Who knew if he'd remember it, anyway? "We got some information though—if you understood what it meant; because I'm lost. At least it confirmed our suspicions."

"It's just another piece to the puzzle. Now we have to start putting the pieces together."

CHAPTER TWENTY-THREE

"So glad to see you've mastered the art of transporting without puking, Wes."

"You are so funny, you should go into stand-up comedy," he replied, holding on to the wall as if it were a lifeline.

"I'm just trying to lighten up the situation. Make you laugh—instead of hurl." I touched his arm in sympathy. "You would think that after almost a month you'd have adjusted."

"You would think," he said, and bent over again. I rubbed his back and looked away, like I used to do for Selena when she would come home after a night of partying. He didn't throw up, but instead took deep breaths.

"We could start taking a car, you know," I suggested, running a hand up his spine and then ruffling his hair in a soothing gesture. "So you wouldn't have to go through this every time we patrol."

"I have to get used to it," he said, straightening and grabbing me by the waist.

I didn't react in surprise, but instead leaned in, bracing him with my arms, since he was sick and probably about to pass out, but I also pressed all of my curves against his body. It felt very right to be against him like that. My mouth went dry as our gazes met and I saw the look of desire in his eyes. My rational mind reminded me we had to keep this professional.

But I didn't move away.

His hands slid down from my waist to rest on my hips.

When I didn't push him away, his hand strayed toward my butt. My breath caught and unconsciously I wet my lips, turning my face up, expecting a kiss . . .

He let me go. "I'm sorry, I got dizzy for a moment."

"It's okay." I turned so he couldn't see my flushed cheeks. "Maybe we should just call it a night."

"I'm fine, really."

"You almost passed out on me."

"No, I didn't." His eyes darkened and I shivered, having the uncanny feeling of Robert looking at me through him. Or maybe it was more he was looking at me like Robert used to when he thought I wasn't watching. Only, Wesley had never made an attempt to hide it.

"Wh-what's that about? Quit being such a man, Wes, and just admit you're sick."

"I didn't grab you because I was sick," he said, running a hand through his hair. "I did it because I wanted to."

Oh, God. And I wanted him to as well. Worse yet, I wanted him to kiss me, and I didn't want it to stop there. When had that happened?

"Wh-why?" I tried to sound curious, like we were discussing politics or something equally boring, and not like I was having very vivid images of kissing him, of him pressing me against the dingy alley wall and having his way with me right there.

Wow. Where had *that* come from?

"I was testing a theory. Looking for a reaction. I'm a scientist and an investigator. It's what I do."

"I don't think scientists are supposed to grab someone's ass to test a theory."

He didn't get a chance to reply, because what sounded like thunder and lightning crashed into a trash can next to us, and it exploded. We both jumped.

I swore. "What was that?"

A dark figure flew down to land in front of us. He was massive, muscles on top of muscles, with a military crew cut adding to the tough-guy appearance. He wore a black cloak with no shirt underneath. Black tattoos swirled on his chest. Literally. They moved and changed shape as I stared in recognition.

"Talon," I breathed.

Wesley grabbed my arm. "*Schermo.*" Another concussive blast struck, but the magic shield he had put up protected us. We were pushed back by the force of it.

"It won't hold forever, Reincarnist," Talon said. "You're too weak."

"I'm still more powerful than any little poseur that comes crawling out of the gutter," Wesley retorted.

Far be it from me to agree with a villain trying to kill us, but I could tell Wesley was already straining to keep the shield up. It was time to take action. "Can he fly?" I asked Wesley.

"You know more about him than I do."

"Let's find out," I said, grabbing him and bolting up into the sky. Talon shot a blast of magic at us, but I swerved and it missed.

"You needed to mind your own business and stay out of this, Old One!" Talon yelled after us. "You can't stop the Divine One from coming."

I flew around a building, putting space between us. "Do you think Fantazia told him about us?" I asked.

"She said she wouldn't."

"And you believe that tramp?"

"Hey, she's not a tramp!"

"Just because she's—"

I screamed as Talon appeared right in front of us. "Where do you think you're going?" he asked, shooting a blast of energy right at me. Lucky for us, Wesley's shield was still up. I still took some of the blow and plummeted, but at the last moment glided around the corner of a building, crash-landing in front of an abandoned warehouse. Instinct had led me to take the fight somewhere with fewer civilians.

"It's not fair that he can teleport, too," I grumbled.

"If he can, then where is he?"

"For God's sake, don't wish him on us, Wes. Maybe he gave up."

"I need a power boost," Wesley panted. "He's right, I can't hold on to the shield and do any sort of offensive spell with the levels I'm at now."

"Well, what are we supposed to do? I still can't teleport long distances, and I don't think we want to chance him following us home and killing us there."

"I . . . I need to take the power from you."

"Huh?"

His face hardened and he stared at me. "You have part of my soul; you have part of my power. It came from me, so I can tap into it. I need to take some of it back."

"Permanently?"

"Well, it's like a blood transfusion. You'll replace it in time."

"Is it going to hurt?"

"Probably not as much as dying will if you don't stop questioning me and just let me do it!" he blasted.

I glared at him. "Fine. Take it." I held out an arm.

"I didn't mean the blood thing literally," he groused, looking heavenward as if asking God why I was stupid and annoying. He put his hands on either side of my head and spouted off something in rapid-fire Italian, of which I only picked up bits. The last Italian word was barely spoken before what felt like an electric current ran through me. And I had been electrocuted before, so I had a basis for comparison. It didn't hurt as bad as Syn's attack on me, but it was damn close.

He let go of me and I collapsed onto my hands and knees, curling up for a moment, concentrating on moving my sore body. Tears were streaming down my face.

"I'm sorry, Lainey," he said.

"Don't talk to me," I growled, closing my eyes. I wasn't really mad at him, just still in terrible pain. "That freaking hurt."

"Not as much as this is going to," I heard. That psycho Talon had appeared out of nowhere and proceeded to blast me with some sort of spell. I flew backward, slamming into a car, my already sore limbs going numb.

"Just stay down!" Talon ordered me, as if I could move of my own accord. "I'll take care of you later. You and I have dealings, Old One. You were not meant to be involved."

"But I am now." I heard the glass in the windows of the warehouse rattle and my skin started to tingle. Wesley was preparing to fight.

"Your theatrics don't scare me, or your reputation. I have gazed upon real power and yours is nothing," the villain bragged.

"And you shouldn't waste time gloating." There was a loud explosion, and I managed to drag myself behind the safety of the car door as glass shards rained down on us.

I shuddered, trying to stay conscious, but the sides of my vision kept going dark and all my eyes wanted to do was close. I heard the sounds of a battle, and knew it was Talon fighting Wesley. Praying he hadn't taken all of what little magic I had, I whispered the Italian words to a healing spell and felt it take effect. I could move again, though I felt like a walking bruise. Wesley had depleted me with his power transfer, but I had a feeling some bones would have been broken had the magic not worked.

I got to my unsteady feet to see Talon shooting some sort of fireball at Wesley. But his back was to me. Seizing the advantage, I flew over, wound up, and punched the psycho as hard as I could in the back of the head, not caring if I killed him.

He must have had a shield up, because my fist would have gone straight through his skull otherwise. As it was, he flew through the concrete wall several feet behind him.

I turned back to Wesley, who looked exhausted and had several bleeding cuts and burn marks on his skin. I probably didn't look too much better.

"Are you alright?" I asked.

"I'm sorry," he said.

"What?"

That was all the warning I got before he did it again: grabbed me by the head and zapped me with his draining spell. This time, my throat burned with my screams and tears streamed down my face. I fell to the ground boneless and whimpering as he released me.

I heard Talon laughing, and he stood up amidst the wreckage. "The Master will be pleased when I bring back your skull, Old One. You're too weak to fight me for long."

"*Alle terre scure con voi,*" Wesley spoke. I recognized the Italian—it was a banishment spell—and then the entire ground shook.

"Sending me to the Darklands won't help, Reincarnist. Our time nears!" Talon screamed. But then his words cut off. A harsh silence followed. I lay still on the ground, unable to move and crying to myself.

"Lainey, oh Lainey, I'm so, so sorry," Wesley said, and I heard the gravel under him shift as he bent over; then I felt his hands hovering over me. "I couldn't do the banishing spell without a little more power, I'm sorry. I had to get him out of here before he killed the both of us!"

"Did you want to kill me yourself?" I spat as he tried to make me more comfortable. "Don't touch me!"

"I could do a healing spell . . ."

"You do another spell on me and I will take your damn head off!" I got on my hands and knees, swearing like a trucker had inhabited my body. I rested there for a moment, willing my body to work. Right now, I had to be tough, not show any weakness. I had to show him I could handle anything this job threw at me and not that I was stinging from betrayal at how he had used me.

"I didn't want to hurt you . . ."

"Then I'd hate to see what you're like when you set out to hurt somebody." I was able to get to my feet.

He backed off. "I had to, *cara*, I'm sorry."

My head snapped to attention. "What did you just call me?"

He looked astonished. "I don't know; it just came to me."

I slapped him on the arm—a girly thing to do, I know, but it was the only violent gesture I could manage in my current state of mind without hurting him. He looked just as shocked as if I'd punched him. "You can't call me that. Especially after what you just did." I smacked him again.

He caught my hand in his. "I don't understand. Didn't I used to call you that?"

I wrenched my hand away and he moved back, but not before I managed to smack him again. "Robert did. But you're not him!" I emphasized each word with a smack.

He looked exhausted. "Lainey . . ."

Turning away, I wrapped my arms around myself, as if that would ward off the pain, and whispered the words to the healing spell again. Nothing this time; I was tapped out. That only angered me further, and I lashed out with a nasty glare over my shoulder. "He never hurt me, and that's all you ever do."

Wesley's face hardened. "Stop it."

But I couldn't. I had to get it out. I turned to face him, my mouth a thin line of barely concealed hurt. "All you do is bring me pain."

"Stop it, Lainey."

"Over and over again."

"God damn it, *stop it!*" He grabbed me with brute force, one hand on my back, crushing me against him, and one on the back of my head, pulling my hair slightly, and he kissed me roughly. His mouth forced mine open. I made a bare effort to resist that we both knew was for show, and then gave in. I had to: it was one of those kisses where you had to give back as much as you were getting or risk being devoured. My hands slid up his back, pulling him close against me with a small whimper of pleasure. He gave a soft groan into my mouth as my tongue danced with his and the tension went out of his body. He was so familiar and yet so different, the same scent of soap and *male*, but he tasted more like that heavily scented tea he drank. I let my hands explore his body, still strong, but in a different way. Just like the way he was holding me was different: still with care, but with a bit more aggressiveness. He wasn't holding anything back.

Why do we always seem to go at it after a fight? I wondered, before he released me, breathing heavy and looking dazed.

"Are you calm now?" he gasped.

I stared, lightly touching my face. I had beard-burn from him, his taste was still on my lips, and he was asking me if I was calm? I was in a tailspin. No matter who he was, he still knew how to kiss. But the kiss illustrated what I had been beginning to realize about the differences between him and the man he used to be.

Elements I had liked about Robert were still in Wesley, but I was starting to fall in love with Wesley for himself.

How bizarre was that?

It felt like I was betraying Robert, but yet not. Wesley was still him, just in new packaging and with little differences throughout, ones I was really starting to prefer. No matter how much I had loved Robert and how much I knew that he loved me, he had always been reserved. Wesley was more open than Robert ever was, even in our closest moments. He didn't hold back.

"Lainey? Are you okay?"

I realized I had been staring off into space ever since he kissed me. "No. I still hate you." My tone conveyed the opposite sentiment, though.

He flashed me a grin. "I could tell."

"Yeah, that was an interesting way of snapping me out of it," I said.

"It was better than slapping you," he retorted, holding

out a hand. "If you're okay now, let's teleport home. I want to get out of here—just in case."

I took his hand. "Okay." He wasn't going to say anything else? Like, let's go home and pick up where we left off?

In a flash, we were back home. He didn't get sick this time, though. I guess my power had helped. My stomach rolled a bit, but my dinner stayed where it was. And I had just been getting used to being able to teleport without feeling queasy.

He kept hold of my hand, like always, and reached up to brush back a strand of my hair, an intimate gesture. "You alright?"

I shivered at the touch. "I'm getting there."

"I'm sorry I hurt you."

"You've said that before."

"It bears repeating." He leaned forward like he was going to kiss me again, and my eyes half closed as I moved toward him.

He stopped, looking at something beyond me. "That's odd. I wonder why Ben's here."

I glanced over my shoulder to see Rath's car parked next to Wes's Escalade.

"He didn't say he was stopping by, did he?" Wesley let go of my hand and moved away toward the door.

"No." I ground my teeth in frustration as another moment slipped away.

"Maybe he saw a shift in the magic grid or has news about the spell . . ."

"Wes!" I caught up to him, determined to not let go of whatever was happening between us.

"Hmm?" he asked, looking distracted.

"Do you want me to stick around?" I touched his arm in what I hoped was a suggestive move.

"Oh, no, that's alright. You've had a long night. I know how draining that had to have been for you. Go rest and I'll fill you in on the details tomorrow."

"O-okay."

"Get some sleep," he said and opened the door. "Mayhew? Why's Ben here?"

I caught the door as it started to swing shut, cursing myself for having seductive powers so severely lacking. I headed up to bed.

Nothing in the world mattered except this moment. There might be pain and nights of loneliness on their way, but they weren't now. I wasn't alone now. In this moment, I had him, and I had what I always wanted: someone I loved returning that feeling. Everything he did spoke of it, from the way he held me, so gentle and careful, to the way he looked at me, eyes full of warmth and love, communicating volumes without a word.

His skin was warm against mine, and I leaned up to taste it, kissing his throat, feeling his pulse under my mouth. His heart beat so fast, like I knew mine did, reminding me how alive I felt, released and finally free, no longer repressed and hidden. I belonged to him and he to me. I was able to express physically what my heart had always felt.

His mouth reclaimed mine, in soft, chaste, open-mouthed kisses in between whispered endearments in both English and Italian. The soft sheets whispered against my skin in tune to our created rhythm. I dared to look into his eyes, making something already intimate even more so.

"I love you, Robert," I said, my voice barely above a whisper.

"I'll always love you, cara. Always."

And then I woke up in the darkness, cold and alone. I raised a shaking hand to my lips, feeling the ghost of his kisses, the phantom taste of him on my mouth. Unbidden, a sob escaped from my throat, and I cursed it. My dream of Robert's and my one night together had only reminded me of one thing—how important it was to take any moment I could grasp.

There was a chance Wesley and I could have something on our own. I needed to know if he felt the same, and if so, what we were going to do about it.

I picked out my sexiest dress and descended the stairs to the lair, hearing heavy metal playing this time. He had multiple personalities when it came to music.

"Wes?" I called out, walking into the room in a way I hoped was seductive and not clunky.

I skidded to a stop, seeing Doctor Rath there as well, flipping through a book.

"Good morning, Miss Livingston," he said cheerfully. "You look nice today. You seem to have recuperated after last night's events."

"Um, yeah," I said, the wind taken out of my sails. I walked over to where Wesley sat and put a hand on his shoulder. "Hi, Wes."

He dragged his glance away from the screen and gave me an almost awkward smile. "Oh, good morning. Did you, um, sleep well?"

"Fine!" I blushed, wincing at how shrill that came out.

"That's . . . good." He cleared his throat and looked back to the screen. "Ben and I are making progress on Jihad's spell. It's an ancient chaos spell, and part of a series of spells and events—that's deed magic—to somehow bring the Ancient Ones back. We're still trying to work that out. And it all ties into that Likghardt prophecy Fantazia was babbling about." He turned again to look at me, and I realized that the way I was standing, my chest was right at his eye level.

He turned quickly back to the screen and I could see the back of his neck turn red. He cleared his throat. "Um, Ben and I are trying to translate a book that mentions the prophecy right now."

"Sounds very mysterious," I said, leaning over his shoulder under the pretense of studying the screen more. Why was he acting so twitchy? "Anything I can do to help?"

"N-no, I think we have it in hand."

"Are you sure?" Doctor Rath said. "I know she knows nothing of ancient languages, but maybe—"

"But there is something you can do for me," Wesley said,

interrupting. "If you can call that antiquities dealer in my Rolodex and see if he has any of these books." He handed me a piece of paper. I took it, brushing his fingers in the process. I swear I saw his face flush before he turned away. "And there's some correspondence upstairs that needs attending, if you don't mind."

"But can't we let that go while all of this is going on . . . ?"

"It'll only stack up."

Okay. "Anything else?" I asked.

"No, that should be it." His attention was back on the screen again.

"Do you want to show me where the correspondence is that you want me to respond to?" I asked. *So I can lock you in the library . . .*

"It's where it normally is." He looked at me as if I were crazy. "If you have any questions, ask Mayhew."

"Okay," I said, defeated. There was no getting through to him when he was in one of these moods.

CHAPTER TWENTY-FOUR

Over the next couple of days, Wesley and Doctor Rath kept busy in research-mode. I tried to help but had been reduced to errand girl: going to online bidding sites and calling obscure booksellers for even more obscure books. I was always the minion, never the partner—something that really irritated me, despite any developing feelings I might have for Wesley.

And even more frustrating, I didn't have much time alone with Wesley. When he was awake, Rath was over at the house. They worked around the clock, barely stopping to eat. Our conversations had become very short and businesslike: "Do you need help with that?" "Will you e-mail Master Mage and ask him if he has the Volumes of Ghilyse?" or even "Run upstairs and see if the book on Sumerian dialects is in the library." Even patrol—a chore that at least one of us had done nightly since I arrived—had ceased. Something was up, but I wasn't in the loop to know what it was.

The first moment I had alone with Wesley finally occurred in the pool. I was swimming laps, rap music blaring on the speakers: it was my favorite type of music for working out. I had hit my stride when the door opened and Wesley walked in. I touched the wall and continued my lap. I was half-expecting Rath to pop up in his wake.

Finishing the lap, I stopped at the shallow end, whipped off my goggles and swim cap, and leaned back against the

wall, breathing heavy. I glanced over in Wesley's direction
to see him getting into the pool. Shirtless, of course.

I knew I was staring, but I couldn't help it. His frame was
less bulky than Robert's, leaner, with muscles that were very
well defined, though not in a body-sculpted way. He had
nicely broad shoulders and a flat stomach.

As much as I was checking him out, he was doing the
same. I was glad I'd gone with the two-piece swimsuit instead of my standard black one-piece.

"I like the blue," he said, as I caught him staring at my
chest. He averted his gaze. I smiled at that and started toward
the stairs. "Don't leave on my account, unless you're sick of
me. I know we've been nothing but work, work, work lately."

"Honestly, I wasn't sure you were even aware of my presence," I said. "You and Rath have been like a two-man show
lately, with me fading off into the background."

He winced. "I've been an awful teacher, I'm sorry. I
should be showing you about cross-referencing spell incantations and dialects, not using you like an assistant. This is
your fight, too, you've been in it from the beginning. And I
mustn't forget that you're my student. You're supposed to be
learning."

I didn't like the student reference. It was as if he was trying to distance us, which was a trick that had made more
sense with Robert, not him. "Yes, I'm your assistant and your
student, but I'm also supposed to be your partner while I'm
training. So I'll be ready to join the big leagues soon."

"Not too soon, I hope," Wesley said, with a slight smile.
"I've gotten used to having you around."

"Nice. I'm a familiar piece of furniture."

"I didn't mean it in a bad way."

"I know. You just have absolutely no tact. It's one of the
first things I learned about you—the second being not to
mess with you when you're in the zone," I said, moving
closer to him.

"The what?"

"The zone. When you're concentrating on solving something, you tune everything else out. An earthquake could happen, fire could break out, I could walk in the room naked and you wouldn't notice." I was purposely baiting him to see how he'd react.

Desire sparked in his eyes. "I'd notice that last bit, I'm quite sure."

"You know what I mean, Wes."

"I notice a lot of things about you," he said, and this time he moved closer to me.

Jackpot. "Really?" I raised an eyebrow. "Like what?"

"You like to flirt with me."

I laughed. "Maybe I'm just a big flirt."

"You don't do it with anyone else."

"What 'anyone else'? It's you, me, Mayhew, and Rath, and you're the only one who's not over fifty." I punctuated this with a flirty grin as I moved closer.

He returned it. "No, you like me."

"Wow, Mister Detective, that's the sum of your keen detection skills? That I *like* you? That seems obvious—we are friends after all." I moved so that our bodies were barely inches apart. "Or did you mean that I've been waiting to catch you alone in a room since the night you kissed me?" I brought my lips to his in a way that was anything but friendly; it was all heat and passion. He crushed me against him, and I ran my hands down the plane of his chest and around to his back, even as I felt his hands stray down to my butt. I ground my hips into his, nipping his lower lip as I did so. He made a masculine noise into my mouth and his tongue tangled with mine. I thought the water would turn to steam around us.

"Does the door here lock?" I asked against his mouth.

And, of course, that's when the alarms went off.

"What the hell is that?" he asked.

"Damn it!" I swore, breaking away from him to fly out of the pool and going to the intercom system on the nearby wall.

"Why does this seem oddly familiar?"

I punched the intercom button. "Mayhew, what's going on?"

A moment later, the system crackled to life and the alarms silenced. "Sorry, Miss Lainey. The new maid tripped the security system."

I restrained myself from punching a hole in the wall. "I thought World War Three was breaking out."

"Sorry, Miss Lainey. Is Mister Charles with you? Doctor Rath is here about the visit to the Other Realms."

"Surprise, surprise. Yeah, I'll tell him." I depressed the button and turned to Wesley. "Your other half is here."

"I forgot about that. Ben's going to help me ascend to the astral plane to ask the Eternals if they know about this prophecy we've uncovered. We think we've translated it, but it doesn't make one-hundred percent sense, so . . ."

Short answer: Wesley was leaving me, going back to detective work.

"Anything I can do to help?"

"Not really. The monks are kind of particular about who visits. They have a strict celibacy vow and don't even want women on the grounds, so you'll have to stay behind."

"But you'll be able to tell if we've averted the apocalypse or how to stop it?"

"I hope so."

"Well"—I picked up my towel and wrapped it around myself—"I guess that trumps fooling around in the pool."

That comment snapped him out of his reflection. "Unfortunately, yes."

"Isn't that the luck? And just when it was starting to get interesting."

He walked close and looked at me for a long time, and I could tell he was weighing ditching Rath and staying.

"Wes, it's okay. Go. Avert the apocalypse," I said, tossing him a towel. "I'll go take a cold shower."

"Not too cold," he said, running a hand down my waist to

finger the ties on my bikini bottoms, like he was contemplating loosening them. He turned to brush a kiss against my neck, right against my pulse point. I shivered, wanting to throw him against the wall and have at it. He grinned at me, as if he sensed my thought, or more likely had been thinking along similar lines. "I'll probably not be back until late. We have to travel to holy ground for me to ascend and . . ."

"I'll be seeing you sometime tomorrow, is what you're saying."

"Likely, yes."

"Okay, tomorrow it is." I gave him a sexy smile. "It's a date."

His eyes burned again. "I'll make sure to turn off every alarm in the house."

"Have fun tripping the cosmos."

"There's nothing to do around here, so take a day off and go have some fun. God knows we haven't had a lot of that." The way he continued to look at me made me want to grab him and go at it again, but I knew there wasn't time. That was all I needed, Doctor Rath walking in to find me doing something very inappropriate with my boss. And it wouldn't be the first time I'd done it.

The first time. A stab of guilt reminded me that Wesley didn't know about what had happened when he was Robert. I had told Robert I would remind him, and then Wesley had shown up and we had gotten off to a very bad start. But it didn't seem right to start something with him we technically had never finished.

"Wes, wait," I said, reaching out to grab his arm. "There's something I need to talk to you about."

"As long as you make it quick." He brushed a strand of wet hair from my cheek, seeing the look on my face. "Lainey, what's wrong?"

I took a deep breath. "You remember the night you were reincarnated?"

He nodded. "As best as I can."

"Well, right before—"

Rath came bursting into the room. "There you are! Are you ready to go?"

I let go of Wesley's arm and moved away quickly, and got a questioning look from him in return. I waved him on.

"It's okay, never mind. We'll talk about it tomorrow. Go avert the apocalypse."

He kissed me on the cheek. "I'll see you tomorrow."

I watched him go, then leaned back against the wall and closed my eyes. My hormones were in a crazy state of flux, wanting Wesley but being terrified about springing the history between me and Robert on him.

Tomorrow was going to be interesting, to say the least.

I took my cold shower, which helped somewhat, and went about my daily business.

"Miss Lainey," Mayhew said, entering the library with a package. "This just came in for Mister Charles."

I took it and read the label. "It's one of those odd books he ordered. I'll take it to the lair."

I hurried downstairs, my thoughts absent, but when I reached the lair I happened to glance at the computer screen, at what Wes and Rath had been studying. There was something in a language I couldn't understand, and then a few sentences in Italian: *L'anima pura sarà consumata dalla mano del drago. L'anima impura lo ristabilirà con se e un sacrificio. Ciò condurrà il senso affinchè il drago apra il portal a quei antichi.*

My newfound Italian skills worked out the translation. *The pure soul will be consumed by the hand of the Dragon. The impure soul will restore it with itself as a sacrifice. This shall lead the way for the Dragon to open the portal to the Ancient Ones.*

It was the apocalypse spell! It sounded like my soul being eaten and Robert's sacrifice weren't coincidence!

Another mention of the pure and impure soul, then more

unknown language, then: *La lucescura trasporterà il mondo a nerezza*. Translation: *The Darklight will deliver the world to darkness*. And then there was more of the same crazy foreign language.

I gasped. Were Wesley and I going to somehow bring about the apocalypse? It certainly sounded so. But how? Maybe that was what he was trying to find out on this trip.

Another phrase I could translate caught my eye. *L'alimentazione del drago sarà indebolita da un sacrificio nobile*. Or: *The Dragon's power will be weakened by a noble sacrifice*. Was someone going to have to die to stop what Wesley and I were unwittingly starting?

I dropped the book on the table and hurried back upstairs, my thoughts in a whirl. Was one of us going to have to sacrifice ourselves to stop the Dragon? I knew with Wesley's powers, he would suggest himself, but God, I didn't know if I could go through that again. And, as he had said before, there was no guarantee this wouldn't be his last life. Dying as part of a noble sacrifice to stop the apocalypse sounded pretty permanent.

But we were heroes; surely we could find a way to stop this before it go that far, right? And if we couldn't figure out what we were supposed to be doing that would bring the apocalypse, then maybe . . .

Maybe we shouldn't be together.

CHAPTER TWENTY-FIVE

His mouth trailed delicate kisses down my body. I sighed with pleasure.

"Don't stop."

He laughed. "Your wish is my command, cara."

"Then stay with me forever."

He looked sad. "I would if I could."

I pulled him back for a kiss. "I'll always love you, Robert."

I woke up the next morning in a sweat. Breathing deep, I wiped a strand of hair from my face with shaking hands. My dream had left every nerve ending in my body on fire. I needed to see Wesley, to find out what he knew about the prophecy and whether there was anything we could do to prevent it. If not, I'd have to leave.

But not before I told him the truth about Robert's and my relationship. And to see if our relationship could change as well.

Wesley was where I figured he'd be: in his lair. But instead of typing away on the computer to some sort of music or paging through some dusty volume, he was sitting on one of the chairs, staring off into space.

"So, what did you find out from your trip to the astral planes?" Uncomfortable silence settled when he didn't respond. "Wes? Are you okay?"

"I remember," he said, forcing his eyes to mine, his gaze so hard it felt like he was looking through me.

I was frozen to the spot. He couldn't possibly mean what I thought he did. "What? You remember what?"

"I remember everything," he said in a voice that was worn and frayed. "No, that's an exaggeration. What I mean is, I remember everything about my last life with you. *Everything*."

"Oh, my God." I sank down in the chair across from him, my legs weak. "That's what I was going to tell you yesterday."

"Why didn't you say something?" His voice was so soft I almost couldn't hear it. "I asked you point-blank if we were lovers and you said no. Why did you lie to me? I told you it was likely I'd forget and you said you'd remember for the both of us. That you'd make me remember."

It was freaky hearing my words to Robert spoken back by Wes.

"And then you turned right around and lied about it," he continued. "I thought I was crazy, I was having these dreams . . ."

"D-dreams?" *No freaking way.*

"But they turn out not to be dreams but memories of our night together. I just don't understand why you'd lie about us to me."

"You don't, huh?" I said, my hackles raised. "You remember everything else so clearly now, do you remember how you asked me? You said, 'Oh, God, we're not lovers, are we?' Like I was some repulsive troll you'd found. Like you just wanted me to agree with you. So I did." I stood up, turning away so he wouldn't see me cry. "And then the damned thing was, I started to care for you, Wesley. *This* you. Robert may have been my first love, but it's you I want to be with now—everything you are. Don't you dare go thinking I kissed you yesterday out of misplaced nostalgia." And with that last shot, I fled the lair, not stopping until I was outside the mansion with the keys to the Mustang in my hand.

Things were so messed up. Wesley had suddenly remembered Robert's and my past that, out of anger and hurt feelings, I had left out. We had been on the cusp of something special between us, and now he was angry and hurt that I had lied.

And we had a potential apocalypse breathing down our necks, that, according to some dusty old book, if we weren't careful, we could start. Personal drama between the two of us was the last thing needed.

I knew now what I had to do.

Rath looked up as I walked into his plush office. "Hello there, Miss Livingston. This is a pleasant surprise. I was just getting ready to make the trip down to discuss the latest intel with the old man."

I took the seat across from him. "I know my training's just begun, but I think we can agree I've experienced more in my short time than most people do in two years."

He nodded.

"Sir, with all due respect, I request a promotion to full member status in light of these events." I met his eyes without blinking.

He studied me. "What does Wesley think of this?"

"I'm sure he'll agree, sir."

"I'm not so sure about that." Rath got up and circled around the desk to perch in front of me. "He's quite fond of you, Lainey. I've worked around the both of you long enough to know that it is reciprocated as well."

I looked away. "I can't work with him anymore, sir."

"Did something happen to bring this on? I must say I expected this reaction when Robert died, but when you and Wesley seemed to be getting along, I didn't think there was going to be any fallout. It's hard to be partnered up with him after he . . . changes, and I know how close you and Robert were."

"I don't think you do, sir," I said, looking down.

I felt his eyes on me. "Let's just say I had my suspicions.

And Wesley did as well, obviously, as many times as he has tried to poke around to figure out what I knew."

"I'm sorry, sir," I said, keeping my eyes on my lap. "It was very inappropriate, I know, and it won't happen again."

"Miss Livingston, we have a policy of no fraternizing between team members because when the affair ends, one way or another, the parties involved no longer want to work together and we have a mess on our hands." He gave me a kind smile. "We have this policy, but I can't count the number of times it gets broken. You're working in close proximity with the same people day in and day out . . . Things happen. I'll tell you the same thing I tell all of them: you just have to find a way to work with each other and forget about the past." He cleared his throat. "However, I know from personal experience how painful it is to be forgotten by him."

I was floored. "Huh?"

"The man that Robert replaced was my father," Rath said, his lined face somber. "I could do no wrong in his eyes. He was happily married to my mother for over fifty years before she died, and I thought her death would kill him. He died one year later. And Robert didn't remember her or me."

"That's horrible," I said. "I'm so sorry."

"I hated him for it, and even when he read about us in his diaries and tried to come to me to make amends, I wouldn't have any of it. It took years for me to become friends with him, but our relationship was never the same. *He* wasn't the same, which I'm sure you understand. Strange that Wesley, who is now young enough to be my grandson, acts more like my father than Robert ever did. Robert was always so guarded and closed off. Wesley's more relaxed and open, and not so serious. I'm astounded that you somehow were able to get through the barriers Robert kept up. But I know what it is to live so close to someone you love, who looks on you like a stranger."

I cleared my throat. "The weird thing is now Wesley remembers about me and Robert."

"How?"

"I don't know. Odd bits about me have been coming back to him for a while now. And today he said he'd been having these dreams that turned out to be memories." I blushed, remembering the type of memory dreams I'd been having, myself. "I've been having dreams too."

Rath studied me. "Your soul, that piece of his that you have, it links you. It may be linking your subconscious minds. And since it's something you both experienced . . ." He trailed off. "I don't understand why you're here then. You should be happy." Was it my imagination, or did he sound slightly bitter?

"It's too much," I said, feeling fresh tears clog the back of my throat. "He's upset with me for lying, and I know he's just going to be suspicious of my motivations. And with the apocalypse prophecy and the Dragon out there somewhere, he doesn't need that distraction right now. With everything the prophecy said . . ."

"Wesley told you about that?" Rath seemed surprised.

"I happened across it. I don't want to bring on the end of the world. I think it'd be best if there was some space between us. And this was inevitable, unless you weren't going to accept me into full membership after all that's happened. . . ."

Rath nodded. "Well, to be frank, Lainey, I thought about promoting you early, but wasn't sure you'd want that anymore."

I wiped my eyes. "It's what I've been working for my whole life. Why wouldn't I want it?"

Rath cleared his throat. "Well, it's just, you and he . . ."

I knew what he was getting at, and it was something I hadn't quite thought through yet. Did I want to be paired with Wesley alone, instead of in a bigger group? Even without the threat of potential apocalypse hanging over my head or Wesley being angry with me, did I really want to throw away my whole individual career for the guy? This was a guy who had already left me once before, though it wasn't exactly his fault. Did I want to be only the Reincarnist's sidekick— or worse yet, his girlfriend? The very thought made me shudder.

But did I want to be alone for the rest of my life, instead? I'd had a brief taste of what it was like to be loved by Robert, who filled that void in my heart. Did I want to walk out on a chance for that again? Was that why I'd come here—to escape that chance of happiness and hurt?

"Well, if you're sure you want to do this, I'm fine with it," Rath said. "You can start tomorrow evening. I can send a car to pick up your things if you don't want to go back for them."

It was settled then. I breathed a sigh of relief. "No, no. I want to go say good-bye. I'll be back tomorrow afternoon to get settled in."

"Alright." He patted my shoulder. "If you change your mind . . ."

"I won't. I'll see you tomorrow, sir." I got up and left without a backward glance.

I didn't go straight back to the mansion. I drove around aimlessly for a while, and then knew my destination.

I ended up at my parents' gravesite. I sat between the two tombstones, resting a hand on either one. I let my tears flow in the safety of my parents' metaphorical arms.

"Mom," I whispered. "Am I doing the right thing? If I stay with Wesley, even if we can find a way to work through this, we could bring down the whole world. Even I'm not *that* selfish. Should I just give up on being with him? I think I could be happy at the EHJ. It's what I've been working for ever since I got these powers. It's what I've wanted since he showed me what a real hero was. But I'm in love with Wesley. He's a lot like Robert, but he's so much more. He's warm and open, and frankly it scares me sometimes, caring for him like this. I don't want to be hurt again by him dying and leaving me, so am I just conducting a preemptive strike?

"I want the EHJ, and I want him, but he won't go to them. If I choose him, I'll be in that mansion for the rest of my life and will always be defined as his—his girlfriend or his sidekick. I won't be known for myself. And if I go to the EHJ, I'll be a part of the team, but I'll be me. And I'll be alone like I've always been. It isn't fair."

I patted the stone with my hand, shaking my head. What was the use of complaining? If my life so far had taught me anything, it was that it wasn't fair.

"Give me the strength to do what I need to do. For everyone," I prayed.

It was late by the time I pulled back into the driveway of the house that wouldn't be my home much longer.

"Where have you been?" Mayhew greeted me with a hiss. "He's been going crazy trying to find you!"

"He should have called his son, then," I said, surprised at the hostility Mayhew was showing. "He knew where I was."

Mayhew's mouth hung open. "You know about Ben?"

"I know about Ben. And he's sending a car over for me in the morning, so call me when it gets here."

"What do you . . . ? Are you leaving?"

"First thing in the morning. Send up the boxes from when I first moved in, so I can start packing." I started toward the library. "Where is he?"

"Upstairs in his room, I believe."

I headed up the stairs, my heart pounding. I didn't want to confront him, but I knew I had to. I couldn't break apart at seeing him and back down. I had to remember why I originally came here: as a step on the path Robert had put me on all those years ago: joining the Elite Hands of Justice and becoming a real hero. Maybe Wesley would still be angry with me. That would make it easier.

I paused outside of his room. I couldn't do it. My heart was beating too fast, my palms sweating, and I was shaking. I needed to get a hold of myself first.

I turned and opened the door to my room. And about had a heart attack.

Wesley was there, sitting on my bed, flipping through my book of his poetry, his hands caressing the well-worn pages. I thought of his hands elsewhere and almost gasped.

"What are you doing in here?" I managed.

"Why did you go see Ben today?"

I swallowed and ran my tongue across dry lips. "He told you I was there?"

"After I searched all around town for you, I finally called him. He said you'd been there earlier, but he wouldn't tell me the reason. He said it was something I needed to hear from you."

"He's over sixty and still afraid his father will ground him."

"He told you?" Wesley asked in surprise.

"Yeah, we had a real bonding experience." I took a deep breath. "I've been promoted. I'm joining the EHJ as a full member. I start tomorrow evening."

Wesley sighed, running a hand through his hair. "Don't do this, Lainey."

"Are you really asking me to give up on fulfilling the goal I've been working toward my whole life?"

"Don't run away from me."

"Why not?" I snapped, a bit irritated he didn't deny that he wanted me to give up on the EHJ. I dealt a low blow: "Now you can forget about what happened again."

He reacted as if I'd hit him. "I didn't want to forget in the first place—you know that. You know how much I wanted to remember. It's not like I did it on purpose."

"But you meant to sound disgusted by the thought of it."

"No! I never was. I was horrified that I could forget I was in a relationship with someone as hot as you. What else might I have forgotten? I was scared I had come back as a void, with no memories of anything."

"Oh," I said. That interpretation made sense. I'd been stupid.

He sighed. "Maybe it's better if you do go. Knowing what I do, I don't think I could live with you every day and still remain friends." He started to walk toward the door.

Ouch. Maybe I hadn't been stupid. "Why's that?" I asked, praying he'd say something that would make it easier to go.

He gave me a sad smile. "I could read between the lines in the diaries to know Robert had feelings for you. And from the way you reacted when I first came here, I knew you had feelings for him as well. I assumed they were never acted on. And the more we were around each other, the more I started to love you myself. With the added strain of remembering what we once had, well, I don't think I could live day in and day out with you and not *be* with you."

He was in love with me, too? That was so not the thing to say to make it easier to leave. In fact, it made it worse. But I could be strong. I could walk away from him—for my career, for the pending apocalypse, and for the possibility, still hanging over my head, that in order to stop the Dragon, a sacrifice had to be made. I couldn't go through him forgetting me again . . .

After tonight?

I reached out for his hand. "Wes, I wanted to tell you about our past. But it doesn't matter now."

He looked sad. "It doesn't?"

"No." I took his other hand and squeezed it. "Because I love *you*, Wesley Charles."

He crushed me to him, lifting me off my feet and swinging me around. I hugged him back, giggling at the obvious joy he felt at hearing me say the words. He set me back down and kissed me with a passion I returned in kind.

I pulled him back toward my bed. "And we had a date today. In a room with doors that locked."

CHAPTER TWENTY-SIX

I woke the next morning to the feeling of a warm male body in bed next to me. Sprawled behind me was more accurate, with one arm tossed over my waist. I smiled and snuggled under the covers, taking a moment to relive the events of the night before. All of them. I turned to face Wesley and found him awake, smiling at me.

"Good morning."

"Good morning." I gave him a light kiss.

"Did you sleep well?"

"When I actually did sleep, yes." I don't think I'd ever felt so rested on that little sleep. Or maybe that was just me gloating. "I didn't snore or drool, did I?"

"Maybe a little. But it was cute."

"Drooling is never cute." My stomach growled. "Wow, excuse me. I don't remember eating yesterday."

"I've got to feed you, then." He got up, taking my hand. "I'd better get in the shower with you. I don't want to chance you drowning in there because you fainted due to hunger."

"Is that your excuse?"

"I think it's a brilliant one."

Mayhew eyed us as we came downstairs hand in hand.

Wesley acted like nothing had changed, talking about the magic research that had been occupying his time as of late.

"It involves opening a portal to let the Ancient Ones—as in, demons—out. The strongest magic users closed the portals ages ago, almost at the dawn of time."

"So you were there, then?"

He gave me a dark look. "Ha, ha. And, well, probably, but that's not the point!"

I tried to stop laughing as he gave me a serious look and continued. "The magic used to seal the portal was powerful, but there is still a way to open it again, though it is very difficult. The caster must bring about certain actions, certain deed magic, but not by his or her own hand."

"That's where the cult comes in."

"Exactly. The Dragon gathers other strong magic-users to do his dirty work, leaving himself powerful enough to cast the final spell. As Fantazia said, all of these other spells, done in the right sequence at the right times, prime the magic forces for the big spell, the incantation that can open the portal again."

I remembered what I had read in the prophecy. "Syn's taking a part of my soul, Jihad killing me and you bringing me back, that was all part of this big spell."

He nodded. "It looks that way. But there are still some variables I'm trying to correct before they happen. The prophecy says . . ."

Before I could admit to knowing about it and the fact that he might have to die again, Mayhew walked back in. "Pardon the interruption, sir, but Doctor Rath called for you. And he said to tell Miss Lainey that the movers will be here at eleven."

I checked the clock. This didn't give me a long time to pack. "Thanks, Mayhew."

"Just tell him she doesn't need them anymore and that'll I phone later."

I stared at him, shocked at his assurance that I was going nowhere. I had been afraid this would happen, and cowardly me, I hadn't wanted to bring it up yet. This time I had been the selfish one, stealing a moment and not thinking about the fallout.

"Wait, I still need them," I said.

Wesley's attention snapped back to me. "Why?"

"I'm still going to the EHJ," I said, knowing this was going to turn bad.

Mayhew must not have wanted to witness the fight, because he left.

"Why are you still going?" Wesley looked hurt. "You were just running from me, and it's obvious we're getting along now."

"First of all, don't assume I was leaving just because we had a fight. And don't go bringing up last night in a snide way."

He sighed. "You're right. I'm sorry. I have . . ."

"No tact, I know." I looked down at the table. "Wes, I've been working toward joining the Elite Hands of Justice since I was a kid. It's been my life's dream. You know that. For God's sake, you're the one training me; it didn't occur to you that someday I'd leave?"

He looked guilty. "I just assumed you'd change your mind."

"As much as I love you, you can't expect me to just walk away from everything I've worked for just to be the Reincarnist's girlfriend. I'm sorry, but you can't." I felt tears spring to my eyes and wiped them away. "I wanted to be a hero, not hook up with some rich guy who'd take care of me."

"What are we doing now? Regardless of romantic involvement, you're my partner. We can still work together."

"Okay, so I'd be the Reincarnist's girlfriend and sidekick," I amended. "I know the luster of the EHJ is gone for you, but it is a big deal to be asked to join. It's what everyone in our set works toward."

"They're nothing but celebrity poseurs! I know you, Lainey, you'll be miserable."

"Then that's something I need to learn for myself." I

sighed. "But don't ask me to give it up for you. And that's not the only reason I'm leaving, anyway. I know about the prophecy, Wes."

He frowned. "Exactly what do you think you know?"

"I saw it while you were out on the astral plane. There was something about the dark soul and pure soul and then a Darklight that would end the world. We can't stay together if we could somehow bring about the apocalypse. Hell, we may already have!"

"Lainey—"

"I can't believe that you would want me to stay while knowing that."

"Lainey—"

"I'm surprised Rath didn't move me back sooner, since he knew about it too."

"You don't—"

"And it's not like I never want to see you again, especially not now, but we just need space until the apocalypse is settled. After that, if we really love each other, we can find a way to work this out. Why aren't you saying anything?"

"I would if I could get a word in!" He took me by the shoulders. "Lainey, first of all, I haven't finished translating that prophecy yet, so I don't know if we have anything to do with bringing the Darklight or not. Remember, the Dragon is still the caster and still involved in some way; he may have to summon the Darklight, not us. We may fight it, I really don't know. And second, the prophecy says the Darklight will either lead the world into darkness *or* save it. So even if we help this thing or somehow summon it, it may be for the good. I'm trying to find a way to prevent things from even getting that far."

I remembered the bit about sacrifice. "Oh."

"You should have said something earlier, love," he complained, giving me a hug. "I could have explained."

"Well, you should have told me about it since I'm part of the equation," I countered.

"True." He kissed me and I forgave him, but it still illustrated that he thought of me more as a sidekick than a partner.

"Don't let the Dragon factor into your decision to go," he said.

"It's still important, and you don't need me around as a distraction, Wes—and let's face it, that's what I would be now." I saw the way he was looking at me, like he wanted to take me back upstairs again. "And I really do want to try the EHJ. Maybe I'll hate it, but I owe it to myself to try."

"You'd be a great distraction," he said, and then sighed. "And you're right, I can't ask you to give up everything for me. That's not fair. Alright, so a little space, and after this Dragon mess is settled, we'll try to work something out."

"You know, your son runs the EHJ, for God's sake, you can make time for a visit. Maybe you'll decide you want to come back to work there," I hinted.

"And hell could freeze over."

I smacked him. "Sarcasm will not win you points."

"I just know how things work in the EHJ."

"Stop sounding like a superior old man."

"I *am* a superior old man." His mouth twitched in humor. "I'll start working on the I-told-you-so dance for when you decide you hate it there and miss me too much." He was messing with me now, trying to tease me so I wouldn't fall apart. I appreciated it.

"Well, when I'm making the world a better place and you get lonely, I'll expect you to drag your antisocial butt in to change your member status back to active for good," I said with a bittersweet smile.

"We'll see, won't we?"

"Yes, we will."

He sobered. "I'm going to miss you, Lainey. And I'm not going to let this be the end."

My heart warmed. "Good. And I'll miss you, too. But you get so into your work, you won't even notice I'm gone."

"Trust me, I'll notice." He slid a hand around my waist. "Now I'll have a whole new set of explicit memories to dream about."

I smiled at him. "I'll dream of you, too."

"Keep sending those kinds of dreams and I'll be rejoining the EHJ sooner than you think."

"And then *I'll* do the I-told-you-so dance." I kissed him lingeringly, knowing that would be all for a while. But this wasn't the end; it was just a pause, if he wanted it to work as much as I did.

I could only pray he did.

CHAPTER TWENTY-SEVEN

I entered the EHJ headquarters with a bit of trepidation. I had been there before, of course, but never with a platinum access card in my hand. I got in the elevator, swiped my card across the scanner, and the penthouse level lit up.

"Welcome, Phenomenal Girl Five," the elevator said in its electronic voice.

"Thanks." I leaned back against the wall and closed my eyes. I was excited to start the job I had been working toward forever, but also sad. I didn't know how or if things would work out with Wesley. He had quit the team, and I had joined it. He had his own life at the mansion, and now I was a good distance away from it.

Don't become that girl, I told myself, *the one who gives up on moving away to a different town or a better job because of a guy. If we really love each other, our relationship can survive some distance.*

The doors pinged open and I was in the largest, most posh penthouse I had ever seen. Everything from the hardwood floors covered with expensive rugs to the priceless works of art on the walls screamed wealth. And in between all that, every technological toy known to man and alien was stuffed in the rooms.

As I stood there gaping, a six-foot-tall woman with long black hair who was more glamorous than a movie star glided up. Aphrodite—she didn't need her powers of enthrallment to snare people's attention.

"Hello, Lainey." She held out a manicured hand. "I'm Kate Hughes, we met at your preliminary interview. Welcome to the Elite Hands of Justice."

"It's great to be here."

"You have your card, of course, and Mindy has entered your codes into our mainframe. Any personal guests have to be cleared by a senior member before security will allow them up. Senior members are, of course, myself, the Magnificent, White Heat, and Doctor Rath."

"Alright." Who was I going to invite here? It's not like I had a lot of friends, except Wes, who had only founded the team. I'd think they'd let him in.

"If you'll follow me, I'll show you around."

She led me through various rooms—living area, kitchen, dining room, training room, and lab—one after the other in a whirlwind tour.

"Where is everyone?" I asked as we left the lab, a huge state-of-the-art facility. How in the world did all of this fit on one floor?

"All in the meeting room. I'm supposed to take you there next. This way."

She opened a set of double doors that led to a chamber that looked like a cross between a boardroom and the headquarters of NASA. Monitors lined one wall, tuned to various news stations and what looked like security cameras. A large glass table occupied the other side, and sitting around it, looking bored, were the rest of the members of the Elite Hands of Justice. All turned to stare at me.

Feeling very self-conscious, I brushed some hair out of my face and stammered, "H-hello."

Six pairs of eyes stared back at me.

"Everyone, this is our newest member, Phenomenal Girl Five, Lainey Livingston," Kate said, going to an available chair, leaving me to stand in front of everyone by myself.

Doctor Rath, sitting at one end of the table, tapped on a small clear keyboard in front of him and a hologram of the building popped up. "Maintenance is bringing your things up to your quarters," he said. "Room G."

"Yes, sir." I didn't even know where the quarters were; we seemed to have skipped that on the tour.

"Did everything go alright with the Reincarnist?"

Well, that was one way of putting it. I nodded. "Just fine, sir."

"So what's the new one like?" asked a woman about my age, with short black hair streaked with magenta, looking up from the bit of machinery she was tinkering with. I recognized her as Mindy Clark, a.k.a. Tekgrrl, who had a way with machinery and could invent almost anything that came to mind. I guess that's one bonus to being experimented on by aliens. "He as much of a stick-in-the-mud as the last one?"

"He's nice," I said. *Did I just call Wes nice?* Not that he wasn't, but could you use *nice* as a descriptor for someone you'd been intimate with?

"Hardly how I'd describe the last one," Simon spoke up. "I'll bet you're glad to escape from your sentence early, Lainey."

"No. I'm happy to have this opportunity, but I enjoyed working with him," I replied, trying hard to avoid looking at Rath. It sounded like I was talking about an old boss instead of my lover.

Oh, God, I am talking about an old boss! What kind of person sleeps with her boss—and then leaves him?

"You don't have to be so polite on our account," Mindy said. "Well all know how he was. You can say what you really mean."

God, let's not. "I meant it. I liked working with him."

"Ugh, why?"

"I did as well," said a well-defined man with warm, latte-brown skin and a calm manner. It was Luke Harmon, also known as Sensei, a martial artist with a photographic memory and insanely quick reflexes.

Mindy shot him a quick look. "He was okay, I guess,

Luke, but he was just so rigid. The new one's at least kinda cute—in a stuffy sort of way."

"Robert had a certain appeal," Kate said with a secretive smile. "And he wasn't always so rigid . . ."

I stared at her. No freaking way did she mean that like I thought.

Mindy rolled her eyes. "Please. If it's male and a hero, you've been there, done that."

"Jealous? I'm the goddess of love, I can't help it if men are drawn to me."

"Goddess of whoredom maybe."

"Ladies—and I'm being generous with the term—we do not need to discuss this," Rath said.

"Yeah, I don't want to hear about how bad the Reincarnist is in bed," Simon said.

"He wasn't." Kate smiled again. "Academic types can be very fun."

I'm sure I turned pale. Rath shot me a look, as if waiting for me to leap across the table and attack. Was he psychic?

"Kate, I don't want to hear about your escapades before me!" said a man with close-cropped brown hair and a serious expression, distracting me from my violent intentions. He was one of the senior members, Paul Christian, a.k.a. White Heat. I hadn't known they were together, and I couldn't picture an eternally young goddess with a stuffy, forty-something scientist who'd given himself heat-molecule-manipulation powers through illegal experimentation.

But I couldn't picture her with Robert, either.

Rather, I didn't want to.

It was before me, I reminded myself. *Can't get mad about that.*

Honestly, if he had a thing for tall, gorgeous stick figures with black hair, how in God's name did he end up with me?

"And I don't want to hear about it, either," Rath said. "Remember who you're talking about, Kate."

"Sorry, Ben." She winked at Paul. "You've nothing to worry about, baby."

"And Lainey doesn't want to hear about it, either," Rath said. "A little decorum in front of the new member please, children."

Aphrodite swiveled her chair to face me. "She's an experienced adult, Ben. I don't think I'll embarrass her." She frowned and then studied me. "Unless you mean . . ." Her eyes widened. "You and he were involved!"

Gasps went up around the table and everyone stared at me again. I felt like I was standing in a spotlight with the words OFFICE WHORE tattooed on my head.

"I didn't mean it like that!" Rath said, giving me an apologetic look.

"Don't try to hide it now, Ben, I am the goddess of love after all. I know when love has blossomed."

Simon looked horrified. "No freaking way!"

Mindy put a hand on her chin, intrigued. "I hope you mean with the new hottie version."

Kate looked me over again. "Not *just* the new one."

Mindy gasped. "Robert was old!"

"Not that old," Paul spoke up. "He was *my* age, for God's sake!"

"Good for him," Luke said.

"Will y'all just leave her alone!" the blond-haired man that had been silent the whole time spoke up in a soft Southern accent. "Way to make a good first impression. Kate goes and blabs about her love life, which is not your business, and happens to mention her own history with the same guy. You sound like a bunch of gossipy teenage girls instead of members of the best hero team in the world."

Rath sighed. "Leave it to Toby to be the voice of reason amongst the chaos."

I recognized my savior: the Magnificent, Toby Latimer. He was, for lack of a better term, an enhanced human. He was stronger, faster, and could take more hits than an average-powered person. He could also jump large distances and control his rate of descent, almost—but not quite—like flying. He was a senior member, and though he was in his forties, he barely looked thirty, since he didn't age as fast as most people.

He smiled at me. "I apologize for the behavior of our teammates, Lainey. Sometimes when they get out of hand, you just have to smack them back down again. And she about rivals me strength-wise, people, so I wouldn't want to get on her bad side."

Everyone murmured apologies and looked chastised.

I squared my shoulders. I wasn't the same slightly chubby, picked-on outsider that I used to be. I was here, and I was going to be strong. "Sorry to ruin your Page Twelve gossip, but that's all in the past, because I'm here to work now." Okay, so not *that* much in the past. Like a few hours ago past.

"And I do not want to hear this mentioned again. I cannot stress that enough," Rath said. "Do any of you want to hear about your parents' love lives?" Everyone looked sickened. "Exactly. Now you know how I felt during that entire conversation. And Kate, other people's love lives are their business and not yours. Unless we need to know who a villain is spending his evenings with, I don't want to hear you mentioning it again, do you understand?"

She nodded. "Yes, sir."

Toby stood up. "I think I'll escort Miss Lainey to her room now and help her get settled in." He walked over. "Right this way, ma'am."

When the door shut behind us, I turned to him. "Thanks. I needed a way out."

He nodded. "I figured. They can be a bit much. This way to the quarters." He led me down a long hallway with a bunch of doors. "It wasn't so much about you as him. The Reincarnist is the subject of many a dispute around here. You either love him, or hate him and want his name erased from the roster forever." He stopped in front of a door.

"G. Here it is." He opened the door to a small but nice room, already filled with my possessions and expensive furnishings. Man, super-movers were fast—but I should have remembered that from going to the Reincarnist's.

"We each have our own bathroom," Toby said, motioning to a door near the closet.

"So where do you fall?"

"Huh?"

"In the Reincarnist like/dislike debate."

"Oh. Rath, Luke, and I all like him. Kate, Paul, and Simon don't. Mindy's wishy-washy. Of course, Rath and I are prejudiced anyway, being kin."

I stared at him. "You're his son, too?"

He laughed. "Not that close. The Reincarnist is my great-great-great-grandfather. That's why my family's so long-lived. We don't come back like him, but we stick around longer than most and don't age near as fast." He sat down on my bed. "I'm normally not a gossip, but since they decided to blab about you, I thought I'd fill you in on the multiple love triangles goin' on here. It's probably for your own safety."

I laughed and sat down on my new bed, too. "Lay it on me."

"Paul and Kate are together, which I'm sure you gathered. It's Paul's turn, I guess." He made a face. "Sorry. That was catty of me. Don't feel too badly about Kate and Robert being together once; she's been with almost every male member of the EHJ since she's been here. She's the latest incarnation of the goddess Aphrodite, whose power is over all aspects of love. If she's giving off her seduction pheromones, unless they are already in love, men can't help themselves."

"So, that includes you as well?"

He laughed. "Well, her seduction works unless you're not wired to like women."

"Oh." His meaning dawned on me. "Well, it's good to meet the one man on this team who has an immunity to her."

"Even if I liked women, I guarantee she wouldn't be my type."

I smiled. I think I had at least one friend here.

"So anyway, Kate's with Paul. But, being who she is, she can't help but grab a little piece on the side, and her current side dish is none other than Simon. And Paul doesn't know—or at least he acts like he doesn't."

"I could see Simon with her."

"He already tried to put the moves on you?"

"We went out once. He asked me out at a party after seeing my date ditch me. I think you can guess who my date was."

"Simon's really got a grudge against the Reincarnist. That's one of the reasons he doesn't like me—my relation to him."

"One of?"

"He's also homophobic."

"You know what they say about homophobic people."

"He does have an expansive set of issues," Toby agreed. "He may try to worm his way back into your good graces since you were with the Reincarnist, kind of like stealing you away."

I made a face. "He wishes."

"Now, Luke was Kate's former plaything, which Paul knows, so they don't always get along. And Mindy has a thing for Luke, but I don't think he notices."

"It's like a soap opera here!"

"Isn't that the way it is on most teams?"

He had a point. It had been all drama with my former teams as well, love triangles and rivalries galore. I was the one who always tried to stay out of it. Not that it had been difficult. "I just hoped it would be different in the big leagues."

"It's not."

I could hear Wesley's I-told-you-so in my head. I silenced it.

"It's so nice to have someone here that isn't sixty or involved in the drama." He patted my hand. "You're a welcome addition."

"Thanks, Toby."

"I'll leave you to get adjusted to the new digs. Fair warning: the newbies do a lot of work around the place and don't get to go on a lot of missions. So prepare yourself for lots of boring paperwork. Call me if you need anything." He exited, the door swishing shut behind him.

Paperwork after patrolling every night and working with the police? I reminded myself that everyone had to pay their dues to be in the big leagues.

I unpacked what remained of my boxes and then looked around. It was an alright room, not as nice as when I was at the Reincarnist's mansion, but nicer than my former apartment.

When everything was settled, my eyes landed on the phone. I wanted to call Wesley, but was that too needy? Should I wait a couple of days? Or would that make it seem like I didn't want to talk to him?

Aw, screw it.

I picked up the phone and dialed the familiar number.

Mayhew answered. It wasn't as if I expected Wesley to pick up; it could sit there ringing next to him and he would ignore it.

"Hi, Mayhew, it's Lainey."

"I recognize your voice, Miss Lainey." He sounded amused. "It hasn't been that long. I assume you want to speak to Mister Charles."

"Of course."

"Just a moment."

For a lot longer than a minute he was gone; then I heard a click and rap music filtered through the phone.

"Hello?" Wesley sounded annoyed that he had been pulled away from whatever ancient text he had been reading.

"So sorry to interrupt your rap and ancient languages time."

He laughed. "Mayhew said it was someone I'd want to talk to. How are you doing? Settling in okay?"

I toyed between glossing over it all and telling the truth. "These people are nuts, Wes."

He laughed.

"I need a scorecard to keep everyone's relationship straight. And FYI, the cat's out of the bag about ours."

"You trying to use my clout or something? 'Let me go on a mission or I'll get my boyfriend here and he'll make you do it because he formed this team!'" He sounded amused.

"No, actually, your blabbermouth ex-girlfriend told everyone."

There was a long pause. "Pardon me?"

"You heard me."

"Who are you talking about?"

"You don't remember?"

"Please, we're not going to rehash the what-I-do-and-do-not-remember game."

"Aphrodite! She announced your sexual prowess in front of everyone, not knowing why that might bother me."

"Well, at least she was complimentary."

"Hardy-har-har. Then she used her love powers or whatever, and figured out that we were together, and blabbed."

"When was this?"

"As soon as I walked in the door!"

"No, Lainey, when was it that I was with her?"

"Some time when you were Robert."

"Oh." He was quiet for a moment. "Well, he never wrote it down and I don't remember it."

"It must not have been too memorable." She was only drop-dead gorgeous, after all. What man would want to remember that?

"Blonde girls trapped in closets I remember; one-night

stands, not so much. But I must say I had terrible taste in women."

"Wesley Charles! I'm going to hang up this phone, fly over there, and hurt you!"

"You know I meant Victoria Dupree and now Aphrodite, not you!"

"I think I'm included in your taste-in-women category!"

"Alright, but I didn't mean you. I meant one-night stands, and let's face it, my love, you are not one of those."

"Really?" I smiled, cradling the phone to my ear. "And what am I?"

"You want me to say something romantic?"

"Yes, please."

His warm laugh filtered through the phone. "My one and only Lainey. My love forever and always."

I smiled. "You're good."

"I try."

I sighed. "I miss you, Wes."

"You want to come back?" He sounded like he was joking, but was that a trace of hope in his voice?

"I'm not giving up that easily. I want this job, even if the people I'm working with are nuts."

"Some of them aren't that bad."

"True. Toby's nice. Did you know he's related to you?"

"No. How?"

"Way far back."

"Ask him the name, and I'll have to read the diary." He paused. "If you start to hate it, come back, please. I won't do the I-told-you-so dance for too long."

"Is there a song too?" I teased. There was a knock on the door. "One of the inmates is summoning me, Wes, I gotta go."

"Play nice with the other kiddies. Tell Ben to make them behave."

"Or you'll ground him?"

He laughed. "I miss you too, Lainey."

"Call me if you find out anything new about the Dragon."

"Of course."

We hung up and I went to answer the door to see Kate standing there.

"Can I come in?" she asked.

"I guess so."

She fidgeted, her ultra-cool demeanor gone. "I just wanted to say I'm sorry for blabbing about your personal life."

"You should be."

"I didn't mean to. To be frank, it caught me a bit by surprise, and I just blurted it out without thinking."

"I do that sometimes, too. And it was a shock to everyone."

"It's because he was such a loner." She clasped her hands in front of her. "Look, the incident between Robert and me was a one-time thing and it was years ago. You were probably just a kid then. I doubt he even remembers it."

"He doesn't."

She shot me a look and then regained her composure. "You asked him about it?"

"It came up in conversation."

She sighed. "I just wanted you to know that it was years before you came along."

I nodded. "Thanks."

"I never would have mentioned it if I had read your aura a little closer."

"My aura?"

"Yes, I can see people's auras and read whether or not they're in love with someone. Yours definitely showed love, but I didn't notice with whom until too late. If he had been here, it would have been easier to read. But it's obvious not even the promise of being with the woman he loves is enough to bring him back here."

"To be honest, I didn't want him coming here right now," I said. "I wanted to make it on my own."

"I can understand that." She turned to go and then paused at the door. "It's still a bit surreal to know the always-guarded

Robert let someone into that protective shell he had. It was a big deal that he loved you." She looked sad for a moment. "So tell me, what's the new one like—Wesley? Besides cute. And don't worry, he's untouchable by me now, since he's with you."

"A lot more laid back," I said. "The same, and yet different in some good ways."

"Ah, youth." She smiled. "Welcome to the team, Lainey Livingston. See if you can get your erstwhile lover to show his face around here again. The senior members weren't thrilled with him for leaving, but no matter what hurt feelings may be there, we'd love to have him back."

"We'll see."

"Yes, we will." She turned and left me to my thoughts.

CHAPTER TWENTY-EIGHT

The next morning I was jarred awake by a knock on my door. Toby burst into the room, way too merry for such an early hour. "Rise and shine, cupcake! We have our daily meeting in about an hour and you'll want to look presentable, not rocking the bed-head."

I sat up and tried to pat my hair down. "What time is it?"

"Seven. Every day we have a staff meeting at eight where we receive our itineraries and discuss any business."

"Itineraries?" I yawned. "Do the villains phone ahead to schedule?"

"My dear, we are not just a hero team but public figures as well. There are public appearances to make, ad campaigns, that kind of thing." He noticed I wasn't making any progress in waking up. "Get a move on, girl! Newbie has to go downstairs and get everyone coffee from Cuppacino."

"We have a Cuppacino downstairs?" Well, if there ever was a reason to get up in the morning.

"I certainly couldn't function without it."

"A job with perks. I love it."

"I'll go with you to get coffee the first time. It's like everyone goes out of their way to be difficult. No one can order a simple caramel macchiato."

"That's my favorite drink."

"Mine too!"

We high-fived like teenagers making a stupid joke. I

disappeared into my bathroom and showered and dressed in record time, not wanting to be late. I came back to find Toby flipping through one of my books.

"Find anything interesting?"

"Your erotica stash." He held up the book. "This one's quite good." He set it down to reach in his jacket pocket and pull out a small silver pen and a pad of paper. "You may want to take notes."

"It's that complicated to get coffee?"

"Wait and see." He opened the door and we walked down the hallway. "First thing you do is go around to everyone and ask what they want. It changes day to day." He knocked at the first door we came to, and it whispered open. Kate leaned against the frame in lingerie that would make a supermodel blush. I stared. Toby didn't even blink.

"I'm showing Lainey the ropes of the coffee run," he said. "What do you guys want?"

Kate tapped one manicured nail on her ruby-red lips. "I want a half caf, half decaf soy latte with one shot of vanilla, two shots of hazelnut, and just a splash of cinnamon. A *splash*, not a whole shot. Sugar-free all the way." I scribbled notes as she turned back behind her. "Paul, darling, what do you want?"

"Irish cream cappuccino, no lid, easy on the foam. And a cranberry nut scone, unless they have morsa biscotti," he called out, walking out of the bathroom with only a towel around his waist. I was surprised to see he had a well-defined body hidden under those stuffy scientist clothes.

Still more than I ever wanted to see, especially this early in the morning, I thought as I scratched out the order with my pen.

"Thanks, guys. We'll see you at the meeting." Toby motioned me on.

It didn't get any easier from there. Mindy wanted a chocolate biscotti latte, which I didn't even know existed; Luke wanted a chai tea, except with oolong instead of black tea, and half soy, half skim milk; Simon, who seemed out of sorts with me, wanted a coconut banana frozen cappuccino with shaved chocolate on top but no whipped cream, and Doctor Rath, thank God, just wanted a double shot of espresso. He likely shared his father's opinion of fancy coffee drinks.

Head reeling, I made my way downstairs with Toby in tow.

There was a line at the Cuppacino kiosk, which happened to be situated next to the gift shop. I gawked.

"Toby," I said, nudging him. "Why is there a gift shop?"

"Lots of people tour this building, Lainey. It's a big deal for the civvies to come here. There's a museum in the west wing that you should check out. See some old pictures of your boyfriend."

"That sounds interesting, but aren't you guys worried that a villain will come here and try to blow the place sky high?"

"Everyone has to pass through security, and I'm not talking about an old man with a metal detector. Mindy invented the most state-of-the-art system possible. Step out of line and it slices and dices and makes French fries." He checked his watch. "Come on, we don't have much time until the meeting."

I pointed at the line. "Hello—can't go until they do."

"Um, wrong, yes, we can. We own this place." He stepped around people, dragging me with him. "Excuse us."

Customers growled at us, annoyed, until they saw who we were. Then excited whispers started up, and I heard the distinct sounds of camera phones going off.

"Good morning, Magnificent," the barista said. "What can I get you today?"

"Ian, this is Phenomenal Girl Five, she just joined us. She'll be getting coffee for us every morning."

"Nice to meet you." The barista eyed me. "I liked the costume the girl before you wore."

"You and every other man on the planet."

"We're going to be discussing costume changes," Toby said. "And we're in a bit of a rush, so . . ."

I gave him the orders, adding a skinny caramel macchiato

with whipped cream for me and a sugar-free caramel mac-chiato with no foam, caramel drizzle, or whipped cream for Toby. Soon we were both transporting drink carriers filled with white cups to the elevator and whisking our way back to the penthouse.

"So, what do they sell at the gift shop?" I asked.

"The usual—snow globes of the building, T-shirts, cups, hats, bags with the EHJ logo on them, books some of our members have written—there's a couple of forensics books down there by Robert actually—photos, action figures . . ."

"There's action figures?" I couldn't help laughing.

"We do market our images, Lainey," he said, not getting my amusement. "You'll be meeting with our publicist over the next day or so to sign off on the likeness rights and to discuss your image."

I was beginning to understand why my boyfriend didn't approve of this. And I wasn't sure I approved, either. Letting random people wander through the building? A museum gift shop with action figures? How was all of that working to help people?

The elevator doors opened, and we walked down the hall to the boardroom and went inside.

"Thank God the coffee's here!" Kate said, holding out her hand for a white cup. I quickly went through them and found hers. No one else reached for theirs, so I walked around the table, handing out cups. I was now the gofer.

"Good, now let's get started," Rath said, taking the espresso I handed him. I found an empty seat next to Simon and sat down. Everyone got out various electronic devices, PDAs, Blackberries, and the like. Mindy had some kind of organizer attached to her arm that looked like it had come from another planet and possibly was alive. Its strange, metallic tentacles kept reaching toward the bits of machin-ery she had scattered around her, and she kept smacking it away. I still had the pen and paper from coffee orders, so I set it in front of me and waited, feeling rather behind on the technology scale.

"Today's agenda looks like this." Rath clicked some keys and a hologram of words appeared before us. "Kate, you have a meeting with *Fashionista* for a cover story."

She sighed. "What now?"

"Love and sex in the modern age."

"Joy." She tapped it into her Blackberry.

"Paul, you have a meeting with several top car manufacturers over the airbag recall. They want some recommendations. And Mindy, NASA wants to speak to you about some shuttle modifications."

She looked up from whatever it was she was working on and snapped her gum. "I'm not doing it unless I get the patent." Tentacles clicked ominously.

"Just take note of what they want and our lawyers can discuss patent rights." Rath moved on. "Toby has a charity dinner tonight, and Simon has a movie premiere and after-party to attend."

"Yeah, and I'm looking for a date," Simon said, giving me a wink.

"Lainey, you have a meeting with our publicist to discuss your image and to prepare you for the press junket later tonight. After that, you will be taking up your scheduling duties, which will be sorting through the various invitations and requests and deciding which ones are of interest to the team. Then you'll be submitting daily itineraries like this one to me."

"Alright." I wrote all of that down. I could keep track of everyone's social calendars; the celebrity stuff everyone else seemed to care about meant nothing to me. "So, when do we patrol?"

They all stared at me. Simon burst out laughing.

"You mean he still makes you do that? Like you're some sort of flatfoot?"

"Robert was a bit old-fashioned," Kate said with a smile. "He needs to get with the times."

"We are linked with every major world leader and some off-world ones," Rath said to me kindly. "If we're needed, they'll call."

"Well, what about the Dragon?" I asked. "When do we work on trying to stop the apocalypse?"

"Miss Livingston, there is always some sort of apocalypse—a villain trying to take over the world or end it," Paul said. "They usually fall through because a plan on that grand a scale never ever works out, but we monitor them and, whenever needed, step in."

"But Wes and I have done nothing but work on that case since I started," I said.

"I'm still working on the situation, Lainey, don't worry," Rath said.

"In fact, I have some contacts I'm visiting today about it," Luke said, turning to look at me, expression serious. "I told Rath to clear my schedule for the week."

"Oh. Okay. Well, if there's anything I can do to help . . ." I was flabbergasted. The heroes didn't go about being heroic unless they were contacted first and scheduled?

"Well, then, if there isn't any other pressing concern, this meeting is adjourned. I'll see you tomorrow, everyone," Rath said.

I could *not* quit my job on the first day. If for no other reason than to prove Wesley wrong.

CHAPTER TWENTY-NINE

Having nothing to do made me antsy. I thought about watching television, but I knew there wasn't much on at this time of day. I also toyed with going shopping in the city, but it was raining, and I hated going in and out of stores carrying an umbrella or getting soaked.

I finally decided the best thing to do was to get the lay of the land, and so I visited the rooms I had seen on my whirlwind tour, taking my time. The kitchen was huge, but it looked like it wasn't used. The obvious reason for this was the take-out containers in the refrigerator. I remembered Kate telling me that our membership cards also acted as credit cards billable to the EHJ, and the team members ate out a lot at the trendier restaurants.

Mindy walked into the kitchen, a bit of machinery tucked under her arm, the strange PDA gone. "Hey, what's up?" She reached into the refrigerator and pulled out a bottle of water.

"Nothing. Just looking around, getting a feel for the place."

"Uh-huh." She cracked open the bottle and leaned back against the refrigerator, taking a drink and eying me. Mindy had a very punk image, from her bizarrely colored hair and leopard print shirt and leggings to her motorcycle boots. But the wild clothes and hair hid a brilliant mind: Even before the aliens came along, Mindy was a prodigy, the genius child of government scientists.

"So, you and the Reincarnist?" she said, taking a long draw. "I don't know what you saw in Robert. He was always so grouchy with me. He didn't like my attitude. But you're probably a nice girl." She said *nice* like it was another word for boring.

"I gave him plenty of attitude. It just so happens he liked mine," I retorted.

"Well, I also wasn't gifted with assets like yours." She looked pointedly at my chest.

"So, it's not so much that you didn't like him, but that he didn't like you."

She laughed. "Got me there. I've always had a thing for the older, brainy types. It's just a question of getting them to crawl out of their labs once in a while or to notice that the person in the white lab coat next to them is a woman." She sighed. "Story of my life, waiting for the guy to notice me."

I remembered what Toby had said about her and Luke.

"So," she asked, "think you can talk the younger and cuter version into returning to the team? Use your feminine wiles and all that."

"He seems pretty comfortable where he is," I replied.

"So he's just going to let you go?" She shook her head. "Big mistake. Simon'll snatch you up before you can even say 'single.'"

"We're not breaking up."

"You're here, he's there. How exactly is that going to work?"

"We haven't really discussed it. We've been a little more concerned with trying to save the world from whatever the Dragon's planning. And I'm not into Simon."

"He told me you went out once."

"Once," I stressed. "Did he also tell you he drooled all over me—literally?"

She cracked up. "Too funny."

"He's a terrible kisser, whereas the Reincarnist has had lifetimes to perfect the art."

"Stop it, you're making me blush." Mindy smiled. "Well, if you're not breaking up, you do have one thing on your side."

"What's that?"

"He's a twenty-year-old guy now. The Reincarnist doesn't seem to be the type to cheat, so eventually he's going to get horny and come here."

I burst out laughing.

She smiled. "And then you can convince him to stay."

"So you want him here."

She shrugged. "Luke wants him here. So do Rath and Toby. Kate and Paul do too, even if they won't admit it. I think we all know we've lost our way. That's why he left all those years ago—the team has become more about celebrity than actual heroism. Maybe with him back, we could find our path again."

"Do you just want him here because Luke wants him here?"

She smiled. "Did Toby the blabbermouth say something?"

I gave her an innocent look. "He might have, after that involved discussion on my love life."

"Yeah, sorry about that." She half laughed and then added, "But Miss Lainey, you landed the impossible guy—so you watch Luke and see if you can give me any pointers."

I wanted to back off the subject a bit, and decided a healthy dose of truth couldn't hurt. "I don't know if I've landed him. I'm here and he's there, as you pointed out."

"You're a hell of a lot closer than I am with Luke. The Reincarnist knows you're alive, a woman, and interested. He's even sampled the goods!" She gulped down the last of the water. "Luke thinks of me as the kid who's always been underfoot." She gave me a mirthless smile. "My parents thought they could teach their freakishly smart daughter better than any school, so they dragged me along everywhere, including to the EHJ. They made all sorts of gizmos for the team back then. I was twelve when I met Luke." She smiled at me. "You remember being twelve?"

I reflected. "I had a huge crush on that actor doing all of

those action movies at the time—and on a guy who visited the School." I thought fondly back to Robert and how he'd changed my life before I even knew him.

"Luke was my intense puppy-love crush." Mindy shook her head. "I was always trying to impress him, acting like I was so mature and ending up looking even more like a kid. You know the drill. I sometimes think I wouldn't have pushed so hard to be in the EHJ if he hadn't been a member." She sighed. "The most he's ever done was pat me on the head and say I was cute."

I winced. "Ouch."

"Yeah. And as far as I can tell, his attitude hasn't changed." She got up. "Anyway, enough about my pathetic love life. I've got things to do and so do you. But it was good talking to you, Lainey. I think we'll get along."

"Me, too."

After she left, I looked at the time. Maybe I'd go check out the museum. As I headed toward the door, I almost ran into Simon.

I jumped back. "You scared me!"

"Sorry." He gave me a dazzling but fake smile. "So, Lainey, I was being serious earlier. I could use a date to this shindig I gotta go to tonight."

"It's sweet of you to offer, but I don't think I'm the party type of girl," I said, attempting to get around him.

He blocked me. "You're young, you need to get out and have a little fun. You've spent too much time with the Reincarnist, you're starting to act like him." He leaned against the wall, getting too close to me. "You need to live a little with a guy who still knows how."

"I'm not interested in the party, but thanks for offering, Simon." I moved his arm away, a little rougher than necessary. "Excuse me." I couldn't believe him. Why couldn't he take no for an answer?

I pushed aside thoughts of Simon and made my way downstairs to the museum. Scanning my card at the entrance, the guard nodded me through—excellent security, people—and I found myself in room after room of memorabilia. Costumes, news clippings, old vehicles, and inventions were all jammed in together. Finally I found the photographs.

I paused in front of one. It was a photo of the founding of the School. I read the names written on a plaque underneath. Finding his, I counted over to the right person. A complete stranger's face. Not Doctor Rath's father, Walter, but the man before him, Herman Whitney. But there was still something familiar: his posture, the air about him. I shivered and moved on to another photo.

Eventually I came across the first team photo of the EHJ. I studied the picture until I found Walter Rath. I remembered learning about him in school, about his exploits in World War II with some of the others of the powered persuasion; how weird was that? I looked at the photo, again feeling that strange sense of the familiar—he looked nothing like Robert or Wesley, but there was something about him that reminded me of them. Doctor Rath bore a striking resemblance to his father.

I was about to leave when a different photo caught my eye. I paused and turned back. It was another team photo of the EHJ, a more recent incarnation, because there was Toby, Paul, Kate, and . . .

. . . . a young Robert.

It had probably been taken shortly after he had been "born." He looked to be in his early twenties but was wearing his trademark suit, a wide grin on his face. My foggy memory again made the connection with the talent scout who had helped me out of the closet when I was eleven, who had once told me that everything happens for a reason.

My heart hurt. God, I missed him.

Without realizing it, my fingertips brushed across my chest, over my heart where he had healed me. I lifted a finger to my lips, kissed it, and touched the glass over the photograph.

"I'm going to make you proud, you'll see," I whispered. "I'll show them what a real hero is."

As I walked into the penthouse, sirens went off like crazy. I looked around for an alarm I had somehow tripped.

Toby hustled past. "Something's up. If all the alerts go off, it means something's going down that we need to investigate. Come on!"

I followed him into the room that we had been in that morning. Everyone else was already there, and Rath looked up as we came in.

"Alpha X is back," he said as we sat down, and the hologram table displayed a picture of what looked like nine-foot-tall man who'd been hitting the steroids too much. "He's wrecking the downtown area and City Hall called to see if we could take care of it. Toby, Luke, and Paul will be our assault team. Mindy, Kate, and Simon will be on crowd control and backup. I will coordinate efforts onsite with the police. Let's go, people."

"Aren't you forgetting something?" I spoke up.

Rath frowned. "No, I don't think so."

"Um, me perhaps?"

He shook his head. "Oh yes, Lainey, of course. So sorry. I don't know where my mind was."

"That's okay." I'd been worried for a moment.

"You're on monitor duty. Make sure nothing else happens while we're gone."

"You're kidding!" slipped out before I could stop myself.

"I don't have time to kid." He gave me a reproachful look. "Let's go, people."

Everyone rushed out of the room without a word, except Luke, who stopped next to me. "It's a newbie thing, kid, don't let it bother you. Newbies always stick around the home front." He clapped a hand on my shoulder and left.

I stood there in shock. I'd left a job where I'd gotten my soul eaten, was murdered, had any bit of magic I had in me drained—not once, but twice—and fought crazy villains on a semi-regular basis to come work somewhere where I did nothing but sit in front of monitors and watch the action from afar, like a civilian.

I can't quit, I reminded myself. *Not yet.*

CHAPTER THIRTY

I'd like to say that my first month working with the EHJ was filled with adventure and excitement. I'd like to say that, but I'd be lying.

Dark thoughts plagued me as I sat "maintaining home base" for the team. That was a fancy way of saying "watching the monitors and listening for important radio transmissions while they were out." That, and coordinating schedules an intern might have done instead of a law school graduate, was the bulk of my duties.

I flipped to the next page in the spellbook Wesley had sent over. Since I had been relegated to the sidelines, I had decided to put my free time to good use and was working to strengthen my magic.

I spoke the Italian words and held my palm up, concentrating, forcing my will into the spell. A small flicker of fire licked my hand without pain. Frowning, I tried to push more strength into it, to make the flame grow. It stayed small, but started to curl into a ball. I was making progress.

"Lainey, clear the way, we're coming home." I heard Toby's voice in my earpiece.

I swore as the spell shattered, along with my concentration. As Wesley would have told me, villains weren't going to let me have absolute silence to work my magic. I moved to check the monitors.

"Everything's clear," I reported, picking up my books and

spell ingredients and stacking them neatly in a small cupboard. Closing that, I walked over to the hologram table and pulled up the readings from today's case. All of the members but me had been called to act as backup to a visiting dignitary who had a hit out on him—never mind the fact he oppressed the women of his country in the name of religion. It wasn't that I wanted to act as his bodyguard; I just wanted to be able to do *something*.

Everyone appeared in the room in an instant, thanks to Mindy's personal teleporters.

"Status?" Paul asked, walking to the holo-table and looking over the readings.

"Everything checked out. Security didn't pick up anything." I punched a few buttons. "Here's a guest list, and you can check it against facial scans the cameras did."

Kate put a hand on his shoulder. "Everything went smooth, Paul. Maybe our presence was all that was needed. Let's not obsess over it. It's over and done with." She didn't sound any more thrilled than I was about helping the chauvinist pig.

"We got paid and we got noticed," Simon said. "And the cash cow got to live. I think it was a win-win situation."

"Why does it smell like sulfur in here?" Toby asked.

"I did a spell," I said in a low voice.

"Which one? The fireball?" Mindy asked, excited. The only bright spot of this job so far was my new friendship with her and Toby.

"You should quit wasting your time trying to become a magic-user and concentrate on your job," Paul chastised.

"Leave her alone, she is doing her job." Luke came to my defense.

"She gets coffee every morning. What more do you want her to do?" Simon said, managing to offend and defend me at the same time.

Rath wandered into the room. He'd had a separate mission that night, one I was more interested in. "Everything go okay?" he asked the team.

I sidled up to him. "Have you found out anything new, Doctor Rath?" He had gone to speak to a real psychic about the Dragon.

He looked as if he wanted to say something but changed his mind. "Not yet, Lainey." He patted me on the shoulder. "Be patient, okay?"

"Did you see Wesley?"

He nodded. "He says hello."

He hadn't said it himself of late. Wesley was getting more and more into his own world of research and magic and forgetting about the outside one. And that included me. Had I had driven him away by coming here?

"Hey, Lainey, we're going to Chi's," Mindy said, referring to the latest hip restaurant that had just opened. "Want to go?"

"Why not? I need to get out."

"I'm in, too," Simon said, eying me. I tried not to sigh. It seemed like anytime Mindy, Toby, and I tried to go anywhere, Simon had to invite himself along so he could spend every available moment hitting on me.

Mindy gave me a sympathetic look. I decided to pay her back the favor.

"Hey Luke," I said. "We're going to Chi's. Want to tag along?"

He gave me a vague smile. "Thanks anyway, Lainey. I've been feeling off-center lately; I just need to take an evening to decompress."

"Well, if you change your mind." I gave Mindy a slight shrug. So everyone's love life was stalled. We could at least make the scene with our loveless selves.

"This sucks."

"Paparazzi; look sharp," Simon said, as we sat pretending to have a good time. He cared a lot about that sort of thing, and we all turned in the direction he was looking and gave bright phony smiles. Simon put his arm around me just as the photo snapped, and I shrugged it off.

Photographer gone, Toby turned to me. "What sucks? The food or the service?"

"So far, I haven't seen either." Mindy held up her empty glass. "Hey! Who does a girl have to screw around here to get another drink?"

Three men looked in her direction and waved to their servers.

"Yell 'I'm a big whore' next time, Mindy."

"Look who's talking, Simon."

He gave her a glare. "I don't know what you're talking about."

"*You're* the one bedding B-list starlets and groupies while at the same time serving as Kate's plaything when she gets bored with Paul. *I'm* the one who hasn't gotten laid in ages."

The guy at the next table over was frantically waving at his waiter.

"And this is her when she's *not* drunk," Toby said to me.

"It isn't like that with me and Kate anymore." Simon gave me a quick look.

Mindy noticed. "Quit gawking at Lainey. She's got a man."

"Like I could forget."

I sighed, trying my best to ignore Simon. "Yeah, I've got a man alright. One I haven't talked to in weeks."

Simon seemed to perk up at that. "Really?"

Toby put his hand up in front of Simon's face. "Shut up. Haven't you called him, Lainey?"

"Yeah, at least once a week. And every single time the phone is either busy, rings without anyone picking up, or Mayhew answers but Wes is supposedly not there."

"It sounds to me like he's dodging you," Simon said, his tone trying to contain sympathy and failing. "I'm sorry, Lainey, but some guys aren't man enough to do the breaking up themselves."

Mindy turned cold blue eyes on him. "Simon. Go to hell."

"Honestly, how you ever manage to get laid is beyond me," Toby said to him. Then to me: "He's just busy, Lainey. You know Rath's been over there every day, working on preventing that apocalypse spell."

"I know." I sighed. "I just don't know how this is going to work out."

Just then the waitress showed up with a tray of drinks. "A variety for you to choose from," she told Mindy. "Compliments of him, him, him, him, and him." She pointed out guys at nearby tables who all raised their glasses at her.

"Thanks." Mindy fingered one drink and a businessman perked up. "Too conservative." She moved on to the next. "Too immature. Too creepy." She paused over a vodka tonic and glanced at the corresponding guy. "Just right." She took a drink and the other men all groaned. She winked at the sender, a guy that bore a passing resemblance to Luke. "I'm going to go thank him. See you, guys."

Toby looked at me. "Is it just me, or did he remind you of someone?"

"It's not just you." I sighed. "She needs to make a move on the actual guy instead of wasting her time on substitutes."

"She's aggressive when it comes to barflies, but with Luke she goes back to being a timid little girl."

I downed the rest of my drink. "I'm over this place. What about you guys?"

"I'm not picking up any vibes," Toby said. "Want to hit the Cabaret?"

"Nah, I have a headache." I said. "But go with my blessings."

"I'll catch a cab with you, Lainey," Simon said. "I'm ready to pack it in too."

Toby raised an eyebrow at me in a silent question, and we headed for the door.

No, I really didn't want to share a cab with Simon, but

there wasn't much harm he could do in that short amount of time.

"It's fine, Toby. Have fun." I kissed him on the cheek. "Go pick up a hot model or something."

"If you're sure," Toby said with another glance at Simon.

"Why are you leering at me?" Simon asked. "Because you know I don't go that way."

Toby sighed. "Please. I'll see you kids later." He walked off in the opposite direction as a cab pulled up in front of the restaurant.

Simon opened the door for me. "Shall we?"

I didn't have a choice.

We rode in the cab in silence for a while, and I relaxed. Thank God. I thought Simon was going to hit on me.

"I understand you want your relationship to work out, Lainey. But you can't force it if it's not meant to be."

"What's that supposed to mean?" And here I'd thought he was going to keep quiet.

"If you were my girlfriend, I wouldn't let a month go by without talking to you. Hell, I wouldn't let a month go by without touching you, even if we were miles apart. I'd find a way to schedule in a little time for you."

I hated Simon. I hated him more when he made sense.

"He gets caught up in his work," I said, but I wondered. Did he think I didn't want to be with him anymore?.

"Is that his excuse?" He snorted. "If he wanted to, he would make an effort. He just doesn't want to. Look, I understand some women can be overwhelmed by men with power, and like him or not—and you know I'm in the 'not' category—the Reincarnist does pack some power. It's understandable that in your naïve state, you mistook attraction to power for feelings of love, and he, arrogant ass that he is, took advantage of you."

"Just stop, Simon."

"He's not here, Lainey, and I am. I can make you forget all about him." He tried to kiss me but I dodged just in time.

"Now who's trying to take advantage of me?" I threw open the cab door as we pulled up in front of the building. "Try it again and I'll break your arm." I got out, slamming the door behind me and not stopping until I was alone in my room.

My eyes caught on the phone.

My hand hovered over it, wanting to call him.

No, I had left countless messages. He had to be the one who made the next move.

I fell asleep facing the phone, willing it to ring.

CHAPTER THIRTY-ONE

I was walking along a tree-lined park. The colors were off, which wasn't a surprise, since this was a dream. The crescent moon was too bright and had a red tint. There were no nighttime noises around me—no crickets, no wind in the electric-green trees, no traffic sounds in the background. My boots didn't even click on the paved path.

Suddenly I was facing a dark passageway, a water tunnel under a bridge. I hate it when dreams skip locations on you.

I tried to peer into the darkness of the tunnel but couldn't see anything.

But I could hear something breathing.

Backing up, I kept my eyes on the tunnel, expecting some sort of monster to come charging out at me.

Hands gripped my shoulders and I cried out as I was whirled around. I faced a pale man. No, he wasn't pale; his skin was more silver than white. Not like a metal robot, but almost like diamonds. Long red hair hung to his waist, blowing in a breeze I couldn't feel. His blood-red eyes bored into mine.

I could feel evil radiating off of him like smoke. I struggled in vain against his vise-like grip. I tried to scream, but in typical dreamlike fashion, I couldn't. I tried ordering myself to wake up. His unnatural eyes still bored into mine.

He opened his mouth and a cloud of black flies poured out, making me gag. He raised one hand and I saw red razor-sharp talons where his fingers should be. My struggle increased as they rose in the creepy red moonlight and then descended into my chest. I was paralyzed, couldn't move or scream, as his claws ripped me open, forcing my rib cage apart as the swarm of flies flew into my chest and heart.

He laughed, a chilling sound without mirth. His hand dropped to my chest, healing it in an instant before grabbing me by the back of the head and forcing his mouth onto mine. I felt flies go down my throat into my lungs. They were filling me, obliterating me, changing me . . .

Then I felt different. Stronger. Better.

Deadly.

I grabbed the stranger, pulling him into an embrace, and began kissing him back. With a growl, he took me to the ground and began doing things to me that made me scream, made me . . .

I woke up, covered in sweat.

I was in my bed at the EHJ headquarters, alone. And I felt scared, sick, and ashamed of myself.

The phone rang, shrill in the silence. Cursing, I fumbled for it, hands shaking.

"H-hello?"

There was silence on the other end for a moment, then: "Lainey?"

I breathed a sigh of relief. For a moment, I'd been sure my evil stranger was on the other line. "Wes? What time is it?"

"I don't know. Are you okay?" He sounded just as flustered as I was.

"Yeah. I just had a bad nightmare, that's all."

"I know."

"You know? How did . . ." Too late, I remembered our soul-dream connection. My face flamed. "I don't know who that was, but it was horrible."

"It was my fault. It was my dream you experienced." He sounded shaken. "It was the prophecy. The Dragon."

"That was the Dragon?"

"The Dragon will try to corrupt the innocent soul to destroy it. If he does, the dark soul will be his servant, and the world will be plunged into darkness. At least, that's the part of the prophecy I've recently translated. That scenario that just played out in our dream—that's the dark end of our story."

"Tell me there's a happy end."

"There is. The other possibility is that the dark soul and the light will come together to destroy the Dragon."

"Next time, dream of that." I looked at the clock. It was four in the morning, but there was no way I was going back to sleep. I didn't want to be caught in a nightmare loop with that playing over and over.

"I'll try to do better next time," he said, sounding a bit more like himself.

"Wes, why haven't you called me back?" I said, angry now that the terror was wearing off. "I've left like a million messages."

"Did you not experience that dream? That's what I've been buried in, Lainey, scenarios like that and worse. Trying to find out what the Dragon is planning to do for his spell to bring back the Ancient Ones, and bashing my head against the brick wall that is Fantazia, trying to get information out of her. Meanwhile, you've been showing up in the papers with Simon Leasure."

"So we've both been stuck with exes. It doesn't mean I enjoyed it any more than you did."

"Did you just call Fantazia my ex?" He sounded disgusted.

"Please, Wes. Even if you don't remember the specifics, it's obvious you two have a history."

"And it's not what you think, Lainey. Fantazia is my daughter."

My tired brain tried to process this information and couldn't. "Huh?"

"She's my daughter from before the Dark Ages. She's the most like me—unlike Ben and Toby's family, she inherited my longevity, except she doesn't reincarnate; she just doesn't age. Ever. Probably it has something to do with her mother, who was a magic-user too."

"Oh."

"Yeah. So you're the only one who has been in the company of someone you've dated."

"It was one date, and you were the guy whose bed I was in at the end of the night, not him. Simon keeps sticking to me like a leech, trying to prove you're some arrogant guy who used me because he could."

"Simon's trying to prove I'm like him?" He laughed.

"Well, you're not acting much better!" I snapped. "Never calling me back and having creepy sex dreams of me with an evil guy!"

Wes sighed. "Let's not talk right now when we're both shaken and exhausted. Nothing good will come of it. I'll be sending you something for protection until I can track down where the Dragon is. Be very careful, Lainey. Be on guard at all times."

"Fine. Go back to your research. Save the world." I was glum as I hung up the phone. Wesley and I weren't getting along, and someone evil wanted to get it on with me to corrupt my soul and destroy the world.

And I couldn't sleep.

CHAPTER THIRTY-TWO

I walked into Rath's office with a stack of papers. "Here's the latest press releases, a bunch of invitations that sound promising, and a few mock schedules for you to consider."

I am secretary, hear me roar. God, my student loans are wasted money.

Rath looked up. "Oh, Lainey. Good. I have something for you." He reached into his desk drawer and pulled out a manila envelope. "I'm sorry, I'm a bit absent-minded. I meant to give this to you after I last visited Wesley, but then I had that conference with the President and the council meeting with the ambassadors from Galaxy Seven, and it slipped my mind."

I took the envelope with a wary look. If Wesley had sent a note with his son to break up with me, I would just have to kill him.

There was a bulge at the end of the envelope, and as I tilted it, something fell out into my palm. I looked down, dropping the envelope.

It was a flat silver 'O' at the end of a long chain. Holding it up for inspection, I could see a faint whisper of writing appear and then disappear, depending on what angle I held it to the light. I ran my finger over the circle—there was no engraving. Magic writing?

"What is it?" I asked, holding it out.

"A circle of protection," Rath said. "As long as you wear

it, no one's magic other than the one who created it can affect you. You're meant to wear it over your heart."

I slid it on, letting it drop underneath my clothes to settle between my breasts. I felt a tingle as the magic took effect, almost as if Wesley himself were there.

"Very few spellcasters can create a circle of protection," Rath said. "It's a big deal to be given one, and just as big to wear one. It means you trust the spellcaster who has given it with your life."

I fingered the chain. "How is Wesley?"

"He's good. Busy. Always trying to track down the Dragon, pick up some kind of clue. It's good you're with us, Lainey, otherwise I would have told him to send you here by now. It's getting dangerous for you to be out and about alone. The Dragon still needs you."

"No missions for me?" I asked glumly. Not that there had been any danger in that happening.

"No. It's best you stay with monitor duty."

"Great."

"We've all had to suffer a year of monotony, Lainey," Rath said. "You'll be off with the rest of us in no time, and someone else will be doing the busywork."

"Let's hope we're still around by then." I turned to go. "When you see Wesley again, tell him I said thanks."

"Of course." Rath went back to his stack of papers. "You could always call him yourself."

"He never answers."

"He's distracted—" Rath broke off and we both whirled as sirens started shrieking in the house. Simultaneously we headed to war room.

"What is it?" Rath called out to Paul, who was bent over a monitor.

"Riot at the Holding Tank," he said. "Couple of guards dead. No one's escaped yet . . ."

"But we'd better get over there," Rath said. "Suit up, people, let's go. Lainey . . ."

"I know. Watch the monitors." I gave him a salute. "Yes, sir."

"Better be careful, Kate, Mindy," Simon said. "Those criminals haven't seen a woman in years. Or are you more their type now, Toby?"

"Simon, make yourself useful and shut up," Luke said, shuffling him along.

"Pretty boys like you are fresh meat in the joint," Toby said to Simon.

"Professionalism!" Rath growled, shooing them all out of the room. Leaving me alone with the monitors yet again.

I got out my spellbook, ready to put my time to good use. I practiced shields on myself and on various inanimate objects around the room. Getting bored with that, I gave up and decided to surf the Internet for any new mentions of the Dragon.

I had just clicked on yet another Web page that looked harmless enough but led to porn, when I heard the door whisper open behind me. I quickly clicked off the Internet and spun around.

"Wow, you guys are back early . . ." I trailed off, not believing my eyes.

"So, this is what saving the world looks like. Funny, it looks a bit like monitor duty."

It was Wesley!

He was giving me a teasing smile. Maybe it was because I hadn't seen him for a month, and had barely talked to him since I left, but my skin suddenly felt hyper-sensitive.

"Wes." I found I could speak. "What are you doing here?"

"We're down to the wire. The Dragon's plan has to go into effect before the next full moon or not at all. I decided it was safer for you to have me here. And being surrounded by other heroes couldn't hurt."

"Why haven't you come to see me? Why did you barely talk to me?" I moved around the table.

"Apocalypse, remember? Besides, I was giving you some

space," he said, and the space between us took on new meaning. "I thought that's what you wanted."

"I did." I moved to stand right in front of him, so close I could reach out and touch him. But I didn't, not yet.

"And now?"

"You're too far away."

"I'm right here."

"It's still too far." I leaned in.

He met me, tangling one hand in my loose hair, the other going to my back as he pulled me in for a mind-altering kiss. I clutched at his shirt, keeping him close. Our bodies pressed together and I found him as turned on as I was.

"I lied," he said against my mouth. "The Dragon's apocalypse does have to happen soon, but that's not why I came here. I missed you too much."

"Show me." I kissed him harder and he reversed positions, backing me up against the wall, pinning me against it while still kissing me. I practically tried to climb him, angling our bodies for a better fit. His hands were going places that were setting me on fire.

He groaned into my mouth and took a step back, grabbing my hand in his. "Which way is your room?"

We made it there just in time.

"You must have really missed me," I giggled.

"I could say the same thing," Wesley replied with a smile, running a hand over my hip. "Maybe there is something to that 'absence makes the heart grow fonder' saying."

I felt my heart flutter. "I like it better when you're with me."

"Me too. And not just for the obvious reasons." His hand traveled lower, and I giggled again.

"I see how it is. You're going to show up anytime you feel like . . . meditating."

He smiled at the old joke. "No, I thought I'd stay here, actually. Unless you don't want me to," he said quickly, reacting to the shock on my face. "If you think I'd be too much of a distraction . . ."

I shut him up with a big kiss.

We were just warming up when I heard raised voices in the hallway, followed by a loud pounding on the door.

"It isn't your place to say!" That was Toby.

"Lainey!" I heard Simon's wrathful voice, and then, "Open up!"

"What the hell is going on?" Wesley asked.

"I don't know. I'll take care of it." I got up and slipped a robe over myself.

"That sounds like Simon, and it had better not be him."

I gave Wesley a warning look and opened the door a crack. "Hello?"

Simon tried to shove the door open but I caught it and held it firm.

"Why the hell are you in here?" Simon's blue eyes were flames of anger. "You're supposed to be watching the monitors!"

"Simon, it's . . ." I leaned back to look at the clock. "Three in the morning?" Wow. Time really does fly when you're having fun. A lot of fun. "Why are you pounding on my door at three in the morning?" Now I was angry.

"We got back an hour ago," Toby said. "It was a mess we straightened out pretty fast, but there was all of this red tape to sort through."

"Literally?"

"No, not literally," Simon growled. "We just got back and found you not at your post."

"You are not team leader, and this isn't for you to say, Simon," Toby said. "And everyone knows monitor duty is a busywork exercise. You once blew it off to go to a movie premiere, for God's sake!"

"We may have needed her!" Simon said.

"I was tired," I lied. Not too much of a lie; it was three in the morning and now I *was* tired. "I was falling asleep at the desk. If it had been something serious, all the alarms would have gone off and woken me up. I set them up to alert me in here if I was needed." My excuse sounded weak, even to my ears.

"Oh, you were falling asleep, huh? You were surfing on-line!"

"Simon, you know Rath's not going to care. Why are you making such a big deal out of this?"

"Yeah, Rath's not going to care. He doesn't dare say anything because she's screwing his old man!" Simon snarled. I cringed, hearing movement behind me.

"You're just pissed because I'm not screwing you!" I retorted, waving behind the door for Wesley to stay put. If he hadn't been ready to kill Simon before, he sure would be now. "And Toby's right, it's not your place to be lecturing me because you're not the boss and you never will be!"

"You're wrong about that," Simon said, getting too close for my taste. "I will be team leader one day, when Rath retires, and then what I say goes. And letting some washed up has-been use you won't carry clout anymore. And for the record, I'm not like the Reincarnist; I don't like fat girls, so get over yourself."

The door was yanked open behind me, causing me to stumble, and Wesley punched Simon. As Toby and I stared, Simon dropped like a sack of potatoes, unconscious.

"Damn!" Toby breathed.

"Oh, my God, Wes, you knocked him out with one punch!" I said. "That is so freaking cool!"

"He needed to be taught manners long ago," Wesley said, leaning against the doorframe. He'd never looked hotter to me than he did just then. The thoughts I was having would guarantee that I'd never sleep that night.

"How have you been, Toby?" Wesley asked, as if we weren't standing in the hallway after a fight. Or a knockout, really. It hadn't been much of a fight.

"Great, sir. Good to see you again. Did you come to visit Lainey, or are you staying?"

"I'm staying, but let's not say anything to anyone tonight," Wesley said. "I want to talk to Ben about it in the morning. And about Simon's attitude problem."

"Sure. No problem. Lainey, I'll take care of the coffee orders in the morning—don't worry about it," Toby said, giving me a wink. "Have a nice night, you two." He slung Simon over his shoulder and carried him off.

Wesley shut the door. "Coffee orders?"

I blushed. "I get coffee from downstairs for everyone in the mornings."

"I see. So, what is it you do around here? You do correspondence, get coffee, and watch monitors that are set to alarm everyone if something happens, and never do any investigations. Yes, I can see how that is a much better use of your time than staying with me where you went on patrol and actually *did* things to help the world."

"Don't go mentioning the correspondence," I said, stripping off my robe and getting back into bed. "Because you made me do that, too."

He got in with me, moving so I could cuddle up next to him, his flesh warm against mine. "I give better benefits, though."

"Mmm, is that what you call this?"

"You need more incentives?"

"Maybe."

He kissed me. "I guess I'll just have to give you some, then."

CHAPTER THIRTY-THREE

I woke up with the smug satisfaction you feel when every-thing is right in the world. The warm male body next to me was a reminder of why life was good. I rolled over to kiss Wes good morning.

And came face to face with the blood-red eyes of the Dragon.

I screamed, horror and revulsion filling me. I stumbled out of bed, backing against a wall, my fear crippling me fur-ther. The Dragon lay languidly in my bed, one pale limb propping up his head, long red hair cascading down his shoulders, a taunting smile playing at his lips. If it wasn't for the aura of evil surrounding him, he would have looked like the cover of a romance novel.

"What's done is done," he said with a slight Irish accent. "I offered you up to the Ancient Ones as a sacrifice and they were pleased. You will help me summon the Darklight that will bring their release."

I looked down at my rounded belly. I was obscenely pregnant.

He laughed as I screamed, and I felt the monster inside me stir . . .

I was still screaming when I awoke, for real this time. Wesley was sitting up in bed next to me, reaching for me, trying to calm me down.

"Lainey, *shhh* . . . it's okay. It's me. It was just a dream."

I was shaking uncontrollably. "D-did you dream it, too?"

He nodded. "The Dragon."

"That's not what's going to happen, is it? If the prophecy is correct? The Dragon will impregnate me with some demon seed?"

Wesley looked away. "That's one translation, yes, that the Darklight will be a child. An extremely powerful child that will one day be able to either release the Ancient Ones or destroy them forever."

"That's just great," I said, feeling my adrenaline wearing off and the cool air on my sweaty skin. "Well, I'm not sleeping with the Dragon, and you are you, right?"

He smiled. "Last time I checked."

Oh, God. Something hit me just then. Last night we had both been so wrapped up in the moment, out of our heads to the point I didn't think we would make it my room, and we had forgotten something very important. I bit my lip, trying to run over my menstrual cycle in my mind to figure out if it was possible that I had dodged a bullet.

Wesley frowned. "What?"

"N-nothing. That dream was just damn creepy." I wasn't going to say anything to him until I knew for sure. There was nothing I could do now, anyway, and besides, we had bigger problems to worry about. I checked the clock and saw that the daily meeting would be starting soon. "Sorry for the rude awakening."

"I was having the dream, too."

"We'd better hurry if we're going to make it to the morning meeting on time."

"What are they going to do? Fire me?" he asked, a mischievous smirk on his face.

"Maybe you're safe from the chopping block, but I'm not."

"No one's going to fire you while I'm around. If anyone gets fired, it's going to be Simon."

"Inferno, fired? Nice pun," I laughed. "You ought to get to

the meeting before he does, or else he'll be blabbing to everyone about your being here and picking on him."

"He won't mention getting punched out in one hit." He frowned. "You're right, though. We'd better be on time."

I watched as he got out of bed. *Yowza.* "You know, there is something to be said for making an entrance," I suggested.

He caught me staring, recognized my desire, and smiled. "There is, eh?"

"It makes a dramatic statement."

"Got to love a sense of drama."

"And I want to wipe away the memory of that dream," I said softly.

A look of understanding crossed his face. "Me, too."

We were late for the meeting.

"Nice of you to join us," Rath said as we walked into the meeting room an hour later.

I slunk over to my seat like a scolded child. There was a now-cold caramel latte sitting on the desk in front of me. I noticed Mindy smiling at me from across the table. She mouthed, "Hell, yeah!" and winked.

Wesley, however, was not intimidated by Rath's . . . well, wrath. I guess you can't be intimidated by someone you have vague memories of diapering. "Good morning, Ben."

"I know you have problems with the team, but you're becoming a poor influence," Rath said. "First you got Lainey to abandon her post and then you made her late to our meeting."

Wesley snorted and repeated what Toby had said the night before. "Please. We both know monitor duty is busywork."

"And I hear there was some kind of scuffle last night?"

Simon glared. "More than a scuffle—he punched me!"

"Knocked you out cold, you mean," Toby chuckled.

"Shut up!" Simon turned his fury on him.

"That was a long time coming," Wesley said to Rath. "I told you he had anger management problems."

"You trying to get me fired?" Simon flew out of his seat.

"Simon, sit down," Kate ordered.

"Stay out of this, Kate!" he snapped, moving toward Wesley. "The has-been is right, this was a long time coming. He's always acted like he's better than me, and he's not! He thinks he's too good for us!" He was in Wesley's face, anger burning off of him, literally. Wesley just looked bored.

"Simon, power down now," Rath said.

"Simon, you're going to set off the fire alarms, and I just got them recalibrated," Mindy complained.

"Just calm down," Paul said.

"Simon, *stop it*." Kate came up behind him and put a hand on his shoulder. "We both know the reason you act like this."

Simon powered down and turned a dark look on her. "No, you don't."

"You have some issues and feelings you need to come to terms with."

"Don't use your psycho-babble on me! I'm so sick of this team holding me back."

"We're holding *you* back?" Paul looked incredulous.

"You never let me speak at the major press conferences. You're keeping the spotlight on yourselves, on the good deeds you do! No one ever sees me except for at movie premieres. If I wanted to be famous like that, I would have been a damn actor—God knows I had offers. But I have these powers for a reason, and I wanted to show the world how good I was. I went through all that trouble with Jihad, and then *he* had to go and ruin it!" Simon pointed to Wesley.

Wesley stared back at him. "What trouble with Jihad?"

"Oh, my God." I was on my feet in an instant. "It was you! You were the one that was working with the Dragon's goons!"

Everyone was up now.

"Start explaining, Simon," Rath said. "And it had better be good."

Simon seemed to realize he had made a miscalculation. "I was just trying to raise my profile, I wasn't *helping* them! Jihad came to me, said they wanted to start a fight. I thought any villain crazy enough to request a battle had to be easy to put down, and who knew what damage they'd do if we didn't show up? So I met with them, started fighting with them, and called you guys. I took out a bunch of major players myself, and was about to take Jihad to the cops when *he* went mental." He glared at Wesley.

"You got me and him killed!" I snapped. "And caused injury to a lot of civilians! And for what? Publicity? You make me sick, Simon."

"And you tipped them that we were off-planet," Rath said, his voice taut.

"Yeah, so they wouldn't start something when we weren't there to stop it. Duh." Simon spoke like we were the ones being unreasonable.

"Syn killed a child that night," Wesley said softly.

"God, you're the stupidest person on the planet," Mindy said.

"You've got explanations to make to the authorities," Rath added.

Simon looked shocked. "But I didn't do anything!"

"I'll leave that up to them to decide. But you're done here."

"This is unbelievable!" Simon ranted to the room. "Well, fine—like I said, this team was holding me back anyway. You'll see. You'll see how well you do without me."

"You're going to tell the authorities about this," Rath repeated.

"What for? My father has plenty of friends in Washington. They'll clear up this misunderstanding and *your* heads will be the ones on the chopping block."

"This isn't a misunderstanding," Paul growled, outraged. "I don't care if your daddy is a senator, you'll speak to the police about this."

"No, I won't." Simon turned to walk out.

He ran into Luke, who had been standing quietly behind him. "Yes, you will." In a lightning-fast movement, Luke struck him in the throat with two fingers. Simon collapsed on the ground, choking and gasping. Mindy threw a collar to Luke, who caught it effortlessly and snapped it on the rogue Hand. "I'll take him downtown, sir," he said to Rath.

"Thank you, Sensei."

We were all silent as the two of them left.

"Wow." Mindy broke the silence. "That was surprising. I knew he was dumb, but . . . wow."

"So, did you come here for any other reason than to see Lainey and reveal that Simon is incredibly stupid?" Rath asked Wesley, somewhat peevishly. I was reminded with a mild amusement how annoying it would be to anyone for them to have their father pop in and suggest they were running things badly. How much worse would it be when you were in your sixties, your father was in his twenties, and you'd capably been running the show for years?

"The Dragon. He's going to make a move soon."

"So you only come around here when you need something? You need our help, and here you are," Paul grumbled.

"Well, you know, you *are* the Elite Hands of Justice. You are supposed to be saving the world and all. If you can manage." Wesley said.

"We do it all the time, why would this be any different?" Mindy asked, looking perplexed.

"Because this is the time it will actually be difficult," Rath said with a sigh. "I've been helping with research on this. We're standing on the precipice of something truly awful if it goes south, people." He looked at Wesley. "It's time we put all the cards on the table."

"Ben, no."

"If it's bad enough that you've come here. It's time she knew, time they all knew what we're up against."

I turned frightened eyes on Wesley. "What's he talking about, Wes?"

Wesley looked like he had aged ten years in a matter of minutes. "I didn't want to scare you, but you remember my dream?"

I grimaced. "Which one?"

"Either. You know what the Dragon's coming for, Lainey. *You.* He's spent all this time and preparation, casting the spell by organizing all the events to prime you. He doesn't have much time left before the sorcery times out."

"You want to share with the rest of the class?" Toby asked. "What's the Dragon need?"

"Me," I repeated, my voice sounding dead to my ears.

"Only partly," Wesley corrected. "He really needs the Darklight, the one that has to be created through a dark soul and a pure one."

Kate stared at him. "A child?"

"Most likely. One created between the Dragon and her," Rath said. "He already began the process of corrupting her by having Syn take a piece of her soul and then having Jihad kill her."

"And I helped," Wesley said. "If I hadn't given her part of mine—"

"We don't know that," Rath interrupted. "That may have stopped the whole thing; her soul isn't one hundred percent pure anymore."

"He's still going through with it," Wesley said. "The translation's a bit off; it could be he wanted just a missing chunk of her soul, or it could be he wanted me to replace it with my somewhat damaged one."

"It's too late to worry about now," I said. "So what do we do?"

"Until the spell times out, you stay inside," Rath said. "One of us will stay with you at all times; this is the safest place for you."

"I warded the building ages ago," Wesley said. "And keep that circle of protection on you at all times."

"How long until the spell times out?" Paul asked.

"A couple of weeks."

"He's going to do everything he can to draw her out," Rath said. "We all have to be on guard. From here on out, things are going to be *really* dangerous."

I fought back a shudder. For superheroes, what exactly did that mean?

CHAPTER THIRTY-FOUR

The alarms went off and my heart raced. I shot Wesley a sharp look. We were sitting in what Rath called the Research Room, which housed all of his—and now a lot of Wesley's—old books, doing our favorite activity as of the last couple of days: reading the vague writings and prophecies regarding the Dragon.

Wesley looked up from the book he was reading. "Is that the general alarm, or is it the full alert?"

I was already on my feet and heading toward the door. "It's the full alert." I raced down the hallway, knowing he'd be behind me. Since I couldn't go out, I had become monitor girl well and true, except it had actually become an important position, since the team was split up into two groups while doing reconnaissance for the Dragon.

I went to the monitors, barely sitting as I hit buttons. Mindy had created tiny devices that acted as GPS systems, transporters, and communicators to link the teams to each other and to home base. Each gadget was barely bigger than a pinky fingernail, and was hidden behind the hero's ear, so no villain could see it, grab it, or end up somehow using it to get into our base.

"Report," I said into the microphone in front of the computer.

The speakers hissed and a tinny sound came through. *"Lainey?"*

Wesley joined me. "Who is it?"

"It's Mindy," I said to him, and then to her: "Mindy, I hear you. Go ahead."

"*It's chaos out here,*" she said, and I could hear blasting and God knows what else going on in the background. "*I can't tell if it's the Dragon, but someone major's running the show.*" A strange sound like snarling could be heard, and Mindy cursed. Her voice was temporarily lost to blasting from the laser gun she had with her. "*It's like a horror movie down here, all sorts of nightmare creatures attacking.*"

Wesley was clacking keys furiously next to me. "Ben and Kate are still with the Power Squad, trying to recruit a new member to take Simon's place." He pulled up a new frequency. "I'll call them, see if I can send them and the Power Squad to her location."

I nodded. "Min? Help's on its way, okay? We're calling in the Power Squad and Rath and Kate. Can you see anyone else?"

"*I'm hunkered down, I can't see anything,*" she said, and I could hear more blasting. "*When we got here, he split us up. Last I saw, Toby was in the air somewhere, and Paul was blasting something that looked like a giant troll. I . . .*" Her voice broke. "*I haven't seen Luke since he was fighting this thing that looked like the Devil with claws.*"

I winced, knowing how much that would hurt her. "Just hang tight, okay? They'll be there soon."

Wesley gave me a thumbs up and nodded. "They've got the coordinates, they're on their way. It's a big enough mess that some other teams are already going in. The Five should be there any minute."

I bit my lip, knowing Selena would be there and that magic was her super-vulnerability, her weakness. "Mindy, some other teams are going to be on location."

"*I'm almost out of power,*" Mindy said, referencing her gun. "*These things are still coming at me.*"

Wesley started typing again. "I'm locating the others, give

me a minute." The computer was running slow as usual. "Damn it, we have the world's most superior technology, and this computer's still worthless. *Lavoro ora*," he said, and laid a hand on the computer. It brought up the locations of the others.

I stared at him. "Teach me that sometime."

"It's tricky. Machinery doesn't like magic." He scooted closer to look over my shoulder. "Paul's too far away from her, Toby's . . ."

He cut off as we both heard Mindy scream, and a loud roar filled the speakers.

I stared in horror at the computer. "Oh, my God. Mindy!" I smacked the button to speak to her. "Min? Mindy? Can you hear me?"

Wesley was talking to someone else on the other computer. He sounded just as panicked as I was.

My fault. All my fault, ran through me. If it weren't for me, they wouldn't be in this situation. Because I knew this was about the Dragon and his scheme.

"Mindy?" I called one more time, tears beginning to well in my eyes.

Silence greeted me.

A new voice trickled in, laced with an Irish accent. "Come to me, little girl. It's inevitable."

An icy feeling raced through me. It was the voice of the Dragon! I recognized it from my dreams.

"I know you can hear me, my innocent," he continued. "It'll be easier on all your little friends if you just submit to me now. Our time is coming, can't you feel it?"

I didn't realize it, but I had backed away from the computer.

"Next time, they all die, not just one," he said, and then what sounded like an explosion followed. I jumped, feeling the tears trickling down my face.

Seconds later, there was a strange sound in the corner, and Luke teleported in, holding a body in his arms. I panicked, remembering Mindy's scream, until a second later, she teleported in too, holding her bleeding stomach.

"Simon—he just showed up to help," she said, obviously thunderstruck and cocking her head toward the body Luke was carrying over to the nearest table. "That thing would have killed me if he hadn't fought it. I can't believe it . . . after what happened, he still wanted to help." She shook her head when Wesley went to her. "No, help him first."

Luke frowned, going to her side. "You need help too, Mindy."

"I'll be okay, I just need to lie down." She stumbled, and I hurried to catch her as she passed out from the pain.

Luke's face paled, and he rushed over to me, sweeping Mindy up and knocking a bunch of stuff off the war room table to lay her down, his normally calm demeanor gone. A hundred emotions played across his face. "There was some kind of monster trying to eat her and Simon." He looked murderous and sick at the same time. "Simon had already done a number on it, but I finished it off."

"With what?"

His eyes were blank. "My hands."

My eyes skittered down to look at his hands, which were coated in strange blood that was not Mindy's or Simon's.

"Simon's fading fast, but he's not gone yet, thank God. I wouldn't be able to work the resurrection spell again. I shouldn't have even been able to do it with Lainey." Wesley was talking more to himself than us. "And I've lost a lot of power since then."

"You can do it," I said, slipping my hand into his. "I'll help."

Toby and Paul teleported in. Toby announced, "Well, the Dragon did the typical my-evil-plan-is-in-place-and-you'll-pay-next-time thing. Everything just disappeared and . . ." He trailed off as he saw Mindy, who had passed out, and Simon. "God, no."

"This shit's getting old quick," Paul said to Wesley, who

was standing over Simon, beginning a spell. "Look at the unholy mess you've brought on us. You stay away for years . . ."

"You all need to leave," Wesley interrupted, his voice commanding. "You're breaking my concentration."

I got up, and he sighed. "It figures you'd be the only one who listens to me. No—Lainey stay; everyone else go. I may need to borrow from you," he said to me.

Oh, joy. But if it would save Simon and help Mindy, I'd take the excruciating pain.

Toby snagged Paul. "Come on, man. Mindy has some sort of alien healing technology in her room, but I'll be damned if I know which of all the gadgets it is. You're a scientist, you might be able to figure it out."

Paul nodded and gave Wesley a look. "We're not finished."

Wesley's blue eyes shot him a challenging look, then he went back to work on Simon, whispering softly in Italian. Toby yanked Paul out of the room.

"Luke, out," Wesley said, looking up, pausing a moment in his incantations.

"I'm staying with Mindy," Luke said.

"There's nothing you can do," I argued, going over to him.

He shot me a nasty look. "There's nothing you can do, either."

"I have some magic, so that's where you're wrong. Believe me, sometimes I'd rather not, what with the horrible pain of being drained, but if it'll help save them . . ."

"If she dies . . ."

"*Now*, Luke," Wesley snapped.

"Wes, it's okay." I realized why Luke was freaking. "What the hell is wrong with you men? Why do you wait until a girl is dying or critically injured before you realize you have feelings for her?"

"Wh-what?" I had at least shocked Luke out of his rage.

He glanced back at her. "I don't . . . I mean, it's not like . . . It's out of the question; she'd never . . ."

Wesley gave me a warm look. "Sounds familiar."

Then he motioned me over and I knew what was coming. But if it would help, I'd do it. "Sorry about this, my love," he said.

I didn't get a chance to brace myself as he reached out for me. The pain hit me harder than it had before, coursing through as one solid wave. I grabbed hold of the table for support, choking back vomit and tears as my head pounded. I could hear Wesley chanting in Italian, and my skin vibrated as the magic took effect.

I focused on Luke. "When Mindy wakes up, you should tell her. Better yet, don't say anything, just take her on this table." I heard Wesley snort. "She'll appreciate it, trust me."

Luke shook his head. "It's not like that at all, Lainey. We're more like brother and sister."

I didn't have the strength to argue with him. "Fine, be more stupid, Luke. I'm going to take a nap now."

I heard Wesley snap, "Well, grab her, Luke!" before I passed out.

I woke several hours later in my own bed with Wesley beside me.

"Did you hit me with a spell and take advantage of me?" I asked, giving him half a smile.

He brushed a strand of hair away from my face. "I wouldn't need a spell, now would I?"

"No." I lifted the covers. "I seem to remember passing out fully clothed, though."

"I just wanted to make you comfortable."

"Then I'd be in a sweatshirt and pants." I tried to sit up and found I still felt too dizzy. "Is Simon okay? What about Mindy?"

He sighed. "I couldn't heal Simon completely, but he is

alive, which was touch and go for a while. His senator father has him being looked after by the best doctors in the country, so I'm sure he'll be fine. He'll live to hold his beloved press conference."

"He did help when he was needed," I reminded Wes.

"True. He has potential—if he would just get over himself."

"I don't see that happening anytime soon," I admitted. "What about Mindy?"

"Toby found some sort of healing orb the aliens gave her, so that helped a lot. It's a good thing, because I was pretty tapped out after Simon. But she's good and resting. She'll probably have to take it easy for a bit."

My stomach flipped again. "This is all my fault."

Wesley frowned. "How so?"

"If I hadn't been here, he wouldn't have gone after them. He was trying to draw me out."

"You can't do that, Lainey. You can't blame yourself. If it wasn't the Dragon, it would be someone else—you know how this life is. And maybe, if you weren't here, the Dragon might have already cast the world into darkness by now. You may be the only thing holding everything together."

I gulped. "No pressure or anything, Wes."

"You're doing fine. Better than fine, actually. You're wonderful." He kissed me softly.

I held on to him and kissed him back, taking strength from his presence and his love. And then I noticed something.

"Wes, did you feel the need to get comfortable as well?" I said, moving a hand in between us, finding bare skin and more bare skin.

His smile was mischievous. "Maybe."

"Wes?" I moved my hand lower.

"Yes?"

"I think you have more making up to do for not talking to me for so long," I said, kissing him again.

Maybe it was selfish to lose myself with my love after everything that had happened to my friends today, but I felt like Cassandra, doomed to see her people's downfall and unable to stop it. I needed something to live for, and he had just what I needed.

CHAPTER THIRTY-FIVE

Wesley had been looking jittery all morning—not that I blamed him. But there was something new to his obvious discomfort, something other than the fact that two of our colleagues were sleeping off grievous injuries from the day before.

"We just bought the coffee, why is it you look like you've drank ten espressos already?" I asked, sipping the caramel latte the barista had just handed me.

Wesley held his espresso but didn't drink it. "It's tension."

"Yeah, you do look tense," I agreed, frowning as I took another sip. "It's the stress of always being on guard for the Dragon. You're not doing enough meditating." I gave him a saucy look.

"It's more than that," Wesley said, not catching the joke. "I can feel the tension in the magic."

"The tension in the magic?" I raised an eyebrow. "Cue the overly dramatic scary music."

"Now is not the time to be making jokes," he snapped.

I gave him a sideways glance as I hit the elevator button to go back upstairs. "Now is the time for you to switch to decaf, Mr. No Sense of Humor." I took another sip of coffee. "I think the milk is off; this tastes weird. Try it."

"You need to take this Dragon threat seriously, and if you think it's off, why do you need me to taste it? Am I your food taster now?" He punched the elevator button again and sighed.

I almost snapped back at him. "I *am* taking the Dragon seriously. That's all I've done from the day I got my soul eaten! People keep getting hurt, including my friends, somebody wants to impregnate me with a demon baby . . . all because some nutjob wants to blow up the world? The only thing decent in all of that time has been this." I motioned back and forth between him and me. "Us. The Dragon's assault will come any day now, according to all those moldy books upstairs you and Rath have been translating, and I'd like for us to not fight each other. I'm sorry for making jokes and trying to forget that dark, lurking evil is, well, lurking. Ready to pounce at any moment." The elevator appeared and we stepped inside. "And maybe I just have morning mouth or something, and that's why the coffee tastes off, which is why I wanted your opinion. I'd hate to throw it away and waste four bucks."

"I have enough money to not worry about your wasting four dollars, love." He took the cup from me and sipped. "And it tastes fine, except for that awful caramel syrup you have them put in it."

"See, my taste can't be trusted." I took the cup back. "And you may have more money than the Swiss National bank, but I don't."

"You will once this chaos is over."

"Is there a cash reward for saving the world from the apocalypse or something?" It occurred to me then what he might be driving at, considering how close he'd acted toward me lately. It was as close as a someone stuck in his own world like Robert or Wes would ever act, and I loved him for it. "Oh, my God. You did not just propose to me in an elevator!" The doors dinged open.

"Alright, I didn't." He stepped out.

I followed. "Without even a ring!"

"What, like this one?" He turned and snapped open a jewelry box.

I stared. "Wow. That is truly a rock."

He snapped it shut again. "But since this conversation never happened . . ."

I caught his arm. "When I tell this story to our kids, it will be infinitely more romantic."

"Roses, champagne, and no apocalypse?" He put the ring on my finger.

"Something like that." I kissed him by way of saying yes to his unanswered question.

It seemed like reality shifted under us, but not in a good way. A wave of dread and revulsion swept through me, and what felt like an electric current tingled in my spine. Wesley turned pale and I knew he felt it too.

"What the hell was that?" I asked.

"It's the reason for all the tension," he answered.

Then the alarms proved him right, howling to life, and we headed toward the war room, everyone else appearing in our wake.

"What's going on?" I asked.

Mindy and Rath sat the monitors, looking terrified.

"This is it," Mindy said.

"The Dragon?"

"Power level's off the charts," Rath said. "It's as if a bomb went off, magically speaking. And the timing is right."

"He's opened a portal," Wesley said from behind us. "It's leaking out all kinds of nightmarish things."

I glanced back at him. "How do you know?"

"I can feel it."

I wasn't going to argue with magic hunches.

"He's right," Rath said. "The Dragon's opened a gateway—not the big one he intends as a final destruction of the world, but something almost as bad. Every team in the country is heading for the site, but you're the only one that can close it." He looked at Wesley.

"I don't know if I can anymore. My power's been depleted, remember?"

"A couple of other minor magic users are heading that way as well," Rath said. "Together you may all be able to close it, but you're the only one with the knowledge to actually do so. You'll just have to boost your power."

I sighed. "Oh, thrill."

"I'm calling Fantazia. It's about time she got involved." Wesley looked around. "Who's going to stay with Lainey?"

"We're going to need most of the team to help with the cleanup," Rath said.

"*Someone* has to stay. This is exactly the kind of distraction he needs for the main event. And we know time is running out." Wesley picked up the phone and dialed, probably calling one of Fantazia's bodyguards.

Rath shrugged in surrender. "I'll stay, along with Paul and Toby."

"They're our heaviest hitters!" Kate said, walking up. "The rest of us aren't exactly long-range."

"Mindy, load them up on weapons," Rath said.

Tekgrrl nodded. "We'll be linked up, sir."

"I'll stand by," Rath said as they exited to prepare for battle.

Wesley put his arms around me. "Be careful, Lainey."

"I think I'm the one who should be saying that, not you. You're the one going off into battle." I was worried. I wanted to be there if he was going to risk his life against demon hordes. And I couldn't forget the prophecy, and the mention of a noble sacrifice, and the fact that he had just proposed to me . . .

"You're not safe, either."

"One of those magic hunches?" I joked.

"I'm not taking all of the power you can give me, just in case. Fire spells are always helpful; if you need to, use one. And keep that circle of protection on you at *all times*."

I pulled the chain out from under my shirt to show him. "It's right here. It always is."

"Good girl." He pulled me to him and kissed me lingeringly. For some reason, his kiss scared me. As if he thought one of us was going to die . . .

"Sorry, my love," he said, and I felt the familiar pain of the draining spell. I swayed, but didn't fall. He hadn't taken enough to weaken me, just to make me dizzy.

"Wes, you need more." I was worried. He'd never be able to close the portal with that, and he also needed to be able to defend himself.

"I'll get more." He looked over my shoulder, and I turned to see who he was looking at. Rath. "Sorry, Ben, but I can't leave her completely defenseless. I know how hard this is on you."

Rath sighed. "It's alright. Go ahead."

I couldn't believe what I was hearing. "You're a magic-user?" I sputtered.

Rath shook his head. "Just barely. I'm like you, I have enough power to do a few low-level spells, but it weakens me. And since my power comes from him as his child . . ."

Wesley walked over to him, and I saw Rath sway under the spell. "I'm sorry, Ben."

"I said it was alright," Rath snapped, and I reached out and grabbed him before he could fall.

"Be careful," Wesley said, and then he picked up a transporter, sliding it onto his belt. He keyed in the coordinates of his destination and looked at me again, as if he wanted to memorize my face.

His behavior was freaking me out. "Wes?"

"Yes?"

"Nice costume."

He looked down at his dark pants and shirt and shrugged. "I told you, I don't wear them. Wait." He said something in Italian, and his black leather coat appeared. "Better?"

"It's very badass," I agreed.

"That's a good thing, right?"

"Definitely." We shared a moment of staring into each other's eyes.

Rath groaned and straightened himself. "I'm leaving before the sexual tension gets too thick."

As soon as the door closed behind him, Wesley grabbed me and kissed me as if the end of the world was coming.

"Damn," I breathed when he finally released me. "That was a life-altering kiss."

He held me tight against him, so close I could hear his heart beating through his shirt and coat. "In all of my many lives, I never had someone affect me like you do. I love you more than any other woman across all of time."

"I love you, too," I said, clutching him. I felt tears run down my cheek. "But don't do this. It makes it sound like one of us is going to die, and we've both survived that once already."

"We're not so lucky to do it more than once."

"Hey, we just got engaged, remember? You're not getting out of it that easy," I teased. "Go save the world."

"If something happens, do me a huge favor."

"Anything."

"This time, tell me we're in love instead of leaving me to guess." He gave me a rueful smile. "And my journal is on your bookshelf next to my book of poetry. This time I wrote down the important things right off."

"Computer passwords, for one?"

He smiled. "I love you." Then he shimmered and disappeared.

"Love you, too," I whispered. My heart felt like it was going to break. I couldn't help but think, because of that stupid prophecy: he was going to have to sacrifice himself to stop the Dragon. I knew he would do it in an instant, because that was the kind of hero he was, even if it truly meant the end of his long life.

Stop, I ordered myself. I would always worry about him in

battles, but death had less of a sting with him. He would always be back. *Always.*

But I wouldn't. Eventually, one day, I would be gone. And he would have to go on. Find someone else. Like he had since the dawn of time.

With those dark thoughts, I turned to watch the monitors.

Rath walked back in with Paul and Toby in tow. "He's gone?"

I nodded. "Now we get to watch from the sidelines."

An hour later, I felt like we were on the sidelines of World War Three.

"Lainey, call everyone on the left quadrant," Rath barked out. "The group by the river is getting beaten down."

"Wesley's team still can't get through," Toby said from his computer. "Someone needs to get over there to help them."

"I'm sending the team in sector three," Paul said.

We were like generals sending grunts into battle as we each radioed our contacts. I felt sick. Heroes were going to die in this one. And it was all because of me. If the freaking Dragon didn't want his chance with me . . .

"We should be there," Paul said. "We have the best security system on the planet and this place is guarded by magic. Nothing and no one's getting in unless we let them."

As if the universe realized what a cosmically stupid thing that was to say, what felt like an explosion rocked the building, though there was no sound. My skin buzzed like crazy. I could almost reach out and touch the magic. I shot a quick glance at Rath, and it seemed to be affecting him the same way.

"Something's trying to get in," he said.

"Nice, Paul. Why don't you just say 'What could possibly go wrong?' while you're at it?" Toby snapped.

"Is it him?" I asked.

"Not powerful enough," Rath said, as another explosion rocked us. "Maybe some of his cultists. Check the roof."

I typed a command into the computer to redirect the security system on the monitor, leaving a channel open in case one of the team needed us. Sure enough, there were two goth-looking types hurling what looked like fireballs at the building. A golden glow would appear, almost like a shield, and block it every time.

A sense of pure evil came over me. I shuddered. "*That's him.*" He had definitely arrived.

This time there was an actual sound, and a furious explosion rocked the building. The alarms screamed.

"Get up there," Rath ordered Toby and Paul. "They're going to breach the shield, and our defense system's not going to hold up to magic like that. Try to hold them off as long as possible."

They both nodded and took off.

I saw them appear on-screen, fighting off our magical terrorists. One of the cultists broke off from the fight and headed straight for the building.

"Kamikaze!" Rath said from beside me.

"What?"

"Death magic is powerful. Especially your own death. It may be enough . . ." Another explosion, this time followed by an electric current I felt race through my spine. Rath swore again. "They just popped our building's protection spell. Anyone can get in now."

I whirled back to the screen. The Dragon was nowhere to be seen, but I could sense his malevolent presence.

And then he appeared in the room in front of us.

I reacted without thinking, pulling back and hitting him with all the strength I had. He flew backward and went through a wall.

"We've got to get out of here," I called to Rath. "Can you call Wesley and tell him to get back here?"

"I can try a distress spell."

"As long as we can do it while fleeing," I said, and we took off toward the entrance.

The Dragon appeared in front of us again. I hauled Rath backward, skidding to a stop.

"I love a girl with spirit," the Dragon said. "But don't run. It will make it worse on your friends."

"Go to hell." I picked up the nearest object, which happened to be a heavy oak table, and hurled it at him, just as Rath whispered something in Italian, and I felt my skin hum as an electric current hit the Dragon.

"Nice," I said to Rath as we headed back the way we came.

"Won't be able to do much more than that," he wheezed, and I could see his skin looked gray. "It took too much out of me."

"Save what you can for defense." I headed toward the nearest window. "We're out of here."

My skin burned as something sorcerous hit me and was negated. The circle of protection burned hot against my chest.

"Bitch!" The Dragon growled, in the room with us again, blocking the window. "That's going to cost you."

"Not with magic it won't," I snapped. "*Ustione.*"

Fires popped up on him for a moment and then disappeared. The Dragon laughed. "Your magic is too weak, little girl. And the circle of protection will help you, not him."

"*Schermo sopra* Ben!" I yelled, just as the magic hit him. My shield took the brunt of it, but some of the blast still got through. He staggered.

I grabbed him and tossed him through the doorway, out of harm's way. The Dragon reached for me and I dodged his grasp, then managed to catch him with a powerful right hook. I followed through, pivoting and driving my left fist into his chest. I felt bones crush under my blow.

"Feisty. But you've got a problem." The Dragon's body glowed red. "Your protection only works on spells directed at you. So if I make myself stronger than you . . ." He punched me in the chest and I flew back into a wall, gasping, thinking he had punched a hole through me. As it was,

I knew several ribs were broken. "Now we're on an even playing ground, girl." He grabbed me and I struggled, finding his grip too strong—it was a new sensation. I started to panic. I was always stronger than men; it shouldn't be like this for me.

"I'm stronger now," the Dragon growled in my ear. He ripped at my clothes and my struggle turned into a frenzy of biting, scratching, tearing, kicking, hitting. This couldn't happen. Never mind the end of the world; I wasn't getting raped, either.

He was on top of my body, overpowering me. I kneed him in the groin and he punched me in the throat. I gasped airlessly, seeing blackness for a moment. Tears burned in my eyes.

He froze. He held me pinned to the ground, studying me with a quizzical expression, frowning. One hand shot to my throat, squeezing the air out of me, as the other moved up to my stomach. He pressed his palm flat, pushing in slightly. I was starting to lose consciousness, and wondering just what the hell he was doing, but I was glad he wasn't trying to rape me at the moment.

He swore in some language I didn't understand and released the pressure on my throat, but kept me pinned to the ground. "What's done is done, but it won't help you! Do you understand?" he screamed in my face. "It won't help!" He looked up to see Rath standing there.

The Dragon frowned and said something in that strange language. A bloody red current struck Rath. I screamed as I felt the magic take effect.

Rath fell to the ground. He whispered something in Italian, and then his eyes went blank. I felt a sob tear my throat. He was dead.

He had made the sacrifice.

The Dragon screamed as a blue glow overtook him. The magic hummed around me, but didn't hurt.

"Damn old man death-cursed me!" the Dragon growled

He looked down at me and I knew it had weakened him. "I don't care if you did wreck part of my plan, the Darklight will still let my Masters back into this world. Soon enough, my dear, you will be expendable. And then you will beg for death before you receive oblivion."

"You're going first," a harsh voice said from the doorway.

The Dragon looked up and I arched my body to see Wesley, eyes black, coat whipping in an invisible wind as the strength of his magic filled the room. My skin felt like millions of ants were running under it.

"You tried to take what is mine," Wesley said, his cold voice sending a shiver of fear through me. "And you killed my son. You're dead."

The blast of power knocked the Dragon off of me and into the wall behind him. Black blood ran out of his nose as he struggled to fight back, but Wesley pushed more will-magic on him, the power visible, radiating off of him like tendrils of black smoke. Wesley held out a hand, fingers splayed, and the tendrils shot off of his body and into the Dragon, lashing him like whips. The Dragon screamed as Wesley spoke Italian in a voice so harsh that I didn't even want to know what he said. He began to float in the air as the power coursed through him, his eyes black with red energy flaring off of them. The hair on the back of my neck stood up. I had never been scared of him until that moment.

The room filled up with tension, with dark power, and the Dragon seemed to realize he had one last chance to stay alive. He started pushing back at Wesley magically, but the strain was showing as patches of his skin began to burn off under the intensity of Wesley's sorcery. The hum and buzz of machinery around us seemed to vibrate the walls, and then the lights popped and everything electronic in the exploded in a blast of electricity and fire.

k blood was beginning to run from the Dragon's eyes

like tears. "It doesn't matter what you've done," he growled. "The prophecy is still fulfilled. The Darklight will return my Masters to their former glory. And I'll be there to see it happen." He slammed a fist into the wall behind him, and then another. A loud crack sounded in the room, and then a swirling black hole appeared behind him, sucking him in. "I'll be back to watch you weep for what you've unleashed on this world," he snarled before disappearing.

"No, you won't," Wesley said. Dark energy flared off of him like a cape or wings, and he followed the Dragon into the darkness. The black hole disappeared.

I got to my feet in a daze.

That didn't just happen, I thought. *Wesley didn't just go into another dimension with the Dragon to die.*

I staggered over to the wall and clawed at it. "No! No! God, no!" I punched the wall with a fist, hearing a cracking crunch, and then another and another, not caring when my knuckles turned bloody. I leaned my forehead against the wall, sobbing in grief. "Come back," I whispered, voice choked with tears. "Please come back."

The only sound in the room was my breathing and the hiss of the fire as the smoke detectors did their job and the sprinklers overhead started to extinguish the blaze. I was aware I was getting wet, too, and didn't care. A wave of sadness, frustration, and anger coursed through me.

I wasn't losing him again. Not this time. I knew I was weakened from the fight with the Dragon, and by giving Wesley some of my power, but I had try.

"*Portila di nuovo me,*" I whispered like a prayer. "*Portila di nuovo me.*"

It was a spell that was too powerful for me, a spell that could burn me out in an instant. But I knew I had to try for Wesley, no matter if it killed me. I loved him enough to sacrifice myself for him.

A sound like a heavy wind came from behind me, and I

whirled to see a black hole opening in the floor and Wesley rising up from it. With a cry, I flew over to him. He caught me with one arm and held me tight. I sobbed against him, shaking and holding on to him for dear life, not even caring that my body was in pain. He was here, he was alive, and that was all that mattered.

"Where did you go?"

"A dark dimension," he said. "We fought and I weakened him further, but before I could kill him, he fled into a place even I am afraid to go. What he met in there was probably worse than anything I could do to him, so there's a bit of comfort in that."

"He can't get back, can he?"

A tension ran through Wes's body. "I don't know, Lainey. The Dark Lands are unpredictable at best, but Fantazia and I will try to ward the gateway between this world and that one, which will make it difficult for him to return if he survives, but I can't promise he won't."

He went over to Ben's body and fell to his knees beside it, cradling his head in his arms. "Benji, I'm so sorry. So very sorry." Tears ran down his face.

"He died to weaken the Dragon," I said softly. "He saved me. He helped save us all."

Wesley nodded numbly and my heart ached for him and for Ben. I stood there, not knowing if I should go to him or let him have time alone.

"He was trying to get the EHJ back on track," Wesley said in a broken voice. "He told me he knew he had messed up along the way, gotten distracted by the celebrity aspect of it all. He wanted to show me he had done a good job as a leader."

After a few moments, he got up and staggered over to me. He slumped to his knees as if his strength was finally gone, wrapping his arms around my waist as he rested his head on my midsection. I ruffled his hair, trying to comfort him.

"It'll be okay now, Wes. As much as it can be, I mean.

The Dragon's trapped in a hell dimension, he didn't get his chance with me, the spell won't work, no more worries about Ancient Ones or us bringing the end of the world."

Wesley sighed, looking up at me. "It's not exactly over."

"Well, he still could come back for revenge because we ruined his spell, but that's kind of a normal day for us. What villain isn't trying to get even with the heroes for ruining his evil plan? But the apocalypse spell is stopped. That's it. Game over. The end."

"Didn't you hear him earlier? It doesn't matter that he didn't spawn the Darklight. The prophecy is still fulfilled. The Darklight is created through the dark soul and the pure one."

"And he didn't get his chance," I said. "He stopped."

"My soul is black," Wesley said, getting to his feet to look me in the eye. "I'm still a good man, but Jihad's death is not the first time I have killed, even in the name of good. Long ago, I had to take out an entire town corrupted by servants of the Ancient Ones. Hundreds of lives gone in an instant because of me. That will stain your soul, Lainey. And that's one memory that sticks forever. I have to live with that knowledge every single life. That's why I don't want to kill, even in situations where it's necessary. It takes its toll on my soul."

Hundreds of people? I shivered, again just a bit scared of him. "But what does that have to do with . . ." It hit me then why Dragon had stopped his attack. When he touched my stomach.

My hand flew involuntarily to it, remembering the bullet that I hadn't dodged after all on the night Wes had come to me and the EHJ.

"It's early on, but . . ." Wesley said.

"I'm pregnant." I said it aloud, just to see if it made more sense that way. Nope. It was still crazy and impossible. But not scary. Not the end of everything I had ever worked for. A baby might be a beautiful thing—if it was a baby of goodness.

He nodded.

Fear filled me. "This child can still bring about the end of the world, because your soul is corrupted?"

He nodded again.

"But it could also save the world." I said, now able to picture a person with Wes's startling blue eyes and my hair and smile, holding my hand. Calling me Mommy. "That's the flip side of the prophecy. That we'd either save the world or destroy it."

A half-smile traced his face. "That's true."

"And you did a fantastic job before," I said. "Ben was a great man."

Tears brimmed in his eyes. "Yes, he was."

"He saved us all."

"Yes."

"So, I'm not worried about what side he or she is going to come down on," I decided, knowing it was true. There was no way Wes and I would have created anything evil with our love. And I was no longer scared of motherhood. I was even, dare I say it, excited. A *family*, my mind gibbered. I'd have a family!

But then a thought occurred to me. "Wait. Since I've been drained of my magic and thrown around a lot, is the baby okay?"

He lowered a hand onto my stomach, on top of mine. My skin hummed again. "She's just fine."

I raised an eyebrow. "She?"

"Magic beats ultrasounds any day."

I smiled. "So what are we going to do now?"

"I think we should definitely stick around here. Now that Ben"—he trailed off and I could see he was trying not to cry again—"is gone, the EHJ needs extra help, especially to make sure the Dragon never comes back. And we'll need help raising someone who could potentially end the world."

"A lot of super-powered aunts and uncles."

"Something like that," he agreed.

"Okay." I slid my hand into his. "I'm in."

He squeezed it. "Me too. Now let's go find out what happened to the others, and see if we can help."

CHAPTER THIRTY-SIX

I stepped out of the car and felt my heels sink into the grass. "Man, I knew I shouldn't have worn these shoes!"

Wesley glanced back at me. "Well, be careful! Don't fall."

I gave him a look. "I'm not going to fall." I lifted up to float above the ground so my stilettos wouldn't sink anymore. "See?"

He shook his head. "You shouldn't be wearing those shoes," he repeated.

"My heels aren't going anywhere, Bossy McAttitude."

He sighed and headed off, me floating along after him. We passed by many gravestones until we reached the right one.

Wesley stopped in front of the large stone, what looked to be part of a family plot. He placed the bouquet of flowers he was carrying down on it. I stood—er, floated—a respectful distance away, letting him have his moment.

He turned to look at me. "It's not too cold out here, is it?"

I smiled. "Wes, she's got heavy clothes and blankets on. She's fine." I cradled our newborn closer to me. "Emily, tell Daddy to stop worrying all the time. How in the world did you manage to raise kids in the Dark Ages, Wes?"

"Don't remember, but maybe that's why I'm paranoid," he said as I floated up next to him. "Ask Fantazia how overprotective I was with her."

"Is that why she's such a rebel now?"

"That's just how she is. Got it from her mother."

I read the tombstone in front of me. BENJAMIN WALTER RATH. BELOVED SON. PROTECTOR OF THE WORLD.

"A fitting memorial for your brother, Em," I said.

Wesley smiled. "Thank you."

I glanced at the other two names on the large stone. BEATRICE ELLEN RATH. BELOVED WIFE AND MOTHER. And finally, the plot I knew was empty. WALTER RATH. BELOVED FATHER AND HUSBAND. NEVER FORGOTTEN, NEVER GONE.

"That has to be a bit weird," I said, running a fingertip over the name.

Wesley sighed. "Not really. I've gotten used to it."

I shivered, running my thumb over my wedding band, knowing that he had done this time after time. Someday, that would be me and Emily. Just names on a stone, ghosts of a life whose memory had faded.

Our baby stirred in my arms and made a cooing noise, reminding me that someday was not today. There were no guarantees in life. Wesley might reincarnate at the end of this life, or this one could truly be his last. We would have a lifetime together. But one day, our daughter would be helping to keep the world safe with a future version of the EHJ. She was our legacy. In her, we would go on. That was a different kind of superpower, and one I hadn't realized I had. In some ways, it was better than all the rest, and it was doubly amazing with the man I'd been lucky enough to get as my partner. All of us can be immortal if we choose to be. All of us can be phenomenal.

Wesley turned to me. "I'm ready."

I smiled. "Let's go."

ELISABETH NAUGHTON

STOLEN FURY

DANGEROUS LIAISONS

Oh, is he handsome. And charming. And sexy as all get out. Dr. Lisa Maxwell isn't the type to go home with a guy she barely knows. But, hey, this is Italy and the red-blooded Rafe Sullivan seems much more enticing than cataloging a bunch of dusty artifacts.

After being fully seduced, Lisa wakes to an empty bed and, worse yet, an empty safe. She's staked her career as an archaeologist on collecting the three Furies, a priceless set of ancient Greek reliefs. Now the one she had is gone. But Lisa won't just get mad. She'll get even.

She tracks Rafe to Florida, and finds the sparks between them blaze hotter than the Miami sun. He may still have her relic, but he'll never find all three without her. And they're not the only ones on the hunt. To beat the other treasure seekers, they'll have to partner up — because suddenly Lisa and Rafe are in a race just to stay alive.

ISBN 13: 978-0-505-52793-6

To order a book or to request a catalog call:
1-800-481-9191
This book is also available at your local bookstore, or you can check out our Web site **www.dorchesterpub.com** where you can look up your favorite authors, read excerpts, or glance at our discussion forum to see what people have to say about your favorite books.

Autumn Dawn
NO WORDS ALONE

As The Only Woman In A Team Of Marooned
Explorers, Whom Do You Trust—
Your Friends...Or Your Enemy?

Crash-landing on a hostile planet with a variety of flora
and fauna intent upon making her their lunch was Xera's
most immediate concern, but not her only one. The Scorpio, sworn enemies of her people, were similarly stranded
nearby, and Xera didn't trust the captain of her team of
Galactic Explorers. He was belligerent and small-minded,
and he'd already caused one unnecessary death—Genson's.
Xera was the translator, and she should have been the
first sent to deal with the Scorpio. Even if she was a lone
woman and they were some of the galaxy's most merciless
soldiers.

For, on this inhospitable world, the warlike Scorpio were
their only chance. And in the eyes of the aliens' handsome
leader, Xera saw a nobility and potency she'd never before
encountered—a reaction she knew her male human com-
panions would despise. A future with Commander Ryven
was...something to consider. But first she had to survive.

ISBN 13: 978-0-505-52801-8

To order a book or to request a catalog call:
1-800-481-9191
This book is also available at your local bookstore, or you
can check out our Web site **www.dorchesterpub.com**
where you can look up your favorite authors, read excerpts,
or glance at our discussion forum to see what people have to
say about your favorite books.

ELISSA WILDS

He says it was foretold, an inescapable way to bring them together. All Laurell Pittman knows is that ungovernable need surges through her body whenever the Axiom is near. Who is this godlike stranger who appears out of nowhere to steal her away from home? If she believes his claim, she is destined to conceive a very special child…and he is the appointed father. As he fights off demons trying to prevent their child's birth and patiently teaches her to use her own undiscovered powers, she finds her heart going out to this Balancer who is equally at home with good and evil, teetering on the edge of temptation, eternally caught …

BETWEEN LIGHT AND DARK

ISBN 13: 978-0-505-52791-2

To order a book or to request a catalog call:
1-800-481-9191
This book is also available at your local bookstore, or you can check out our Web site **www.dorchesterpub.com** where you can look up your favorite authors, read excerpts, or glance at our discussion forum to see what people have to say about your favorite books.

Christie Craig
Divorced, Desperate and Dating

Sue Finley murdered people…on paper. As a mystery writer, she knew all the angles, who did what and why. The only thing she couldn't explain was…well, men. Dating was like diving into a box of chocolates: the sweetest-looking specimens were often candy-coated poison. After several bad breakups, she gave it up for good.

Then came Detective Jason Dodd.

Raised in foster homes, Jason swore never to need anyone. That was why he failed to follow up after experiencing the best kiss of his life. But when Sue Finley started getting death threats, all bets were off. The blonde spitfire was everything he'd ever wanted—and she needed him. And though this novel situation had a quirky cast of characters and an unquestionable bad guy, he was going to make sure it had a happy ending.

ISBN 13: 978-0-505-52732-5

To order a book or to request a catalog call:
1–800–481–9191
This book is also available at your local bookstore, or you can check out our Web site **www.dorchesterpub.com** where you can look up your favorite authors, read excerpts, or glance at our discussion forum to see what people have to say about your favorite books.

KIMBERLY RAYE

Slippery When Wet

The Flag Is Up

Jaycee Anderson is the first female to take the NASCAR Sprint Cup circuit by storm, and after finishing fourth overall last season, she has her eyes on the prize: knocking Rory Canyon out of the number three spot. She'll do anything to see the job done, too, even transform herself from a tomboy into a glamour queen if that's what it takes to get sponsorship and the edge. Rory's the kind of infuriating chauvinist who's just begging to get the pants beat off him by a woman — on the track, at least; Jaycee's fairly sure he's never had to beg anywhere else. Not with the millions of female fans who buy his shirts and caps and posters. Rory's just the type who gets Jaycee's own pistons pumping, her wheels spinning, and her engine burning oil. With their past, she's surprised they haven't already seen a smashup that ended in flames. But this track they're running has some deadly curves . . . and it's getting more slippery by the minute.

ISBN 13: 978-0-505-52773-8

To order a book or to request a catalog call:
1-800-481-9191
This book is also available at your local bookstore, or you can check out our Web site **www.dorchesterpub.com** where you can look up your favorite authors, read excerpts, or glance at our discussion forum to see what people have to say about your favorite books.

✂ □ **YES!**

Sign me up for the Love Spell Book Club and send my
FREE BOOKS! If I choose to stay in the club, I will pay only
$8.50* each month, a savings of $6.48!

NAME: _____

ADDRESS: _____

TELEPHONE: _____

EMAIL: _____

□ I want to pay by credit card.

□ **VISA**   □ **MasterCard.**   □ **DISCOVER**

ACCOUNT #: _____

EXPIRATION DATE: _____

SIGNATURE: _____

Mail this page along with $2.00 shipping and handling to:
Love Spell Book Club
PO Box 6640
Wayne, PA 19087
Or fax (must include credit card information) to:
610-995-9274
You can also sign up online at **www.dorchesterpub.com**.
*Plus $2.00 for shipping. Offer open to residents of the U.S. and Canada only. Canadian
residents please call 1-800-481-9191 for pricing information.
If under 18, a parent or guardian must sign. Terms, prices and conditions subject to
change. Subscription subject to acceptance. Dorchester Publishing reserves the right to
reject any order or cancel any subscription.

GET FREE BOOKS!

You can have the best romance delivered to your door for less than what you'd pay in a bookstore or online. Sign up for one of our book clubs today, and we'll send you *FREE* BOOKS* just for trying it out... **with no obligation to buy, ever!**

Bring a little magic into your life with the romances of Love Spell—fun contemporaries, paranormals, time-travels, futuristics, and more. Your shipments will include authors such as **MARJORIE LIU, JADE LEE, NINA BANGS, GEMMA HALLIDAY**, and many more.

As a book club member you also receive the following special benefits:
- **30% off all orders!**
- **Exclusive access to special discounts!**
- **Convenient home delivery and 10 days to return any books you don't want to keep.**

Visit www.dorchesterpub.com
or call 1-800-481-9191

There is no minimum number of books to buy, and you may cancel membership at any time.
*Please include $2.00 for shipping and handling.